ANOTHER LITTLE PIECE

ANOTHER LITTLE PIECE

KATE KARYUS QUINN

HARPER TEEN
An Imprint of HarperCollins Publishers

HarperTeen is an imprint of HarperCollins Publishers.

Library of Congress Cataloging-in-Publication Data
Quinn, Kate Karyus.
Another little piece / Kate Karyus Quinn. — 1st ed.
  p.   cm.
Summary: A year after vanishing from a party, screaming and
drenched in blood, seventeen-year-old Annaliese Rose Gordon
appears hundreds of miles from home with no memory, but a
haunting certainty that she is actually another girl trapped in
Annaliese's body.
  ISBN 978-0-06-213595-7 (hardcover bdg.)
  [1. Identity—Fiction.   2. Amnesia—Fiction.   3. Family life—
Fiction.   4. Supernatural—Fiction.   5. Immortality—Fiction.]
  I. Title.
PZ7.Q41946Ano 2013   2012022161
[Fic]—dc23

Typography by Torborg Davern
13 14 15 16 17 CG/RRDH 10 9 8 7 6 5 4 3 2 1

First Edition

TO ANDY, FOR OFFERING TO BE MY DP . . .
AND
FOR EVERYTHING ELSE THAT CAME AFTER

BEGINNINGS

THE FIRST PERSON

The field didn't end so much as trail off, beaten back by the rusted-out trailer and circle of junked vehicles surrounding it. As if they had forgotten how to be still, the girl's bare and bloodied feet tripped and stumbled over each other. Slowly, slowly, the momentum that had brought her through the night and into the cold gray dawn leeched away. She tugged at the garbage bag she'd refashioned as a poncho. It was worse than useless at keeping her dry, but its constant crinkle had been a steady companion, and now that she'd reached her destination it seemed wrong to let it be lost to the wind.

Standing still, she studied the No Trespassing sign spray-painted on a weathered chunk of plywood, waiting for something to happen. Certain that something would. She didn't know where she was, or even her own name, but she felt sure of this.

She smelled the smoke only a split second before a girl

stepped around the side of the trailer. Perhaps the same age as herself, this girl divided her attention between bouncing a baby on her right hip and taking little puffs of the cigarette pinched between her fingers. Mid-exhale their eyes caught and held.

They might have let the moment pass, pretended they'd never seen each other at all, but then the baby released a wild wail that was instantly answered by the screen door flying open and a heavy woman with an uneven gait thumping down the stairs. Her body moved slowly and awkwardly, but her eyes were quick and took in everything. The hastily dropped cigarette. The baby's hand curled tight around a chunk of his own hair. And the stranger with the bare feet, garbage-bag wrapping, short-cropped hair stuck flat to her head from the rain, and, hovering over her left eye, the red starburst scar that resembled a crack in a car windshield.

THE THIRD PERSON

"Annaliese, let me interrupt you right there," Dr. Grimace and Gloom said. His eyes squinted at me in an attempt to be piercing, but only succeeded in creating the network of wrinkles across his face that had earned him his nickname. "Now the girl with the scar—you also refer to her as the stranger. You do realize this person is you?"

"Yeah."

Predictably the creases multiplied. The doc hated one-word answers.

"Then why are you referring to yourself in the third person?"

The third person. I liked that. I felt like a third person in this new life where they called me Annaliese and knew everything about me. Except the one missing piece—where I'd been for the past year. Unfortunately, no matter how many different ways they asked me, I couldn't answer this either. My memory only went back five days. One day made of walking. And the last four spent within the white-and-green walls of the hospital.

"Annaliese? Do you not understand the question? The third person is when you refer to yourself as *she* or *her*, as opposed to *me* or *I*." Dr. Grimace and Gloom explained this in an almost singsong way, like he was breaking down a difficult concept for a small child or the mentally deficient.

He'd placed me in the latter category before he'd even examined me in person. Several examinations and interviews later, he could still only see the brain scans showing extreme damage to the cerebral cortex, and not the girl in front of him who against all odds could not only breathe, walk, and talk but had somehow also retained all of her metal faculties . . . with one small exception: any knowledge of who she was. To them I went missing for a year. For myself I might be gone forever. And without myself, how could there be an I? I didn't say any of this to Dr. Grimace and Gloom.

"You told me to write my story down. You didn't say to write it a certain way."

Dr. Grimace and Gloom knew more about the human brain than just about any other person on the planet. Everyone said this, in an awed voice, like he was some kind of rock star doctor. He was pretty impressed with himself too. "I am a physician specializing in the field of neuroscience, specifically trauma and neurocritical care." That was how he'd introduced himself. Not, "Hey, I'm the brain doctor."

Maybe he was a genius when it came to brains, but he didn't know anything about teenage girls, and my answer nearly killed him. The wrinkles in his face quavered and burned bright red.

"That is true." He shifted slightly on the hard chair he'd dragged across the room and parked beside my hospital bed. "However, what I am attempting to get at is the reason why you chose to write it this way, especially when you are now speaking of yourself in the first person."

"Yeah, well, it's different when you're writing something down and talking out loud, isn't it?"

His eyes closed, and his nostrils flared as he took several deep breaths. In. Then out. In. Then out. "Fine," he said at last, as if it pained him to concede this small point. "Let's move on to the sheriff arriving. You explained to him that you were searching for something specific."

I looked down at the bound pages of the journal. It was a gift from the parents. They said I had liked to write. That I'd even won some sort of poetry prize. They seemed really impressed by that. When I stared at those blank pages, the only poem that came to mind began, "There once was a girl from Nantucket."

So I skipped the poems and instead filled seven pages writing this girl's—my—story down in painstaking detail. But now Dr. Grimace and Gloom just went and skipped ahead to the sheriff coming. He didn't want to hear about how after the heavyset woman came flip-flopping out of that trailer, she—in the same breath—said I looked like trouble but I'd best come on in and sit down anyway, turned to her daughter and told her to stay out of her damn cigarettes if she knew what was good for her, and ordered the baby to stop crying. And all three of us had nodded and yes-ma'amed her, because she was the kind of person to make you do that sort of thing. Even that little baby, who must have been older than I'd first thought, lisped out a little, "Yes'um."

I closed the journal. He already knew this story, or the parts he wanted to hear about anyway. And I didn't need the journal to recall what had happened. When your memory only contains five days, you don't worry much about forgetting the little details. My head was like a pantry where all the nonperishable memories got stored. I opened it, and there they all were—lined up in a neat little row—no need to push things around, or hunt for anything. Easy accessibility was nice, but at other times I opened that memory pantry hungry for something that wasn't there.

"Annaliese." He said the name I still didn't recognize as my own as a verbal nudge, prompting me to answer his earlier question.

"I told him I was trying to find myself," I answered in a flat voice, annoyed he was making me say it out loud, making me hear again how stupid it sounded.

BEYOND STRANGE

All five of us were in the cramped main room of the trailer. I sat in the middle of the sagging couch, with Deenie, the mom, on one side, and her two kids, Lacey and baby Robby, still tugging at his own hair, on the other. They'd introduced themselves when we came inside, and having no name to give in return, I gave them nice manners instead. "Pleased to meet you."

When the sheriff arrived, he took the recliner chair and immediately kicked back in it, apparently not afraid to be seen lounging on the job. "Well, EMTs will be here shortly. Couple kids ran their cars into each other over near Route Fifty-Six, and they need to finish sortin' that out. In the meantime, we can relax some and get the basic information I'll be needing for paperwork and whatnot."

A bit of the tension that had been holding my shoulders stiff released. The way he spoke, where a car crash was something that could be sorted out and a girl appearing out of nowhere caused no more trouble than filling out some forms, took some of the terror from my situation.

"Now," he said in a low drawl, almost sleepy sounding, "what's yer name, sweetheart?"

The name problem. Again. My shoulders went tight once more. "I don't know."

Deenie stepped in here. "She looks like the girl from that *Dateline* we saw on TV the other week. Remember, Bobby?" It took me a moment to realize this was the sheriff. "What was that girl's name? Something kinda funny—like a regular name that somebody tried to fancy up."

The sheriff—I couldn't think of him as Bobby—frowned at her, not for interrupting but for dropping that detail about them being together. I wanted to tell him that I already knew. When Deenie had gone to refill the plastic Thomas the Train cup with more water, Lacey had told me. The sheriff was Deenie's steady boyfriend, despite having a wife and a full-grown boy at home. Lacey didn't really care about that; what upset her was that the two of them worked together to scare away the boy she liked. "They got the whole high school thinking I'm a narc."

"Nobody knows how to have a quiet affair no more," the sheriff finally grumbled, but he didn't seem too upset about it either.

"Affair?" Deenie shot back at him. "Hmph. Five years in and he's still calling it an affair."

"Five years in and you still don't know I never can stay awake more than ten minutes after you turn one of them news shows on. By the way, Bethany says hey."

"That's his wife," Lacey informed me, with a roll of her eyes that seemed to say, *Can you believe these people?*

I was so caught up in this back-and-forth that I let my guard down. In retrospect it was a fine interrogation technique. When the sheriff abruptly turned toward me and asked, "So, *Dateline* girl, whatcha doin' way out here anyway?" I answered truthfully, without hesitation.

"I woke up, I'm not really sure where, and I had this feeling, and I kind of started following it. I didn't know where I was or who I was, but I felt like maybe I could find some answers . . . could maybe find myself here."

They all stared at me, and I realized that while they were strange, being so open about their messy private lives, they were not a girl with bare feet and a funny scar, wrapped in a garbage bag, who had followed a feeling to their door.

I was beyond strange.

"Find yourself, huh?" the sheriff said at last. "I think

that's what Tim Butler's wife said when she ran off with that orthopedic-shoes salesman."

His voice was light and teasing, but there was no missing the look he exchanged with Deenie. It said she had been right. This girl was trouble for sure.

KIND OF NORMAL

"And what did you mean by that?" Dr. Grimace and Gloom asked.

I'd meant exactly what I'd said. The afternoon before I'd arrived at the trailer, I'd woken up in a one-room wooden cabin with a dirt floor. The only thing in it other than myself was a plastic milk jug full of water and a garbage bag beneath my body acting as a bed. I wore a T-shirt and jeans that despite being covered in faded stains had the clean smell of soap. I wasn't scared. Scared would come later. At that moment I was just confused. I couldn't think why I would be there. Or who I was. Or where I should be. The whole thing felt unreal.

Pushing aside the sheet of plastic that covered the doorway, I'd stepped outside. That's when I felt it. The pull. Something telling me to walk. Like some internal GPS had been activated, I'd crossed through a wooded area strung thick with spiderwebs, waded through some swamplands while the frogs and crickets croaked and chirped in alarm all around me, and then there was that long field that stretched through most of the night until I reached the trailer.

I shrugged. "I don't know. I was just trying to figure out what was going on."

The doctor said nothing, but his eyes turned into the tiniest little slits and his frown twisted into a sneer. "I have been a physician for more years than you have been alive. Do you have any idea how many brains I have studied in my career?" His voice changed with this sudden shift of direction, becoming more directly challenging. Menacing.

"I don't know." I shrugged again.

"Guess."

"A hundred?"

"Seven hundred." Pause. "And fifty-two."

"Oh."

"Out of those seven hundred and fifty-two brains, only four have behaved in ways that I could not understand. In all four of those cases, I determined after extensive testing that those brains were aberrations to the point of no longer being technically human."

Spittle flew from his lips, and he was no longer Dr. Grimace and Gloom. He was Dr. Crazypants. Dr. Nutso and Insane. Dr. I Will Kill You While You Sleep. I inched my fingers toward the call button on my bed rail.

"I have remained silent concerning these findings," he

continued, "because those brains all came from cadavers. But yours is the fourth brain. And that makes you my first living monster."

My fingers, instead of pressing the button, went to the indentation on my forehead. What had he seen in my brain underneath the skin and bone?

He stopped, clearly wanting me to say something. Maybe my confession. Or defense. I had neither.

The rage seeped away into the silence, leaving him grimmer than ever. Leaning back, he studied me over steepled fingers.

"People prefer to believe in miracles over monsters. And so tomorrow I will give my recommendation that you have survived some traumatic event through unusual and, yes, perhaps even miraculous means. You'll be released to your parental guardians immediately. But first . . . first I want you to tell me one thing. One honest answer from you."

He leaned forward once more. "I want to know what it feels like."

I gulped. I didn't know if I wanted to go home with my parental guardians—those strangers I met yesterday after the DNA tests went through and I was officially declared Annaliese Rose Gordon. I did know that I didn't want to stay here, near Grimace and Gloom and all the other doctors who might not have said it as directly as him, but with all their questions seemed to also imply that I was some kind of monster.

Looking directly into his beady little eyes, I answered as truthfully as I could.

"I don't know." The three-word phrase that had quickly become my signature exited my mouth before I could recall it, and Dr. Grimace and Gloom's brow darkened. Hurriedly, I added, "I mean, I don't know anything about myself except from these last couple days, and I know what happened to me is weird and no one can explain it, but somehow I just, I don't know, I feel normal, I guess."

"Normal," he repeated.

I nodded miserably. "Yeah, I mean, kind of normal."

PASSED

He left without another word.

I didn't sleep that night.

Wondering if I had passed his test.

Wondering if he was right about me being a monster.

Wondering exactly how he expected a monster to feel.

How he expected me to feel.

I still felt normal.

Whatever normal was.

It wasn't until the seven a.m. nurse-shift change, when the night nurse said good-bye and good luck, that I realized I was leaving. Going home. Whatever and wherever that was.

All of the many doctors I'd seen during my four days at the hospital made a point of coming by my room and wishing me well; some even told me to keep in touch. Only Grimace and Gloom stayed away. I guess we'd already said our good-byes.

HOMECOMING

HI, MOM

Hi, Mom.
Hi, Dad.
I know you love me lots.
Of course, I love you lots too.

What else can I say?

School's fine. I'm fine.
Yeah, the weather's gray.
I know whatever I need, you're there.
Of course, I'll always come to you.

What else can I say?

Bye, Mom.
Bye, Dad.
I know you trust me.
Of course, I'll be good.

I'll be good.
That's what I told 'em.

What else could I say?

—ARG

They found me in Oklahoma, which was strange, because Annaliese Rose Gordon's home was in the northeastern part of the country. Western New York to be more specific. Buffalo, if you were looking to stick a pin in a map. According to the GPS stats, that was a distance of almost thirteen hundred miles. From the way everyone kept shaking their heads and saying "Oklahoma" in the same way they might have said "Mars," I guessed this was far beyond the range where anyone had ever considered looking for Annaliese.

Here's another GPS-derived fact. Those thirteen hundred miles can be traveled by car in about twenty-one hours. A little less than a day to get from one part of the country to another seems reasonable, but that doesn't include stops. When you account for stopping early and often, those thirteen hundred miles start to stretch across several days . . . and they begin to feel like forever.

My parental guardians explained their reasons for this mode of transportation very earnestly. Well, *she* explained. The mom. She is the talker. And the crier. And the hugger. And the everything else. The dad is there for one thing and one thing only. Backup. He stands behind her. Sometimes holding her up. Sometimes bracing her. Sometimes just there. Waiting. Waiting in case she sticks her hand out, and then he will be there, ready to take it in his own.

They are a good team.

The explanation for the drive went like this:

Air travel would be too traumatic after everything I had gone through.

Traveling by car would give me time to adjust.

We've always loved family road trips.

After three hours I added another possible reason: to quiz me endlessly.

The mom insisted on calling my memory loss amnesia. As if I were a character in a soap opera. She thought I just needed the right trigger to snap me out of it. It started with a picture quiz. I correctly identified the Gerber baby, but couldn't place my own baby picture.

It got worse from there.

Ronald McDonald—yes. The clown from my fourth birthday party—no. I easily named every character from *Friends*. My own best friend—"Gwen is such a nice girl," the mom told me, as if this detail might jog my memory—no recognition at all. In the animal-kingdom category I got Kermit the Frog, Lassie, and Dumbo all correct. But Snowball didn't come close to Here Kitty Kitty, the rather cumbersome name that I apparently gave my own dear cat at the age of five.

The game officially ended when I incorrectly identified a woman with iron-gray curls and a closed-lip smile as Queen

Elizabeth. Turns out that one was my nana.

Next we played something called, "What's Your Favorite...?"

The first topic was food.

I was trying, even though my palms were sweaty and a headache had formed behind my left eye. It would've been easy to tell the mom where to shove her questions. Except the mom was a really nice lady. And she was trying to be upbeat, chirpy even. But with every wrong answer, she'd deflate a little bit. She tried to cover it. She'd pat my hand and tell me it was okay. She was always touching me—patting, rubbing, squeezing my hand, arm, or leg. And that's when she wasn't hugging me. That was okay, too, though. She was a good hugger. As soon as her arms wrapped around me, there was this sensation like everything was going to be okay. So far this was the one thing that we had most in common—we both really wanted everything to be okay.

So favorite foods. I knew she picked this topic first because I was so skinny. I knew she thought I was so skinny because she said it every time she looked at me. And she'd shown me Annaliese's school picture from the previous year. It had been taken only a few days before she'd disappeared, just a few weeks away from her seventeenth birthday. There was a roundness to her cheeks, not fat, just a sort of youthful glow. But now, as the mom made sure to remind me, it was almost exactly a year later, I was once again only weeks away from a birthday, but the glow and roundness had been replaced by hollows and eyes too big for my face.

"Well, I don't really know about favorite," I said at last, wanting to play along. "The hospital food was pretty bad."

The mom jumped on this. "It was terrible! Wasn't it terrible, John?"

That was the dad's cue. He knew his part too. "Awful."

For a moment we were a family, united by our shared disgust for hospital food. Buoyed by my success, I added, "It was so bland—that was the problem."

Another hit. "Yes! It's like they have a flavor extractor back there in the kitchen."

"Must take out color too, 'cause my green beans last night were gray," the dad added, backing the mom up in her comedy attempts.

We were all smiling at one another. It felt good. No, great. It felt great. If I could take that moment and plant it in the ground, I would wait for a tree to grow from it, and then I would build a fort in that tree where I would live forever. That was how good it felt.

"I need something to wake my taste buds up again," I said.

"Ooh, yeah," the mom agreed excitedly. "How about Mexican for lunch?"

"Or better yet," I said, "curry. That would really hit the spot."

The smiles dimmed. "Curry?"

I'd said something wrong. "Yeah, like Indian?"

"Indian?"

"Uh-huh?"

Every one of our words had question marks attached, as if we would recant them in an instant if asked.

"You never liked foreign food. That's what you always said?" This was the mom again.

The dad stepped in. "Your favorites were spaghetti and tacos, which we always thought was funny because they are foreign foods." This was a statement. At last. He would not rewrite history for me, just because I couldn't remember it.

I said nothing, feeling like I'd been caught playing a part. The monster trying to disguise herself as someone's daughter.

The mom suddenly gasped. "Annaliese, do you remember where you had those Indian foods? Do you think it's possible that a—what's a person from India called, John?"

"An Indian."

"Of course, of course. Indian. I always think cowboys and Indians, but they're Native Americans now. Except they live on Indian reservations, don't they? I mean, we don't call them Native American reservations. Or should we?"

"Sweetheart." The dad's voice was soft, a reminder that she had gone off track.

"Oh, right. Do you think it was maybe an . . . an Indian that took Annaliese? Annaliese, what do you remember?"

"Nothing," I said immediately. Except there was something. Pointing to the word *vindaloo* on a menu. And the taste. I kept a tissue clutched in my hand to dab at my nose, running from the heat, but I didn't stop eating. Using pieces of naan, I sopped up every last bit of sauce until the bowl was clean.

"Chocolate," the mom abruptly broke in. "You love chocolate. We love chocolate. Do you re—?"

She stopped herself from asking if I remembered, not wanting to hear that I didn't. Pulling one of her overflowing bags from the backseat, she rooted around in it until she found a package wrapped in brown paper. Carefully, as if it held precious contents, she unraveled the paper until at last she revealed four bars of chocolate.

"I bought these before you . . . well, I've been holding on to them. It was—it *is*—our thing. Monthly chocolate taste tests. We'd find different places on the internet to buy from, all over the country, little specialty places and—" Her voice cracked as she stared down at those chocolate bars. Her hair fell forward, hiding her face, but I could tell she was struggling against tears. There was a charged feeling in the car, like the way the air feels before a thunderstorm.

Wanting to make it better, wanting to bring her daughter back, I snagged one of the bars off the pile, peeled away the paper and foil, and took a huge bite. The chocolate was hard and at first tasteless, and as it melted between my teeth and found its way onto my tongue, it wasn't sweet, but instead bitter and salty.

It felt like chewing on my own tongue, like my mouth was filling with blood. I tried to swallow but my throat had closed up. No, it wasn't closed, but merely already occupied with my last hospital meal of orange juice and Cheerios coming up. My hand flew to my mouth, but it was too late. My insides erupted. Even after everything was out—spattering the backs of the car seats, the floor, my clothes and shoes—I couldn't stop gagging. Finally in desperation I sucked on the fabric of my own shirtsleeve until it absorbed most of the terrible chocolate blood taste from my mouth.

The dad had pulled onto the side of the road by then, and they'd both gotten out of the car, throwing all the doors open. Together they stared at me like I was some kind of wild animal that had wandered into their car, and they were waiting for me to realize I didn't belong here and go back to wherever I had come from. I simply sat there, staring at my puke-spattered sneakers.

Finally, the mom handed me a tissue. Only then did I notice my runny nose and the tears leaking down the side of my face.

"I think I must have gotten carsick," I said feebly.

"Annaliese was never carsick."

The mom didn't seem to notice that she had referred to Annaliese as if she was a different person from me, a person who now existed only in the past tense.

Thirty-four. "She's our daughter." The whispered words came from the dad when he thought I was asleep, in one of the two queen beds that filled our tiny motel room. At first I thought he was talking to the mom, but then he said it again, again, and again. Repeating that phrase. To keep myself still, I began to count each set.

It wasn't simply a statement, but a mantra. He was trying to convince himself. Eventually the flow of words became a trickle before stopping entirely, replaced by the sound of his steady breathing.

I didn't sleep again for the rest of the night.

One interview on the *Today* show. Three with each of the local news stations. It was necessary to remove the reporters camped out on the front lawn. Annaliese's disappearance had been a major news story, but my reappearance was more than that. Annaliese Rose Gordon. The name was at the top of internet search phrases, and that meant that people were talking about me, and they wanted to know more. The reporters were there to feed that appetite. The mom and the dad did most of the talking, and at the end I delivered my one line: "I'm happy to be home, and just want to get back to normal."

Sixteen. That was the number of counseling sessions I attended. Some alone, some with the mom and the dad. The mom was behind it. On the ride back to New York she'd read some book about families in crisis—apparently unable to find one specifically about having one's amnesiac daughter returned after disappearing for almost a year—and this book stressed the importance of finding the right counselor for YOU. The emphasis was theirs.

Two. The number of hours I spent touring Annaliese's old school. She was only a few months into her junior year when she'd disappeared, and I would be picking up where she had left off. The parents trailed behind the principal, and I trailed behind them as he gave us a guided tour, helpfully pointing out the classrooms I would go to on Monday morning. It felt like another test. One I failed again and again as they asked, "Remember this?" And then they reached my old locker—preserved exactly as it had been at the mom's insistence that I might return any day.

"Go ahead," they said. "Give the lock a few spins, maybe the muscle memory will remember what you don't."

So, I tried. But my muscles didn't remember any more than the rest of me did.

Forty-five to zero. That was the score at the end of the Homecoming football game. At the school we'd seen the signs advertising Saturday's game and the dance that would follow. Annaliese's disappearance came a month before last year's Homecoming, but according to the mom, the dress for the dance was hanging in the closet—the tags still on and waiting. When we returned home I checked, and there it was. Perfectly preserved inside a clear plastic bag, a pink dress with spaghetti straps and matching pale-pink crystals, hanging at the back of the closet. Of course, I couldn't go to the dance this year. As the dad quickly pointed out, quelling the gleam in the mom's eyes, it was too soon. After a moment to swallow her disappointment the mom agreed, adding that with all the weight I'd lost, the dress would've hung on me anyway.

The game was another matter. It was the perfect opportunity for me to get my feet wet, while still having the mom and the dad at my side.

Five seconds. That was how much time remained on the game clock when I decided to stop counting, and begin my new life as Annaliese Rose Gordon for real. It wasn't that I started feeling like Annaliese, but more like it shook me awake. For the first time I knew for sure that the worst wasn't behind me.

No, the worst was straight ahead, and I was headed right at it.

GAME CHANGER

There were only seconds left on the clock, and the other team, losing and desperate to put some kind of number on the board, launched a Hail Mary pass. It wasn't a game changer, but you could feel how badly the other side wanted it, needed it, to ease that long ride home. And as if God himself were behind that ball, it was the first the quarterback threw that didn't jelly-roll through the air but flew straight and true, landing right in the outstretched hands of . . . one of our guys.

Number sixteen, the name RICE written across his back, tore down half the field and danced into the end zone to score the final touchdown of the game. Rice Sixteen ripped his helmet off and, shaking his head, sent long, shaggy hair flying. The setting sun flared, gilding him.

And that's when I felt the first hunger pang. Even from my spot halfway up the bleachers, I could see the beads of sweat on his golden-brown skin. Except it didn't resemble sweat so much as the juices dripping from the crisped and crackling skin of a roasted chicken. I wanted to sink my teeth into him. My stomach growled with hunger at the thought. Saliva collected in my mouth. I swallowed loudly.

As if he knew, Rice Sixteen's gaze turned toward the stands and latched on to me. Surprise, shock, and something I couldn't name rippled across his face—and then the other players surged around him, hiding him from view.

Nausea replaced hunger. Drool turned to dust. Had I really wanted to take a bite of another person?

In that moment it became clear: there was something seriously wrong with me. But was this something new to Annaliese or a problem she'd already had? I turned to the mom, already knowing she wouldn't react well to the question of whether I'd had a problem with cannibalism before I'd disappeared, and trying to think of another way to phrase it. Instead, she was the one who had a question for me.

"Annaliese, did you recognize Logan?" Her eyes, even I had to admit, looked amazingly similar to my own. A cloudy shade of blue that shifted chameleonlike depending on what other colors were in close proximity. Right now they were twin wishing wells, begging me to toss a penny in and give her a chance to make my dreams come true.

"Who's Logan?" I asked. The light faded away, and the mom's eyes sank back into the dark circles beneath them. Not for the first time, I regretted causing this nice lady so much pain.

She wasn't giving up that easily, though.

"Logan Rice? The running back?" She pointed toward the field, although Rice Sixteen had, along with the rest of the team, headed back into the school, leaving the field empty.

"Were we friends?" I asked, trying to remember, trying to understand my disturbing reaction to him. But I already knew the answer. That boy was one of the popular kids—the kind with the inner spotlight, drawing others closer. I'd already figured out enough about Annaliese to know she couldn't have been anything but another mosquito, hovering nearby.

"Well, no, I don't think so," the mom admitted hesitantly.

"He's one of those boys who everyone knows, and I thought you might remember him."

Next to me, the dad snorted. "She doesn't remember us, you think she's gonna remember a boy she probably never even talked to?"

The mom didn't say anything in response, just made this soft little mewing noise that was her response to being hurt. Hearing it, the dad, as he always did, immediately apologized. And then we stood, and were carried out with the rest of the crowd.

When we'd arrived at the game halfway through the first quarter, I'd caught whispers of "That's her. There she is. Annaliese." Now, though, in the parking lot, my classmates were braver . . . or drunker. They yelled "Welcome back" at me in the same rowdy way they did "Go, Panthers," with a long "Whoooooo" tacked on to the end of the phrase, as if my return was something to be celebrated along with their football victory. With the slightest encouragement, they might have picked me up onto their shoulders and paraded me through town like a trophy.

I couldn't think of anything worse. The mom's fingers brushed against mine, and I gladly grabbed hold of her hand. When we finally reached the car, she sat in the backseat beside me and kept the same steady grip the whole way home.

It would have been comforting, except I couldn't escape the thought that maybe I should warn her. There was a chance I might one day try to bite that same hand off.

ANSWERS AND QUESTIONS

A COULD-HAVE-BEEN

A could-have-been destroyed.
Although "might have" only in my mind.

How awful to have mini moments of maybe slain.
A betrayal—the worst kind.
One that exists only in my mind.

How tragic to know
I'm not second best.
I wasn't even in the running.

How horrific to make such mistakes.
To mourn a fantasy,
and find it meant so much.

How . . .
how pathetic.

—ARG

DETONATION

By eight thirty that night I was in bed, staring up at the ceiling, where star-shaped stickers arranged into smiley-faced constellations glowed dimly in the darkness. It was early to be in bed—even I knew this—but I couldn't stand to sit in front of the TV watching it while they watched me.

As I lay there, I did what I'd done during every free moment since I'd woken up in that cabin a few weeks ago. I tried to remember. Dr. Morgan, the hospital psychiatrist, told me not to try so hard, that the straining could actually make it more difficult for the memories to resurface. *Resurface.* That was the word he used, and even then, I thought of them as bobbing beneath murky waters, just out of reach. Still, I couldn't stop going on my fishing expeditions.

I don't know what time I drifted off to sleep, but when I woke, the red numbers on the bedside alarm clock told me it was ten after two. In the desk chair at the other end of the room, the mom slept, hunched in on herself, her neck folded so that her chin rested on her chest. It looked horribly uncomfortable, but every night she was there, until around eight a.m., when she tiptoed back out, believing I was none the wiser. I'd come to find the sound of her soft, rhythmic snores soothing in their constancy, like listening to a recording of waves breaking.

Tonight, though, the noise grated against my nerves. I tossed and turned, trying not to think about the way my stomach had clenched with that sudden hunger at the football game. I stared into the darkness, wishing for a distraction. And suddenly, there it was. Whirling blue-and-red lights leaked between the blind's slats and splashed across the ceiling.

I lay still for several long moments, gazing at the lights, waiting to see if they would wake the mom. When they didn't, I slipped out of bed and down the stairs. For pajamas I'd taken to sleeping in my hospital gown, feeling now, as I did then, that it was the only thing that truly belonged to me. Reaching into the closet by the front door, I pulled out the first thing my fingers grabbed hold of—a gigantic puffy parka that covered me to midthigh. Even though it wasn't that cold out, I pulled the fur-edged hood over my head, figuring it would counterbalance my bare feet.

The front door opened soundlessly and I slipped into the night to watch the spectacle taking place across the street. I didn't know how I'd slept through so much of it. Music with a heavy bass beat pounded from the house, and, almost as if they were running from that punishing beat, the interrupted partygoers streamed out the front door, taking off in various directions. Of course, the reason they were fleeing wasn't the music, but the two cop cars sitting in the driveway. The cops didn't pay any attention to the mass exodus of teenagers, except to pull aside those who were obviously staggering.

In the middle of this a girl cried. Loudly. Histrionically

even. Despite the tsunami-size tears sliding down her cheeks, it was obvious she was faking. It wasn't that her acting was all that bad; maybe it's just impossible to buy the crying of someone clad in a string bikini, especially when she stands in a way meant to show off her body to the best possible effect. And that effect was impressive. She looked like her body had been made for bikini wearing. Or maybe vice versa. Either way, this girl could not simultaneously rock the bikini and look believably distraught.

I drifted across the lawn, wanting to hear what the girl was saying—"But I told you, I was in the hot tub; how was I supposed to know they'd broken into the liquor cabinet?"— when I realized the maple tree that grew out of the patch of grass between the sidewalk and road was staring at me.

When I took a step closer, the tree separated from the person leaning against it. No, not a person. A boy. The same one from the football game. Rice Sixteen.

Except this wasn't the grinning, confident boy from before. This was a different, stripped-down version. It wasn't just the absence of his uniform and pads, which had been exchanged for a dripping pair of swim trunks. It seemed like something internal had been removed as well. He didn't lean against the tree, so much as sag. The expression on his face was limp, too—his mouth slack, the staring eyes heavy-lidded. Despite his muscled bare chest and legs on display, nothing about this boy made me hungry.

I took a step closer and the reason for his inertness reached my nose. He was drunk. I wondered if he even knew who I was, but the answer came quickly enough when he whispered my name.

"Annaliese? That really you?"

Good question, I wanted to tell him, but I figured he was looking for a more direct answer, so pulling back the hood, I said, "Yes."

"I thought you were dead. Everyone thought you were dead."

Actually, the first words the mom said to me were "I knew you were alive. I always knew." Again, though, I didn't want to complicate things. I nodded.

"Please, don't be mad at me," Rice Sixteen said, and his voice cracked. His head dipped into his chest, and it reminded me of the mom, still sleeping in the chair upstairs, making me wonder if he'd fallen asleep as well, but he looked back up at me and there were tears running down his face. These tears were real, and they flowed faster than he could wipe them away, until finally he scrubbed at his face in frustration. All the while the words were coming at me. "I'm sorry, so so sorry. Please believe me. If I'd known you were alive, I'd have said something, but I thought you were dead, so why let people talk, why make things harder, when it wouldn't change anything. And I know it's my fault. I shouldn't have left you out there. I shouldn't have—we shouldn't have been together at all—not like that. Especially not out in the woods. I shouldn't have—I shh-shh-shh—"

He stepped away from the tree and lurched toward me, arms out, still babbling about what shouldn't have happened—although it was impossible to say exactly what that was. His volume increased, his earlier whisper giving way to full-voiced desperation. Then his arms clamped around me, and his big head flopped onto my shoulder. Suddenly, I was the tree holding him up, and I felt similarly rooted to the ground, helpless to shake him. His words were impossible to decipher now, just sounds mixed in with syllables. Not knowing what else to do, and realizing that we were starting to attract attention, I told him, "It's okay."

It's easy to grant forgiveness when you don't know what it is you're forgiving, but apparently it's harder to accept it, because he stumbled away from me, wildly shaking his head.

"No! You don't understand. I heard you. I pretended I didn't, but I did. You said, 'I love you,' and I walked away. We'd just done it and I walked away and left you alone in the woods. I walked back to Kayla, and I left you there, still . . . still lying there, and I pretended I hadn't heard you say it."

His words were a grenade. You could see the shock waves spreading out from the epicenter, hitting the people who had quietly gathered around us. There were gasps of shock. A shriek of anger. More than a few giggles.

But the main detonation was inside of me. Because his words triggered a memory. My first from the time before I woke up to my new life.

I walk through trees, not a forest, but a dense little copse that separates two subdivisions of oversized houses, giving the occupants on either side the illusion of privacy and seclusion. The bass thump of party music pulses in the distance.

At the deepest part of the almost forest, where the motion-sensored security lights of the houses can no longer penetrate, I slow my pace. I'm listening, looking for something. Then there it is, the crunch of dry leaves. Not the crisp crackle that even my softest footsteps produce, but a softer *shuska shuska* of the same leaves being ground into dust. Another step and I hear ragged breaths, interspersed with an occasional low groan. Not even lifting my feet, I slip closer, until they come into view.

There really isn't much to see. His dark hoodie covers his upper body, while his jeans are only jerked down to his knees, leaving an inch or two of bare leg exposed before his baggy boxers cover the rest of him. Beneath him she is almost invisible, her dark hair disappearing into a tangle of dead leaves. Only her pale white legs give her away as being there at all. Jeans bunched around her ankles force those legs to jut out at awkward angles on either side of him. Her little silver heels, silly with the jeans, even sillier here in the dirt, are still firmly fastened to her feet by their rhinestone-studded straps.

I'd hoped they'd be done by the time I arrived. High school

boys can't be counted on for a lot, but a quick finish is almost always a guarantee. I wonder what the hell he is waiting for when he gasps, "I'm gonna . . ."

"Yeah, okay." There is no mistaking the relief in her voice. Clearly, they've been here long enough for all the romance of this encounter to be as ground into the dirt as shiny silver shoes.

The corner of my mouth kicks up into a half smile, as if I think it is funny how quickly this girl has been stripped of her romantic illusions. Inside, my gut is twisting. This is the least of what I plan on stealing from her tonight.

The boy doesn't notice the relief in her words. He has too much going on, what with trying to stay quiet and stalling his imminent orgasm, to worry about subtext. Still, he persists in his questioning.

"But you, you came, right?"

"Um . . ."

"You didn't, did you?" His movements stall completely. "It's just I don't wanna . . . if you didn't."

Finally, she grasps the problem. "No, no. I did. Really. A . . . a couple times actually."

There's no way he'll believe that, I think, at the same instant he says, "Oh, wow. Wo-ow." Overcome by the idea of his own sexual prowess, he gasps and shudders. And into that moment she whispers the words "I love you," so softly I'm left wondering if I've heard them at all.

He heard them though. As much as he must wish he hadn't. An inability to orgasm first and catlike hearing are apparently the double curses of this particular youth. Finished, he keeps his body held stiffly above hers for what feels like an eternity. Long enough for her to hope he might say those same words back. Long enough for her to believe this wasn't a terrible mistake.

At their feet, his cell phone beeps, announcing an incoming text. He grabs for it and his pants in one graceful movement, pulling the jeans to his waist, the phone to his eyes.

She knows then. As she sits up slowly, her long, dark hair swings forward, hiding her face and the tears threatening to fall.

"It's Kayla. She's looking for me." It's an apology. Of sorts. And a request.

She grants it. "You should go."

"Yeah."

But he doesn't. He hesitates. Tilting his head back, he studies the shadowed treetops, then his eyes follow the long lines of the branches to where they join the trunk and from there sweep all the way down to the roots in the ground that jut out toward Annaliese. His whole body jerks back, like he's surprised to see her there. No, like he's awakening from a dream. Already he can't quite remember how he got here, what it was that drew him to Annaliese, a girl he'd never even noticed until two weeks ago.

His hand scrubs through his long hair. "I didn't mean for this to happen."

A small sob shakes Annaliese's body. She chokes most of it back, only allowing a tiny hiccup of sorrow to escape.

"Don't cry, please. I didn't mean . . . I'm not saying it was bad. It was great, probably the best I've ever . . ." He stops. As if hearing the words out loud and realizing how terrible they sound. "And you had fun too, right? I mean, you came, like, how many times? Not like you were counting, but . . ."

His phone beeps with another text message. Reading the message, he curses softly. "Kayla says someone saw me heading out here. She wants to send a search party."

These words finally spur Annaliese into motion. She reaches forward, grabbing hold of the jeans still bunched round her ankles. "You should go." Without looking, she can sense his hesitation. "Really. Go."

He takes two shuffling steps backward, but his eyes are still fixed on Annaliese, needing some further dismissal or release. "But you're okay, right? I mean, I know you said it wasn't your first time or anything but . . ."

Of course it was her first time, you idiot. I want to beat the words into him, anything to transfer some of the responsibility away from myself.

Annaliese forces a little laugh. "Really, I'm fine. It's no big deal."

And that's enough for him. Mumbling, he edges away. "Okay, yeah, okay. See ya around then."

His words linger behind, even after his body has faded into the darkness.

I shift slightly, but not enough to give myself away. Not yet. Usually when it's this bad, and goes this wrong, they start to cry right about now. It seems unfair to cheat her of that too.

But Annaliese surprises me. She stands up, brushes herself off, and then pulls out her cell. Flipping it open, she begins tapping away at the keys. Her hands tremble and a few sniffles escape, but mostly she manages to hold it in. Probably waiting to cry until she reaches the safety of her own room, where no drunken partygoers might accidentally stumble across her.

Unfortunately, there will be no safe haven for Annaliese tonight.

Or ever again.

I step out of the trees.

"Hey," I say.

She blinks in surprise, and then recognition.

"Oh, it's you."

I say nothing. Experience has taught me less is more.

"You were right," Annaliese says now. "Love and lust are different."

"I'm sorry," I reply, placing a hand on her shoulder. The apology isn't for the bargain that didn't go her way. And the hand isn't for comfort. It's a restraint, because this is when many of them try to run away. "It's time to pay."

"Now?" She doesn't know what the payment is; none of them do up front. Some guess. Not exactly, but they know it will be a price higher than they wish to pay. Annaliese, though, has no idea. She has been sheltered and thinks that evil is something you see in movies and on the nightly news. Her reluctance is because she sees my demand as an inconvenience, rather than something she should have been dreading and fearing ever since we made our unnatural deal.

"It has to be now."

She nods, but I need a verbal agreement to complete the circle and take away her will the same way she took his. "'Yes, I will pay.' I need to hear that."

"Yes, I will pay," Annaliese immediately repeats, no need for my fingers on her shoulder to dig into the skin, pressing the answer out of her. And with those words, I release her, knowing she'll stay.

Rolling up the sleeves of my sweater, I block Annaliese out. There is no reason anymore to reassure her, and right now I have to focus on myself. This is always the hardest part. I flick the straight razor open. It's from another time and place, and yet still so familiar, still full of memories of a father long dead. My hand squeezes the wooden handle tighter.

"Please," I murmur softly. This isn't for Annaliese, but directed toward a higher power I no longer believe in. I used to finish the phrase with "forgive me," but I dropped that decades ago—along with any hopes for absolution.

Then I make two slices through my skin. One for each arm. Starting at the edge of my elbow and tearing straight through the soft flesh until I reach the edge of my palm. The razor falls from my fingers into the dirt at my feet. My hands hang limp at my sides, and blood streams from my fingertips, a slow drip that will quickly turn into a steady red waterfall.

Annaliese stares in horror. Her mouth moves, but no sound comes out. "Yes, I will pay" are the last words that Annaliese will ever say.

"Now pick up the razor and cut my heart out," I tell Annaliese. And because she has no other choice, she does exactly as I say.

HEART IN HER HAND

The memory stopped abruptly. Like a plug had been pulled. The world that replaced it felt less real, and somehow not as substantial in comparison.

With a detached sense of horror I watched the mom slap Rice Sixteen across the face repeatedly. He accepted each blow, not even looking at the mom, his eyes focused on some point beyond her. Maybe he was reliving the same memory I'd just witnessed.

The dad finally pulled the mom away, wrapping her in a full bear hug to do so. After a moment she slumped in his arms and went silent, at which point I realized that the low keening noise I'd been hearing was coming from her. The whirling police lights caught her face, twisted in the despair that I'd always sensed hovering just beneath her skin.

My detachment left me. She looked too much like Annaliese. Not the one I saw in the mirror, but the one who'd slashed through skin, and then cracked apart ribs until she held my hot, wet heart in her hand.

As my eyesight blurred, I felt sick with fear that I was returning to that otherworld in the trees and dead leaves once more. It was almost a relief, as the world went black, to realize that I was merely having a good old-fashioned fainting spell. My surroundings faded away, and then quickly returned as the force of my body hitting the ground jerked me back to consciousness. Still, I kept my eyes firmly shut. I'd seen enough for one night.

Two fingers slid across my neck, seeking a pulse, at the same time a low male voice asked, "Are you okay?"

My eyes fluttered open. Spots blurred my vision, and I could feel the darkness rushing back at me. I leaned into it like it was one of the mom's hugs. But before my last bits of consciousness fully released me, I saw two eyes staring down at me. One was dark and searching, while the other was a blinking red pinpoint of light, burning straight through me.

BEGINNINGS. AGAIN.

LOVE IS . . .

Love is flannel pj's.

Every fall picking
the perfect print
and pattern
at Jo-Ann Fabrics.

Mom sews them
top and bottom
zigging and zagging
through the machine.

The buttons
Mom sews by hand.
They're better that way,
she says.
Lasts forever that way,
she says.
Even though I always
outgrow them after a year.

But this year
I wanted snaps.
Bright shiny silver snaps
that tinkled softly against
my tapping fingertips.

Mom said they were cheap
that they wouldn't last forever.
I don't care about forever.
That's what I said.

So Mom marched them
down the middle of the
once button-
now snap-front
top.

Bright shiny silver snaps
right where
boring sturdy buttons
would've been.

Love is warm flannel pj's.

On cold nights
Mom throws them in the dryer
while I am in the shower.
When I get out
they're warm and
soft and ready.

But the snaps are hot.
The first time they leave

little red marks.
After that I know
to hold them away
to let them cool.

Love is flannel pj's
handmade
and warmed.

But love is also snaps
bright with silver shine
that burns.

—ARG

Morning came too soon. I woke at eight a.m. Outside my window birds chirped. Farther off in the distance I could detect the low roar of an airplane. It was like every other morning since I'd been returned to this place, except for one thing. The chair where the mom usually slept was empty. The pillows that she always arranged so that they sat slightly overlapping one another in the crook of the chair's arm lay stranded on the bedroom floor, two tiny oases of disorder in an otherwise perfectly tidy room. No doubt they were in the exact spot they had fallen last night when she'd awoken and realized I wasn't asleep in my bed.

Funny. She thought she'd found her daughter, but Annaliese was more lost to her than ever.

Was that why she hadn't returned to the room last night, realizing the futility of safeguarding the very person who had caused her daughter to disappear?

I shook my head, forcing the order of events back into place. No one else knew what I had seen. No one knew what had happened to Annaliese. It was the one thing that had been repeated during all those TV interviews we'd done. Her disappearance was still a mystery. There were suspects—*persons of interest* are what they called them—but no arrests had been made. And there had definitely never been any mention of finding another body or even blood. But then again the mom had been quick to close off any line of questioning that went near that subject.

"The police are still looking into it, and we continue to pray that the person who did this will be found and brought to justice. Right now we are focusing on the future."

Those had been her exact words every time. They had been a warning. The details of my own disappearance were not for me to know. And if it was the gruesome scene that I can now imagine all too well, then it makes sense that the mom would want to protect her daughter from that knowledge.

Protect Annaliese. That is always her mission. An unending one. And that's what she had been doing last night. Attacking Rice Sixteen for taking her daughter's virginity. For leaving her alone to be attacked and taken . . . and for blurting it all out for everyone to hear. I'm sure it was a combination of the three.

And that look on her face as the dad pulled her away.

Jumping out of the bed, I decided to find the mom, make sure she was okay. I now knew—if I could believe the terrible thing I'd seen last night—that she wasn't my mom, and that whoever—or whatever—I was, she had every reason to hate me for taking away her daughter and bringing an impostor back. And yet, I already knew the mom well enough to guess she'd prefer an impostor to having no daughter at all. And without knowing myself at all, I, too, preferred to have the mom, not just because my only other option was to be alone in the world, but because the stranglehold style of love she practiced was the only real and consistent thing I'd experienced since waking up.

Quickly, I threw on a pair of jeans and a long-sleeved thermal T-shirt. I tucked my hospital gown into the farthest corner of the closet beneath a pile of shoes, where the mom was least likely to discover it. The brand-new clothes the mom had purchased after seeing how Annaliese's old clothes hung on my emaciated frame were stiff and scratchy against my skin. I'd been mixing in pieces of Annaliese's wardrobe, shirts worn soft from years of usage—my favorite a faded T-shirt reading YOUTH POETRY FEST—but now it felt like I had taken too much of hers.

Before leaving the room, I grabbed a fresh pack of Listerine breath strips and placed two of them on my tongue. After the chocolate incident in the car, the dad had gone to the nearest gas station and he must have bought every variety of mint-flavored anything they carried—including a car air freshener. The breath strips were the only thing that had been able to make the gagging stop and let me think about the possibility of chewing and swallowing food again.

Although not chocolate. Never again chocolate.

Since then I'd developed a bit of a habit. I was up to three packs a day. Without them, that horrible flavor of chocolate mixed with death kept coming back, coating my tongue and closing my throat.

It was always at its worst first thing in the morning, but this morning was a new high—or low. Popping another breath strip into my mouth, I pocketed the rest of the packet and tiptoed down the hall to the parents' room. They always left their door wide open, I think as a way of saying that there was no room I wasn't welcome in. Still I'd never done more than glance in from the doorway of my own room farther down the hall. It had never been necessary to go looking for the mom before.

The room was empty, the bed neatly made. No clothes on the floor, or flung over the backs of chairs. Yes, the mom was a bit of a neat freak, but this room looked, if not unlived in, then definitely unslept in. And not just from last night. Of course, I'd known the mom had been spending her nights in my room, but it had never occurred to me to wonder where the dad was sleeping.

I don't know why this upset me. There was certainly nothing sinister about a tidy and empty room. It looked lonely, I guess, and made me panic again, certain that the mom and the dad had figured out I wasn't actually their daughter. Maybe they were out right now looking for the real Annaliese.

How ironic. The replacement, the forgery, afraid of being replaced by the real thing.

My thoughts chased me down the stairs, through the empty kitchen, and into the family room. I stopped there, frozen by the sight of the mom, curled up on the couch, asleep.

A few months before I was found, the mom had taken up knitting. It hadn't been her idea, but a solution suggested by one of her doctors to deal with a condition she'd developed after Annaliese had first gone missing. Trichotillomania, they called it. She pulled out her own hair. I guess it started with pulling at the hair on her head, but then she became numb to that pain, so she began to pluck out her eyelashes. Soon she had almost none left. The knitting kept her hands busy.

She'd explained this to me matter-of-factly, while she'd frowned down at the needles in her hands. Watching her, I could see there was no enjoyment in the task, only frustration. Still, she was faithful to the project. The lumpy woolen blanket, just a series of knots in some places, stretched wide enough to cover everyone sitting on the couch. But she wasn't done with it yet. Maybe the mom thought that if she kept knitting away, she might yet shape it into something beautiful, redeemable.

It covered her now. The needles and a ball of yarn were stuck into a corner near her feet. I was about to turn away, leave her to sleep, when I noticed something clutched in the fist she had curled up over her head. Leave it, I told myself, even as my feet crept closer and I leaned over, holding my breath so that a blast of Listerine wouldn't shake her awake. If I had been looking for reassurance, something to say that she was still holding me tight even if she hadn't slept by my bed, then perhaps I found it.

There were two plastic-covered strips in her hand. One aged, yellow, and almost comically tiny. The other much newer. I recognized it instantly. They were the identifying bracelets the hospital puts on patients. The first must have come from a newborn Annaliese. I could almost see the mom's careful concentration as she slipped a sharp pair of scissors between the plastic and the tender skin of her newborn's leg.

Holding them together like that, she would be reminding herself of the happiness she'd felt both times, bringing her precious daughter home. This was what I wanted to believe. And it fit. The mom was the type to keep hospital ID bracelets as keepsakes.

But then another thought intervened. What if instead she was comparing and contrasting? What if she was wondering what exactly she had brought home this time?

FENCE

I slipped out using the sliding glass door that led into the backyard. It whined softly as I pushed it closed behind me, but the mom still didn't stir. Deliberately I forced myself to turn away and contemplate the view instead. It was your typical suburban backyard, I suppose. A cement slab for a patio, with a grill and glass-topped table. Flower beds ran alongside the house on either side. The rest was grass.

Another row of houses lined up behind ours. Backyards flowed into one another, and grass stretched in all directions, like a gigantic communal backyard. Except for the one fence. Not a box, closing in a single backyard, but instead a straight wooden line, shielding our house from the one directly to the left. It was so strange, the one-sided fence, and there was no doubting its meaning. Clearly, there was some kind of bad blood, a neighborly feud even. It didn't seem like the type of thing the mom and the dad would get caught up in.

I walked beside the wooden divide, lightly trailing my fingers along. My feet were once again bare, and the grass felt cold and stiff against my soles, but I kept placing one foot in front of the other.

At the edge of the yard, the fence stopped, and I with it. Only a few small steps around would take me to the other side. Into enemy territory. My fingers moved ahead of me, finding the rough edge—and getting a splinter for my trouble. Jerking my hand back, I felt irrationally as if I'd been attacked.

A scream of anguish came drifting across the empty lawns. Although distant and muffled, it pierced me. I knew that scream.

It was the mom.

Turning, I ran toward the house, my own small hurt forgotten. Another cry. Picking up speed, I reached the door too quickly, and my bare feet skidded against the cement slab, stopping me from slamming into the glass door. My hot breath came too fast, fogging the glass, but even through the haze I could see the mom.

She was still in the exact same position on the couch. Asleep . . . perhaps even peacefully.

As I backed away from the door, the splinter in my finger throbbed and my battered feet ached. I retraced my steps along the fence line, trying to understand what I'd heard. Or had it been imagined? It would almost be a relief to know my mind was playing tricks on me; perhaps then I could discount the memory from last night too.

But only a few steps from the fence edge, I heard it once more. It still sliced into me, but I breathed through that and focused on moving toward the sound. The screams led me away from the mom sleeping inside, and over to the other side of the fence.

What had I expected to see? Something threatening, I suppose. Or, at the very least, something obviously odd and out of place. But there was the same cement slab. The requisite grill was missing and the outdoor table was orange with rust, and chairless. A tangle of weeds and rotting leaves filled the flower beds, but the grass was the same, if maybe a little longer.

The place was completely inoffensive, except for one small detail. The storm doors leading into the basement, instead of being sealed tightly closed, overlapped slightly, just enough for the sounds of the mom's wail to escape into the sunlit morning.

It was a recording. From this distance the hiss of background noise become obvious, giving it away.

And now I understood the enmity. What kind of sicko taped that and then replayed it for their own amusement? And now I also remembered the red blinking light that I'd seen before finally passing out. Not just a sound recording then, but video too. And the cameraman himself had been pretending to check on me, when really he'd been moving in for a close-up.

Anger surged inside me. I banged a fist against the metal door, and then lifted it up. The recorded cry cut off abruptly. It only increased my rage.

I shouted down into the sudden silence, "I know what you are!"

Of course, I had no idea who was down there, or anything about them except the evidence of the recording and a very hazy memory of a face. The one eye that hadn't been red had stared at me in a way that had seemed kind, compassionate even. But maybe I was remembering wrong.

"Monster," I added, spitting the word down toward the darkness. A hot potato of a word, I tossed it and then ran away—before whoever was there could pass it back to me.

BASEMENT

Before opening the sliding glass door, I popped another three breath strips to wipe away the sour taste that had risen once more.

Inside everything was the same. I couldn't stop myself from being disappointed that the mom hadn't already woken up, and hadn't been anxiously scanning the room for my presence. Uncertain where to go or what to do next, I was about to wake her . . . when the basement door swung open and the dad stepped into view.

He gave a little jump of surprise, obviously not expecting to see me standing there in the middle of the room. Even though I had yet to make a peep, the dad put his fingers to his lips, signaling that I was to remain quiet. I nodded my understanding. The dad frowned back at me, so I repeated the same gesture, letting him know I was on board. He didn't notice because now he was frowning at the mom. His gaze swung to me again and the grimace was gone. Resignation had taken its place as he beckoned me to follow him, and then disappeared down the basement stairs.

As I tiptoed past the mom, I got it. With her out of commission, it fell to the dad to look after me, and this was clearly a task he'd rather avoid. The feeling was mutual.

After closing the door so softly it was no louder than a sigh,

I turned to check out the basement. Every wall was lined with floor-to-ceiling storage shelves. And every shelf was stacked full. Mostly canned goods, but as I slowly came down the stairs I could make out three units with nothing but jugs of water, another one full of jarred spaghetti sauce, one dedicated to all types of boxed macaroni and cheese, and finally one that was devoted to all things Little Debbie. All together, there was enough to feed an army.

The organization would have worked for the military too. Except for the spaghetti sauce. On the third shelf down, exactly three jars were missing. No, not missing. They'd been relocated—with some haste—to the cement floor. The dad must have been in the middle of cleaning it up. A broom and the shattered glass sat in a pile pushed to the edge of the room. A bucket of pinkish-colored water waited in the middle of the splatters and streaks of sauce.

The whole thing looked almost bloody. Like a crime scene. Except I knew blood. Blood wasn't really red; it was black disguised as red. This was reddish orange. It smelled sweet too, with no hint of blood's sour metallic tang.

I popped another three breath strips, while the dad stood there staring at the mess. Taking a step farther into the basement, I noticed another room. Of sorts. More of a drywall border with a doorway cut into it. The light was dimmer on the other side of the wall, but I could just make out three cots lined up in a row. One was neatly made up with sheets and a blanket. A digital alarm clock glowed beside it on the floor. It looked lived in, in a way that their bedroom had not. I had a horrible feeling that this was where the dad had been sleeping.

"Your mother started this during the whole Y2K scare," he finally said softly, still not looking at me. "You know what that was?"

I did. Although, like all my memories, it was detached. The fear that the computers and all the things that helped run everything from banks to electric companies would fail because they weren't programmed to change from 1999 to 2000. Some people had panicked, but in the end it was all for nothing.

I knew this, but I didn't remember who told it to me, any more than I could remember where I was when that New Year was rung in.

"Yeah," I answered at last.

"It was only half as much then. She was embarrassed afterward, said it was silly. . . . Anni—" He stopped, and quickly corrected himself. "*You* would bring your little toy grocery cart down here and pretend to go grocery shopping. And I would joke with your mom about it. You know, saying, 'More cans of peas, the end is near!' Or something like that. It was funny. Harmless. But then 9/11 happened, and, well, after that . . . She never said anything, but every few weeks another shelf would appear, and food to fill it." His voice was thick, like he was crying, or trying not to.

I opened my mouth to say I was sorry. Sorry for making their worst nightmare come true. If a basement full of nonperishable items can't keep your child safe, then what could? And that's when I guessed what had happened here. What—or who—had sent those three jars of spaghetti sauce crashing to the floor.

"Was she upset last night?" My voice shook. I felt nosy asking, like it was none of my business.

Maybe he felt that way too, because he hesitated a long time before finally answering. "Yes. After we got you into bed, your mom was . . ." He shook his head. "I've never seen her like that. Not the whole time you were missing." For the first time since I'd joined him down here, he looked at me. Straight on. Actually, it might've been the first time the dad really looked me in the eye at all.

"You have to understand, it was bad. The way you went missing, everything we knew . . . Your mom doesn't want you to know the details, but suffice to say, no one thought you were alive. Almost from the beginning they were searching for a body. Except your mom. She couldn't believe it. And I let her have that hope, because I was afraid of what would happen if she didn't. It's because of her that we kept looking. If she hadn't, we never would have found you."

Now it was my turn to look away. Suddenly shaky, I sank down onto the bottom step and laid my cheek against my knees.

The mom had been better when I was missing. The belief that she would find her daughter had fueled her. Now that she had me, it was worse. I was wrong. I'd thought an impostor might be better than no daughter at all. But the mom had never really lost Annaliese, because she'd refused to let her go.

"She was so angry last night," the dad continued. "She attacked that boy, and I had to hold her to keep her from going after him again until the cops drove him home. Even then, it took a long time before she calmed down. I went to make her some tea, and get her pills, and that's when I heard her down here. She threw a few cans first, and then started in on the jars. More satisfying, I suppose." He hesitated once more and I waited for him to tell me this was all my fault.

It *was* all my fault. I should've stayed lost in those endless fields of Oklahoma. Or even better—I should've taken that garbage bag and wrapped it around my head instead of my body.

The dad's hand landed on my hair, gently, as if to comfort me. His palm half covered my ear and so I was certain that I misheard his next words. "We are so sorry, Annaliese. We failed you. We thought we could keep you safe, that all this would protect you somehow." He laughed, but the sound was hollow. "We didn't know you were at a party that night. We didn't know you were with that boy. We didn't know that you were with any boys at all. I guess . . . I guess we didn't know you. And we're sorry for that. We should have done better. We should've known."

I wanted to tell him that Annaliese was a typical teenager who in a moment of rebellion had made a mistake. And that she wasn't with that boy. Or any other one. She had been the girl they believed her to be . . . but she wasn't. Not anymore.

I didn't say any of this though.

Lifting my head, I took his hand in my own. "I'm sorry too. And I'm gonna do better." Finally, I forced my eyes to meet his again. "Dad."

And with that one word, I hated myself even more, because he finally smiled at me, as if I truly were his long-lost daughter.

TWO BOYS

SEVENTH SEASON

Winter to spring to summer to fall.
The seasons change
and change nothing at all.

This is my seventh season of loneliness.
I begin to despair it will never end.

—ARG

It was decided that my return to school would be delayed a week. Or perhaps more. We were going to "wait and see." Those were the mom's words, although she never specified exactly what we were waiting to see. In the meantime I was supposed to rest and relax. This was code for "stay in the house away from other people."

I didn't mind. So far other people hadn't brought out the best in me. Plus it made the mom happy.

My fears of the mom turning on me were unfounded. If anything, she clung to me tighter than ever. The only difference was that I held her right back. We were a perfect little circle of neediness, one completing the other. And if there were instances when I felt a bit suffocated by it all, well, they were brief and passed quickly.

Each day the mom had a project to keep us busy. The dad, who had returned to work that Monday, would pretend to look disappointed because he was missing out, as she announced at breakfast that we would be scrapbooking baby pictures or bedazzling T-shirts. There was also baking.

On Tuesday we made oatmeal raisin cookies.

On Wednesday we ate the cookies during a Disney-movie marathon. We took turns picking. The mom chose *Dumbo* and *Bambi*. I couldn't help noticing that they were two movies where the moms got top billing.

As for me, I went with *Pinocchio*. Three times. I told the mom I couldn't get enough of the song about wishing on a star. That made her happy. She liked thinking I was still a girl who believed in dreams. But it wasn't true. What I really couldn't get enough of was the end, when Pinocchio became a real boy, and not just a puppet who'd found a way to move without strings.

Thursday I woke up on the couch. Some sort of ringing noise had woken me, but in my groggy state I couldn't place it. My head pounded.

I hadn't been sleeping well. My nights were filled with nightmares. Or memories, maybe.

The first time I had one, I'd cried out in my sleep. The mom was instantly out of her chair and at my side, looking for the injury, wanting to fix it. I lied and told her my stomach hurt. I didn't want her to know I'd been having a bad dream. Didn't want her wondering what the dream was about.

I started going to bed early, so I could get a few hours of sleep before she set up her nightly vigil. Then I'd sleep for a few more hours after she crept out at eight to see the dad off to work. Last night, though, our movie marathon had run late. I'd been so exhausted, I couldn't even remember falling asleep.

But I remembered my nightmare. One clip played over and over on a constant loop, and I spent the night trying to escape it.

Now, as I stumbled to my feet, moving toward the ringing

63

noise, the scene played again.

I was back in the trees. With Annaliese. She had a bright red apple held in her two hands. It glistened slightly. As if she had plucked it from a dew-drenched tree. Her long fingers, pale white against the harsh red, seemed to clench the apple tighter as it came closer to her mouth. Snow White ready to bite into the poisoned apple.

And that's when I knew. But it was too late.

Her mouth was opening wide to take a bite, and an instant before her teeth sank in, a drop of juice fell from the apple. Not the juice of overripe fruit, but blood. Blood, still warm from the heart it had been pumping through. Her mouth snapped shut, straight white teeth closing over red. And then everything went red . . . until the clip started once more.

Rubbing my eyes, I tried to focus and pull away from the dream. I'd followed the noise into the front entryway, and now, looking up, I saw a white box stuck to the wall right above my head. Smoke detector, I thought. But no. Those were round and went beep. This was square and the sound was more like *dingdongdingdongdingdong.* At the same time my brain finally identified the doorbell, three loud knocks made the front door shake.

After an initial backward jump of surprise, I rushed forward to open it, then stopped. I wasn't supposed to answer the door, or the phone, or do anything that might put me into direct contact with anyone other than the mom or the dad. And where was the mom? How long had that doorbell been ringing? I spun around, expecting to see her only a few steps behind me. Nothing.

Whoever it was knocked again.

It occurred to me that maybe it was the mom. If she wasn't inside with me, then the only thing that made any sense was that she was on the other side of the door, trying desperately to get back in. Maybe she ran to grab the mail, and had locked the door behind her. An automatic response. Lock me in. Keep everyone else out. Except now she was locked out.

A smile was on my face, ready to make some small joke, as I pulled the door open. It fell away almost instantly.

It wasn't the mom leaning on our doorbell, but rather an overweight boy with a freckle-covered face and a head of curly red hair. He didn't seem to notice that my own smile had been fleeting as he grinned up at me.

"Hello again, my girl." The words came out in a silky tone that didn't quite match the little-boy pitch of his voice.

"Don't call me that," I snapped at him without even meaning to. The words were automatic, the same way I instantly answered "fine" to the mom's constant query of "You okay, hon?"

He laughed; his round cheeks dimpled and shook in a way that was oddly sinister. "That's my girl. And they said you'd forgotten. Brilliant angle. Always were clever." Reaching up, he gently flicked a finger against my cheek. I shivered. "Now be a good girl and tell me where you've been the last year. Physician wouldn't tell me nothing. Fucking typical, right?"

I couldn't imagine Annaliese being friends with this boy. He had to be at least two or three years younger than her, but his manner was so familiar. And he'd mentioned a physician. Maybe they shared a doctor? That seemed unlikely. He didn't act as if he simply knew her, but as if they had a long-standing relationship. The type where you saw things about someone that they couldn't even see about themselves.

"I'm sorry," I said, uncertain. "I really don't remember. . . . We're not . . . are we friends?"

Now his smile faltered, although he regained it quickly enough, along with a hard laugh. "Shit. You really can't remember, can you?"

I could no longer miss the malice in him. Hard eyes stared out of his soft, round face.

"I'm sorry," I said again, no longer caring who he was, only wanting to get away. Closing the door, I added, "For whatever I did."

He slammed against it, pushing both of us into the house. I stumbled over my own feet and hit the ground, but he didn't let up. He was short but round, and he positioned his considerable bulk over me, planting a dirty sneaker on my chest.

"What you did? What you did!" The pressure against my

chest increased. "What you did was fuck everything up."

His voice cracked on *everything*, and I let out a nervous giggle. His foot slid forward, nudging the base of my chin.

"Something funny?"

I gave only the slightest shake of my head in reply.

"Good." His foot eased back slightly, just enough that I could swallow without him detecting the motion through the tips of his toes. "'Cause I didn't think it was funny when you disappeared without a trace in the middle of a switch. And I didn't think it was funny when I got a note from the Physician telling me to take this fat little fourteen-year-old and wait. Wait. Those were his fucking instructions. Wait. So I've waited. And waited. Nearly a whole damn year I've waited. And that hasn't been funny either. But what's really not funny is that you left it till the last minute. You come back with the clock ticking down to the last few weeks, and then . . .

"KABLOOEY!" He leaned down so his face was in mine. I shook. He laughed.

"Yeah, you don't remember what happens then. Now, that is funny. But you probably wouldn't think so. Way I remember it, you sure weren't laughing the last time you thought you'd found a way out. So you better get your next stooge lined up, 'cause I'm more than ready to be finished with this fat suit." He looked down at himself with a sneer of disgust and poked at his round little belly.

"Please go away." I could barely get the words past my trembling lips.

At this his eyes flickered away from me, and then back. It wasn't guilt that made him look away. Rather, he seemed to be calculating something.

A moment later, his foot finally lifted from my chest. As it hung in the air above me, I wondered if he'd decided to kick me in the face. He was capable of it; I had been able to feel that right through the sole of his shoe. Instead he knelt beside me. Instinctively, I leaned away, but there was nowhere to go. His fat fingers grabbed the back of my head, twisting into my short hair.

"Anna, I love you. Don't you remember *that*? And you love me. We belong together. We're the same. You know it. Even if you don't remember. You know it."

The switch from fiery vengeance to equally fiery lover left me blinking at him in surprise. And then his lips were on mine. His tongue too. Forcing its way in when I opened my mouth to protest.

I bit down, trapping his tongue between my teeth, hard enough to draw blood. That tiny bit of blood filled my mouth. Gagging, I unlocked my jaw. He jerked away, but not quick enough to miss being splattered by the bile my empty stomach spewed out.

Even after there was nothing left, I continued retching while my shaky hands fumbled for the pack of breath strips. I could hear the boy cursing in the background and closed my eyes against him as I crammed a whole handful of the strips into my mouth, not letting them melt, but chewing them so that they squeaked and crunched between my teeth. Pressing my forehead against the cold tile floor, I focused on the burn, desperate not to think about the way his tongue had felt in my mouth. Or how horribly familiar the taste of blood had been. And definitely not about my sneaking suspicion that this boy didn't know Annaliese at all. That maybe he knew me. Whoever I'd been before I became Annaliese.

Something bounced off my curled spine, before hitting the floor beside me with a soft thunk. "We belong together, Anna. Always have." His sneakers scuffed across the floor, away from me, and then the door closed.

I was alone.

Stumbling to my feet, I twisted the dead bolt and then the smaller lock on the door handle itself. Trembling, I sank down once more. Beside me a bulging manila envelope lay on the floor. He had left it for me.

Picking it up between two fingers, I flung it across the room. But a few minutes later, I was crawling after it, needing to know what was inside. I shook the contents out. A pack of cigarettes fell first, followed by a lighter. Something else was still in there, wrapped in paper towels and wedged into the bottom of the envelope. I left it. The cigarettes were already in my hand, the cellophane crackling as I tapped the box against the palm of my hand. Red letters against a faded white background read Winston.

"Winston tastes good . . . like a cigarette should." I murmured the words, not sure where they came from. Tearing the cellophane wrapper away, I slid one from the pack. It felt right perched between the V of two fingers, and even better when I brought it to my lips in perfect coordination with the flickering lighter and a deep inhalation to start it burning.

I sucked the smoke into my lungs. The acrid tang obliterated everything else, and this felt right too. The entire ritual, like a form of meditation. So, I was a smoker. Exhaling, I reached toward the smoke, trying to snatch it from the air.

No, I wasn't merely a person who smoked. I was the smoke itself. A smoke person. It was real, and it wasn't. There and then gone. Ashes to ashes. Dirt to dirt. Smoke to smoke.

Already I could feel myself drifting away.

"Not smart for a boy made of wood to take up smoking," the mom had said, the second time we watched *Pinocchio*. It was the part when they were on Pleasure Island. I had laughed.

The red tip of the cigarette glowed in front of me as I exhaled a long plume of smoke, and at the same time I pressed the burning tip against my thigh, an inch above my knee. The thin flannel of my pajamas burned away too quickly, and then there was skin.

The pain was real. Vicious. Even so, I pressed harder, grinding, until it went out. With a hiss of agony I pulled it away, and then brushed the ashes aside, wanting to see the red-blistered skin below.

I touched the spot gently with the tip of a finger. It was ugly and angry and already oozing something viscous and clear.

Perfect.

This would leave a scar. A permanent mark to say: I Was Here.

BOY WITH THE RED EYE

I stumbled around. Up and down, from one end of the house to the other. I must have been through the kitchen five or six times before I saw the note on the table.

> Annaliese,
>
> Had a doctor's appointment this morning. Wanted to let you sleep, you looked so tired. I left some waffles and bacon warming in the oven. Please do not leave the house or open the door to anyone. Will be home soon.
>
> Love and hugs and kisses,
> Mom

There was something about the brevity of the note that bothered me. The mom had given me a shoe box stuffed full of letters that she'd written to Annaliese while she was missing. It was another suggestion from a shrink. The letters didn't say much. Mostly that she missed Annaliese and thought about her all the time. Still they managed to ramble. None of them were this short or to the point. The only part of this note that felt like the mom was the "love and hugs and kisses" at the end.

I didn't really care. The important thing was that I hadn't been abandoned, and soon the mom would be home. She would keep that horrible boy away from me. Or maybe I should worry about keeping him away from her, so he wouldn't tell her about the real me. The me stowed away inside of her daughter.

I sank to the floor with that thought.

But I didn't stay there long before getting up again. I was all business this time.

Turning off the oven, I took the plate of waffles and bacon out. They were toaster waffles, but she had pretoasted them for me. For some reason this struck me as funny. I laughed a little desperately, even as I shoved the food down the whirring garbage disposal. After it was gone, I dirtied a plate with a few strategically placed crumbs and a few dots of syrup, and then placed it in the sink.

Getting rid of the cigarette-smoke smell came next. After checking several times to make sure there was no sign of the boy,

I flung the front door open. Using it like a giant fan, I swung it back and forth. When I was done, the sheer drapes covering the little window next to the door still stank like smoke if you stuck your nose right into them, but I could only hope the mom wouldn't do that.

My last task was disposing of the manila envelope. I slipped out the back door, intending to bury it in the trash can. The cigarettes had lost their appeal at the same instant I'd gained a new scar. But there was something else still there at the bottom of the envelope. I feared that wrapped lump. The redheaded boy wanted to hurt me, that much was certain. The cigarettes were up-front about their dangers, a warning helpfully printed right on the package. That made them the lesser danger. The other thing would hurt more.

I'd had enough hurting; I wanted no part of whatever was at the bottom of that envelope.

I lifted out a few sacks of trash, until I found the perfect one, heavy and reeking with rot. Holding my breath, I carefully untied the bag and eased it open just wide enough to reach inside. With the envelope clutched in my fist, I plunged my hand into the heart of the assorted waste.

If I had uncurled my fingers, and left the envelope there, the whole thing would've been lost in a distant landfill within the week.

Cursing softly, I jerked my hand back out, and the envelope

with it. It wasn't the best time to be indulging my curiosity. It might've been the worst. Still, I couldn't let it go without seeing what was inside.

I tore the envelope apart and stuffed it into the trash bag, and then the cigarettes and lighter went in too. That left me with a wad of paper towels, sealed with duct tape.

I gave it a squeeze. Layers of softness gave way and then stopped, where something hard and solid sat at their core.

As I stared down at the misshapen lump, red began spreading out from my hand, racing across the paper towels, slowly yet steadily consuming the white.

Blood. My whole hand was sticky with it.

I tore the red parts off, like I was unwrapping a cursed mummy, but the blood continued its advance. When the last bit of paper towel fell away, a single-edged blade folded into a wooden handle sat in my hand.

I recognized it instantly. This was the blade I'd given Annaliese. The one she'd used to cut me open.

Names were carved into the wooden handle. The blood still oozing out around the razor had filled the tiny crevices and outlined them in red. Eight names in all. Anna began the short list; Annaliese ended it.

The razor slid from my hand and fell to the ground.

Only then did I notice the deep cut across my palm. It wasn't from the blade tucked away inside the handle. Instead, the culprit was resting at the top of the trash bag I'd opened—the jagged tin disk from a can of peas. I hadn't even felt it slicing my hand.

"Are you okay?"

The question came from a boy. Or a man. A man-boy.

His face—the stubble on his cheeks, the lines around his frowning mouth, the bags beneath his gray eyes—all spoke of age. But his body, long and gangly, made up of limbs leaning this way and that, was like a foal just born and stumbling around on his new legs.

I might've smiled at him, despite my bleeding hand and everything else going on, if only to see what he looked like without the frown. It didn't fit him. But dangling from the flexed fingers of one of his long arms was a video camera.

This was the boy from next door. The boy with one red eye, who liked to record and replay people's screams.

When he noticed the direction of my gaze, his face went red beneath his darkly stubbled cheeks. "I wasn't, I mean . . . it's not what you think." He shifted the camera behind a jangling leg.

"Okay," I said. And maybe it wasn't. Maybe I'd been wrong about him. Then I could maybe be wrong about myself too.

I wanted to ask him questions and find out for sure, but there was no time. I heard the sound of the garage door opening. The mom was home.

Swiftly, I scooped the razor off the ground. And in that

same instant I made a decision.

"Do me a favor?"

Before he could answer, I tossed the razor in his direction. The throw went wide and high but the boy's free hand snapped out. Quick as a frog's tongue catching a fly, he gripped it in his fist.

"Hold on to that for me, please. Don't tell anyone you have it. Don't show it to anyone. Just keep it for me."

I heaved the open trash bag into the can, and then turned to the boy for his response.

His eyes, which had been watching me so intently, skittered away, focusing on the razor instead.

As I awaited his response, I felt irrationally anxious, like I'd just gathered my courage to ask him to the prom. Stupid. I clenched my still-bleeding hand into a fist.

After what felt like an eternity, he looked into my eyes. The hand holding the razor flew out at me, and I thought he was giving it back. But then the razor slid up his sleeve, leaving him free to simply offer a handshake.

"I'm Dex."

Not wanting to press my bloody palm against his, I instead ran for the back door, calling over my shoulder, "I'm Anna."

It was only after I'd sprinted up the stairs toward the bathroom—jumping into the shower before the water was fully warm—that my words had time to catch up with me.

"I'm Anna." That's what I'd said.

Anna was what the redheaded boy had called me too.

Anna was the first name on the razor handle.

Anna was me.

But how had I gone from Anna to Annaliese? And who were those other six girls in between?

Hot water poured from the shower and over my head, but I shivered and shook. No matter how hot I turned the water, the shakes continued. The burn in my thigh ached, and the cut across my palm stung every time one of my fingers had the slightest twitch. Clenching my teeth to keep them from clacking together, I stood under the burning stream until the water went cold.

EAVESDROPPING

Dear Annaliese,

I miss you. I wish I had a place to send this letter so that you could hear that . . . wherever you are. But wherever you are, I think (and hope) that you already know this. I also hope you can soon find a way to come home. I miss you. Oh. I already said that. Well, we both know that you are the talented writer in the family. Your father and I were both so proud when you won the Poets of Tomorrow contest. I know you thought it was embarrassing, but I still think it was beautiful. Maybe wherever you are, you have a bit of paper and you are writing your poems and they are helping to get you through. If you don't have paper, maybe you could compose them in your head, because you need to get through, Annaliese. You need to get through, because I am here and waiting for you.

Love and hugs and kisses,
Mom

The minute I turned off the shower, before I could even reach for a towel, the mom was tapping at the door.

"You okay in there, Annaliese?"

And just like that. BOOM.

"Leave me alone!"

The words tore through my throat, leaving it raw in their wake. I could almost see them as they pierced the door and hit their target on the other side. And the mom so defenseless, her arms constantly held open.

As I toweled off, I heard nothing else. I imagined the mom knocked over by my words. Eventually, she would gather herself enough to crawl away, lick her wounds in private.

I didn't give the mom enough credit. This was the same woman who'd attacked Rice Sixteen, with her hands curled into claws. I remembered this as I opened the door to find her standing ready and waiting for me. There were no red and teary eyes, or trembling lips. She wasn't angry or prepared with a how-dare you-speak-to-me-that-way lecture either.

What I got instead was more of the steadfast love and concern that flowed from a seemingly bottomless well.

"I'm sorry, sweetie, I shouldn't have left a note. But you were sleeping, and I didn't want to wake you. And I knew you wouldn't want to be dragged along to the doctor's. . . ."

It would've been easier if she'd yelled at me. Because that soft tone brought back the fear I'd felt when I'd woken up.

Not today, but the first time. In that little wisp of a building. And I was alone.

Where had she been then?

And when Annaliese lay in the dirt and dead leaves, losing her virginity. Losing her fantasy of love. Had the mom thought she was safe in bed? Had she even known Annaliese wasn't home?

Or when Annaliese held a hot heart in her hands? The mom should have been charging through the woods, screaming her name, and ending the nightmare.

Where the fuck had she been then? Where?

"Maybe I did want to go," I said. No, I shouted it—right into the mom's face. "You didn't tell me because you don't want to let me out of this house. You want to keep me a prisoner here."

It wasn't what I meant to say. I wanted to tell her to never let me go. To let her know she'd allowed the redheaded boy in, and I was afraid of him. I was afraid of everything. Except at the same time that I wanted her to be my shield, I also wanted to push her away. It was like when she was there, I had to breathe for both of us. Or maybe it was her trying to breathe for me. Either way, there wasn't enough air.

The mom's hand went to her eyes. Not to brush away a tear, but to pluck at her eyelashes, pulling a few small hairs loose.

It seemed to focus her.

"Annaliese, you are not a prisoner. If you wanted to leave the house, why didn't you say so?"

She was so calm. So reasonable. It was absolutely maddening.

"I am a prisoner. You know I am. You won't let me go to school, you won't even let me check the mail by myself."

She flinched, caught by this undeniable truth. It wasn't enough. Not yet. She needed to know that she'd hurt me.

"This isn't a house. It's a tomb. You brought me home to bury me in here. And I won't. I won't."

The mom shook like my words were an earthquake. She still wasn't running though.

"Annaliese, sweetie. That's not—"

"I won't," I said again, interrupting her.

She threw her hands up. "You won't what? What is it you won't do?"

I honestly didn't know. *I won't and you can't make me.* That was the whole of it. But I had to give some answer, and so I held up my palm, showing the mom my wounded hand.

She gasped as if my pain was her own. And it was only when she pulled me to her in a trembling hug, her cheek pressed against mine so that our tears ran together, that I realized. This was what I had wanted the whole time. I hadn't wanted to hurt the mom. I'd only been waiting for her to kiss it and make it better.

"She needs to go back to school."

"You told me so, right?"

A sigh. "I didn't say that. Giving her an extra week was the right decision at the time, but now . . ." Another sigh. "For both of you, Shelley."

There was a long moment of silence. Then another sigh. This time it came from the mom.

"She won't tell me what happened this morning. That cut on her hand . . . I shouldn't have left her here alone."

It was his turn to sigh. "We both decided it would be more difficult, and complicate everything further, for her to be at the doctor's office. To explain why we were there."

"Maybe we were wrong. Whatever we do, why does it end up feeling wrong?"

He didn't give an answer. It wasn't a question that needed one. Instead, they sighed together, united in their wordless exhalations. Hers a soft sigh of sadness, his almost a groan of despair.

John and Shelley. Funny, it was the first time I'd actually heard her name. He was usually "dear" or "your dad." She was "babe" when he was joking and "hon" when he was worried. She was "hon" a lot. Never did they use each other's names as he had now. It was as if when they had a kid, they'd left their material lives and names behind.

The mom and I hadn't spoken after our earlier showdown. Or meltdown. After we both caught our breath again, she put me to bed. Tucking me in, and sliding her cool fingers across my forehead as if she was taking my temperature.

"Sweetie, talk to me," she'd said.

Confession is good for the soul, they say. I'd imagine this is true. But my sins were too convoluted. And from the little I understood—too damning.

I'd rolled over onto my side. Away from her hand and into my pillow.

She'd stood there a long time before finally leaving.

I didn't sleep. My heavy eyes wanted it, but I was afraid of Annaliese. Afraid of what else I might dream. Of course, even awake I was fighting nightmares. So with the covers pulled up to my chin, and the afternoon sun streaming through the blinds, I practiced saying the alphabet backward. Over and over again I whispered the letters, until I could do it without hesitation. Until I could do it without thinking, which meant that my mind was free to think about the razor with the names. That was when I stopped.

After placing a fresh layer of breath strips on my tongue, I headed downstairs to find the mom. The basement/doomsday-bunker door was open, and as I prepared to call a hello, voices came floating up to me. I took one step down, intending to announce my presence, but somehow my legs folded beneath me and I sat on the top step instead.

I almost wanted the mom and the dad to discover me sitting there, eavesdropping. Maybe they'd tell me what the whole doctor's office thing was about. It had to be something bad. Like that the mom was dying. Or maybe the dad. But probably the mom. That would be worse. I decided then and there I was glad they hadn't told me, and I wouldn't demand answers.

They didn't come up though. They didn't say anything else either.

Waiting, I stretched forward and let my head fall between my open legs, studying the dusty underside of the basement stairs. That was when I saw them. Three little balls stuck to the bottom of the stair. Chewed gum, I first thought. But no. Faint blue lines ran through them. I squinted, trying to see clearer.

It looked like notebook paper wadded up into spitballs. Almost as gross as chewed gum, but I reached for them anyway. A tiny tap was all it took to send them tumbling into my hand.

Carefully, I peeled the first one open. The wrinkled bit of paper was only a few inches wide and jagged on three edges as if torn from a notebook. Slanted cursive lettering ran perpendicular to the lines. And in the bottom right-hand corner were the initials ARG. Annaliese Rose Gordon.

It was a poem. They all were. Three little scraps of poetry. Three little bits of Annaliese, crumpled and hidden away where no one would ever find them. Except I had. The last bits of

Annaliese. Maybe the truest parts of her. And they fit into the palm of my hand.

SPYING

I sat on the steps, learning the poems. Rote repetition had quickly turned a challenge like the backward ABCs into nothing but background noise, no more distracting than the hum of the refrigerator. The poems, though, became more insistent with every reading. I could hear Annaliese's voice in my head.

I had forgotten where I was, and had thoroughly forgotten the mom and the dad still in the basement. A creaking noise and some wet smacking sounds brought me back to my surroundings. While I had been lost in Annaliese's poems, the mom and the dad had stopped talking . . . and moved on to doing something else. They could be chewing, breaking into those Little Debbie treats, but I was pretty sure that wasn't it. The mom's next words confirmed it.

"John"—her voice was breathy—"we can't. The door is open."

"We can. She's sleeping, you said so yourself. A nice long midday nap, probably the best rest she'll have all week."

"But if she wakes up—"

"We'll hear her."

"But—Oh! Jo-ohn."

Covering my ears, burning red with embarrassment, I tiptoed away before I could hear anything else.

I kept going until I was outside, walking along the fence line, up our side, and then around onto the other. I almost expected the boy—Dex—to be waiting for me. He had a knack for showing up. But the only sign of him was the storm door I'd shouted down into before, cracked open, as if he were inviting me in.

I tapped gently. The hollow metal clanged loud enough for the whole block to hear it. No one came running though. And there was no response from inside either.

Anyone else would have left, and I especially should have, considering the things I'd said the last time I'd stood here. Having come this far, I found I was reluctant to leave. Besides, I reminded myself, he had my razor.

Boldly lifting the door, I called in, "Hello?"

Still nothing.

"Dex? It's . . ." I wasn't sure whether to call myself Anna as I had before, or Annaliese. All I could see were the cement-block steps leading into the gloom below. Cautiously, I stepped inside and then took one stair after another until I was underground. Unlike the mom's bright fluorescent-lit basement, the only source of light here came from three glowing computer monitors lined up side by side at the opposite end of the room. They all ran the same screen saver, the words *free will* rotating round and round.

I spotted Dex in a little cubby space built into the gap beneath the stairs that led up to the house. A gigantic beanbag, covered in furry black fabric, filled and overflowed from the cubby, as if it were a growing thing that refused to be contained. And Dex was apparently involved in a fight to the death with the overgrown pillow. His body was hidden, seemingly being eaten, while his long limbs stuck out in all directions jerking and twitching as if in his final death throes.

But it wasn't a battle. Feeling foolish, I abruptly called off my rush to his rescue. The world was a more frightening place than most people knew, but it appeared we were still safe from the scourge of evil pillows.

Dex was just dancing. Sort of dancing. He twitched in time to whatever song was being pumped from the iPod into the gigantic headphones clamped tight over his ears. His eyes were squinched tightly closed, as if to fully take in the music, he had to seal off all his other senses.

I stood watching him for longer than I should have. I actually leaned in, until I could make out his lips barely moving, forming little oohs and aahs along with the music. Inching a bit closer, until the fur on the beanbag almost brushed my shin, I could just barely discern a beat and a high voice singing, "MEEEEEEEEEEEEEEEE."

Even as I leaned in, wanting to hear more, recognition hit me. Queen. "Bohemian Rhapsody."

An involuntary gasp escaped. Not for the song, but because

the world in front of me had lost its color. And then it faded away completely.

SEVENTEEN

I'm in a car. Sardined into the backseat with five others. We three girls have our heads pressed together, our Farrah Fawcett–inspired shags tangled one into the others as we croon the tragic verse to Mama about having just killed a man.

Maaammaaa. Ooooo-oooooo.

The boys, whose bony knees we balance on, would normally be playing air guitar, but here in the car they hold on to us girls—supposedly for safety.

Today I am seventeen, and we are celebrating. They don't know how many times I have been seventeen. I am always fifteen going on sixteen going on seventeen. But eighteen never comes. And this song, from the moment I first heard it last week, makes me feel both the miracle and tragedy of that strange fact all in the same instant.

"Bismillah!" We all shout the word together. None of us know what the word means; maybe it means nothing at all. But for me it defines something inside myself, something I've never had a word for—until now.

"Jane," the girl beside me whispers into my ear. "I think

Darren really likes you!"

I don't answer. Darren and I will end up together—we always do, even when he isn't Darren and I'm not Jane. But I don't want to think about that now. Instead, I sing louder.

"Bismillah!"

SORRY

Dex's eyes flew open and met mine. I'd been as lost in the music as him . . . but in another time, and another place. His body stiffened and then went completely still, the music draining, as if I'd tripped some hidden plug.

Clumsy, my feet scraped against the cement floor as I backed away. Not quickly enough to evade Dex's arm stretching out to grab my hand and pull me toward him. It was the hand I'd sliced earlier, now carefully bandaged by the mom, and I winced, waiting for him to squeeze. But Dex took it gently, not demanding at all. It was almost old-fashioned, like he might ask, "May I have this dance?"

Instead, when it was clear he'd prevented my retreat, his hand dropped away from my own. Our dance was over before it had begun.

Or maybe not. In a rippling move, Dex extricated himself from the beanbag chair and stood up, his mouth right at my eye level, reminding me that he'd yet to say a word to me. Or I to him. Funny, he hadn't demanded to know why I was there, and I hadn't felt the need to fill the silence with explanations.

Now I tilted my head back, so that my eyes could see into his. As if this was the signal he'd been waiting for, he tilted down toward me, so that our eyes, noses, and mouths were all lined up and on the same level.

Except, I couldn't hold his gaze. It was too direct. Too knowing. I was afraid of what he might see.

Maybe he was thinking along similar lines, because the moment I took a step back, he did the same. Our movements felt almost choreographed.

"Sorry, I—"

I was going to explain that I'd knocked, that I'd come for my razor, that I hadn't meant to watch him, and that I shouldn't have called him a monster the other day. Or even more than that. There was so much I was sorry for.

But my apology had stalled, when he'd said the same words, with me: "Sorry, I—"

We'd uttered each syllable at the exact same instant, oddly in sync.

For a long moment we stared at each other. Then he smiled at me and I beamed back, a big goofy grin I held for so long that my cheeks started to hurt. And while we smiled and looked deep into each other's eyes, I thought that I might kiss him or tell him all my secrets. Or both. There was something about Dex that made me want to confess and kiss. Kiss and confess. Like the two things went together.

I decided then that it might be better to avoid Dex. He was a strange and unpredictable boy, and that seemed like a dangerous combination for a girl like me.

I was about to make an excuse to leave, but Dex spoke first, and that changed everything again.

FRIEND

WISTFUL

Wistful.
Wanton.
Woeful wonderment.

More words.
All meaning:
I WANT.

—ARG

"You probably don't remember, but you were my first kiss," Dex said with a crooked smile. "I mean, I know you don't remember anything now, but before . . . well, before everything, I'm not sure if it's something you particularly thought about. It probably wasn't a big moment for you. We were in seventh grade, and most people have already kissed by then, or it seemed that way to me. I'm a late bloomer, that's what my mom used to say." His face, so open and bright, suddenly went still. "She doesn't say that anymore; that was from my before."

I didn't want to know about the circumstances of his before, any more than I did my own. Befores were a bloody business, and I wanted to go back to hearing about kisses.

"Most girls remember kisses, even the ones that aren't their first."

"Point taken," Dex said with a grin. He collapsed into his computer chair, and did a little spin in it, before facing me again, serious once more. "I think what I really meant was how well remembered it was. Let's say it was a love letter. No, that sounds too serious. A like letter—instead of a kiss."

"A like letter?" I said, skeptical but amused.

"A note of affection?" Dex kicked a second chair in my direction, and I grabbed hold of it before it went flying past.

"Okay," I said, sitting down. "Let's stick with a like letter."

"A like letter it is. One that's been written on the back of an envelope. If it were a love letter, it would be scented stationery, monogrammed too. But a like letter—you just scribble it down on whatever's handy."

A giggle escaped me. I hadn't known that I giggled. It was a nice surprise. "Thank you. I have a very clear picture of it now."

"But wait, the picture isn't complete yet. There are actually two different versions of these back-of-an-envelope like letters. The first is creased and bent from being folded up to fit into a pocket. One corner might have a coffee ring, and somewhere in the middle there's a pink blob from a jelly doughnut. This like letter's often reread over breakfast."

"I see," I answered softly.

I did see, or I was starting to. Dex must have been in love with Annaliese. Or in like. Or something. Did he think this was his second chance with her? For a second I imagined giving it to him. A second chance at a first kiss. Quickly, I shook the thought away.

"Now, the other version of this letter," Dex continued, oblivious. "It's stuck between the pages of *Moby Dick*, left there after having been used as a bookmark, and then forgotten right along with Melville's masterpiece. And I'm guessing this second one was exactly how it all played out for you way back in seventh grade when you gave me my first kiss."

If that was true, then Annaliese was an idiot.

"I don't know. I wish I did," I said, unable or unwilling to squash my wistful tone.

Dex, who had once again been spinning in his chair, came to an abrupt stop. "Wait, did I make you feel bad about not remembering stuff? 'Cause I was joking around." Stepping one foot in front of the other, he walked his chair forward until our knees were touching. "Seriously, I'm sorry."

I looked down at our knees instead of at him, his sincere concern shaming me. "It's fine. It's just . . . I can tell it meant a lot to you."

"Oh shit, oh no." Dex sprang to his feet, the chair flying away behind him, and then he planted his hands on the armrests of my chair, leaning forward and boxing me in so that I couldn't escape his gaze. "Look, I think we can be friends, I'd like us to be friends, but there's something you have to understand about me if that's gonna happen." He took a deep breath, and I braced myself for something terrible. Would this be the before he'd alluded to earlier?

"I talk a lot," Dex said, as if confessing a dark secret. "And that means a lot of what I say is total and complete shit. Just utter nonsense. I put words together to hear myself talk—well, to make other people hear me talk; I'm not really into talking to myself. So all that stuff I said about the letters, it was just that. I don't have this grand passion that I've been holding on to since seventh grade. That would be nuts. And also, no offense or anything, but at that age I'd already discovered internet porn, so the kiss was not the most exciting sexual moment of my life up to that point. It was the same for you, I'm sure. Well, not the internet porn. But hell, maybe."

He didn't want Annaliese. He wanted to be friends with me. My heart thumped with the joyful rhythm of a dog's tail slapping the floor beside his master's feet.

Dex pushed himself away from me, falling into his chair once more. "Here's the story. Bullshit-free. The Braverman twins started it all. Amelia and Danny. She invited all the girls in our class to their joint birthday party, and Danny invited all the boys. I think there might have been some idea of keeping the two parties separate, but that lasted all of ten seconds. So we ended up playing spin the bottle combined with seven minutes in heaven. Heaven was the closet where the twins stored their soccer equipment, and seven minutes was more like whenever everybody got tired of waiting and decided to throw the door open.

"To be completely honest, when it was my turn to spin, I aimed for Kayla Robins. All the boys were aiming for Kayla Robins. She was—I want to say she was hot, she is definitely hot now, but to think of a seventh grader that way seems kind of wrong. Let me put it this way—she had this Dr Pepper lip stuff that she wore on a string around her neck so that it hung right between her—well, right between nothing. She was flat chested and remained that way until the next year when the hormones kicked in, I guess, and she was suddenly va-va-voom. . . ." Dex stared into space for a moment, lost, I could only assume, in a vision of Kayla's curves.

I, meanwhile, remembered exactly where I had heard the name Kayla before. It was the name of the girl who had texted Rice Sixteen the night he was with Annaliese. The beautiful girl who every guy wanted had dated the same boy Annaliese wanted badly enough to trade her very soul for him.

"But my lips never touched those of Kayla Robins, and I doubt they ever will," Dex continued cheerfully, and I was thankful to be pulled out of my own thoughts. "The bottle landed on one Annaliese Rose Gordon instead. You didn't jump up and down with joy, but you also didn't wrinkle your nose and turn to your friends and roll your eyes. I found this to be fairly encouraging. Seconds later we were in the dark closet. I took your hands in my own damp and sweaty ones, and we kissed. We were probably in there for all of thirty seconds before Jason Snyder flung the door open. Lucky bastard, spun that bottle and pointed it straight at Kayla Robins. Or maybe not so lucky; she told everyone his braces scraped her lips, and that his breath smelled like bananas. You'd think that wouldn't be so bad, I mean I could think of a lot worse things to taste like, but in junior high . . ."

Dex shook his head. "I think people still call him Monkey Boy to this day."

"Wow," I said in response, a huge grin on my face despite the fate of poor Monkey Boy. "So that's it, huh?"

"Nope, there's one more thing I forgot to tell you about—the magical words we exchanged in those final moments in the dark."

This time I saw the mischievous twinkle in Dex's eyes and wasn't worried about any declarations of love. "And they were?"

"You said to me—and I remember this exactly—'It kinda smells like feet in here.'"

I couldn't help myself. I burst out laughing. And in that instant Annaliese's skin fit me perfectly. I forgot it was her head being thrown back, her hands covering her mouth, trying to stop the helpless whoops shaking her whole body. Dex had told the story so perfectly that I was almost there too, remembering it with him. I was Annaliese. Almost.

Like birds, my laughter fled. One second there; the next, nothing but distant specks in the sky.

I wasn't Annaliese. I never would be.

I shot to my feet. "I should go."

Dex, who had been laughing with me, changed gears quickly, following my new, more urgent mood. He stood as well, and before I could make a move toward the storm doors, he took my injured hand in the same gentle yet insistent manner he had earlier. A stray bit of sunlight found its way through the cracked door and brought to life the dust motes dancing between us.

His long, jangling body was still. Already I was learning to identify this as a sign he was preparing to say something serious. "I meant what I said earlier about us being friends." His voice was pitched so low, I had to lean closer to hear his words. "I'd like to be friends with you. I don't have many, in fact the number right now stands at zero. Okay, that's not totally true, there are several chat rooms where the screen name Dexterious is a welcome addition to any thread. But here in the nonemoticon world, I'm a bit of a hermit."

I squeezed Dex's hand with my injured one. It only hurt a little. "I could use some friends too."

I'd hoped for a lightening of the mood, or at least a smile, but, if anything, Dex became even more serious. "As your friend, there is one thing that I have to tell you. Your mom hates me. She put the fence up because she couldn't stand seeing me. And I don't think she'd want us to be friends, or even long-distance pen pals."

"No," I said immediately. Even though I'd seen the fence, I couldn't believe it was directed at Dex, now that I'd met him. Now that I knew him. "That can't be right; she's protective, but she's not like that. I don't even think she's capable of hating. . . ." An image popped into my head: the mom striking Rice Sixteen over and over, and the look on her face.

He'd hurt me. And yes, she hated him.

"What did you do?" I asked, knowing it had to be something big, something awful.

And I was right.

"I watched you die. I watched you die, and it was because of me that the rest of the world was able to watch it too."

SCREAM

The video clip lasted all of one minute and twelve seconds.

It began with the camera moving, scanning the crowd. Dozens of teenagers milled outside in air cold enough to turn their breath frosty. Almost every one of them clutched plastic cups of beer, a sort of security blanket. Eyes were glazed and laughter was plentiful, but shrill. Wherever the camera's mechanical gaze landed, people shaded their eyes against the glaring light that was its constant companion.

"Dude," one guy grumbled, after his jerk of surprise caused him to slosh beer onto his shirt.

Another girl blinked blearily, before stumbling away.

"Hey, over here," a different girl catcalled. The camera turned her way and she was ready, lifting her shirt. There was only the quickest flash of flesh, before the camera pointed down, illuminating the camera operator's shuffling feet.

"Not cool," his voice said. He must have tossed the words over his shoulder, because the camera was already on the move again, this time finding a couple huddled in a corner. But not making out, like the other shadows surrounding them.

The girl repeatedly stabbed her index finger into the boy's chest while she ranted at him. They were too far away for the mic to pick up her words, not over the pounding music and noise of the crowd.

Like everyone, they turned to the camera as the light hit their faces. She immediately extended her middle finger, and it didn't take an expert lip-reader to translate the "fuck you" her lips formed. The boy merely looked grateful for the interruption.

He was wearing his sweatshirt with the hood pulled over his head, and even if I hadn't recognized his face, I would have known for certain when he turned away again. Rice Sixteen. The camera almost made the big white numbers at the center of his back glow.

I recognized the girl too. She was the girl in the bikini at the party last weekend. The one crying to the cops. So this was Rice Sixteen's girlfriend. Kayla Robins.

My fingers fumbled the pack of breath strips as I pulled them from my pocket.

The video continued, and the screaming began.

It started with one scream. There was terror and pain in that scream, and something else too. Something so deep and dark I didn't even have a word for it.

The crowd fell silent. For three seconds there was only the

scream and the stereo blasting some guy rapping about his bitches.

Then came the reactions.

"Who the fuck was that?"

"Is this a joke? 'Cause it's not funny, guys . . . okay?"

Someone else started sobbing. Maybe it was more than one person.

And all the time, the camera roamed, pushing through the crowd, which seemed to be turning in the other direction, toward the house, away from the terrible scream that only grew louder.

The camera scanned the outer edges of the yard, where citronella candles stuck into the grass like tiki torches cast flickering shadows onto the line of trees that stood like sentries at the gate between the party and something terrible.

At thirty seconds she stumbled from the trees. The girl in red. I'd known it would be Annaliese, and yet seeing her hit me with a physical zap of shock. Still screaming, she stumbled and lurched her way forward; it seemed impossible that she didn't fall, that she could keep coming.

"Oh my God," a girl cried.

And then it was impossible to make out any other words, because others had joined Annaliese in her scream. It seemed like the whole world was yelling and screaming in a terrible chorus of fear and pain.

And as she came closer, the blood became clearer. It was everywhere. Streaming from her forehead, it obliterated half of Annaliese's face. Her mouth, open wide in an O, was nothing but a red, moving wound. The blood dripped from her hands too, even as she held them out in an obvious plea for help.

No one moved forward. I couldn't see, but could sense the crowd shrinking away. Only the camera came closer, the zoom finding Annaliese's eyes as she turned toward its light the same way everyone else had. Blood coated her eyelashes, and against this the whites of her eyes seemed unnaturally bright. Unblinking, she stared into the camera, as if trying to communicate something that her desperate scream could not.

And then everything went dark. The camera still ran, because there was sound, but every last bit of light had been extinguished.

The screams crescendoed, now mingled with sobs, curses, pleas to God.

Three seconds later the lights were restored. Even the candles flickered back to life.

The camera searched for another thirty seconds, scanning the trees, and across the neighbors' yards, and then turning back to search the panicked throng of bodies.

It was only when a siren sounded in the distance that Dex must have realized it was over. The screen went black.

Annaliese was gone.

I watched it more than once. More than twice, more than—well, I lost count. All the while I popped my breath strips, blindly, my own version of popcorn and a movie.

One time I watched it with the sound up extra loud. Next with no sound at all. I went frame by frame, watching eyes slowly widen, and tiny droplets of blood form and drip down one by one.

By the end of it I knew nothing more than I had after watching it the first time. Nothing I saw could tell me what had occurred between my last memory of Annaliese being told to cut out my heart, and her running screaming from the woods.

I turned away from the screen, searching for Dex. He'd told me that when the police had arrived, they took all of his equipment, even his laptop. Twelve hours later the one-minute-and-twelve-second clip was posted on YouTube with the name "Real-Life Horror Movie." An anonymous email address sent the link to the entire school. It took less than fifteen minutes for YouTube to pull it down, but the damage had been done. It spread like the most virulent of viral videos.

Despite the one commenter who had written, "Bad fake blood, needs more viscosity. But that girl can act. Someone call Wes Craven," almost everyone else turned it into a virtual prayer wall.

The police denied a leak in their own department and went after Dex, saying he must have uploaded it from his laptop. They came to his house and confiscated all his tapes, computers, and electronic equipment, including an electric shaver. In the end they couldn't prove that the YouTube leak had originated from him.

"They couldn't prove it"—that's what Dex said. He didn't say that he didn't do it, and I didn't come out and ask. It didn't feel like a question a friend should ask. Especially not after Dex had treated me like a person who didn't need to be packed away in Bubble Wrap.

In doing so, he gave me the courage to finally admit that I couldn't run from this. I suppose I could continue to hide, but sometime during my numerous viewings, I instead decided to put the pieces together and find out exactly when Annaliese stopped and I began. And where the other girls on the razor fit in too. And the redheaded boy.

It was a lot. It was possible that it would never all make sense. But I would try. And for that Dex deserved a thank-you.

There was no sign of him anywhere, so I scribbled the words onto a scrap of paper that I found on his desk and signed it simply, *A.*

DAY OF SCHOOL

I JUST IMAGINED

I just imagined
conversation
one hundred thirty-two
with you.
The words are
not important,
but instead the way
you looked
at me.

You saw me.

I know in reality
you don't think of me
that way.

You don't think of me
at all.

—ARG

On Monday, the dad drove me to my first day of school. Or first day back to school.

He'd insisted on taking me, saying it was on his way to work and there was no need for the mom to go out. Saying it was the way they'd always done it, saying pretty much whatever he had to until finally the mom relented.

It was strange, but lately the dad had been pushing back against the mom more. Not really against, because it was all in the mom's best interest. And in the case of school, mine too, because we all knew the mom would've insisted on walking me in and then would've waited to make sure I remembered how to open my locker, and then she'd want to be certain I made it to my first class okay. There was a very good chance she'd end up hanging out in the parking lot, knitting, until the end of the day, just in case I needed her.

So, the dad saved all of us from that.

The mom gave me an extra-big hug before I walked out the door, and then she waved the entire time as the dad carefully backed out of the driveway. I can only assume she kept on waving until we disappeared from view, but when I turned to look back, the dad stopped me.

"Don't," he cautioned, placing his hand on my shoulder. "If your mother sees you looking back, she'll think it's a sign of uncertainty, and the next thing you know she'll be running down the street after us, saying we need to wait another week." The dad said it with a smile, like it was a joke. And I laughed as if it were funny, and not sad and true.

So I didn't look back. I needed school, and I needed to get out of that house. My sanctuary had turned into a prison.

It began after I'd returned from Dex's basement. The mom was in a panic. I'd been gone for almost two hours, but luckily she'd only known I was missing for thirty minutes of that time. This meant she'd searched the entire house—top to bottom—twice, and was ready to call the cops. Lucky for the cops—not so lucky for me—that's when I strolled in.

"Annaliese," the mom shrieked, as if I'd jumped out of thin air . . . as if she hadn't expected to see me. The phone slid from her hand and hit the floor. You could tell she didn't remember she'd been holding it. I watched as it crashed and skittered across the hardwood floor, but her eyes never left my face.

"Annaliese," she said once more, this time on an exhalation and the end of a sob. That's when I braced myself for her to throw herself at me and wrap me into one of her anaconda hugs. Instead her body went boneless, and she dissolved into the floor. "Oh God, I thought we'd lost you again."

The dad and I were at her side instantly.

"I'm sorry."

"It's okay now, she's right here."

"I'm sorry."

"She went for a walk."

"I'm sorry."

"Annaliese is home. She's okay."

"Please, I'm so, so, so sorry."

And I was sorry. Even more so because I had been with Dex, and I knew she hated him, and I also knew that I would see him again. But I would never again let the mom wonder where I was, or let her think for an instant that I was missing. If we all had our personal hells, I'm pretty sure hers was one where she constantly searched for a missing daughter who never came home.

Eventually the mom calmed down enough to swallow one of the pills the dad gave her. Then he picked her up, and carried her to their room.

When he came back down, I expected him to yell at me. He looked like he wanted to, and it might've made me feel better as well. But he only sighed and sat on the floor beside me.

For a long while we just breathed. I guess we had both gotten pretty worked up, because it took some time before we were inhaling and exhaling normally again.

"I'm sorry," I said, although by this point the words felt like a cheap shirt that has lost its shape after too many washings.

The dad must've agreed, because he waved it away with a flick of his fingers. "I'm not going to tell you to never leave the house. I know it can be hard . . . that your mother can . . ."

He stopped, and tried again. "We've already talked about where we went wrong the last time. We don't want to repeat past mistakes and make you feel like you need to sneak around behind our backs."

That one got me. I wanted to tell the dad that maybe sneaking around wasn't so bad. That maybe lying to their faces was the kindest thing a child could do for a loving parent. Spare them the worry. Spare everyone the fights.

But I didn't say any of this. The dad didn't want to hear it, any more than the mom wanted to hear that there were some things parents couldn't protect their children from.

"So please let us know anytime that you go out. If we're home, find us." The dad colored a little here, no doubt thinking of what I would have found had I gone looking for them this afternoon. "And if we're not home, call our cells, or leave a note, or something. Don't disappear again. Please."

I wanted to tell him that I hadn't disappeared. That I'd only been next door.

But again I didn't say this, because Annaliese had disappeared, and I'd been the one to take her.

"I won't," I said instead. "I promise."

During the next three days the strength of that promise never had a chance to be tested. The mom did everything but handcuff our wrists together. And if she had known that when I gazed out the window it wasn't to "enjoy the last leaves before they fell," but in hopes of catching a glimpse of Dex . . . well, she might've had handcuffs delivered express.

"Here we are," the dad said as we pulled into the school parking lot.

Students milled around the front doors, and nerves replaced the relief I'd been feeling.

"Have a good first day," the dad said cheerfully, unaware of my sudden change of attitude. "And don't forget your mom will be waiting here, right after school." *Don't make her wait*, was the hidden message there. *Don't let her worry.*

"I won't forget," I answered. "I promise."

Opening the car door, I stepped out, and headed straight up the steps and into the school.

Once again, I didn't look back.

THE WARNING BELL

The first bell for homeroom was only ten minutes away. The halls were crowded with students gathered into tight clusters.

I walked in.

Everything went whispery kind of quiet. All eyes were on me. The same students who had cheered my return at the Homecoming game now stared at me with hard eyes that looked hostile and betrayed. And then I caught the edge of a whisper.

"Anna lies."

My heart jumped and lodged in my throat. They knew. They were calling me Anna. Somehow they found out I wasn't Annaliese.

I managed to keep walking. The area directly around my locker had been quarantined; no one wanted to catch the sickness that was me. I smelled the red nail polish before I saw the word painted across the front of my locker.

AnnaLIESe

I gasped. Not with horror, but relief. They weren't calling me Anna. They knew nothing about the blade with the girls' names carved into it. They knew nothing about what had happened to Annaliese before she came running out of those woods.

"Whore." This new word came bouncing along the top of the crowd like a beach ball kept aloft by so many invisible hands.

That's when I remembered that they did know something of what had happened to Annaliese. The part with Logan. The part that he'd very recently, very publicly confessed. By now everyone would have heard . . . and that changed everything. I had been poor little Annaliese, the victim of a bloody and gruesome attack. But with the addition of s-e-x, I'd become something else—a girl who'd done the nasty in the woods with a boy. A boy who'd been dating someone else. And in the vicious high school world, that was a girl who got what she deserved.

Just like that, Annaliese had gone from victim to vixen.

A flash of color caught the corner of my eye. The redheaded boy. He smiled right at me and winked. Somehow I knew without a doubt that the words on my locker had been his doing. Only he knew exactly how much hearing the name Anna would rattle me.

Shaking, I pulled the locker open. All of Annaliese's books, folders, and notebooks from last year were there, neatly stacked and waiting for her. I shoved my book bag in, hanging it from a hook, and peeled off my stiff new jean jacket, letting it fall to the bottom of the locker. Finally, I grabbed the books I needed for my first few classes and the notebooks that went with them. Then there was no more procrastinating. With a deep breath, I turned, closing my locker behind me.

The mob had shifted, pretending to go about their business. But they were still watching, and they had me surrounded. I avoided looking toward where I'd seen the redheaded boy, but I could sense him still standing there, enjoying this.

I juggled my books so they were tucked into the crook of my right arm, freeing my other hand to pull the breath strips from my pocket.

That's when a girl broke away from the crowd. Her mouth was smiling, but her eyes were hard and unfriendly. I recognized her. The girl in the bikini at that party. The girl in the video with Logan. The girl from Dex's story. Kayla Robins.

"Annaliese." She pronounced it normally, but in a way that

was snide, as if just like Benedict Arnold my very name had become synonymous with an insult. "Everybody wants to know. Did they find the horrible person who did this to you yet?"

Several people snickered. Even if I hadn't already identified her as Rice Sixteen's girlfriend, I would've known from her tone—this wasn't a question from a concerned classmate. I could've walked away then, or told her to fuck off. But she had this scene scripted out, and if I didn't say my lines now, she'd find me later and we'd have to do it all over again.

"No," I said, keeping it short. I didn't return her smile.

"Oh, that's *terrible*. And you don't remember anything, right? 'Cause you have amnesia? Right?" Her hand fell on my arm, like she was trying to comfort me. I shook it off.

"Permanent brain damage actually. But yeah, I remember nothing."

"Oh, Annaliese, don't be mad," she cooed. "I had to ask because it sounds so crazy, like a soap opera or something totally made up, and we're all just trying to understand. But I guess weird things happen, right? Like my trashy truck-driver uncle told me this story the other day about how for the past year he's seen a prostitute working the truck stop on the Ninety right outside Fredonia, and he says she looked exactly like you. Isn't that weird?"

The bell rang, saving me from answering.

But Kayla wasn't finished. She leaned down and hissed in

my ear, "Now we're even." The tips of her fingers connected with my sternum. More of a poke than a push, but to someone who'd been simultaneously hollowed out and flattened, it had the effect of a knockout punch. As Kayla flounced away, books fell from my numb arms. I collapsed against my locker, my liquefied legs melting beneath me, and slid all the way to the floor.

Shoving a breath strip into my mouth, I stared at my fellow classmates' jittery knees and shuffling feet, which were so much less certain than their hard faces.

The late bell rang. Time to be in homeroom, or be counted late.

The feet moved, purposely scattering my books even farther, bending the notebook covers, and leaving tread marks on the pages.

I sat there watching, waiting for it to be over so I could collect my things without their eyes on me. Except before the hall could empty, everyone froze all over again.

This time their stares weren't fixated on me, but on something at the other end of the hall, coming toward them. They craned their necks, straining to see, and I found myself looking too. A part of me half hoped it was the mom, coming to kick their asses for making me cry. The thought was almost enough to make me smile.

But it was Rice Sixteen who came bursting through the

crowd, his head swinging this way and that as he wildly searched for something.

Or someone.

His gaze landed on me, and he stopped in his tracks. Holy crap. He was looking for me.

Or maybe not. He looked up over me, at my locker. His lips moved as he read the word painted in red, like he was sounding it out. Maybe he was an illiterate jock. Or maybe it had never occurred to him that his confession might cost me more than it did him. Either way—he was an idiot.

Never taking his eyes off the locker, he took six deliberate steps, until finally he was close enough to plant his fist in the metal. The clang reverberated through the crowd. They swayed indecisively, afraid this might blow up in their faces, but even more afraid they would miss the explosion and have to hear about it secondhand.

The final bell rang.

"Get to class!" An adult's voice. Finally. Striding down the hall was Mr. Hardy, the smiling principal who had greeted me when I'd been on the tour with the parents. He wasn't smiling now.

Everyone scattered; there would be nothing more to see.

And then there was only Rice Sixteen quietly collecting my books from where they had fallen, and me slowly rising to my feet, realizing I hadn't even made it to first period before everything went kablooey.

Mr. Hardy's glance swept across the scene. "This is a fine mess you've created," he said while he stared at my dented name-calling locker. Shaking his head, he turned to Rice Sixteen. "Go see the nurse, Logan. Get your hand cleaned up, and then you will join me in my office immediately afterward."

It was funny to hear him called Logan, especially when he was once again wearing that same hoodie with RICE 16 across the back.

He didn't even acknowledge Mr. Hardy's order, just picked up my last notebook and added it to the stack in his arms. Then he turned toward me. I reached out to accept the books, but he placed them at my feet instead.

Standing to face me once more, his eyes met mine for an instant before being obscured by his hoodie, which he was now pulling up over his head. He held it between us, and then repeated the same actions, but in reverse. The hoodie came up, over my head, and down. RICE 16 was now printed across my back.

His warmth and smell surrounded me. A girl could lose herself in this hoodie. Lucky for me, I had nothing left to lose. I pushed my arms into the sleeves.

"Logan," the principal warned, but he sounded slightly less pissed off.

"I'll find you at lunch," Logan said to me, and then headed down the hallway.

Mr. Hardy turned to me. The stern expression was replaced

by a more assessing one, and I found myself squirming beneath its intense scrutiny.

"Sorry," I squeaked, thinking this was what he was waiting to hear.

"I'm sure you are." He sniffed, and then transferred his attention to a clock on the wall. "Now why don't you hurry to the last few minutes of homeroom, or if you would prefer, we can call your parents to pick you up."

Call them. Tell them to take me home. Yes, please. Except I didn't have a home, not really. Or parents. I was supposed to be looking for answers. Trying to figure out why I would've wanted to take Annaliese's life. And the only way to know that was to continue living it, even if it meant staying at this horrible school.

"Homeroom." I immediately started walking, wanting to put as much space as possible between myself and Mr. Hardy.

"Excellent choice," he said, from behind me. "We wouldn't want the parents to know too much. They might start wondering exactly what they brought home."

His words were quiet but absolutely clear, as if he'd hissed them directly into my ear. When I spun around, though, Mr. Hardy was at the other end of the hallway, his shoes clacking against the linoleum floor.

I stared after him for a long moment, then hunkered down into Rice Sixteen's hoodie and took off running through the long, empty hallways.

UNCERTAIN

I survived the rest of the day. The student body seemed shaken, uncertain how to deal with me in my RICE 16 armor. I had become something too complicated for them to sum up with one word painted in red nail polish.

So for the most part they avoided me. And I avoided Logan. I spent lunch hiding in the bathroom. It wasn't the most original place, but Logan wasn't the most original boy. He didn't find me.

Unfortunately, the redheaded boy did. He stood directly outside the door, waiting when I emerged with the bell. Before I could think to run, he'd grabbed hold of my arm.

"Leave me alone." I jerked away and started walking fast. With his stubby legs, he had to trot to keep up.

"If you had any sense, you'd thank me," he hissed. "You're in position now."

I didn't want to know, and yet still I asked. "In position for what?"

He smiled. "To wear the glass slippers, Cinderella. Then you live the fairy tale until it's time to sell it to the next little ash girl."

"I don't even know what that means."

"Oh right, your amnesia. I mean brain damage. Let me spell it out for you. You date Logan. Every girl wants to be you. You pick one of those girls and tell her that she can live the dream too. And then she gets to be you . . . for a short time at least. Until it's time to pay. Then you get to be her."

"I don't know what that means," I said again—except that this time I was afraid that I did.

"Right." He rolled his eyes, and then grabbed my hand and pressed something into it. "Found this in the hallway during the fight, must've been with your books."

The hall widened, and he moved away from me. I stopped, wanting as much distance between us as possible. Then I opened my hand. He'd given me a pen. Or half of one. It was a clicker type. I had the top half, and someone had wedged a bit of paper inside. I steadily tapped the pen against my palm until two little balls rolled out. As soon as I saw them, I knew. These were more of Annaliese's spitball poems.

POPPING

TRY

To the born losers
who watch the golden
girls and boys
effortlessly achieve.

And to the lost,
those lonesome wanderers
roaming roads at night
peering into windows
where all is bright.

To those on the outside
shut off from the
smiles and light
of the luckier ones.

To those who have
given up
'cause their dreams
never took flight.

To those who cry themselves
to sleep.
Who for one reason
or another
can't help but weep.

To all out
there who know
they were
born to merely

try
and
try
and

die.

—ARG

"Annaliese!"

A short roundish girl with a headful of curly hair that she'd scraped back into a little pom-pom of a ponytail came barreling toward the car.

It was Tuesday, and amazingly I was at school once more. I'd been half certain the mom would've heard what happened and never let me near the place again. Instead, totally clueless, she'd asked, "How'd it go?"

I'd hesitated before answering. I didn't want to upset the mom. And she had that look on her face too. The one where she couldn't decide between hope or fear. She was an optimist, dog-paddling like crazy to keep from drowning in a glass she'd insist was half full.

Finally, I settled on: "Okay, I guess. Kind of strange, but I survived."

That was the right answer, because the mom laughed. "You sound like a typical teenager." And for the mom, that was the best thing I could be.

Now I looked to the dad to see if this girl outside our car alarmed him. After yesterday, I was prepared for the worst. "It's okay. That's Gwen. She's your friend."

Not really reassured, I nodded and slid out of the car.

"Annaliese," she said again, a gigantic smile on her face. When

I took a step toward her, she took one back. "Don't get too close. I'm recovering from a nasty stomach bug, and I do not want to deal with your mom if I get you sick. She still hasn't forgiven me for giving you the chicken pox in third grade, even though she never did prove it was me, since half the kids in our class had it, but that's all water under the bridge, right?"

Words flew from Gwen's mouth at intense speed, and she kept moving at the same time, walking backward, step for step with me, as we advanced toward the school.

"So I heard about what happened yesterday. Kayla Robins catapulted herself into superbitch territory. They're not even together anymore. Logan and Kayla, I mean. They broke up a few weeks after you disappeared, and she's dated, like, five or six guys since then. And he hasn't dated anyone. So, everyone thought he was pining away for her, but then confession time and, oops, suddenly everyone thinks that maybe he was pining for you. It is all such stupid drama, and I am so sorry I wasn't here for you. Mr. Hardy actually called my house to say he was very disappointed, and that he'd been counting on me."

She rolled her eyes. "I told him, 'Mr. Hardy, I'm sorry, but I'm sick. I didn't plan on getting sick, but it happened, and I know you wanted me to help Annaliese get through her day, but I don't think it would've helped anything if I puked on her shoes.' He didn't have anything to say to that. I mean, what could he do, accuse me of faking sick? We both know my attendance record is stellar. Anyway, that's when I realized how weird it was for him to call, and that something really awful must've happened. So I said, 'Mr. Hardy, did something happen? Would you like to talk about it?' He got pretty upset, all, 'Don't psychoanalyze me, Miss Durkin.' I wasn't trying to psychoanalyze him, of course. Jeez, as if I would need to; I had that guy's number my first day here. But I only said, 'I'm just a sounding board. Completely confidential, of course.' The sounding board bit is what my mom always says to her patients. It usually helps them open up."

We had reached the front doors at this point, and without pausing in her narrative, Gwen held them open for me. Then she ran up and walked beside me normally.

"My parents are both psychologists, by the way, in case you were wondering. They have in-house offices and I've spent most of my life overhearing their sessions. When I was little they thought it was cute, but now they get very upset about it. So if you see them, don't tell them that I eavesdrop more than ever. Okay?"

Before I could answer, she was talking again. "Anyway, I think Mr. Hardy would really benefit from therapy, and I was about to say so, but then he said, 'Miss Durkin, I have no intention of gossiping with a student. I only called to determine whether you would make good on your commitment tomorrow, or if I should find someone else.' As if you had so many friends, and he had specifically chosen me as some great honor, when we both knew that I wasn't just your best friend, I was your only one."

Gwen grabbed hold of my arm, pulling me to a stop.

"Sorry, was that mean? It's not that people didn't like you, they just didn't know you. Now me, on the other hand, my lack of friends is definitely a personality problem. As in, I have too much for most people. By the way, have you noticed how everyone is staring at you but kind of pretending not to?"

I had noticed, and was sort of getting used to it.

"It's okay," I said, amazed to get some words out.

As if reading my mind, Gwen said, "Sorry. Again. I talk too much. When you used to get annoyed with it, you would say to me, 'Gwen, silence is golden.' Which is a lot nicer than 'shut the hell up,' which is what most people say. Anyway, that was your signal, and I'd be quiet for at least five minutes."

I had to laugh at that. Gwen laughed too. I actually didn't mind her chatter; it was a lot like Dex's steady stream of words. Having someone else willing to carry the conversation was a relief for a girl with too few memories and too many secrets.

"You can talk, I don't mind. I guess you just have a lot to say."

Gwen slapped both hands over her mouth, and her eyes popped open. "Annaliese. Oh my God! That was a memory. 'You've got a lot to say.' You always used to say that. I mean, when you weren't telling me 'silence is golden,' you would always say, 'It's okay,

Gwen, you have a lot to say.' Did you just remember that?"

I waited for all the color to leach away, the way it did when my memories resurfaced, but there was nothing. I had absolutely no memory of Gwen.

Now it was my turn to apologize. "I'm sorry, I don't really—"

Gwen wouldn't let me finish. "Don't apologize. Memory is a fickle thing. And don't try to force it. But I can tell, it's coming back." She gave my arm a friendly squeeze. "You're coming back, Annaliese."

"Maybe," I said with a shrug, as we finally reached my locker.

She started chattering about how after her phone call with Mr. Hardy, she'd had to know what happened, and sent a flurry of emails and texts to find out the whole story. I'd stopped listening, though, because when I opened my locker, a note fluttered out and settled on my toes, and as I bent down to pick it up I watched my fingers go from pink to gray ... right before the memory carried me away.

TWO NAMES

"Jaclyn, stop avoiding me. Please, whatever it is, just talk to me."

I laugh as I spin the combination of my locker. But it's forced, and I can't meet her eyes. "Jess, please yourself. Everything is fine. Better than fine. It's perfect. I found a guy so great that Mom lifted the no dating rule. What more could I want? And I haven't been avoiding you, I've been busy. Steven takes up a lot of my time."

"Steven." She spits out his name. "Jaclyn, look at me."

She grabs my hand as I reach for the latch to pull my locker open. Having no other choice, I look into the face that is identical to my own. Choosing a twin was a miscalculation on my part. Jess knew almost immediately that something wasn't right. Maybe that's what I'd been hoping for. After all these years, for someone to finally suspect.

"Jac?" Her eyes stare into me, digging. "Are you even in there?"

Pulling away, I force another little laugh. "Are you high again?"

I yank the locker open, and as I do, a piece of paper comes floating out, landing at my feet. I don't need to look closer to know what it is.

It's time, and it doesn't matter who suspects. It changes nothing. Jaclyn's birthday is only a month away, but she will never blow out her birthday candles.

Quickly, I grab the paper before Jess can. As I knew there would be, two names are written on it.

Two girls, and I have to pick one. It gives the illusion of having a choice.

Glancing down once more, I focus on the first name. *Annaliese Rose Gordon*. Long but pretty. Not that the name matters, any more than the face or body does. They are all temporary.

"What's that?" Jess asks, suspicious.

"Nothing." I crumple the paper into a ball. "It's nothing."

MAKE IT RIGHT

"What's this?" Gwen asked, plucking the paper from my hand. "Oh." She shoved the paper back at me. "A note from Logan. Supergreat." Pulling a face, she also stuck out her tongue, in case I hadn't caught the heavy sarcasm.

The note was short.

Sorry about yesterday. Meet me at lunch today? Please. Logan

I sighed and shoved it into my pocket.

"Seriously?" Gwen raised one eyebrow at me. "That's it? You don't want to squee and jump up and down for a bit? I mean, I know you don't remember, but you were seriously in . . . well, you would've said 'in love.' Actually you did say it, many many many many many times. It was the only thing you ever talked about. You were totally obsessed with him, and he barely knew you existed. At the end of sophomore year, when you finally got up the nerve to ask him to sign your yearbook, he didn't know how to spell your name. Granted your name is not the easiest, but that's not why he needed you to spell it out. It was his way around not admitting that he had no friggin' clue what your name was at all."

"That wasn't his fault," I said, not even sure why I was sticking up for him.

Gwen groaned. "You used to defend him too. Well, let's hear your defense for why he took your virginity and then left you for dead."

"It wasn't like that."

"You *remember*?"

Too late, I realized what I'd inadvertently admitted.

"No, no, of course not. I just know what he said about it, and now I think he's trying to make things right."

As I said this, I knew that I would be meeting Logan for lunch and wearing his hoodie too. I needed to find out his version of what had happened between him and Annaliese, see if it lined up with my still fuzzy theory that some sort of love spell had been cast, and that he'd somehow been forced to feel something. Just the idea of it was crazy, and that was what made me believe it was true. And if it was, maybe that meant I should try and make amends for my part in the whole him-and-Annaliese mess.

Gwen had gone silent. One of my few allies at this school was now mad at me.

"I'm not in love with him. I have no memory, so he's just another person I don't know."

The warning bell rang. Gwen still said nothing. I pulled Logan's hoodie out of my locker, making sure to hide his name and number. "I probably shouldn't be late two days in a row."

Gwen nodded and walked beside me until we reached my classroom door. "This is me," I said. Trying one more time to salvage the situation, I added, "I'll see you between classes then?"

The kids in my homeroom watched us with interest, blatantly trying to listen in, but Gwen didn't seem to notice them anymore.

"You never told me." Her eyes met mine, and for the first time I could see the hurt there. "You just stopped talking about him, and I thought it was because—" Suddenly Gwen seemed to notice our audience. "I knew you hadn't stopped liking him, so I figured you didn't want to talk about that kind of thing with me anymore."

There was something she was trying to say, without saying it, but I didn't have enough information to know what that might be. Once again I felt the need to fix it. For Annaliese or for myself, I didn't know.

"Maybe I felt weird about it 'cause he had a girlfriend? Otherwise, I'm sure I would've said something. I mean, we were friends, right?"

Gwen took a step back. "You know, I'm having trouble

remembering too." The bell rang, and Gwen spun away, ducking into a classroom three doors down. A moment later her head popped out again. "And you have his hoodie, you don't need me for protection."

Just like that, I was on my own again.

LUNCH

SCHOOL COUNSELORS SHOULD

School counselors should
have offices with doors
and walls.
Not cubicles
made of flimsy gray fabric.

School counselors should
be better prepared
for appointments
not running off to
find files
and leaving students
to overhear.

School counselors should
think of who might
be listening
when one of those students
is a boy
talking about
his father leaving

and mother working two jobs
and his dream
to be the first
to go to college.

School counselors should
see someone peering
over their inadequate divide
and recognizing
the football hero
of the school
on the verge of tears.

School counselors should
know that this is how
girls fall in love
with boys
they never ever
would've
considered before.

—ARG

I found another one of Annaliese's poems wedged into a fold at the bottom of my backpack. Funny how those words made Annaliese more real than all the framed pictures scattered throughout the house did. This was a part of Annaliese that no one else had ever seen. She had wadded up her poems and hidden them away. It was telling that she hadn't simply trashed them. It was as if she'd known to preserve this small part of herself for later.

And now, along with everything else that was once hers, they were entrusted to me. I wanted to have the words tattooed across every inch of my skin. Except even that didn't feel permanent enough. Bodies were too disposable.

These were the thoughts that occupied me as I sat at a cafeteria table completely alone. I'd gotten there early, fleeing from the redheaded boy, who I'd seen approaching as I retrieved my lunch from my locker. Now the tables around me filled up, making mine seem even larger. And emptier. I could feel myself shrinking into Logan's hoodie, hoping people might see only that and forget about the girl inside.

Next to me a chair screeched. Peering around the edge of the hoodie, I watched Logan sit down.

"Hey," he said, his voice sounding unnaturally loud, as the entire cafeteria went silent.

"Hey," I replied, my own voice so low, I could barely hear it.

"So I wanted to say I'm sorry. For the thing on your locker. And the thing with Kayla too. Just so you know—we're not together anymore, but we were dating when you and I . . ."

"Yeah, I figured."

"Oh." Logan glanced down at his empty hands and then back up at me. "Well, sorry. Again."

I shrugged. Logan nodded. We stared down at the table.

He jerked his head toward my lunch, still packed away. "You brown-bagging it?"

I nodded.

"All right. Let's get out of here then."

Grabbing my lunch bag, he stood and headed for the doors, leaving me to follow. I didn't like his way of doing things. Telling me to have lunch with him. Telling me where to have it. The way he assumed that not only would I want to be with him, but alone with him as well.

I followed him, though. I didn't have any better options.

Logan stopped in front of the hall monitor stationed outside the cafeteria doors.

"Hey, Ms. Haley, can we get a pass? I left my lunch in my sports locker."

Ms. Haley's gaze went from Logan to me and back again. "What's that in your hand?" she finally asked.

"Oh, this is hers."

"Then why is she coming with you?"

Logan opened my lunch bag, and pulled out a Baggie with two of the mom's oatmeal raisin cookies inside. "'Cause I'm trying to convince her to let me trade her something for these. C'mon, Ms. Haley, you know Coach doesn't want us missing any meals."

"Coach," Ms. Haley muttered with clear disgust, but she scribbled something onto the stack of hall passes in front of her and handed one over to Logan. "If you get into trouble, you're not leaving this cafeteria early until you graduate, and I don't care what Coach says."

"Thanks, Ms. Haley," Logan called over his shoulder, already walking away.

"Thanks," I said too, adding a little smile of apology for Logan forcing her to bend the rules and not even having the courtesy to properly thank her for it. And then I was annoyed with myself for doing it. Catching up with Logan, I jerked my lunch away from him. "I can carry this myself."

Logan blinked at me in surprise. "Did I do something?" He shook his head, realizing he'd left that question a little too open. "Not before, but, like, now."

"Yes." I was exasperated. "You announced in a very nonprivate time and place that we'd had sex, you punched my locker, you dressed me in your hoodie and ordered me to have lunch with you, and when I didn't show, you left a note in my locker.

And when I did show, you told me we had to go somewhere else."

Logan frowned. "I thought you'd want to get out of there."

"I did. That's not the point. Why are you doing any of this at all?"

Logan's eyes fell away from mine, drifting down to his sneakers. "You hate me, don't you? For everything. I mean, you should, it's just . . ."

He stopped, shaking his head. His long hair fell forward, hiding his face, but I could see his throat working, fighting the tears. *Please don't*, I wanted to say, *it's not fair.*

He held it together, though. I could see him physically working to shake off the urge to cry as he reached his hand up, behind his shoulder. His fingers worked, searching for something and finding only air. As he snatched his hand back, burying it deep in his jeans pocket, I realized what he'd been reaching for. The hood that was pulled over my own head. The hoodie was more than simply a piece of clothing to him, it was a second skin. And he'd given it to me, not just for protection, but as his penance and pound of flesh all in one.

I reached out and touched his arm. "I don't hate you. I don't even know what happened between us, except that we . . ." I trailed off, suddenly feeling embarrassed, remembering that I had watched him and Annaliese.

We stood there in the middle of the hallway, with my hand still on his arm, and if I hadn't been that close, I might not have even heard his next words. "My mom said she'd never been ashamed of me before." His voice cracked, and I felt the muscles in his arm flexing as he struggled to control his emotions once more. "I don't want my mom to be ashamed of me. I gotta fix this."

Now my own tears threatened. Thinking of Annaliese's poem, and Logan's mother with two jobs. Thinking of the mom, the way it mattered too much what she thought of me. The way I feared she'd know the worst and hate me for it.

"Then let's fix it," I said.

THE DEEP END

It turned out Logan didn't have a lunch at all. Instead he led me to a vending machine tucked away in a corner between the pool and the main gymnasium. According to him, it wasn't meant to be used during school hours, but everyone did. Feeding a few dollars into the machine, he chose a bag of Fritos, another of Doritos, pretzels, and a package of Starbursts. Popping open the Fritos, Logan pointed toward the door to the pool.

"Mind the smell of chlorine?"

I didn't, and we settled in the poolside bleachers to eat.

Neither of us said anything at first. The silence was the kind you eyed nervously, trying to think of a way to make it go away, while the tiled walls created an echo chamber that multiplied every foot shuffle, bag crinkle, and crunch of a chip, effectively filling the room with the sound of us not talking to each other.

Sitting beside Logan as he methodically worked through his bags of junk food, I found my thoughts drifting to Dex. Admittedly, it wasn't the first time. Ever since our meeting it was as if a new current had been created that wanted to carry me back to him. Remembering he'd said we were in the same class, I'd been looking for him at school. I hadn't even known how much I'd been counting on seeing him here, until I realized either he no longer went here or he was avoiding me. I hated to think the latter might be true. And suddenly, I had to know the truth.

With what I hoped sounded like an offhanded casualness, I added my voice to the echoes. "Does a guy named Dex go here?"

The way Logan jumped, my question might've been a bullet ricocheting off the walls.

"Are you kidding? Someone already mentioned that creep to you? Shit. If someone showed you the—" Logan stalled, and I helpfully filled in what he didn't want to say.

"The YouTube video?"

His mouth fell open, and then it snapped closed. "Who did it? If anyone at school is found with a copy of it, they'll be expelled. Everyone knows that."

"Nobody here has shown it to me," I said, carefully sidestepping the question, afraid Logan might decide to punch another locker on my behalf.

He looked relieved, and I knew then that the little video clip I'd watched scared the hell out of him. "Well, if somebody does try and show it to you, walk away. You don't want to see that." His gaze was distant, and I could almost see the one-minute-and-twelve-second clip playing in his head. I wondered how many times he'd watched it. Maybe only once and it remained burned into his memory. Or, perhaps, he had made himself watch it again and again. Not like I had, trying to understand, but as another way of finding a path toward forgiveness.

"And don't worry," Logan added. "You won't run into Dex. He left school in eighth grade, got homeschooled or something. I don't know, I didn't go here yet, but everyone says he was the same freak then. I guess his only friend killed himself, and he had some kind of nervous breakdown or something, and that was the last anyone saw of him. Well, until he started showing up at parties sophomore year. Always with his camera too. No matter how many times he got kicked out, or had beer dumped over his head, he kept coming, so everybody just started to ignore him."

Logan's fist clenched around his bag of pretzels. "I don't know why he put that video online. I don't know how anybody who was there and had seen it would want to do that." His voice caught, and I watched him make another aborted attempt to grab for his hood.

"This is where we used to meet," Logan said suddenly. He wasn't looking at me, but at the smooth water in front of us. "Not during lunch, that would've been too obvious. We would skip out during class. Just for ten or fifteen minutes at a time. You used to be really nervous about it, but kind of excited too. Like you couldn't believe you were doing it. You said you'd never skipped before."

The words stumbled from Logan's mouth in a halting kind of way that left me wondering if he was forcing them out, or had just been holding them in for so long that he now couldn't quite release them.

"I don't remember," I said, not as a reminder, but to let him know he could let go of these memories—there was no one holding on to them anymore—except him.

"I know you don't, that's why I need to tell you." He turned away from the water, facing me.

"Maybe you should try and forget it too."

Logan shook his head. "Don't you think I tried? The whole time you were missing, I tried. And it kinda worked, but then you came back and now you're here and I can't keep pretending. You ever hear somebody say something is eating them up inside? I never really knew what that meant—or I thought I did, like being stressed about a test or shit like that—but this, this is nothing like that. Knowing what happened between you and me, it feels like actual fucking teeth taking these, like, gigantic bites out of my guts and stuff."

I wanted to make a joke. Tell him he sure put away a lot of junk food for a guy who was suffering from a parasitic guilty conscience. Except teeth. And bites. Those words recalled my nightmare vision of Annaliese's white teeth closing around a dripping red heart. It was just a dream, I told myself. Or maybe an allegory. Annaliese's life wasn't the only one ruined. So many other lives had also had a bite taken from them.

"So how did it start?" I asked, wanting to give Logan this bit of himself back. "Where did the whole you-and-me thing begin?"

Standing, Logan stepped onto the bench below ours and started to walk along it with careful precision, one foot in front of the other, as if it were a balance beam perched over shark-infested waters. He should've looked like a hippo in a tutu, a big guy mincing along like that, but the natural athleticism that had made him a star on the football field transferred here. It was more than just gracefulness. There was a confidence and oneness with his body. He made walking look like something special.

"We were in Spanish together. Mr. Fields's class. As a teacher he's known for two things: the Mighty Taco parties he throws the last day before Christmas break, and his constant vocab pop quizzes. The Mighty Taco thing is cool, but those quizzes were brutal. And he was one of those teachers who would get all bent out of shape if you weren't prepared. Like he would tell you to take out paper and a pen, and two seconds later be shooting these Spanish words at you, and if you missed one 'cause you were still digging around for something to write with, he wouldn't go back and repeat any. So, I flunked a few of them, just because I'd missed half the questions, and they were like fifty percent of your grade or something. I couldn't really afford to mess up anymore."

Reaching the end of his row, Logan neatly pivoted and began moving back in the other direction.

"One day, I came in and realized it'd been a while since our last quiz. Before I even go to sit down, I start looking in my pockets for a pen. And I got nothing. That's when I walked past your desk. You always sat like totally front and center, and I'm more of a last-row, near-the-windows kind of guy. I passed by your desk and saw you had all these pens lined up. The little clicky kind."

He mimed a clicking gesture with his thumbs. "So, I grabbed one from the pile, and said, 'Mind if I borrow this?' You kind of stared at me and turned real red, and I figured, well, not to be a jerk, but you know, lots of girls like me, and I thought you were stunned speechless or something. But then you grabbed it back, and said, 'Not this one.' Then you took one of the other pens there, and honestly they all looked alike, and you did the weirdest thing. You unscrewed it, and kind of peered inside, like you were making sure all the parts were there or something."

I wondered which of her poems had been inside that pen Logan had almost taken. If it had been one about him—and most of them so far seemed to be, even though he was never mentioned by name. She must have been mortified.

"Then you put the pen back together, held it out to me, and said, 'You can keep it.' And I said, 'Nah, I'll get it back to you at the end of class.' Then I went to my seat, and it turned out there wasn't a pop quiz that day after all. And I didn't give your pen back, because I totally forgot about the whole thing. And I didn't think about it until maybe three or four weeks later, when I was walking past your desk again, but this time I didn't notice your pens. I . . . this is gonna sound nuts, okay?"

Having reached the end of the bleachers once more, Logan stopped. He leaned into the tile wall in front of him, letting his forehead rest against it. He looked exhausted or defeated, as if he had literally hit a wall. But then he was in motion once more, rotating 180 degrees so that his back was against the wall. Logan slowly slid down and then backward until he was lying on the bench, staring up at the ceiling.

"Lots of things are nuts," I said softly, letting the acoustics carry my voice to him.

"Yeah, but this . . . The night before that Spanish class, I had these dreams. You know those kind of crazy dreams where they feel so real, like realer than real, and then you wake up, and you're still kind of in the dream, and you want more of it, but as you start to think about it you begin to lose it, and the more you try to remember, the more you forget, until the only thing that's left is your hard-on?"

He paused then added, "Sorry. Didn't mean to say that."

"It's okay." Wanting to get past the moment, I quickly added, "So the dreams were about . . ."

"Annaliese. Yeah."

He didn't seem to notice that he'd just referred to Annaliese as someone other than me, and I didn't stop him to correct his mistake that wasn't a mistake at all.

"The dreams suddenly came back to me; I remembered them completely. It was . . . I didn't even know I could imagine stuff like that, and I'd been watching late-night Cinemax since I was eleven. And Annaliese, she's just staring at me, and then says, 'Did you need a pen again?' And well, the pens had played a part in the dream, and it was like she knew or something, I mean, of course she didn't, but the way she was looking at me . . . I had to get out of there. So, I just said no, and my voice cracked like I was a fucking freshman again, and I ran for my desk, practically falling into my chair."

Logan sat up and let out a long breath, as if he'd finished something difficult. Then he lay down once more.

"Of course, that day Mr. Fields did have a pop quiz and, of course, I didn't have a pen, and I didn't even fucking care. I was like, screw it. But by the end of the quiz, I kind of got my head back in the game, and then Mr. Fields says to find a partner 'cause we're gonna practice our conversational skills. It was weird. He never did that kind of thing, said it was just an excuse to goof off. But whatever, I would take it, because I knew that I had to talk to her. And that's how it was, all the time after that, until she disappeared. I had to talk to her, see her, touch her, be with her. It was like I couldn't stop thinking about her."

Logan's foot tapped a few times against the wall, and then he spun onto his feet, and with a few quick steps was in front of me once more.

"Did I say *her*? I meant *you*. I couldn't stop thinking about you." He looked into my eyes. "I still can't stop thinking about you."

And then he knelt in front of me, grabbed hold of my shoulders, and drew me in for a kiss. It was passionate. But not with love. Or desire. With desperation. As if this kiss could bridge the gap between now and everything that had happened since he'd had sex with Annaliese on top of last year's fallen leaves.

I pushed him away. Gently.

I might as well have slapped him. He stumbled back, down the bleachers and to the edge of the pool.

"I'm sorry," he whispered. "Maybe I'm losing my mind, because I really can't stop thinking about you."

Annaliese would've gone to him, wrapped her arms around

him, and pulled him from the edge. I wasn't her, though, and I didn't want this boy kissing me. Even if it was the only thing that might save him.

"But it's not in the same way, is it?" I asked, in response to Logan.

If he gave an answer, I didn't hear it. I'd already walked out the door.

NOTEPAD

Even though I'd left Logan behind, his hoodie still covered me. It had been protection and a kind of comfort, but now it was a weight and a reminder. His smell—a mixture of cologne liberally applied, sweat, and something else that I couldn't quite pinpoint—clung to me even after I put the hoodie back into my locker. This was what guilt now smelled like.

I stopped in the middle of the hall, trying to remember which class came next. But not really caring. English, math, biology. It all felt like repeats. *Julius Caesar*, the cosines, the chromosomes—I knew it all and had seen it presented better.

A girl's laughter pushed me back into the present. It wasn't at my expense for once. She wasn't even aware of me. A boy had tripped and fallen. Maybe she'd pushed him. When I looked, he was on hands and knees, already struggling upward to scramble away. I only saw him out of the corner of my eye, because my attention was on the laughing girl. Her orangey tan skin, bleached blond hair, and heavy-handed black eyeliner. At the same time I took in all these little details, my stomach growled. The strange hunger pang I'd experienced when I first saw Logan had struck once more. I gulped, starving.

I spun away. Away from the girl. Away from the thought. And right into the redheaded boy.

"Hey, watch it," he said loudly, but a second later he was whispering in my ear. "The hunger's getting worse, isn't it? The Physician give you the names yet?" He studied me for a moment. "Okay, you look confused, so I'm thinking that's a no. Don't worry, little Anna, they'll come soon." Pressing something into my hand, he pushed me away. "Watch where you're going next time."

I stumbled back, relieved to be released. With any luck he'd leave me alone for the rest of the day. Leave me to my fantasy of being a normal girl. A normal girl like Annaliese. Annaliese before she met me, anyway.

But being hungry for your classmate's flesh makes it hard to pretend. And that's why I pressed through the crowd, reached toward the redheaded boy, and grabbed hold of his arm. If I was going to look for the truth of who I was, then I had to stop running from him.

"Wait."

His eyes lingered for a moment on the point of connection between my hand and his arm. I expected a smirk or a triumphant grin. He had the power. The answers. And I'd come running after him. But when his gaze moved to meet mine, his smile was almost warm. I'd reached for him instead of flinching away. That's what made him smile. The very simple fact of a touch—voluntarily given—made this horrible, frightening boy happy.

I smiled back, thinking it might be easier if we weren't enemies. And I kept my hand on him even though he made my flesh crawl.

"What's your name? You call me Anna. That's my name, my real name. Isn't it? What's your real name?"

It was the wrong question to ask. His smile flatlined as he jerked from my grasp. "I don't have a real name. Not since I watched the boy I once was turn to dust, and his name went the same way. Just like your beloved Anna. Anna is dust blown to the other end of the earth by now and sunk to the bottom of the sea. Anna is nothing. And I call you Anna because without me you're nothing too."

The bell rang, and I ran. Not to make it to class on time, but to get away from him. It wasn't until I sat down, and the American history teacher began one of his painful lectures where he tried to compare Benjamin Franklin to Snoop Dogg in an effort to make him more relevant, that I finally unclenched my trembling fingers and remembered the object the boy had pressed into my hand.

It was a cell phone. Hiding it beneath my desk, I began to click through the different menus and options, looking for whatever he had wanted me to find. It took nearly the entire class, but I found it in the notepad section. Another poem.

Reading it, I knew with a terrible certainty that this was what Annaliese had been tapping into her cell phone in those moments after Logan had left her in the woods, right before I'd approached her. These were in essence Annaliese's last words.

I walked out of class. Didn't even make up an excuse, just got up and left. Without consciously planning it, I went back to the pool.

I pulled out the cell phone and read Annaliese's poem again. Her body lived. Her poems lived. But Annaliese was gone.

If I asked the redheaded boy, he would probably say that she was nothing too.

If I asked the mom, she would say that Annaliese was something special. And she would back that up with a hug, solid and reassuring. You don't hug nothing.

And if you asked me . . .

I looked down into the depths of the pool. The water was clear and blue, not a speck of dirt anywhere.

Annaliese was gone. Anna was dust. We might never be found.

STERILE

IT WAS TRUE

it was true
he wanted me
just like I'd wanted him
to want me

or not

i was a craving
like a hamburger
with fries

and now he is full
and I . . .

I am eaten

—ARG

ICE CREAM

"Do you want ice cream? I feel like ice cream! Let's go and get some ice cream." As I got into the car after school, the mom was bright and overly chipper. Every time she said *ice cream*, she put so much stress on the two words that it felt like a code for something else.

But it was a beautiful Indian summer day, and having ice cream sounded so good that I couldn't resist. We ended up at Anderson's, sitting out in the dipping afternoon sun, licking vanilla ice-cream cones with sprinkles. It felt like a moment you'd be willing to steal someone else's life for, and even that thought wasn't enough to ruin it for me.

Of course, when you steal those moments, you also have to deal with all the other ones that come in between. Like the mom blindsiding me.

"I talked to your principal," the mom said as we walked back toward the car.

"Oh?" I said, silently adding *shit*.

"He told me about the fight yesterday." She paused long enough for all the good feelings to curdle. Long enough for me to realize she'd been buttering me up for this interrogation.

I wasn't giving anything away until I had a better idea of how much she knew.

"He said Logan Rice defended you?"

Okay, so she knew everything. I wondered if she'd given the principal ice cream first too, to get him to spill it all so quickly.

"I didn't want you to worry," I said, which was true. Except I should've known that she'd find out anyway.

"Well, I am worried. I'm worried that you're not telling me things." Another pause. This one shorter. Not that it mattered. I already knew what was coming. "Again."

And there it was.

I wanted to tell her that if she weren't so neurotic, maybe I would tell her things, and maybe Annaliese would've too. Except I knew it wasn't true. No daughter would've told her mother she traded her very soul to make a boy notice her.

So I gave the mom something instead.

"Logan and I had lunch together today."

"You did *what*?" It was like I'd said I had lunch at the local prison.

"I know you don't like him."

"That's not—" The mom shook her head, and then seemed to remember we were standing in a parking lot, talking over the top of the car. She pulled out her keys. "Get in."

We both climbed into the car, but we didn't buckle up and she didn't start it. Instead, the mom grabbed hold of the steering wheel, her hands clenched tightly at precisely ten and two. To someone walking past, it probably looked like we were in the middle of an incredibly tense driving lesson.

"I wish that Logan had come forward at the beginning, when you first disappeared, with the information that he had been with you. The detectives said that it would only have helped confirm the timeline, but you never know, when the whole thing was fresher in his mind, he might have remembered some small detail that could have helped us find you sooner. Other than that, I have no reason not to . . ."

I could see her mouth trying to form the word *like*, but she couldn't quite seem to get it out.

"I don't think he's a bad boy. And he seems sincerely sorry. I wish you and he hadn't chosen to embark on a sexual relationship. And his having a girlfriend at the time certainly doesn't speak well of him, but it seems it was consensual, and for that I can't blame just him. I have to blame you as well."

It was a lot of words for the mom, and when she got them all out, she burst into tears.

"If it helps," I said softly, "I don't like him like that. Not anymore."

"Oh, honey," the mom said with a half sob, half laugh. "It actually does kind of help. But it would help even more if you would not like any boys for a while. At least until you finish high school, or college." She was joking. And totally serious.

I pretended only to hear the joke, and laughed, and tried really hard not to think about Dex and how I was determined to see him soon. And how even though we were friends, there was a part of me that couldn't help thinking about kissing him.

The mom wiped her eyes and started the car. It seemed the grilling was over, but then her hand landed on my leg instead of the gearshift and gave it a little pat.

"So, is school okay then, Annaliese? The other kids haven't made it too difficult? Mr. Hardy said that Gwen was there today, and, well, I admit I was never her biggest fan, but she was always a good friend to you."

"It's fine," I said with a little shrug, not wanting to get into the whole Gwen thing, not wanting to think about her at all, and what kind of friend Annaliese might have been to her. "Probably no better and no worse than it ever was before."

The mom's eyes filled once again, and I wondered if I should've been more falsely upbeat about the whole situation. She quickly blinked the tears away.

"Sorry, no more watering pot today," she said, giving my leg a reassuring squeeze. "Sometimes you sound so much like your old self, it just . . ." Her voice broke and she shook her head.

I waited for her to finish. I wanted to know what came after *it just*. Did it just make her wonder who the hell I was the rest of the time?

But she released my thigh, and then we were backing out of the spot and driving home. And it was—like so much else in my life—just forgotten.

The sun is warm against my face, burning as I listen to the waves wage their constant campaign of attacks and hasty retreats against the shore. My toes curl into the sand, seeking the comfort of something solid. But none of this is enough to hold me here in the now. I am falling.

The hands find me. Six of them press against my back. Slowly they leach away the pain, leaving only the memory.

It is a bad one. Filled with blood. And regrets.

This is not unusual. Many of them are bloody. And all of them are bound by the common theme of regrets, remorse, and wrongs that can never be righted.

The three women at my back take their hands from me one by one, slowly allowing me to stand on my own.

"You are okay now?" one of the *brujas* asks in Spanish. I don't speak the language, and yet I understand her perfectly, and the other two as well. And though they never speak English, they understand me just as easily.

Turning to face them, I take turns touching their hands, letting them feel that I am fine.

When I woke in their small cottage many days and weeks—or maybe even months—ago, they were gathered around me. I'd woken up screaming. In the middle of a dream about a scream that I couldn't stop. One by one they touched the tip of a finger to my lips. The scream faded away to ragged breaths, and then more regular ones as they hovered over me. They were nearly identical with their weathered faces and gray hair hanging loose and heavy over their shoulders before flowing to their bare feet and the packed-dirt floor.

A bucket of cool water appeared along with ragged bits of cloth that wiped at my face and came away red. Cooing a chorus of sympathy, they'd washed away the blood that had crusted over my eyes, coated my lips and teeth, and left stripes running down my arms all the way to my fingertips.

Brujas. The word appeared in my mind then, and I knew they were witches, and I knew this was not something to be afraid of, and I knew they would take care of me. "Thank you," I rasped through raw vocal cords. Then I closed my eyes and fell into a peaceful sleep.

In many ways it feels like I have stayed in that peaceful sleep—except for when the painful memories intrude.

They tell me not to fight it, that there is no future without the past. But I must fight, or perhaps run. Every time the past comes rushing toward me, I only want to get away. What those memories reveal makes it impossible to believe the future can hold anything good.

No, I'd rather stay here in the now, with the sun, the surf, the sand, and most importantly—the peace.

The *brujas* understand this as easily as my untranslated words.

They are hiding from the past and future as well. This is a between time, they tell me, and between can be a dangerous place.

"We will keep you with us as long as we can," they promise. "As long as we can."

I hope it will be long enough for my hair to grow long and gray like theirs. But they always look toward the horizon when they make this promise, as if watching for something coming, something that will take me away. They whisper softly then. Words not meant to reach my ears, but the ocean breeze brings them to me anyway. "Our brother, the Physician. He will return. We must prepare or she will be lost."

Another memory comes; it burns in my chest. They are coming faster now. My eyes close, as the *brujas*' hands find me once more.

SOFT EDGES

"Annaliese."

I opened my eyes, not to the three *brujas*, but to the mom, gently shaking me awake.

We were still in the car, now parked in the dark garage. The leather seat beneath my cheek felt immaterial, like with only a few blinks it might turn to sand and me right along with it, all of us crumbling away.

I grabbed hold of the mom's hand, needing to feel something warm and solid. She couldn't draw away the pain the way the *brujas* in my dream had, but she squeezed back and then continued to hold tight. I didn't release her until the cool, quiet garage became more real than the beach with the constant hush and crash of the waves.

"Come on," the mom said, as I wiggled my fingers free. "Let's get inside, and you can take a real nap."

After finally brushing the sand away, I had no interest in letting sleep catch me again, but I didn't say this to the mom. She looked so exhausted and almost literally drained—her face a chalky white color. When she suggested I might want to take a nap, I knew she was the one who needed it, but she wouldn't be able to take one until I was safely tucked away.

So I made a big show of yawning and stretching, agreeing that yes, I was really tired and a nap sounded perfect. After she pulled the covers up to my chin and planted a tender kiss on my forehead, I listened to her walk back downstairs. I hoped she'd keep going, all the way to the cots in the basement, but twenty minutes later when I came easing down the staircase, I found her on the sofa. She looked completely out, like she'd collapsed and immediately fallen into a deep sleep.

I almost turned around, resigned to staring at the bedroom walls, unable to betray the mom who may not have originally brought me into this world, but who now helped hold me here.

And yet, like the *brujas*, her eyes too were always on the horizon, looking for the next thing that would come to carry me away.

The past was coming for me, the now could only keep me for so long, and the future . . . I had little hope of it holding anything good. But that tiny bit of hope was enough to send me hunting for a way to secure it. And for some reason I felt like Dex might be able to help me with that search. Or maybe I was just looking for an excuse to see him again. To see what it felt like to have a friend.

"I'm sorry," I whispered to the mom.

I probably could've slid out either the front or back door, both directly within her line of vision, without her knowing a thing. But if she stirred, I was screwed. Then not only would I miss out on seeing Dex, but she would know that I was trying to sneak away, and any semblance of trust would be gone.

Slipping through the storm-cellar doors, just like the ones I used to get into Dex's, was a perfect alternative. If the mom caught me going into the basement, I could simply pretend that I'd been attempting to raid her Little Debbie supply.

The door creaked loudly as I closed it behind me. I stood on the top step, waiting and listening. Not a sound to be heard. She was still asleep. Flicking on the light, I headed down.

As I'd hoped, our storm doors were in the exact same place as the ones next door. Thank goodness for suburban conformity. Unfortunately, one of the mom's overloaded doomsday shelves blocked the cement steps leading to my escape. Stacked full of canned goods, I knew there was no chance of moving it.

I wasn't giving up that easily. If I couldn't go around, then I would go through. Painstakingly, I began to remove six rows of cans from the second shelf up, carefully restacking them on the floor, until at last there was a hole big enough for me to wiggle through. A padlock held the door closed on our end, but with the key inserted into this side of it, all I had to do was turn it and then climb out and into the backyard.

I darted across the lawn, ducking low when I passed by windows, in case the mom had woken and was looking out. Then I was on the other end of the fence. Remembering that Annaliese's cell phone had an alarm function, I dug it out of my pocket. Thirty minutes, I decided. Less time than I wanted, but enough in case the mom took a short nap.

His storm doors were flung wide open, and I leaned over to gently tap on one.

"Hey, Dex, it's me," I called into the darkness.

A moment later I heard footsteps, and then Dex's head popped up, a big smile stretched across it. Something expanded inside of me, joyful and hurting all at the same time.

"Anna." The smile was in the way he said my name too. "Come in. Come in." He disappeared down below again, and I followed.

There was something different about the basement; I felt

it as soon as I stepped fully inside. Not like the furniture had been rearranged. The desk, the metal cabinets, and the man-eating beanbag chair were all in the same places . . . but it seemed changed somehow.

"Soft edges," Dex said, so close to me that his breath tickled my ear.

"What?" I asked, turning toward him, not to hear him bet-ter, or to see him, but to put my lips in closer proximity to his. I wanted his lips to cover over Logan's. *I've had too many unwanted kisses in my life.*

I frowned, wondering where that thought came from, and knowing I wasn't just thinking of the redheaded boy and Logan.

Maybe Dex saw my frown, or maybe he simply had no thought of kissing me. He took a step back, not a great distance, but enough to put us out of kissing range. This time when he spoke, I couldn't feel his breath against my skin. I missed it.

"I put foam edges on all the hard surfaces," Dex said, pointing toward the desk and metal cabinets. "And I found some foam mats for the floor too. I just thought, well, everyone can use a soft edge when they fall."

"Did you fall?" I asked.

He shrugged. "No, but I might in the future, and having my head cracked open like an egg on this cement floor is not the way I want to go."

It seemed so much like the mom, worrying about every little

thing that might happen and trying to prevent it and everything else from happening. Except Dex wasn't like that at all. Even talking about his head smashing, he was smiling and seemingly carefree.

As this all worked its way through my mind, Dex had taken a half step closer, and then he held my hand in his, tracing along the edges of my fingers. "You have lots of edges too. Before—when you were Annaliese—you were all rounded corners, but now, you call yourself Anna and have all these sharp jagged parts."

I knew that he wasn't merely talking about the weight loss or a name change, that he realized the changes in Annaliese—in me—went deeper than that. But if he knew exactly how deep, I doubted his mouth would still be smiling.

"If you asked my mom, she'd probably say I should be baby-proofed," I said with a soft laugh, hoping to draw Dex away from the true depths of my secrets.

"Hmmm," he said as his hand left mine to travel up my arm, past my wristbone, elbow, and shoulder. Trailing his fingers lightly across my neck, he left goose bumps in his wake, until he cupped my cheek. Here comes the kiss, I thought.

I was wrong.

Tenderly his thumb found the scar on my forehead and brushed against it. Once. Twice. Three times. Each time so tender. As if he were wiping some faint smudge away. If he pressed a little harder, he would feel the way the bone beneath the skin cratered in too. One of the doctors had shown me on an X-ray where a chunk of brain matter was missing. Something had quite literally put a hole in my head, and yet Dex's touch made me believe he could wipe it away. That he could make it all go away. I could simply be Annaliese.

His fingers drifted down, skimming over my eyelashes, and brushing my lips, as he leaned in for a kiss that I had quite possibly been waiting my entire life and several others for when—

Ba-beep. Ba-beep.

I cursed myself for setting that stupid alarm. How was it possible that thirty minutes had gone by so fast? Then Dex pulled out a cell of his own and his eyes scanned the small screen. Flipping the phone closed, he returned it to his back pocket. Then he looked at me. It wasn't a "now where were we?" kind of look. He was studying me. No, assessing. Later, I realized he was deciding if he wanted to let me in. If he could trust me.

"It's a text from my mom. She says the house is open. Want to come inside while I prep dinner?"

I checked my phone. Fifteen minutes until the alarm went off. It would've been smarter to head home. Instead I said, "Sure."

Dex's hand found mine, and he pulled me up the stairs. Strangely, the door into the house had a lock. Three, actually. Dex took care of them quickly, flipping through a series of different keys for each one without letting go of my hand once.

It was dark inside the house. Darker than the basement, and when Dex flipped a switch on the wall, I saw why. All the windows were covered with thick curtains that looked as if they'd been stolen from a theater. They were thick and red, and blocked out every last bit of light, making it permanent midnight.

I gripped Dex's hand tighter as we moved through the house. Layoutwise it was a duplicate of the mom and dad's, but it felt different. Smaller and hollow. Most of the rooms were empty, with only a scattering of chairs, or a few random stacked boxes to give any hint of occupancy.

"We've lived here almost four years now," Dex said, as if he knew I'd been wondering. "An old friend of my dad's helped us find this place."

There were no further explanations, and then we were in the kitchen. Next door, the mom's kitchen had a round table at its center. Here there was only a single metal folding chair with a cross-stitched cushion. I leaned in closer to read the words *God Bless This Happy Home*.

"Hungry?" Dex asked, releasing my hand. He pitched his voice softer than normal. Not whispering but muted, like he didn't want the sound to carry. It made me nervous, and I looked around, wondering who exactly he didn't want overhearing him.

"I'm good," I said, keeping my voice low too.

"Probably a good choice, because I'm not much of a chef," Dex said, swinging open the pantry door.

Peering over his shoulder, I saw a selection similar to the mom's basement emergency supply of nonperishables. Dex reached for two cans of Chef Boyardee ravioli. Then another of green beans. Sliding these across the counter, he went back once more for a handful of vanilla wafers.

Next he reached into the fridge and pulled out a bottle of water, a Pepsi, and a Diet Pepsi. I couldn't help but think of the nutritious dinner the mom would prepare for me later that night.

She knew I liked mashed potatoes, so she'd been making them almost every night. Not the instant kind either. Russet potatoes, peeled and boiled, and then mashed with lots of butter and cream. There would also be roasted chicken or broiled steaks, as well as some other vegetable to round things out. I guess the mom figured we'd have plenty of time to eat Chef Boyardee when the end of the world came.

"My dad ran out when I was a kid," Dex said, interrupting my thoughts. "So, it's been me and my mom since then."

He'd opened all three of the cans and was now dividing the contents between two plates. "Moneywise, things were hard growing up. Stupid little things really, like my sneakers were Walmart brand instead of Nike. Around the holidays my mom always worked overtime, so I could get the new Xbox system or whatever. At the time I didn't think about how hard that was for her, how exhausted she must've been. I was just so happy to have that Xbox, you know? Then around the end of seventh grade, everything changed."

Taking a glass from the cupboard, Dex poured the contents of the Diet Pepsi into it. "The doctors thought she had a nervous breakdown or was manic depressive, or some other type of crazy that could be treated with medicine and therapy. And money." Dex stopped and looked up at me.

Every time my eyes met his, it was a shock, but this time the anger crackling in them made my breath catch.

"Lots and lots of money. And the whole time I knew what the problem was, and it wasn't that she was crazy. She was dealing in her own way, and if that meant shutting herself away from the world, away from everything, including sunlight, and air, and me, well then, I would help her do it."

Okay, now this dark, empty house made a strange kind of sense. Except for one thing. "You don't see your mom?" I asked softly.

Dex shook his head. "Haven't since we moved here. We have a routine. She texts me with the all clear, and I get meals ready for both of us. She doesn't like to do the cooking, because she doesn't want to see the labels on the food. There are too many pictures and names."

"You said you moved here four years ago," I said, and then hesitated. I wanted to know more about what Logan had told me but didn't want to ask directly. So I tiptoed around it instead.

"Is that when you left school too?"

Dex gave me a crooked smile. "It's okay, Anna, you can ask questions."

I could feel myself blushing. "I heard you had some kind of breakdown. And that you had a friend who . . ." Logan had said it was a suicide, but I couldn't make myself say the word.

"Tim killed himself." Another smile, but this one was pained. "Everyone thinks he's why I left. Except for the people who knew something was wrong with my mom, and they thought she was the reason. And they were connected, but . . ." As Dex turned to open another cupboard, he left the unfinished thought hanging in the air. Taking his time, he pulled out a plastic lid and snapped it onto the second plate.

"But?" I prodded gently.

He didn't answer me, didn't even acknowledge the question. Instead, he swept the empty cans into the trash can beneath the sink, and then washed his hands, rubbing them together beneath the running water for such a long time that I wondered what exactly he was trying to rinse away.

When he turned back toward me, though, he didn't look like someone with a guilty conscience. In fact, for someone who had just finished relating his somewhat tragic history, while preparing an equally depressing dinner, Dex looked pretty happy.

"But," he said, taking one slow deliberate step and then another in my direction. "We all make our own choices, Anna.

Every single day—no, every moment—we get to decide how to live our lives. I could've killed myself. Or locked myself away. I didn't. I found other ways to deal." Dex stood directly in front of me. Reaching out, he touched the tip of his finger to the tip of my nose.

"Actually, you've shown me other ways."

And then, at last, he kissed me. A soft, flitting, there-and-then-gone hummingbird of a kiss. It seemed like it wouldn't be possible to savor something so temporary and fleeting. But I closed my eyes, letting that brief brush of lips reverberate and ricochet through me.

Opening my eyes again, I saw Dex watching me. Worried. And hopeful. Always hopeful. My heart fluttered, as if that hummingbird kiss had become trapped inside me. I leaned toward Dex, wanting another kiss. And another. And another. A whole flock of hummingbird wings beating away inside me.

The alarm on my cell phone chirped instead, and we jumped apart.

"I have to go," I said, my voice breathy and foreign.

Dex nodded. Taking my hand, he led me to the back door. Like the basement door, it had multiple locks, although these were all on our side, so Dex only had to flip them. Then he slid the door open, but instead of releasing my hand, he tugged me closer once more.

"I was going to tell you why my friend died, and why my mom

is like this, and why I record life more than I live it, but I decided to kiss you instead. I'll tell you some other day, okay?"

I nodded, but inside something was opening up. I was afraid to have his secrets, but mostly I was amazed that he would give them to me so easily. That he saw something in me worth not just kissing but truly trusting as well.

Impulsively, I stretched up and kissed his cheek. And then I ran out the door of his empty house, so giddy I was almost skipping.

Home again. Home again. Jiggity jig. I came bounding down the storm door stairs, and almost crashed into the shelf. Wiping the big stupid smile off my face, I ducked down to wiggle through the little hole I'd created.

That was when I saw them lining the back of the top shelf. A row of spitballs.

I'd actually forgotten Annaliese for a few moments there. Forgotten that my joy was at her expense.

I couldn't bring myself to read them. Not with the memory of Dex's lips still making mine tingle. But I couldn't leave them behind either. I gathered them, squeezing them into a tight ball at the center of my fist.

If I had been floating before, I'd returned to earth. Hard. No more skipping. Through the basement and all the way until I reached my room, it was more like trudging through six feet of shit.

Until now, some part of me had thought Annaliese was a

stupid girl to make a terrible deal just to get a boy, the way she had. She'd given herself away.

But that one kiss had changed things.

As guilty as I felt, and as horrific as it was to remember . . . I could almost do it all over again.

For that hummingbird kiss, I would let Annaliese eat her heart out once more.

KNOWING

FIRST KISS

First kiss
or first kiss that counts
that didn't come from a
spinning bottle
pointing at me
and someone making a face
'cause their lips will have to
meet mine.

First kiss
or first kiss that
wasn't just a scene
that I dreamed
writing the word
love
into your mouth
moments before it
touched mine.

First kiss
or first kiss that

was nothing like I
thought it would be.
wetter and warmer
worse and better
with your hands everywhere
and mine hanging by my side
and then your tongue
licking mine.

First kiss
or first kiss that
after a slow start
and some uncertainty
made me realize
why this is something
people do.
And why it is so much more
than simply your lips
on mine.

—ARG

I know immediately. I am somewhere strange. This bed isn't my own. The blanket is scratchy, and the pillow has a strange sour smell.

Dim light leaks through a crack in the curtained windows, enough for me to see another bed lined up with mine and a night table between them. On the opposite wall sits a small television with rabbit ears.

A motel room. There's no relief in identifying it.

Something terrible has happened, but I can't quite remember what. Or I don't want to remember.

Oh God, someone please help me.

Silent tears slide down my cheeks.

Oh God, someone please help me.

I open the drawer of the bedside table, and pull out the Bible that I knew I'd find there. I am torn. Should I read, search for some passage that will explain or provide some comfort? Or just have the immediate release and small satisfaction of tearing out the damn pages one by one.

Still undecided, I flip it open.

Words blur before my eyes.

Love is patient. Love is kind.

I throw the book across the room, hitting the door just as it is opening.

A young man walks in. I know him. And I think I remember why I am here. Except I thought that was only a nightmare.

Oh God, please let it be a nightmare.

"Look what you've done," he says, throwing a newspaper at me.

Dully, I let it hit me and then flop down to the dingy bedspread. The large capital letters of the headline seem to scream at me.

FOUL PLAY NOW SUSPECTED IN CASE OF TWO MISSING GIRLS

The smaller words below the headline refuse to come into focus. But I can't avoid the big picture. A girl smiles at me. It's her school picture. The smile was forced and didn't reach her eyes. Most people wouldn't know that, and wouldn't notice. Pretty girl, they would think.

"That's me," I say, touching a finger to the inked image of Anna Martin.

"No, that's Anna," he sneers, snatching the paper away with one hand and grabbing hold of my arm with the other. He drags me across the room and into the bathroom. I blink against the too-bright fluorescent lights as he pushes me in front of the mirror. "*That's you.* Katie Campbell."

A girl winces back at me. Pale and terrified, she looks nothing like the girl in the picture. The young man was right. This is not Anna. I recognize her, though. She'd been my brother's girlfriend. She'd been my friend too. She'd been Katie Campbell, but now I was Katie and she was . . .

The girl in the mirror shakes her head, warning me not to think of that. To think of anything else but that.

"You *were* the missing girl," the horrible boy says. "And now you're the other missing girl. The one who is also the suspect."

BLURT

Another night. Another dream. Another memory.

Before bed I found a few more of Annaliese's spitball poems, along with some notes hidden in the toe of an old shoe. I shouldn't have gone looking for them, but I couldn't stop myself. I always found at least one during my hunts, as if some part of me remembered where they'd been hidden. As usual the poems left me unsettled. It was no surprise that when I finally fell asleep, I dreamed.

It was one of those where you think you are sleeping, so when you wake in the dream, it tricks you into believing you are waking into real life. Except in the dream I was Anna.

Anna. Annaliese. Anna. Annaliese.

The two names echoed in my head for the rest of my sleepless night, a puzzle that I was still determined to solve. When the sky began to lighten it was a relief to put the mystery aside and face the more straightforward trial of getting through another day of school. At this point, the distraction of avoiding both Logan and the redheaded boy was better than waiting for the next memory.

Of course, since I wanted distractions, I went through the whole day without seeing either boy. Not a single person talked to me either, and hardly anyone even stared anymore. The next day—more of the same. It was starting to seem like I would've been better off staying in Annaliese's bedroom, staring at the walls and sucking on breath strips, when Gwen grabbed hold of my arm. She dragged me into an empty classroom and shut the door behind us.

As she flicked the light on, I saw it wasn't a classroom at all, but instead a room not much bigger than a closet with a piano shoved into a corner.

"Please sit," Gwen said, gesturing to the piano bench.

I was supposed to be in class. I sat.

"What is this?" I waved my hand, indicating the room.

Gwen looked around too, as if surprised to find herself there. "It's a practice room. For band, or chorus, or, I don't know, musicky people. Who cares. The real question is, Why are we here? And the answer is: I owe you an apology. A big one. I was talking to my . . . well, a friend that I met while you were—"

Flustered, Gwen stopped. She quickly regrouped. "You know what, it doesn't matter who I was talking to. What matters is she made me realize that it wasn't fair to be mad at you, because you are not Annaliese."

My heart and stomach clenched together. Fearful. Hopeful. I'd been found out. Finally.

But then Gwen kept talking. "I mean, you are Annaliese but not the same Annaliese. I can't be mad at you for something you don't even remember. That's nuts. And if you hadn't been taken away and lost your memory, I think we would've worked things out eventually. I mean, I want to believe we would've. I have to believe it, so I can be friends with you—the new Annaliese."

"What if I'm not the new Annaliese? What if I'm not Annaliese at all?"

It wasn't what I'd meant to say. But once it was out, I didn't want to take it back.

"What do you mean?" Gwen asked, looking confused but also intrigued. She perched on the bench beside me and took my hand.

That was all the invitation I needed. Don't blurt it out, I thought. And then I did exactly that. I told her everything. Everything I knew. Everything I suspected. The words tumbled from my mouth, pushing and shoving at one another, eager to get into the open.

Except once they were out, they were less substantial. Less believable.

Everything I knew was actually nothing. It was all suspicion. Somewhere along the line, as I'd turned my half-formed theories over and over in my mind, they had gathered weight. Enough weight for them to—without my ever noticing—slip over the line from good guess to hard fact.

I knew the redheaded boy from another time, from before. And I thought he was someone else. Had been someone else. Like me.

I had been many girls. I stole their bodies somehow. Maybe with a weird ritual that involved making them cut out my heart. Then I was them. Or controlling them. A puppet master of sorts, except I was inside the puppet. And there were no strings.

And Logan. Some sort of lust spell had been cast on him. To make him fall for Annaliese.

Then there were the Spanish witches on the beach, taking care of me.

And the witches' brother. Some guy everyone called the Physician. Somehow he was behind all this, making things happen.

It sounded absurd. Or worse, crazy.

And the thing that it was all built upon, that had made it oh-so-easy for me to believe it, was my feeling that I was NOT Annaliese. My feeling that I was a girl named Anna.

I stopped talking midsentence. Feeling foolish.

Gwen was surprisingly silent. For several long moments she gazed at me with an expression of polite interest. I recognized this from my short stay in the hospital as a classic shrink look. By the time she was ready to speak, I had a good idea of what she would say.

And I was right.

I only half listened as she spoke of the intense emotional trauma of my abduction and whatever had happened during the time I was missing. Perhaps my mind had created those other personalities as a way of coping. My current feeling of no longer being Annaliese was completely understandable as well. After such an ordeal, it was totally normal to feel divorced from the person I had been before. Honestly, I would make a fascinating case study, and in a few years when Gwen was doing her thesis, if I felt up to it, if I would consider putting some of this on paper for her, that would be really great. No need to make any promises now, of course, just something to think about.

By that point I couldn't even look at her. I was embarrassed, yes. But that didn't explain the tears pressing against the backs of my eyes. Or the disappointment crushing my chest.

Gwen kept talking, offering to recommend someone to help me work through this. I let my fingers run along the piano keys in front of me, and then without even thinking about it, I began playing. The music flowed effortlessly from my fingertips, while every other part of me wrestled with the question of whether Gwen was right.

It would be a relief to simply be crazy. Or traumatized, as Gwen would have it.

"Annaliese!" Gwen's hand covered mine, bringing the music to a crashing halt.

I stopped. I was being rude. After all, Gwen had listened and she was trying to help.

I turned toward her, preparing to apologize, when I saw her face. Gone was the look of complacent concern, and in its place . . . what I had expected to see from the beginning.

Horror.

"Annaliese," she said once more, the name trembling from her lips. "You don't play piano."

"I . . . oh," I answered, looking down at my hands still poised over the keys, ready to begin playing once more.

The color washed away, making the whole world the same black-and-white as the piano keys, and then the memory carried me away.

THE INSTRUMENT

My fingers—once Evie's fingers—stumble across the keys, clumsy and uncertain.

Her first piano teacher always said Evie had a love/hate relationship with this instrument. She told her to find another that she felt less ambivalent about.

But the teacher—her mother—didn't really mean it.

Evie's mother played piano. Her grandmother too. It is more than tradition. It is destiny. Evie will play piano as well.

And love it . . . even if she also sometimes hates it.

Except these stupid hands can no longer play, and her daughter is no longer here, not truly.

The instrument didn't seem so important when I first chose Evie. Now, though, it is the key to making everything finally fall apart.

I lift my stupid hands and confess. "I don't know how to play."

Evie's mother slams the lid down—I barely jerk my fingers away in time. "Then you will learn again. Because no matter what tricks you try, Evangeline, you are my daughter and you will play piano."

What if I am not your daughter? The question goes unasked. As always. It is the one thing I can never bring myself to say.

But I wonder. Are teenage daughters that interchangeable, or simply so foreign that one can easily be swapped out for another?

It is another question I avoid.

SUSPECT

Gwen's white face was pressed close to mine and her hands grabbed hold of my shoulders. "Annaliese, what did you just see? Do you remember something from your kidnapping? Did the person force you to learn piano?"

I blinked at her, confused by our different versions of the

truth. Then I took out my breath strips and placed one on my tongue before answering. "I—"

Gwen cut me off before I could get any further. Probably for the best—I had no idea what to say.

"Now, go slowly, Annaliese. Absorb every detail you can remember; even the smallest thing might lead us to the person who did this horrible thing to you."

I almost laughed at that. Did Gwen truly believe someone had taken me away to torture me with enforced piano lessons? If only that was the nightmare I had to live with. A smirk escaped me, and Gwen leaped on it.

"Annaliese, you're not protecting this person, are you? I mean, you've heard of Stockholm syndrome, right? Feeling a kind of bond with your kidnapper is nothing to be ashamed of, or to hide, or—"

I cut Gwen off. "I don't know what happened to me. Really." I opened my eyes wide, trying to look like someone innocent, sincere, and honest. "If I remembered being taken, or the person involved, I would tell someone."

I stood. "If I miss class completely, Mr. Booker might send a note to the principal, and he and my mom are real chummy lately, sooo . . ."

"But Annaliese," Gwen gasped, looking more certain than ever that I was hiding something. Ironic, given that she was the one person whom I had told everything.

And that, I now saw, was why I had chosen her. I'd known she wouldn't believe me, but I had needed to say it all out loud. "Thanks for listening," I said, pulling the door open. "You're a good friend."

This last bit quieted Gwen. Giving her a final wave, I quickly took off down the hall.

TOTALLY HOPELESS

Annaliese —

Yesterday at the pool was amazing. Or mucho bueno, as Mr. Fields would say.

I need to see you again. Not just see. I need to do much more than see you. Please say you want to do more than just see me too.

Same time, same place today?

Logan

Gwen hunted me down at lunch, and I spent the entire time convincing her not to tell her mom, my mom, or her rabbi about our earlier discussion. I argued about my right to privacy, patient/doctor confidentiality, and how it would freak everyone out for nothing. But the one thing that finally swayed her was a simple declaration.

"If you tell anyone, I will never trust you again."

Gwen looked for a moment like she would cry, and then very softly promised that she would keep my secrets—at least until I was ready to share them.

I could see her remembering the fight she'd had with Annaliese, and I wanted to say something comforting, but the bell rang, and once again it was for the best because I hadn't been able to think of a single thing.

Coming out of the lunchroom, we almost collided with Logan. This was the first day I'd gone through without the protection of his hoodie. I could see him noting its absence.

"I waited for you," he said, completely ignoring Gwen. "I have something that I thought you'd like."

"Oh, I'm—" My apology never came, as Gwen linked arms with me.

"C'mon, Annaliese, we'll be late for class."

She dragged me away, all the while glaring at Logan as if he were responsible for all the evils in the world, including forcing piano lessons on the unwilling. Even after we turned down several hallways, she held on to me.

"What a doofus," she said at last, and instead of defending Logan, I giggled. Looking like I had given her an unexpected present, Gwen giggled back at me.

For a moment, life was so simple. And sweet. To be seventeen and walking the crowded halls of a high school, clutching your best friend's arm while you giggled over stupid boys.

Sometimes it was just so fucking wonderful to be alive.

Then from behind me I heard someone muffle a cough. I glanced over my shoulder, and there was Logan. He'd been following us the whole time, and the look on his face . . . My cheeks flamed and I ducked my head, unable to meet his eyes.

Then I was Anna again. A girl in borrowed skin that hurt like hell.

Gwen had noticed Logan too, and she whirled to face him. "Can't you take a hint and leave her alone already?"

I tried to tug Gwen back toward me and away from Logan. Away from this whole scene. Gwen shook me off, and when I caught sight of the look on her face I could see the hard and angry words bubbling up inside her. I knew then that she wasn't going to stop until she told Logan exactly what she thought of him. And those words would cut him to ribbons.

"Gwen," I said, trying to stall her.

She didn't even hear me, because Logan spoke at the same moment. His voice was low and ragged where mine had been high and squeaky. Even though he stood a foot taller than Gwen, with his shoulders sagging and his chin against his chest, he had to almost look up at her beneath hooded eyelids.

"No, I can't," he said. "I can't leave her alone. I left her alone once. It was the wrong thing to do and I won't do it again."

Gwen blinked at him. Once. Twice. Uncertain.

Before she could regroup, I stepped forward, inserting myself between them. "I'm sorry about lunch," I said, going back to what he'd said outside the cafeteria, trying to pretend that this whole little confrontation had never happened. "I didn't know you were waiting. I have study hall right now, if you want to talk or something."

"No, no, it's okay." Logan shook his head, sending his shaggy hair flying. "I don't want you skipping for me."

I shrugged. "It's just study hall. Anyway, I'm tragedy girl. I can get away with pretty much anything right now." It was a joke. Logan winced. Clearly he was nowhere near the someday-we'll-all-laugh-about-this stage. I wasn't either, but I forced a smile anyway. "But if *you're* worried about cutting class . . ."

"Oh please," Gwen said, pushing her way back into the conversation. "He's a jock. That means he's practically required to cut." Gwen linked her arm with mine, marched us forward, and grabbed hold of Logan's bicep with her other hand. "And I can talk myself out of anything. So where are we going?"

Over Gwen's head, Logan's eyes met mine. He looked confused but no longer stricken. It was a good change. I shrugged and smiled encouragingly. After a long moment Logan smiled back.

"Outside," he said. "The storage shed by the bus lot."

The warning bell rang. We ignored it. Gwen dropped our arms so we weren't blocking our scurrying classmates actually trying to make it to class, but we still stayed in the same three-across formation with Gwen at the center.

Once outside, Logan took the lead. We wound through the parking lot until we reached the chain-link fence with the buses lined up in neat rows on the other side. A worn path in the grass led us to a gaping hole. We wriggled through one by one and made our way toward a long, squat building. The path looped past the tightly padlocked front doors and around to the back, where a smaller door that didn't quite seem to fit in its frame swung open easily beneath Logan's fingertips.

"Wait here a minute, okay?" Logan asked, and then he stepped into the dark interior and closed the door behind him.

We stood silently, stamping our feet and shivering against the breeze that came whipping around the shed. My previous sleep-impaired nights made my eyes ache, and I rubbed them with the backs of my fists. A small sigh escaped me.

"What's wrong?" Gwen immediately asked. "You're annoyed

that I'm here. That's it, isn't it? You wanted to be alone with him."

"Gwen, no. I'm glad you're here." Glancing toward the closed door, I lowered my voice. "I'm trying to be nice."

Gwen's head tilted to the side. She peered at me so intently it looked like she was working on her X-ray-vision skills. "You really don't like him anymore, do you?"

"I really don't."

"And it's not because you're secretly in love with your kidnapper?"

I grinned. "No, it's not. Although if I was secretly in love I'd probably say that anyway."

"You know what? I don't even care." Gwen smiled back. "I think I would rather you be in the grip of a terrible case of Stockholm syndrome than have a crush on Logan. It was awful. You were awful. Sorry, but you were. You dropped out of Advanced Placement Spanish so you could be in class with him. You switched to art from music 'cause he took art, but then you didn't even get into his same art class. You kept a tally every day of the number of times you passed him in the hallway. You didn't think I knew that one, but I did. And I kept thinking it would stop, you would get tired of stalking him, but you never did. And then I thought, please don't ever let him like her back. I know that sounds mean and selfish. I guess it was, because I thought if you were with him I would lose my friend. And not lose you like we wouldn't hang out anymore, but lose you like you would cease to exist. You would have become one of those girls who has no thoughts or opinions or ideas that didn't come directly from her boyfriend."

Ceased to exist. I almost choked. It was amazing how Gwen could trip right over the truth and not even notice it. Luckily, I didn't have to find a reply because the shed door opened and Logan stepped back outside. He had an old suit jacket on over his T-shirt and a bouquet of red carnations clutched in his fist. His face went a little red as he thrust the flowers toward me. Before I could reach out to take them, he jerked them away. Glancing toward Gwen, he looked like he had just remembered she was there. Quickly, he pulled the intertwined carnation stems apart into two bunches.

"Flowers," he said simply, this time holding one bouquet out to me and the other to Gwen. As if realizing his presentation was a little graceless, Logan cleared his throat and tried again. With a rough smile this time. "Beautiful flowers, for two beautiful ladies."

I expected a snort of disgust from Gwen, but instead her face turned pink and she murmured a quiet, "Thanks."

For an instant I had an idea of playing matchmaker between the two, but then Logan's gaze turned toward me and I knew it would never work. His dark eyes drank me up, like he'd been walking through a desert looking for water and I was a shining lake that might also be a mirage.

"I'm sorry about the other day, by the pool," he said softly. "I didn't want to make you feel . . ." Logan shook his head and started again. "I wanted to give you something. So I've been trying to think of something I could give you, trying to think of what you'd want. And I remembered Homecoming. You missed it. Every year. You told me. Freshman year you were too nervous to go. Sophomore year you had strep throat. And last year . . ."

Logan stopped, swallowed, glanced toward Gwen and then back to me.

"Last year you were excited to go. You'd bought a dress, and even though I was going with Kayla, I promised you a dance. It was stupid. I couldn't dance with you at Homecoming. Everybody would think it was a pity dance. But I couldn't tell you we wouldn't dance, 'cause I could see you were all excited about it. Really I kinda hoped you would forget I'd promised it or maybe get sick again or something—anything—that would get me out of that dance."

"Oh boy," Gwen murmured. "So that explains why you walked offstage when they were trying to crown you Homecoming king."

Logan's shoulders lifted in a half-shrug, half-sigh gesture. "Yeah, I guess." With another shrug/sigh, he focused on me once more. "So maybe this is lame, but I thought I could give you that Homecoming dance. I mean, if you still want it."

He was so sincere and there was something in his face that was almost little-boy sweet. Any other girl's heart would've been going pitter-patter, but mine only felt wrung out and small. Still, I offered my hand to Logan, accepting his offer for the girl who had once counted how many times she passed him in the hallway.

His hand swallowed mine, and then with a tug I was carried along into the storage shed. As soon as Gwen stepped in behind me, Logan reached back to close the door, sealing out the one wedge of sunlight and leaving us in darkness.

"Stay there," Logan said as he dropped my hand. I heard his footsteps moving through the darkness; just as my eyes had adjusted enough to let me pick up his outline a few feet away, the lights came on. Not the bright fluorescents I'd expected but white Christmas lights strung in a crisscross pattern, blinking and twinkling across a small cleared space at the center of the room. Long strips of green-and-white streamers twirled gently between the strands of light, creating an almost seaweed, under-the-sea effect. The towering boxes stacked to the ceiling everywhere else made it feel secret and hidden, like we'd stumbled into some alternate world where high school dances lived on in between prom and Homecoming and Christmas balls. Logan pressed Play on his iPod and the tinny sound of "Lady in Red" filled the room, completing the scene.

Gwen gave me a little push, and it was enough to send me stumbling forward into the seaweed streamers and into Logan's arms.

When he drew me in close, instead of pulling back I let my head rest against his chest so that the thump of his heart mixed with the song and little points of light pulsed against my closed eyelids. We didn't actually dance so much as sway in time, making the tiniest rotations through space.

As the song began to fade, I opened my eyes and blinked away the tears that filled them. I didn't want to explain them. I couldn't explain why this kind and thoughtful gesture had opened up a deep well of longing and sadness and despair that truly made me feel undersea.

The song ended, and I hesitated a moment before pulling away, trying to find the best way to tell Logan that this would be our last dance.

I still hadn't found it when Logan's arms gripped me a little tighter, and the whole world went sideways. A streamer tickled my forehead and Logan grinned at me dipped low in his arms.

"My mom taught me that," he said, slowly tilting me back up.

"Do it again," I said. Not because I enjoyed being swept off my feet, but because I could picture him with his mom, practicing that dip. And because he was so proud of his smooth move. But mostly because I could tell in the way he was smiling at me that there was nothing I could say to let him off the hook. I was the hook, and as long as I existed, he was hung.

The world spun once more, with Logan dipping me faster and lower this time. His jacket came flopping open at the end, and a bit of white paper drifted to the floor. Logan didn't even notice. Eyes closed and lips pursed, he was focused on obtaining something else. The paper was the perfect excuse to deny him. As I leaned sideways to snatch it up, Logan's kiss found my left ear. Startled, his eyes flew open and he straightened abruptly, pulling me with him.

Quickly, I held the small card I'd retrieved up between us.

"Some sort of praise Jesus reminder?" I asked, staring at the picture of a glowing guy in a robe. It was a lame joke that came out snarkier than I'd intended. I'd meant to lighten the mood and instead I'd deflated it.

"No, it's a prayer card." Logan grabbed it from my hand. "It was my gran's. It's a prayer she used to say hoping my dad would come back after he left."

"Oh." I felt even worse. "Did it work?"

Logan shook his head. "No. He walked out on us when I was three, and then when I was nine we found out he was dead. So by then it was pretty certain he wasn't coming back—ya know? Gran, though, she kept right on saying this prayer as if he were still alive." Logan held it out to me, and I took it once more, this time flipping it over to see the prayer on the backside.

"So why did she keep saying the prayer?"

Logan shrugged. "Well, it's Saint Jude and he's the saint of hopeless causes. Gran said that Dad was as hopeless as they came, and she thought Saint Jude would appreciate that fact. It would be a miracle, she said, but that was okay 'cause she believed in miracles and she was gonna keep on praying for him."

I held the card out, and Logan tucked it into the back pocket of his jeans. Our eyes met for a long moment. Too long. I could feel Logan gearing up to say something big.

"Annaliese," he said.

I cut him off. "We should go."

"Oh yeah, that's right." Logan cleared his throat, and then looked away from me. "You guys go. I'm gonna clean this up first."

"Okay." I nodded and took a step back, relieved it was going to be this easy to get away. Except, of course, it wasn't, because Gwen stood between me and the door, and she wasn't ready to leave yet. She had a follow-up question.

"Wait. That prayer card. Your gran gave it to you so you could continue to pray for your dad?"

I tugged at Gwen's shirt, annoyed that she always had to psychoanalyze. Or maybe I just knew what Logan would say, and I didn't want to hear it.

"Nah. Never cared about my dad enough to say any prayers for him."

"It was for Annaliese then," Gwen said, even though she didn't need to say it aloud at that point.

"Yeah," Logan quietly confirmed. "It's for Annaliese."

Not *was* for Annaliese. *Is.* Present tense. He was still praying. And things were more hopeless than ever.

DESPAIR

That feeling of despair stuck with me. It didn't help when, in the middle of my last class, the sun streaming through the window lit up a pretty blond girl sitting nearby and that terrible feeling of hunger came alive inside me once more. It was stronger than it had been the last time. More insistent. Like something was in me, demanding to be fed.

I stared down at my desk and didn't lift my eyes again until class was over. Even then I tried to avoid directly looking at anyone. I actually ran for the doors, and then through the parking lot until I was safe inside the mom's car.

"Let's go," I said, clicking the seat belt into place.

"Bad day?" Of course, she had to ask, but at least she put the car in reverse while doing so.

"I don't wanna talk about it. Please."

There was a long pause, and I could almost hear the mom internally debating whether to force me to talk about it for my own good, or to simply honor my wishes as she slowly backed out of the parking space. The latter must have won.

"Okay, then. Different topic of conversation. I've been meaning to discuss your birthday next week. . . ." The mom paused, switching gears from reverse to drive. "Obviously, we missed your seventeenth birthday, so your dad and I were thinking—"

I would never find out what they had been thinking because at that moment a blur on a bike came hurtling between the rows of cars straight at my door.

The mom braked. Hard.

The bike skidded sideways, as if purposely trying to throw its owner beneath the car's tires. As he fell, I saw a shock of red hair, and I knew. It was him. The redheaded boy. Somehow he had done this on purpose, and I wished with everything inside me that he would be crushed and die. It would be a slow painful death, I was certain, and this only made it better.

But—as Gwen would no doubt be quick to remind me—imagining something doesn't make it so. We didn't hit him.

The mom jumped from the car to fuss over him. I just sat there, coating my tongue in a thick layer of breath strips. A few people rushed over wanting to know what was happening, but they quickly drifted away when they realized there was nothing exciting to see. No hideous dents, broken bones, or blood. To their disappointment and my own, the only harm done was a few new scratches on the bike.

The mom helped him off the ground and then, to my horror, into the backseat.

Once he was in the car, I got out. Ostensibly, I was helping the mom fit the bike into the hatchback, and not avoiding breathing the same air as him.

Standing close to the mom, I could see that she was barely holding it together. A tremor ran through her whole body, while the skin on her face looked too tight, especially when she forced her mouth into a smile and announced, "All's well that ends well," over and over and over again. I felt bad then for wishing the redheaded boy dead. It wasn't fair of me. The mom didn't need blood on her hands just because I was already drowning in it.

"Do you two know each other?" the mom asked as she—more carefully then ever—steered the car toward the parking lot exit.

"I'm just a freshman," he demurred, easily avoiding the question.

I said nothing, refusing to take part in whatever game he was playing. Maybe the mom interpreted my silence as shock from the accident, because she took up my end of the conversation.

"Well, I don't see any reason why freshmen and juniors can't occasionally mix. So Annaliese, this is Eric, um . . ."

"Swanson," he helpfully supplied.

"Eric Swanson. And this is Annaliese."

"Oh, everyone knows Annaliese."

Despite looking for it, I couldn't detect any malice in his voice, but the very fact of this statement was enough to shake the mom. For a second I was afraid she might break down crying, and it made me feel oddly protective of her. I didn't want Eric to see her exposed like that. But the mom pulled it together.

"Oh, of course. That's, well, with everything, I guess everyone would . . ." She trailed off, and, unable to take it any longer, I stepped in.

"Are we dropping you off at home, Eric?"

"If you wouldn't mind," he said in a small voice, and then added with a little sigh, "My mom thought she might get out of work early today, so maybe someone will actually be there for once."

The mom gasped while I closed my eyes in defeat, instantly understanding how this would play out. There was nothing to be done but for him to come home with us, and his mother would pick him up after work.

And that's how twenty minutes later, I found myself seated at the kitchen table having an after-school snack of milk and cookies with Eric.

"These are good cookies," he mumbled around his fifth snickerdoodle. "But chocolate chip are my favorite."

"Oh mine too," the mom said. She had regained some color since returning home, and the shakes had tapered off so that there was only an occasional quiver. Still, she looked ready to collapse, and it seemed like she barely knew what she was saying. "But Annaliese can't have chocolate."

"Oh no." Eric practically oozed sympathy, but there was an edge to it. "Are you allergic?"

"I just don't like it."

"But it's so good. The way it coats your mouth and melts against your tongue. It's so yummy." His eyes were on me, watching as I had to swallow against the sickness rising in my throat.

Somehow he knew what chocolate did to me. Thrusting another couple of breath strips into my mouth, I hated him more than ever.

"May I use the bathroom, please?" The perfectly polite question was asked with a smirk, but the mom was beyond noticing and simply pointed him in the right direction.

As soon as he left the room, it felt easier to breathe. I couldn't stand being near him for another minute, and was about to tell the mom that I needed to go lie down, when she started to sway. Jumping up, I caught her right before she fell. As I shifted her onto the chair I had just vacated, her eyes fluttered open once more.

"Oh, dear. I think I'm a bit light-headed."

"You should lie down," I told her, giving away my own Get Out of Jail Free card.

"No, no, that poor boy," the mom protested, but I was already helping her up, and then into the family room toward her favorite sleeping sofa.

"Don't worry. I'll stay with him until his mom comes."

I expected more objections. The selfish part of me even hoped she would rally once more and insist on staying with Eric. Instead she collapsed onto the couch.

"Oh, thank you, sweetheart. I'm just so tired."

I covered her with a blanket and then, without planning it, pressed a kiss to her forehead. Tears came to the mom's eyes, and I found matching ones in mine as well.

"Go to sleep. It's okay."

Her eyes were already fluttering closed, but she managed to mumble, "I love you, Annaliese."

She was more asleep than awake; I didn't have to answer, but the truth came out anyway. "I love you too."

I turned away, trembling a bit myself, and saw Eric watching from where he lounged in the doorway. Lifting his hands, he made a show of giving me a round of silent applause. My whole body went hot. With fury. But also with shame. Maybe it was all just for show. I couldn't tell anymore.

I pushed past him, through the kitchen to the living room. Unlike the big fluffy couch and two recliners in the family room, the living room love seat and two upholstered chairs were hard and uncomfortable, which suited me fine right now. As I'd known he would, Eric followed me and sat down in the chair closest to my own.

I glared at him. He smiled back serenely.

"I hate you," I said, wanting a fight.

"You love me." A taunt. He was spoiling for a fight as well.

"I don't believe you. You're a disgusting, horrible person. Everything about you is revolting. Even if you weren't in that fat body, you'd be gross."

His rounded cheeks went red. "It's baby fat!"

It was a direct hit, if not exactly the one I'd meant to score. Still, I'd found his tender spot, and I dug deeper. "More like cookie fat. How many did you just have?"

A growling noise came from deep in his throat. "I wouldn't be in this body at all if it wasn't for you messing up the Annaliese exchange."

The Annaliese exchange. Like a parcel changing hands. I needed another breath strip. But that was my weakness, and I ignored it. I went after him again.

"Then you've been in that fat boy for almost a year. Enough time to lose some weight, I'd think. Ever hear of Slim-Fast?"

He surged to his feet, fists clenched, and I stood as well, ready to plant my knee in his crotch.

Except the doorbell rang, and we froze.

"Annaliese?" the mom's sleepy voice called out. "What was that?"

"It's okay," I yelled back. "Eric's mom is here, I think."

The doorbell rang again. Apparently, Eric's mother was the impatient type.

"Get out." I pointed in the direction of the front door.

But Eric wasn't quite finished with me. "In less than a week you move on, and I'll be right behind you. This will all be dust." He swept his hand out, taking in the whole room. "Or it might as well be, 'cause you'll never see it through those eyes again. This will all be over, and you and me—*we*"—I could see him savoring that word, rolling it around in his mouth like a fine wine—"we will be brand-new and together again."

"I'm not going anywhere," I said, but the words sounded uncertain even to my own ears. What had the mom said about my eighteenth birthday next week? It had seemed inconsequential in the moment. A year older—no big deal. But if everything I'd been remembering was true, then I would never be a year older, and a birthday was more than a big deal—it was the Ides of March.

"No? And what about the hunger? That need to sink your teeth into someone's skin? I'm gonna let you in on a little secret. That's the tip of the iceberg. It gets worse. Let it go too long, and you'll be so hungry you could tear your own mother's face off."

I said nothing. I didn't have to. My shudder gave me away. And he knew it.

"Why are you doing this?"

He pointed at himself. "I'm not doing anything. The Physician's the one handing out the little notes with our new names on them. He's calling all the shots, giving us our marching orders. Always has. Me? I just like playing the game."

"You keep talking about this Physician. Who the hell is the Phys— he?" I couldn't say the name twice. There was too much power in it. It made my tongue tingle.

"He scares you, doesn't he?" Eric laughed. "He should. I've only seen him twice. Once when I first started this whole thing, and the second time when I asked him to let you join me. He never looks the same, but he lets you know it's him."

"And what about his sisters, the *brujas*? How do they fit in?"

Eric's eyes narrowed. "What the hell are *brujas*? I don't know what's going on in that cracked skull of yours, but the Physician doesn't have any sisters. Don't you get it? He's not a normal person. He's a god. Or the devil. Or maybe both. All I can say for certain is he knows everything. He can make things happen. And he owns us."

He took a step toward me. "Owns us body and soul. So if he tells you to go—you'll do it. You don't have a choice."

Eric grinned as he walked away, victorious. But it wasn't enough for him; he couldn't resist stopping for one final dig.

"Soon," he said. I heard his footsteps on the tile of the front hallway and then the sound of the front door yawning open.

"Eric, are you okay?" It was Eric's mom. She sounded frightened—not for him, but of him.

I went still, listening hard.

"I'm fine. Don't touch me! I told you what would happen if you touched me again!"

"I'm sorry. You said you'd been hurt, and—"

The door shut, cutting off their conversation. I was grateful for it. I'd heard enough. I didn't want to think about who the previous Eric had been. About what else had been lost.

Even worse, I could not—would not—let myself contemplate how much more there was to lose. The more I understood, the less I wanted to know. But that was a luxury I couldn't afford. There was a deadline, and I needed to keep working at putting the pieces together.

A week, he'd said. No, less than a week. The clock was already ticking.

BLOODY

CAN'T SLEEP

*Can't sleep
my mind is a muddle
full of dreams better left
undreamed.
So I sit at the window
staring out at the nothingness
of a sleepy suburban street.*

*The clock ticks.
It's so much past midnight
and I should get back to bed.
Instead I turn to the sky
and the single star somehow
shining through the gloom
just waiting to be wished upon.*

*No cars rushing by
no other windows bright with light.
I may be the only person to see that star
and make my wish only to*

watch it
fade.
Sucked into the cloud's shadow.
Winking away—a burnt-out bulb.

Perhaps the star was never there.
I only saw it for a second.
I want to yell out into
the cold and silent night,
"Hello out there,
did anyone else
see that star disappear?"

—ARG

The mom slept right through dinner, so the dad and I ended up ordering pizza and wings. He tried to pretend it was fun, the two of us having a pizza party. He even put his laptop at the center of the table and we watched what the dad called the greatest movie about golf ever created: *Caddyshack*.

"It's so funny," the dad insisted several times during our viewing, but I never actually heard any laughter come from him. I did, however, catch him glancing more than once toward where the mom slept.

She was still out when the movie ended.

"Looks like she's gonna sleep through the night," the dad said.

"She looked really tired. I guess she needs the rest." It was the same thing I'd been saying all night, but the dad once again nodded as if I'd imparted some bit of sage wisdom.

"True, very true. Well, then, should we pop in *Caddyshack II*? It's not as good as the first one, but not many things are. Hey, we could watch *Tin Cup* instead. That's another great golf movie."

Even an idiot could see the dad's heart wasn't in it. He wanted to be at the mom's side, making sure she was okay. I wanted him there too.

Unlike the mom, the dad wasn't a worrier. But he was worried now, which meant that whatever sickness or disease the mom had was serious. Equally clear was their commitment to keeping me in the dark.

I decided to let the dad off the hook. "Actually, I'm pretty tired. I think I'll just go to bed."

I thought he'd jump at the chance to get rid of me and rush to the mom's side. Also, I hadn't forgotten what I'd overheard in that motel room during our road trip home. Despite our few heart-to-heart moments, it still felt like the dad wasn't completely convinced that I was his daughter. And even if his doubting instincts were right on, I couldn't help but be a little hurt by them. He surprised me though.

"Oh, c'mon. It's not even nine o'clock. You don't expect me to believe you're already tired."

Actually, every last nerve ending in my body buzzed with leftover adrenaline from my earlier confrontation with Eric. Caught, I shrugged.

"It was the golf movies, right?" the dad asked with a teasing smile. "You hated the game. Couldn't even stand mini golf. But I thought maybe I'd been given a second chance to make a believer out of you."

Stupidly, I stared at him, feeling like he'd tipped me upside down, and all my misconceptions had come tumbling out. Had the dad just said that my being different from Annaliese could actually be a good thing?

"A second chance?" I asked, wanting to hear it again.

But the dad misunderstood. He took it as a criticism. "Not

as if you weren't perfect before, or that I wanted to change you. No, it was more me with you that could've been better." The dad reached forward to fiddle with the laptop, popping the DVD out, rubbing at a nonexistent smudge on the screen. "Don't get the wrong idea. That wasn't your fault either. It was mine. When you were a little girl, we were buddies. We'd watch *Caddyshack* together with you tucked into my side. Every time I laughed at something, you would look at me, and then you would laugh in the exact same way. I don't know when it changed. You became a teenager, and you groaned at my jokes, and rolled your eyes when I suggested watching a movie together. Not always, but enough times that I stopped."

The dad finally looked back up at me. He grinned sheepishly. "Couldn't take the rejection, I guess. But now I'm insisting. We're watching a movie together. You and me, kid."

We ended up watching *Caddyshack II*. I don't know why the dad had said it wasn't good. I thought it was pretty great.

HEADLINE

I climbed into bed, my mouth still burning from the dad's hot-sauce-enhanced microwave popcorn. Rolling over, I looked up at the smiling stars and grinned back at them.

Something crinkled beneath my head. I reached under my

pillow, and pulled out a yellowed piece of newspaper. *Indianapolis Star* said the big letters at the top. And below that, the all-too-familiar headline.

FOUL PLAY NOW SUSPECTED IN CASE OF TWO MISSING GIRLS

The oasis of comfort I'd found with the dad crumbled. An illusion. So much less substantial than the truth in my hand.

There was my name in print. Anna Martin. And my picture too. This smiling Anna was me. The real me, original recipe. I was almost certain. But her face was only familiar from the dream.

Tears filled my eyes, blurring the picture. I thrust the paper away, not wanting to get it wet, but then pulled it back, needing to see one more thing.

Friday, January 14, 1973

1973. I'd been forever young since 1973.

On the razor there had been seven names in addition to Anna, but if I was never older than seventeen, that meant becoming a new girl almost every year. The seven names on that razor had seemed like so many, but if my suspicions were correct, that was only a small portion of the hearts that blade had met.

In 1973 I'd been a sixteen-year-old girl named Anna who had disappeared. Now I was a seventeen-year-old girl named Annaliese who had disappeared and then miraculously reappeared. Perhaps only to disappear once more.

Automatically, I reached for my breath strips, but before I could pull one out, I threw the package across the room.

No more covering up the terrible taste. I couldn't hide from the blood any longer. But before I could face the truth, I had to find it. The room began to fade before me, and this time I didn't flinch.

TOGETHER

I make two long slices through my skin. One for each arm. Starting at the edge of my elbow and tearing straight through the soft flesh until I reach the edge of my palm.

The razor falls into the dirt at my feet. My hands hang limp at my sides, and blood streams from my fingers, a slow drip that will quickly turn into a steady red waterfall.

Annaliese stares in horror. Her mouth moves, but no sound comes out.

"Yes, I will pay" are the last words Annaliese will ever say.

"Now, pick up the razor, and cut out my heart," I tell her. And because she took someone else's free will, Annaliese has no choice. She does exactly as I ask.

The first bite she tries to chew. They all try to chew. Her jaw works, making little headway on the tough tissue. Then with a grimace and a gulp, she swallows. Bringing the heart to her mouth once more, she sinks her teeth in.

This time they are my teeth too. And together we gag on the blood. Together we lock our jaw, swallow, and bite again.

Now I can feel the heart still warm in her hand. And through Annaliese's eyes, I watch Jaclyn—the girl I had been—stagger forward. I catch her in Annaliese's arms, carefully cradling the heart in a loose fist behind her back. New me holds old me in a macabre embrace, sealed with blood. And tears. A good-bye of sorts.

With the next bite, Jaclyn will begin her disintegration, until by the last bite there will only be a razor on the ground to mark where she'd stood.

The next bite doesn't happen.

Something sharp and silver shiny comes flashing out of the woods, a madwoman behind it. She chants a single word. A curse. No, an accusation.

"Sodomite!"

Amazing the things you can hear in that one word. Hate. Fear. Anger. And love.

This last is for her daughter. For Jaclyn. Too late though. Jaclyn's heart has already been cut from her chest.

"Sorry." I try to say the word, but it is too early. I can't control Annaliese's vocals yet.

The pickax in the hand of the woman I'd spent a year calling mother drives straight into my skull. Blood floods my eyes, and

I wipe it away only to dodge the slicing silver coming at me once more.

Oh God, oh no, oh help, please, please, please . . .

The words run in my head, on a loop. But they aren't mine. I gave up on God years ago. This is Annaliese, still stubbornly clinging to her body, and her life.

I have already decided it is over.

Finally.

Let the executioner swing. I am ready for the end.

But Annaliese is not.

The scream that has been bottled inside her comes roaring from our lips—the high-pitched whistle of a teapot boiling.

It shouldn't be happening. Annaliese's will should be suspended—just long enough for me to replace it with my own. But instead, what should have been a killing blow—the sharp metal tip of a pickax piercing her gray matter—has somehow set her free once more.

And we are running. Wiping more blood away, attempting to catch the light bobbing in the distance. The trees grab at us, trying to pull us back, trip our feet, and then they fall behind.

We are in the light. We slow, stumble. Lights and eyes everywhere. Staring.

Help. Annaliese tries to form the words. Can't get them past the scream that won't stop. A monster we created, now stronger than both of us.

We take another step forward. Hoping. Wailing. Waiting to be saved.

Please.

Everything goes dark. At the same instant, one finger presses against our windpipe. Cutting off our scream, our air, but not our life.

Before the darkness extinguishes our thoughts as well, I find one last prayer inside myself. I pray that it isn't him. *Please, anyone but him.* Please don't let the Physician drag me forward into another stolen life. Please let this be the end.

EMERGENCY

After that last memory, sleep eluded me. I drifted off eventually, but it was a restless and haunted slumber. When the dad shook me awake, I was relieved.

"Is it time for school?" I rasped, peeling my eyes open.

"No, no," the dad said. "It's still night. You can go back to sleep, but I wanted you to know—" He stopped, and I could actually see him trying to pull it together. That wasn't like the dad.

I sat up, worried now. "What's wrong?"

"Nothing is wrong," he answered automatically, but then, shaking his head, quickly backtracked. "Nothing that can't be fixed. That's why I woke you, to let you know your mother is sick and I'm taking her to the hospital. You'll be okay here, won't you?"

I ignored the question. "Sick?"

"No. I mean, yes. It's not . . ." He shook his head again. Harder this time. Sounding just as tense but less scattered, the dad tried again. "It's nothing life threatening, but she needs to get to the hospital."

"Oh, okay," I said, uncertain. I didn't understand how it could be that serious, but not life threatening. I wasn't going to argue, though. "I'll be all right."

"You're sure?" the dad asked, but he was already standing.

I nodded, not trusting my voice as tears suddenly pressed against the backs of my eyes. I didn't want to be here alone. Not at night. Not with the memories coming hard and fast, and my dreams consisting of nothing but nightmares. I liked knowing the mom was close, ready to rush in and stroke my hair and tell me everything would be okay.

"All right then." The dad stood silhouetted in the doorway. "I'll make sure all the doors are locked. Just stay inside. We'll be back soon."

I jerked my head up and down, but the dad's footsteps were already on the stairs. I could hear his voice, but not the exact words. I didn't need to. He was assuring the mom I was okay, that I would continue to be okay, and that they needed to take care of her so she could take care of me.

Maybe the mom could only nod in response too, because I couldn't catch any sound from her. Then the garage door opened, ejected the car out onto the street, and closed again.

They were gone.

I hugged my knees to my chest, staring into the darkness. The smart thing—the brave thing—was to go back to sleep and hopefully dream once again. Or I could pull out the newspaper clipping and see if the past came to swallow me up and spit me out, the way it had so many other times. The more pieces I remembered and put together, the better I could understand what was going to happen next week on Annaliese's birthday. And if there was any way to stop it.

I promised myself I would do one of those things. In a few more minutes. As soon as I calmed down a bit.

Calm never quite came. Sitting up in bed, I dozed a few times, but as soon as my chin touched down on my chest, I'd snap awake once more. The red numbers on my alarm clock seemed frozen in place, until all at once they would jerk forward fifteen or thirty minutes in time. In this halting way the night crept on, until a little after three a.m. when I finally heard a car on the road. Like a child, I ran to my window and peered around the edge of the blinds, hoping to see the mom and dad returning.

The car slid past the house, and I watched the taillights

disappear into the night. I scanned the dark street, looking for a light somewhere, and as if in answer, the light over Dex's garage door flickered on. Pressing my nose against the glass, I waited for something else to happen, hoping the light wasn't just a motion-activated one triggered by a skulking cat. Again, my wish was granted. The garage door slid upward, and a moment later a small car came inching out.

Without even thinking about it, I ran. Down the stairs, out the front door, and then across the lawn and into the street. The cold stung my bare feet and the wind whipped through my thin pajamas, but I didn't care as I flung myself across the hood of Dex's car.

The car jerked to a stop. I looked up to meet Dex's astonished gaze. It occurred to me that I might look a little insane. Or maybe he was remembering how the last time we'd been together we had kissed. Hoping it was the latter, I waggled my fingers at him and then mouthed the word *hi*.

Dex's eyes widened a fraction, and I thought he might finally tell me that I had gone too far, but then a huge grin spread across his face and he laughed. A second later his window came down and he leaned out. "I don't know whether to make a very bad hood-ornament joke or ask what the hell you're doing."

"Maybe you could just ask if I need a ride?"

The grin faded. "Anna, you don't know where I'm going. And if you did, you wouldn't want to come along. Trust me."

"But I do want to come. Please, Dex. The mom . . . My parents are gone. At the hospital. I don't know when they'll be back and I don't want to be alone anymore. Please, I'll stay in the car. It's not like I'm dressed for it anyway." I offered my bare foot as evidence.

He cursed softly and then was out of the car, lifting me off the ground, into his arms.

"Dex," I said, thinking he was going to carry me back into the house. But before I could add another *please*, he was opening the passenger-side door and sliding me in. He shrugged out of the long black trench coat that had been wrapped around his thin frame and laid it over my shoulders, tucking it around my sides before pulling the seat belt across me.

"Thank you," I whispered a moment later as Dex clicked his own seat belt into place.

He shook his head. "Let's save the thank-yous for now. You might—" Another shake. This one harder.

Instead of finishing his sentence, he put the car into drive and we began to move up the long, quiet street. Beneath us the muffler wheezed and rattled, mostly drowning out the talk radio station's quiet conversation. The car had clearly seen better days, but with the heat pumping warm and steady at my feet and the steering wheel moving smoothly beneath Dex's hands, I didn't mind in the least.

I stared straight ahead, watching the headlights slice through the darkness. We bounced along narrow back roads, nearly deserted except for the sporadic car that sped past us with its high beams blazing and blinding. I began to think that Dex had no destination at all. That he was driving in an attempt to chase away the long, lonely hours of the night. Maybe this was part of the secrets he had hinted at the other day. But even as this crossed my mind, Dex had started to pull onto the shoulder of the road, easing us to a stop.

He took a deep breath before letting his hands fall from the steering wheel and into his lap. "We're almost there. But first, I feel like I should tell you something about why we're out here in the middle of the night. So the question is: How much do you want to know?"

Nothing. Everything. Those were the two responses that first came to mind. Each of them equally selfish in their different ways. Instead, I decided to answer the way that I thought Dex would if I asked him the same question.

"As much as you want to tell me."

"Okay then." Dex nodded and smiled, and I knew I'd said the right thing. Reaching into the backseat, he grabbed hold of a flashlight and handed it to me. "Then the first thing you need to know is that country roads are the darkest places on the planet."

"The darkest? Really? Darker than the middle of a forest or an underground cave?"

"Well, no. But notice I didn't say '*literally* the darkest place on the planet.' The use of *literally* would have made hyperbole verboten."

"Verboten?" I clicked on the flashlight so Dex could see my raised right eyebrow. It was a neat trick I'd recently discovered while brushing my teeth.

Dex raised his own right eyebrow back at me. "It's a German word. Means 'forbidden.' Most good things are."

"German or forbidden? No, wait." I shook my head. "Don't tell me. Let's preserve the mystery."

Dex nodded. "Agreed. Although, if you ever saw how much bratwurst I can pack away, that case would be quickly solved. But let's move away from these sidetracks and back onto dark country roads."

"Aye-aye, Captain." I saluted with the flashlight, knowing I was being silly and not caring. I was also smiling too big, laughing too loud, and finding excuses every two seconds to let my hand brush against his leg, his hand, his arm. I felt punch-drunk from a combination of sleep deprivation and the tingly memory of the last time I'd seen Dex.

As if reading my mind, Dex leaned in and kissed me. The flashlight fell from my hands, but before I could kiss him back, he was already pulling away.

"Sorry, we shouldn't. Not here." Dex mumbled the words, avoiding my eyes as he reached down to pick up the flashlight. He pressed it back into my hands, gently. "You're gonna want to keep this handy. We're looking for a rusty old mailbox, but then again, most of the mailboxes out here are old and rusty. The one we want, though, has a few other unique characteristics. The door on it doesn't close all the way, and it sits on a squared-off piece of wood. 1306. That's the number on the side of the box. Black numbers printed on white stickers. And there's a drawing of a shark trying to eat the numbers. Or maybe bite them. Or kiss them. It's not a very good drawing." There was a flash of a smile, but then Dex was back in serious mission mode. "I need you to shine the flashlight out as we drive by and let me know when you see it. I think it's the fifth or sixth one coming up, but I can never remember which one exactly . . . thus the flashlight. Once we find it, I'm gonna leave a letter in that mailbox, and . . ." Dex shrugged. "That's it really."

Gripping the flashlight with two hands, I flicked it on and then pointed the beam out my window. "Let's do it."

Dex stared at me for a minute and I thought he was going to say something else, but he put his hands on the steering wheel and we were on the road once more. The mailboxes hung near the edge of the road, beside driveways that disappeared into a tangled wall of trees. Supposedly there were houses on the other ends of those driveways, but most of them were set so far back you couldn't see any hint of them from the street.

My flashlight illuminated three different mailboxes before I found the right one. I saw the numbers first, their white backing almost making them glow. Triangle-shaped teeth slashed through the white edges, and from those teeth grew the gigantic shark that seemed to be attempting to swallow the mailbox whole.

It was exactly as Dex had described. Except for one thing. The sense of menace. How a dilapidated mailbox covered in graffiti could convey that sense, I couldn't say. But I felt it. I could almost smell it too, seeping into the car, the sickly sweet smell of decay.

"Dex," I whispered. "This is it."

The car jerked to a stop, and Dex leaned in to see the mailbox too. "Yeah," he answered, also whispering. "That's it."

I held out my hand, wanting to get this over with and leave as quickly as possible. "Give me the letter. I can reach out and pop it in."

Dex shook his head. "Thanks, but it's kinda one of those things I need to do myself." He pressed against me and I thought he wanted to check once more that it was the right place, but this time his lips brushed my cheek. "I'm glad you're here."

"I'm glad I'm here too." And I was. Although I would be even happier when it was time to leave this place. I could almost feel that mailbox throbbing at my back. I grabbed Dex's hand and gave it a tight squeeze, feeling oddly worried for him. "Good luck."

I watched anxiously as he crossed in front of the car, cutting through the headlight beams. Then he was beside my door, between the mailbox and me. I saw the letter, bright white in his hand as he lifted it, and then it was flying into the air, detached from Dex, whose body slammed into my door. Once. Twice. The third time Dex crumpled, and that's when I saw the man.

He stood over Dex, his face hard and twisted, and oddly gleeful as well, while his fists slammed into Dex's stomach again and again and again. Finally, he let Dex fall at his feet. With a grin, he kicked him. I tried to scream, but all that came out was a tiny squeak of despair. The man grabbed the back of Dex's shirt and hauled him up, only to fling him against the hood of the car. Dex's eyes, wide and scared, stared at me through the windshield; then the man grabbed him again, flipping him up and over. Full of menace, he glared at Dex. Then, with slow deliberation, he reached down to wrap his hands around Dex's throat.

"I got you, you little shit. Leaving me these letters. Trying to scare me. Weren't ya? Well, who's scared now? Who's scared now?"

My vocal cords finally functioned again. "Dex!" The word came tearing out of me. At the same time I lunged across the front seat. Dex's coat tangled around my legs and I kicked it away while I punched the horn wildly. It was enough to startle the man. Enough for him to loosen his grip on Dex and let him take a choking breath. It was also enough to turn his attention to me.

Our eyes met. His were dark and oily. I pressed the horn again, a long, low bleat of distress. Those horrible eyes narrowed. Releasing Dex, he turned, reaching for the passenger door. His hand reaching in through the open window. I stomped on the gas. The engine roared, but we didn't move. Fingers brushed my shoulder as I jerked the car into drive, and then we shot forward. Maybe my false start had given Dex some warning of what I was going to do, because he managed to hold on as we went careening down the dark road.

I kept going long enough to make sure the horrible man was far behind us. Finally pulling the car to the side of the road, I flung the door open and ran to Dex.

"Anna," he said. He slid from the hood and onto the ground in front of my feet. "I'm sorry."

"No time," I said shortly. Grabbing hold of him, I half carried, half dragged him to the passenger side of the car and dropped him in. His legs still hung out, and I quickly folded them in before slamming the door shut. Then I was back in the car and we were flying down the road once more. I drove too fast, still feeling like we were being chased. I didn't ease up on the gas until we reached a small town. Old-fashioned streetlights lined the road on both sides and chased the deep, inky darkness away.

Taking my first full breath since the man had appeared, I slowed the car and pulled into an empty parking lot behind a bank. We sat there for a while, both of us struggling to breathe as if that man's hands had been around both of our throats.

Finally, I turned to Dex. He looked horrible. Shrunken and broken.

"Dex." I reached toward him but didn't actually touch him, not wanting to hurt him further. "Are you okay? Do you need a doctor? Or the hospital? Or—"

"No," Dex answered quickly, his voice raspy. "I'm hurting right now, but it's nothing a little ibuprofen won't cure."

"Okay," I said, and then, even though I'd told him that he only had to share what he wanted to, I couldn't help asking, "Who was that man?"

He coughed and then looked up at me. "Kenneth Ray Jr. That's his name, I think. It's what I found on my internet searches. The real question, though, is: What is he?"

"Okay, what is he?"

"He's a monster. He . . ." Dex turned to me, and his eyes glimmered with unshed tears. "You might not believe me. I don't have any proof, but I know because . . . because sometimes I just know things. He takes kids. Little girls. I don't know how many. There's one he wants to take but hasn't yet, and I thought if he was scared, if he thought someone was watching him, then maybe he'd leave her alone. I wanted to save her. Be some kind of hero. Save her from—"

I threw my arms around Dex, cutting him off. Not wanting

to hear any more. A monster who took girls. It sounded horrible. And all too familiar.

Dex hugged me back and I shuddered, scared that Dex might somehow know things about me too.

"You okay?" He didn't whisper, but merely breathed the words softly against my skin.

I wanted to tell him no. I wanted him to see that I needed saving too. That I wanted him to be some kind of hero for me. I kissed him instead. It was meant to be soft and tender. Comforting. But Dex's lips parted beneath mine, pulling me in deeper. It wasn't comfort he wanted. Dex was drowning. But I wasn't his lifesaver. And he knew it. I was someone to sink with.

I went willingly.

When it was over, his lips pressed against my forehead, so that I felt his next words before he said them.

"I'm a fuck-up."

I jerked away. Wanting to see his eyes. And wanting him to see my own, and the truth in them. "No."

Dex's hands fluttered up toward me. His fingertips swept across my forehead, tracing my eyebrows, and then trailed downward, until his palms gently cupped my jaw and framed my face. It was the sort of thing you did when you hadn't seen someone in a long time, or were planning not to see them again.

"No," I said again, meaning something different this time. Meaning, *Stop. Don't say what you're going to say. I can live without your secrets if you can live without mine.*

Except I could see that he desperately needed to tell his secret. To make it my secret too. And I realized that I'd been wrong before when I'd thought he wanted to tell me his secrets because he saw me as trustworthy. It wasn't that at all. He wanted to tell me because he thought I was strong enough to hear them. And I wanted to be strong. I wanted to be the kind of girl who had all the best adjectives attached to her name. Strong and good and honorable and all the rest. But right now I would settle for strong.

So I shut my mouth and let Dex talk.

"I see death. I see people die. How and where and why. I see it every day. And usually I can't do anything to stop it. Usually I don't even try. Sometimes it's not horrible. Sometimes it really is just someone's time and it can be quiet and peaceful and . . . it still makes your heart ache, but in the way it does when you see the sun rising on a cold winter morning, pushing its way up above the bare tree branches, and you try to capture it on camera, but it's not the same, it doesn't—it can never—do it justice. And that's okay, because it's not meant to be held on to forever. It's only there for that moment."

Dex's index finger slid across my cheek, wiping a tear away. But there were more coming, and he couldn't catch them all. Still he kept trying, even as he continued to talk.

"Other times it's disease or bad timing, and it's wrong and

unfair, and you wish there was some kind of appeal system. The whole thing feels cruel and random, and you start praying because you have to believe there's a bigger plan, a bigger something happening that's too much for our small minds to understand. You believe this or you kill yourself. So, I work very hard at believing, and some days it's more work than others."

I could barely see Dex through the ocean pouring from my eyes, but I heard his sigh and knew the worst of it was yet to come.

"But then there're the few times when you see something evil. And if that is part of the bigger plan, then there's no more believing anything other than the plan sucks. Unless maybe me seeing it is part of the plan. Me stopping it *is* the plan."

The word *evil* thudded around inside me. Everywhere it touched, I hurt.

"I usually avoid kids. It's hard to see them die. Even if they're really old when it happens. It's like seeing time fast-forward. But I was waiting in the checkout line at Wegmans, and she was at the register next to mine, whining about wanting candy. Her mother told her no, and then she had a total meltdown. Temper tantrum on the floor—kicking, screaming, the whole deal. The mom was mortified and dragged her out of there. I shouldn't have turned to look, but I did. I saw her little face, red and tear-streaked. And then I saw how she would die." Dex shook his head, correcting himself. "No, how she would be killed."

His eyes had been locked on mine this whole time, and his

gaze was still directed toward me, but I could feel it turn inward. Could tell he was watching it happen once more.

It turned out that our secrets were more alike than I'd known. We both had uncontrollable nightmares in our heads. Real ones. Except I was the one who brought about my own nightmares. I deserved to see them. Whereas he saw everyone else's and sometimes tried to stop them. I'd known he had secrets. I'd assumed that all secrets were like my own—dark and damning. Although perhaps not to the same degree. But his secrets weren't merely lesser sins, they were something else entirely.

As if my thoughts had triggered it, the color peeled away like strips of faded paint. Dex's hands suddenly felt burning hot against my face. I tried to pull back, but it was too late—I was already somewhere else.

REMOVE

A black rectangle is all I can see. Then words appear.

REMOVE LENS CAP.

The black slides away, and a picture takes its place.

A child. Tear streaked and terrified.

Then a beep.

REC. The three red letters appear at the bottom left corner of the screen.

The picture zooms out. The child becomes smaller, dwarfed by the man straddling her small body.

My head won't turn, my eyes won't close. But I can shift my focus. Stare at the date at the far corner of the screen.

November 17. In my peripheral vision, the man's body begins to move.

No. Look at the date. I do the math, desperate not to see her little pink sneakers thrashing, the little red lights on them flickering against the looming, dark trees.

Another part of the screen records the time.

Three minutes, twenty seconds.

This is when she stops crying.

It zooms in again, this time finding the man's face. In profile, so I can only see half of the satisfied smirk, and one remorseless eye.

SEEING

"No!"

The word ripped from my throat. I blinked at Dex's face in front of mine. Too close. I was already pulling. Pushing too. We were too close. I couldn't get far enough away.

"You saw it. You were seeing it too. With me."

I tugged at the door handle and lunged for the opening, not

even feeling it when I hit the cold cement. Dex reached for me, but I evaded his grasp, skittering backward on all fours. I put my hands over my ears. Afraid of what else he might say. What else he might make me see.

"Anna, please. Wait." Dex stepped from the car, but he was slow, wincing with pain.

I scrambled to my feet, and then I was running.

"Anna, please!" I heard behind me, and then maybe an "I'm sorry."

Or maybe those were my words, ricocheting against my own skull.

DAWN

OKAY

Okay
truth time.

I am the other girl
a boyfriend stealer
or maybe just borrower
. . . for now at least.

He can't get enough of me
that's what he says.
And I hope it means
he's had enough of her.
I want him full-time
and official as my bf
and for her to be the ex.
Because I can't get enough
of him either.

With every stolen
—or borrowed

(like a cup of sugar
from the neighbor
next door)—
kiss
I only want him more.

I tell myself it's
okay.
Because I love him more.
I tell myself she's the
twenty boys by twenty kind,
but for me he is the
one and only.

This is how we take
what's not ours.
This is how we make
the bad things we do
okay.

—ARG

I ate cornflakes by the handful straight from the box, shoveling them in as if I hadn't eaten in years. The crunch between my teeth acted like a sort of white noise, blocking out everything else. Like the memory of walking down the street, frozen from the cold as Dex followed beside me in his car, begging me to get in. I finally did after he promised not to touch me. Or talk to me. Or look at me. Even so I sat in the backseat, with my eyes squeezed closed for the whole ride home.

Now I opened my eyes to find the dad standing directly in front of me.

He looked as surprised to see me as I was to see him. Like I was some forgotten houseguest who should've had the decency to leave by now. The dry cereal became glue in my throat.

"Annaliese." He rubbed his eyes. "Don't you have school?"

I swallowed. I'd completely forgotten. He must have too, because he was my ride, and the school day had started over three hours ago.

"I was scared," I said at last, because it was true and because it would make the dad immediately back down.

And he did. "Of course. I—" He seemed almost not there, as if half of him was with the mom still. "I'll call the school, let them know there's a family emergency. But right now I've got to get back to the hospital. I only came to pick up a few things."

238

He was already drifting out of the room, moving in one direction and then another, as if he'd forgotten how the house was laid out.

"Is she okay?"

My question stopped him. And for a horrible moment I thought maybe the mom was dead, and he couldn't tell me, couldn't even process it himself. But when he turned, he merely looked guilty, not grief stricken.

"She will be. They said she can probably go home later today, or maybe tomorrow morning. Everything will be okay. When your mom is home, we'll talk. But right now . . ."

Again he moved away. This time, I let him go.

Whatever the mom had, the dad still wasn't telling. Sitting at the kitchen table, I could hear him in his room above me, opening and closing drawers. He was probably trying to gather everything the mom could ever possibly need or want.

As he came down the stairs, I dashed into the living room and, reaching behind the couch, grabbed the mom's knitting bag. Running back into the kitchen, I caught the dad as he opened the garage door.

"Knitting," I said, thrusting the bag at him. "If she gets bored or anxious."

The dad stared at the bag and then me, as if he'd never seen either of us before. Finally, he took it from my hands, giving my fingers a little squeeze in the transfer.

"I told her I'd bring you for a visit, but she doesn't want you to see her in the hospital. Your grandmother—you never met her, she passed away in the hospital of pneumonia when your mother wasn't much older than you, and your mom thinks—honestly, I don't know what she thinks, except that she really hates hospitals."

The dad looked at me helplessly. He was caught between us. And I could see how lost he was without her. He always seemed like the strong one, holding the mom up, but in truth he depended on her as well.

"It's okay. I really hate hospitals too."

The dad smiled at that. Almost a real smile. Then he was gone, and I was alone once more.

I grabbed the box of cornflakes, but I wasn't hungry anymore. Instead, I shoved a few breath strips into my mouth and went upstairs, past my own room and into the mom and dad's.

Methodically, I walked around straightening the drawers the dad had dug through in his haste, leaving some of them half open. This finished, I drifted toward the computer desk, stuck into a dark corner behind the bed. This had been my destination from the beginning. Sinking into the faux-leather chair, I gave the mouse a few wake-up shakes. The computer blinked to life.

A cheery screen of sunflowers lifting their faces to the sun greeted me. At the center a blinking cursor waited for me to enter my password. I tried different ways of typing Annaliese. All in caps. Then lowercase. It was useless.

I turned to the little nooks and tiny drawers built into the desktop hutch. Receipts. Those tiny pencils you use to keep score when playing golf. And then a scrap of paper, crinkled and torn at the edges, as if it had been curled up into a tight little spitball and then only much later carefully unrolled and smoothed out.

It was one of Annaliese's poems.

The mom or the dad had found it. Read it. There was no telling when, or what they'd thought of it . . . but I could almost feel the panic of seeing the mom with the poem in her hands, while she asked what it meant.

"Just a school assignment. Based on a book we read, from a character's point of view." The lie comes easily.

Mom looks down at the poem in her hand, studying it. This is what it must feel like to be strip-searched. I force myself not to squirm. "Let me guess. The Great Gatsby? Right?"

Nodding. My head bobs up down up down up down, while at the same time saying, "Yes, yes." Eager to accept this easy answer. Anything to not explain about Logan and the crush and the strange deal that was made and has in some insane way worked better than I'd ever hoped. There is no way to explain that . . . even if I wanted to. I snatch the paper. From now on I'll have to be more creative in where I hide these.

My eyes opened. I didn't even remember closing them. Was

I imagining that, drawing on what I knew of the mom and Annaliese? Or was it a memory, hidden somewhere inside of Annaliese's stolen body even more cleverly than she'd hidden her poems?

They were unanswerable questions, and I shook them away. Carefully, I tucked the poem back into the spot where I'd found it. I fell into the chair and, not really hoping for anything, lifted the keyboard. There sat a yellow Post-it note with the phrase *dogdays58** written across it in the mom's careful script.

I typed it into the waiting computer, and the desktop full of icons appeared. Opening the internet browser, I hesitated, my fingers hovering over the keyboard. Then I typed in my name. My original name.

Anna Martin.

There were too many of them. Anna Martins were lawyers and dentists and even an aspiring actress on IMDB, but none of them were missing girls.

Anna Martin, I typed again. This time I added the other girl's name: Katie Campbell. And the few other things I knew. 1973. Indianapolis.

And there it was. The very first result. An article from 1993, revisiting the case after twenty years. Anna and Katie were still missing, and Katie's mother was still searching. She believed that her daughter had been just as much a victim as Anna. The only proof against Katie was Mrs. Martin's statement that Katie had been in Anna's room, going through Anna's things, on the same day the girls disappeared. That was the last time anyone ever saw Katie. Mrs. Campbell said everyone knew Mrs. Martin had a drinking problem, and that Katie had been Anna's best friend. She also said she left the porch light on, and would until her daughter came home. There was a quick recap of the case, mostly the same as what I'd read in the older article. But one thing had been added.

Three years after the girls went missing, the case had gone cold, and detectives held little hope of finding them without any new leads. Then on August 17, 1976, the Martins' family home was burned to the ground with both parents and the older son inside. After finding traces of gasoline, detectives determined that it was arson. No suspects were ever named, and no connection to the case of the missing girls was ever found.

"It's a shame," Mrs. Campbell said, pointing to the spot where the house had once stood, across the street from her own. "That whole family gone. And Anna—if she's still out there . . . I keep my light on for her too. I'm still waiting for both her and Katie to come home."

I clicked the browser window closed, and stumbled from the room. My head swam. I grabbed hold of the wall, wishing it could keep me anchored here, but it couldn't and I drifted out and away into the sea of memories.

LEMONADE

I hear Mrs. Campbell's voice. "If you girls want some lemonade, you need to help me squeeze. You know how bad my hands are on these rainy days." I can taste that lemonade. She likes it sour. "Put too much sugar in, you might as well get one of those mixes, make it that way." Katie always sneaks more sugar into her glass. But I like the sourness too.

"Mrs. Campbell makes her own lemonade. Mrs. Campbell makes cakes from scratch. Apparently, Mrs. Campbell has a big crank in her basement to make the sun rise and set every day too."

My mother. She doesn't like Mrs. Campbell. She doesn't like anybody. She mutters beneath her breath all the time. Mean things like that. People are either not good enough or trying too hard. She stares out the window, a cigarette in her hand. Or a drink. Sometimes both.

Lipstick. Dark red. It leaves a perfect mark of her kiss on my cheek. But that doesn't happen often. More often it marks her cigarette butts overflowing the ashtray. And toward the end of the day it stains her teeth. She hates being told when that happens. When did I start finding joy in watching her scrub at her teeth with her finger, trying to wipe it away? She looks foolish then. And human. Sometimes I want to take it back. Do something to earn a kiss instead. But what? What she wants is a mystery. Maybe it doesn't exist.

"She's a sensitive lady." That's what Daddy says about her moods. And although moods suggest something passing instead of constant, this is what we all call them. My brother and I. "Mom's in one of her moods," he'll say. At some point I start answering, "Same shit, different day." It makes him laugh. Every time it makes him laugh. It's too easy to get a laugh out of him, but those laughs never feel cheap.

"Johnny was always easy." My mother again. The subtext being, *Anna was difficult.*

"Well, boys and girls are different. Give it time." My daddy's reply there. He doesn't say much really. Just a few stock phrases he recycles over and over again. "This is the life" is for sitting by a warm fireplace with a whiskey or outside in a lawn chair with a beer. All complaints are met with "Give it time." He is a doll with a pull string in his back.

"You'll understand when you're older." She is looking at the TV when she says this, but not really watching it. Her eyes are pointed in that direction but seem to be focused somewhere else, like there is some other show playing, beyond the *Press Your Luck* board, that only she can see. "Things happen in life.

Things don't go the way you plan. And even when they do, it doesn't feel the way you thought it would."

CLOSER

I hesitated outside Dex's door. What I'd seen last night with Dex had been someone else's nightmare, and one that hadn't even happened yet. Now, in the light of day, I felt embarrassed. And cowardly. He'd let me in, and I'd . . . run away.

The right half of the door flipped up, and a moment later Dex's head popped out like a groundhog that had the power to make spring come early. Without him saying a word, I knew.

I'd been forgiven. Relief poured through me, bringing tears to my eyes. More tears came. A flood.

"I'm sorry," I choked out. "I'm so sorry."

"No, no, no." Dex winced as he came up the stairs toward me. "I'm sorry. I never should have brought you there. I felt terrible, and then when you saw . . . I didn't know you would see. You gotta believe me. It's never happened before. I don't really know how it did happen. I mean, you haven't read my mind before . . . have you?"

I shook my head, unable to find my voice.

"Okay, good." Dex smiled slightly. "I didn't think so because you've never slapped me, and I've totally had some thoughts that, well . . . you probably would've slapped me."

I laughed a little shakily, but the tears kept coming.

"Come on, let's get inside." Dex took my hand, not pulling me but simply giving the comfort of his own. "It's starting to rain."

Actually it was more like sleet. Cold and stinging.

Squeezing Dex's hand tight for courage, or maybe so he wouldn't run away like I'd done, I prepared to give back. To share with him as easily and freely as he did with me.

"Sometimes I see things too. Horrible things. Horrible like what we saw last night. But my visions aren't showing me other people. They're of me. I'm the one doing the horrible things. Not in the future but the past. I think I'm remembering what I was."

I released Dex's hand, allowing him to escape. To run. But he held tight.

Maybe he didn't understand.

"I think I'm— No. I don't think. I know. I'm not Annaliese. Annaliese is dead, I guess. Or . . . I don't know. She's gone. Because of me. I tricked her. I took her. And now I'm tricking her parents too, 'cause they think I'm their daughter. But I'm not. I'm not their daughter. I can't even make myself call them Mom and Dad, because it's not fair when I'm not her and I'm not even . . . I'm not even a real girl. What I am is a . . ." I gulp, and then force the rest out. "I'm a monster."

Still he didn't turn away. Didn't slam his door. Icy rain

dripped from the tip of his nose as he studied me. Intently. I stood patiently, letting the rain soak through every layer of clothing while I awaited his verdict.

Finally, he tipped his face up toward the dark sky. He sighed, and his breath hung like a ghost between us before fading away.

"I saw Annaliese die. I saw it years before she disappeared. The funny thing is . . . I still don't know how it happened. What I saw was almost exactly what I got on tape. Annaliese covered in blood, running out of the woods. Screaming too. I can't forget that. I've tried, but it must be superglued inside my skull somewhere. As terrible as the screaming was, it was worse when it stopped. Like someone hit Mute." Dex ran his hand over his face, sluicing a layer of water away.

"And I wanted to stop it, but I didn't know how. When she—when you—came back, I thought it couldn't be her. And whatever or whoever you were must be bad news. That's what I figured. My plan was to stay away. That worked for all of— what? One week? At first, I think it was guilt that drew me back. That first time, with the camera. I couldn't even look at her—at you—without the lens between us, but then I watched the footage from that night when you passed out. Over and over. And I saw something else there."

Both of his hands clasped my trembling one and squeezed. "I saw you. And I had to see more. Know more. Find out who you really were."

My teeth were chattering, but not with the cold. "And what did you find?"

Dex's gaze left the sky to meet mine again. "Not a monster. Nope, not a monster at all. Just a girl. A really complicated, secretive, but also brave and—"

"Brave?" I shook my head. "I ran away. I totally freaked out."

"But you came back. Lots of other people have run from me, and that's the last I've seen of them. But you didn't fall apart or hide away forever. You've been broken and you've survived. I admire you, Anna. And I . . . I can't get enough of you."

The rain turned to snow. Almost as if someone had flipped a switch. Snowflakes pinwheeled lazily through the air, drifting down to earth, where they settled softly with a sigh before disappearing completely.

I reached out, finding Dex's other hand. It wasn't enough. I stepped closer, pressing my body against his. My hands slid beneath his shirt, finding his stomach, chest, back. His skin felt so hot against my freezing fingers, it warmed me from the inside out. Our mouths found each other. We gorged on kisses. And then we were stumbling down the stairs, still caught up in each other.

Our kissing continued until our chattering teeth made us remember our wet clothes. Then, suddenly shy, we turned our backs to each other and pulled clinging pants and shirts from our bodies. We wrapped ourselves in gigantic afghans knitted in undulating waves of bright color. As one we flopped onto the oversized beanbag chair and curled into each other. The blankets kept us each warm in our separate cocoons, but our fingers poked through the open loops of yarn to find each other.

Fingers intertwined, we fell asleep, as if we'd both come a long distance and had finally found a safe place to rest.

FUTURE

I LOVE YOU

*I practice the words
and wonder
where people find
the courage
to ever say them
aloud.*

—ARG

CUT

The *brujas* are frightened. I have never seen them this way before. Even when the hurricane came through. The wind shrieked and the walls of our small hut shook. While I cowered, they sat calmly. Tonight, though, they woke me, saying, "He is coming. Run."

Whoever he is, he is worse than a hurricane.

Under the moonlight, they dig into the garden, pulling up the tomato plants and peppers. A plastic garbage bag finally emerges, and from it a T-shirt and jeans. Faded red blots and streaks cover both garments, but they smell clean like detergent and the freshly churned dirt that kept them hidden. The *brujas* dress me like a child, and I am as passive as one, only watching as they slide the clothes over my body and gently pull them into place. They cluck their tongues in concern when the jeans slide down, barely clinging to my bony hips. One finds a frayed piece of rope, and another slides it through my belt loops and knots it tight at my waist.

Then the hair cutting. Their knives slice and they explain. Spanish words spill out, each saying something different, words and voices overlapping. Yet, as it always is with them, I have no trouble understanding.

I must run. He is coming. The Physician. My hair will be scattered to the wind, and with it my memories. All those hard-earned memories—lost. I will have to find them again later. On my own. Without the *brujas* there to draw away the pain. But maybe this time I will remember it differently. Maybe this time I will see another way. When I came to them, there was not much of me left. Too much time had passed. Too much of me had been lost. But they gathered the pieces of the others. The girls. And with them and what was left of me, they were able to knit me back together. They'd hoped I would stay with them, but had always known it was not to be. We are all of us not quite human, but I am on a different path and must follow it.

They fall silent as the last chunk of hair is lost. I almost wish they would keep on cutting, until I am only bits and pieces, all scattered to the wind.

"What will happen to me?"

Again they answer as one in their varying ways.

"You are hanging by a thread."

"That was once a thick rope, fully binding you."

"Many would be content, trapped in eternal life."

"But you pulled and tugged, never accepting it."

"Always looking for a way out. Slowly breaking it down."

"This is good work. This is hard work."

"And now there is only this thread."

"Now no more pulling."

"Now no more tugging."

"We helped you rest. We made you strong again."

"Now you must cut it."

Tears of frustration fill my eyes. "Cut the rope and then what? Fly away?"

They exchange glances. "No." They say it as one.

The middle *bruja* steps forward, takes my hands. When she speaks, it is in heavily accented English. "No fly away. If you no cut rope, then you swing. Always swinging." She moves her hand back and forth, indicating the motion. "Swinging above dark and dangerous waters. Or you can cut rope. But no fly. You fall. Fall down down down. Down all the way into dark and dangerous waters. Fall and try not to drown. Your choice. Swing or fall. Now choose."

"No," I say. "No."

They ignore me. They push me out toward the rising sun. A battered Toyota truck waits there, its fan belt already whining in protest against the long ride before us. The driver stares straight ahead. For our entire journey he will pretend I am not there, and when I leave him, in his mind this will become true.

I climb in, and they hand me a plastic jug of water through the open window. My fist clenches around the garbage bag that had held my clothes. I'd taken it, wanting to hold on to the last bits of earth hidden in its folds. Wanting to hold on to this place and time.

As we drive away, I cannot help looking back, hoping for some final good-bye. But the *brujas* have given me their last words. I am on my own.

"Choose."

The voices echoed in my head, even as my eyes flew open and I jerked upright. Everything was dark, as if my eyes were adjusting from the glare of a tropical sun. Across the room, the screen saver on Dex's computer glowed, drawing my gaze toward it.

Choose. That same word bounced from one corner of the screen to the next, never resting. Wrapping the blanket around me, I stumbled toward the computer until the mouse was in my hand. I clicked it and almost sighed in relief as the screen faded away, and the desktop picture took its place.

The computer clock said it was seven p.m. It felt later. Like days had passed. It had only been three hours. The basement door that led into the house creaked open, and then shut again. Locks clicked and clacked back into place, and then Dex came down the stairs, a laundry basket in his arms.

Feeling shy, I pulled the blanket tighter. I had not been myself. Not in the usual not-myself-because-I'm-not-Annaliese kind of way. This was different. I'd been a different self I hadn't known existed. A truer self. But now that part was gone and without her I felt . . . naked.

"You're awake!" Dex's grin was wide and warming. "Sorry, stating the obvious. I was worried you'd still be sleeping, and I didn't know whether you would rather stay asleep or be woken up . . . but problem averted."

Dex set the basket in the middle of the room, reached down for a small bundle, and handed it to me.

"I dried your clothes. Hope I didn't shrink anything."

I took hold of them with one hand, not wanting to lose my blanket. They were still warm. "Thank you."

"You have to go, right?" Dex asked while turning away, giving me privacy to get dressed.

"Yeah," I answered, quickly tugging on my jeans. "If the mom and the dad get home . . ."

"I peeked out when I was up there. Your house looked dark. No searchlights or anything."

"I just don't want them to worry." I pulled my long-sleeved henley on. "Okay, I'm dressed."

Dex turned toward me, and even though we were both clothed again, I still felt shy and uncertain. I'd told him I was a monster. That was a nakedness that could never be covered up again. I found myself not quite able to meet his eyes.

"Hey." His soft voice was suddenly close. "You okay? With everything? With us?" He didn't touch me or crowd me. And just like that, I was fine. Dex was still Dex. And despite all the times behind me when I had chosen wrong, this time my choice had been right.

"Yes," I said, even as I moved into his arms. "And I'm sorry for running away before." I whispered the words into his chest.

I felt Dex's lungs expand with a deep sigh. "Don't worry, I've had worse reactions. In the past, people I've told my secrets to have had . . . side effects."

"Side effects?"

"Well, not side effects exactly. More like contagion. There's a reason I don't go around warning people, and it's not because I'm worried they'll think I'm crazy. It's because when I tell someone how to avoid their death, they get this." Dex pointed two fingers at his eyes. "The all-death, all-the-time channel playing constantly inside their head. And as it turns out, there are people who would rather not subscribe to that station." He stopped and swallowed heavily. And that's when I guessed.

"Your mom."

Dex nodded.

"And your best friend who killed himself?"

Another nod, and a sad, ironic smile. "I saved them."

I squeezed his hands. "You did."

"Thing is, some people would rather not be saved."

I wrapped my arms around Dex even tighter, squeezing as if I could push all the hurt out. "You can save me. No, even better. You can show me." I grabbed his hands and pressed my palms against his. "Show me something. Like you did with the little girl."

"No, I don't think that—" Dex tried to pull away, but I held tight.

"Come on," I said, not sure why I was pushing so hard for

this. I had more than enough nightmares of my own; I didn't need to be sharing his. Except I could tell that Dex needed to share them, and for some reason he was able to do that with me. "It doesn't have to be a bad one. Pick a peaceful one. Can you do that? I don't really know how it works."

Dex sighed. "It works like a TV that you can never turn off. Once I've seen someone's death, it becomes almost like a channel in my head that I can flip to at any time. Mostly it's repeats, but sometimes something changes and the death becomes different from how I'd first seen it. That's what happened with my friend Tim. I told him that I saw him die in a motorcycle accident, and when I finally convinced him that what I'd seen was true—it changed. I saw him die, but now he was old. But then he started having the visions too, and . . . the vision changed again, but it was too late to stop him."

I peeled my hands away from Dex's and then, taking a tiny step back, struggled to keep my voice steady. "I saw it."

And I had. Just like with the little girl, it was like watching through a video camera's lens. But there were three separate recordings this time. The mix of smashed metal and blood from the motorcycle wreck. An old man in a hospital bed quietly passing away with a sigh. And finally a young boy staring down at a black gun in his hand. The moment dragged on forever and then, so quickly I didn't even have time to flinch, he brought the gun up and—BANG.

My whole body trembled from it, but this time I didn't run. This time I saw that Dex was trembling too and I flung myself at him, throwing my arms around his neck. My fingers climbed into his hair, pulling his head toward mine, so that my lips brushed his with my next words. "Save me, Dex. Save me and I'll save you."

Then there was kissing. And more kissing. And there might have been more than that too, except we both heard a car drive past.

"Come on," Dex said, and grabbing my hand, we ran up the stairs and outside. The snow had stopped falling, and only a thin layer that didn't even cover the grass remained. "Stay here," Dex whispered. Then he ducked around the side of the house, his footsteps crunching softly. I waited, knowing he would give me some sign if it was the dad.

"Hey," his voice came several long moments later. "Come on out. I don't see anyone. It's all clear."

As if we'd been separated for years, I flew around the house and back into Dex's arms. This time we kept the kissing brief. Ten minutes tops before we made ourselves pull away.

"Will I see you tomorrow?"

"I don't know. It depends what happens with the mom. I'll try."

He kissed the tip of my nose. "Try."

I kissed him back. "I will."

We stood there grinning at each other a moment longer, neither of us wanting the moment to end.

"Okay, you go." I gave Dex a little push.

"Traditionally I'm the one who's supposed to see you to your door."

"But you're injured."

"Oooh, now she remembers. You didn't seem all that concerned earlier when you jumped me and—"

I placed my hands over his mouth, and he nibbled at my fingers.

"Stop that!" I took my hands back with a smothered giggle.

"Okay, we'll both walk away. High-noon style. Twenty paces in opposite directions. Except we'll skip the shoot-out at the end."

Spinning, Dex presented his back to me, and following his lead I did the same.

"Now walk," he said. "And no cheating."

Very seriously, I took careful steps with perfect upright posture, not peeking once, until I reached the fence line. Then, knowing I would dive right back into Dex's arms if I didn't keep going, I ran, my feet sliding a little on the slick driveway.

The motion-sensor light flickered to life as I reached the porch, illuminating Logan Rice standing at my front door, a load of schoolbooks in his arms. My goofy smile faded as my mind raced, wondering how much he had heard.

He wore a hoodie. Not the one he'd given me but a new one, with white stripes down the arms that glowed in the dark. But it did little to illuminate his face.

"What are you doing here, Logan?" I wrapped my arms around myself, suddenly feeling the cold.

He held out the pile of books. "You weren't at school. I brought your books."

I reluctantly accepted them. "Thanks. You didn't have to; it was only one day."

"I thought you'd be worried about falling behind again. You're still trying to catch up."

It was so thoughtful. Annoyingly so. Why couldn't he be a dumb jock who'd taken Annaliese's virginity and never thought of her again?

"Sorry. I mean, thanks again." I tried to edge around him toward the door. "I should get inside. It's cold out here."

Logan didn't move. "Where were you?"

Even as the guilt squeezed me tighter, I wanted to scream at Logan for ruining my moment with Dex. I could've sat alone in the house for at least an hour, hugging that memory, before all the other stuff came seeping back in, but now he'd taken that hour away. The other stuff was here standing on my doorstep.

"Logan, I—"

"Dex Matthews lives over there. Is that who you were with?"

"Why ask, if you already know?"

"Because I want to understand. I told you who that guy is, what he did. He's a level-A creep. He should be rotting in jail right now. Or just plain rotting."

"Go away, Logan. My parents don't want you near me."

He didn't budge. "Yeah, from the looks of that fence, they don't want *him* near you either."

"Well, I like him. Okay? I like him. A lot. Is that what you wanted to hear, Logan?"

My words went pinging right off him. "Annaliese, listen. I did this backward. But I can fix it. I can make your parents like me. And you too." As if I was the afterthought. "I want to take you to dinner. At my mom's. She said she'd cook for us. And she wants to meet you."

The mention of his mom drained some of my anger away. Yeah, I understood the mom thing. "Logan, that's nice of your mom."

"You'll like her. And you'll see, I'm not this dumb jock. I'm gonna go to college. For accounting. Or something like that with numbers. I'm pretty good with numbers. And when I get out of college, I'll have a good job, the kind that can support a wife and a whole family. And a house too. A real nice one, you know, like the kind with one of those really big Jacuzzi bathtubs? And maybe one of those big staircases too, like you see in the movies. I'm gonna get all of that."

"Logan, why are you telling me this?" Of course, I knew, but I had to ask. Had to hear the worst of it.

"Because I want our future to be together."

I wished I hadn't made him say it out loud.

In that moment Annaliese's love for Logan felt like a curse. And I knew that no amount of being nice to him was going to end that curse. I had two choices. I could either tell him straight out that I was never going to have any interest in him, or I could be with him, for my last few days. Be his girlfriend. And if for some reason the redheaded boy was wrong and life didn't end at eighteen, then maybe we'd be together forever, through college, and kids, and whatever else.

If the last few hours with Dex hadn't happened, maybe I would've forced myself to be with him. Both of us doing penance by being with the other. But that was no longer an option.

And then it got worse. Logan bent until he was down on his knees in front of me, and grabbed hold of one of my hands still wrapped around the books. They went crashing to the ground, but he didn't seem to notice.

"I love you, Annaliese. Be with me."

It was ridiculous. Absurd even. But neither of us was laughing.

I took my hand away. With Logan kneeling I was finally able to reach the front door. He didn't stop me as I slipped my key in and then eased the door open. Only as I crossed the threshold did I have the nerve to answer him.

"I'm sorry," I said, feeling those words in every part of me. "I don't love you. And I never did."

I didn't wait for Logan's answer. Stepping back, I closed the door in his face.

NAMED

I waited.

Long after Logan leaned on the doorbell while softy calling out to an Annaliese who didn't exist anymore. Long after I watched his slow retreat, the way he looked shrunken in defeat, walking along the sidewalk to his car parked at the curb a few houses down. Long after he sat in his car—for so long that I began to feel afraid—before finally starting it and then, with a clash of gears and a stomp to the gas pedal, racing off down the street. Long after it was quiet and I knew he wasn't coming back, and long after I wished he would so maybe I could tell him no some kinder, better way.

That was when I opened the front door, just wide enough to scuttle out on hands and knees, grab the schoolbooks still scattered on the porch, and pull them back into the house with me.

I carried them up to my room. Not with any real intention

of doing homework, but more to give the appearance of having done it. A small gift for the mom and the dad. A small lie.

History, biology, and algebra. They were all thick and heavy textbooks. I dumped them on the desk. Algebra bounced off biology and fell to the floor, its pages spread open in surrender. I grabbed it one-handed, letting the pages flutter, and a bit of white paper drifted out from between them.

Everything inside me froze. It was just a torn piece of paper with a bit of writing on it. It might have been a note from the teacher. Except I knew it wasn't.

"Run!" I heard the *brujas* echo in my head. I wanted to, but it would be like running from the sunrise. Some things we are not meant to easily escape.

There was a watermark on the back side of the paper. I focused on it, believing it was the less harmless option. Holding the paper at an angle, I tilted it this way and that, but it was like trying to read underwater; the words wavered before my eyes and never quite came into focus. It was an address. Maybe. I could just barely make out Albion, NY. I wondered if that was near, and if it meant something. Really, though, I was stalling.

I flipped the paper over. The handwriting was familiar. Horribly so. Dark and crabbed and deadly serious. It didn't ask, it coolly commanded. This wasn't Eric. It was the one above him. Above us both. The *brujas* called him their brother. Eric referred to him as the Physician. I was too afraid to call him anything at all.

Lacey Lee Beals. Oklahoma.
She will arrive. Prepare.

I knew what it meant. This was the next girl I was meant to take. Worse yet, I knew exactly who she was. The girl from the trailer at the edge of nowhere. A cigarette in her mouth, and baby brother on her hip. I'd thought she'd looked about my age.

I realized now that her name had also been on the paper along with Annaliese's name. I'd chosen Annaliese, and when that hadn't quite worked out, I'd followed a feeling to Lacey's door. I'd gone right toward option B without even knowing it. And now here she was again.

I looked down at the paper. It wavered before my eyes, and I saw other papers. Other names. The roaring began, and instead of holding back, looking for an escape, I threw myself into it.

A FINE EDGE

The wind blows my hair into my face, making it difficult to see. Impatiently, I push it back, wanting to get this finished before the lunch bell rings. Turning my back to the wind, I flick the lighter and then, cupping my hand, hold the bobby pin steady in the bluest part of the tiny flame. When it's hot enough, I drop the lighter. Then, keeping the wooden razor handle steady, I scratch the letters *y* and *n*.

Jaclyn is now official.

"Hey, Senorita, finally done with that?" He lounges by my side. White teeth, white skin, white hair. I call him the albino, but it doesn't bother him the same way that Senorita does me. I'm not going to fight with him today, though. Tomorrow I will be someone else, and soon after, he will be too. Then we'll find new names to call each other.

"It's nice out today, isn't it?" I turn my face to the wind. It smells like spring.

He snatches the razor from my hand. "Jaclyn this time, huh?" His forefinger runs down the list of names. There are seven of them now. "Ooh, I remember this one. She was musical. Very sexy."

Musical. That's one of his jokes. At my expense.

The girl had played piano, but I couldn't. He told me to relax, let the body take over and do what it knew. This worked for him. Every body he took over he owned completely. The football star could still throw the ball, the artist knew how to sketch, and the musician could strum his guitar. It never worked that way for me. The body I was in never quite fit. He didn't really care though. He liked to watch me struggle to explain.

As for the piano-playing girl, he didn't miss the music at all. He thought the grand piano at her house had been a sexy prop. We'd stretched out on top of it.

"It's not believable," I'd told him. "No one would really make out there." He didn't listen, said we were setting the scene. But then, he wasn't the one with the hard wood digging into his spine. Anyway, it worked. Her mom flipped, and we ran away, hand in hand, never to be seen again.

"Must be nice to have a choice." His voice has that whiny tone. I know it well.

I hold in a sigh. I want my razor back. Last night I sharpened it to a fine edge so that it will glide through flesh and saw through bone with only the slightest bit of pressure. But I let him hold it, let him look, and try to be conciliatory. I tell him the truth. "I hate choosing."

"Oh, boo-hoo. You hate to choose. Once the choice was always mine, and I gave it up for you."

I only half listen. You spend enough time with a person and you start to repeat conversations. We've had this one many times before. He knows I dread that slip of paper arriving in my locker. Two names, and I must pick one. It's made so simple too. The two possibilities are presented like fresh lobster in a tank, claws bound. My only job is to boil the water.

But sometimes the girls are different. I meet them and feel a connection. Jane was the first one like that. When I met Jane, it was like she was me. Or it felt that way. I didn't have to choose her. The choice was already made. When I am these girls, I feel a little bit less like an impostor. A bit more like my real self. That's why I scratch their names onto the blade handle, beneath my own. I remember all the girls, no matter how much I want to forget. But the ones on the blade . . . I remember them like I remember Anna—as if they are still a real part of me.

It's been several years since I felt that connection, but it was there once more when I met Jaclyn. And that's why I'm adding her name below Evie's.

Sensing my waning attention, he flips the blade out. I'd known he would eventually. Drawing blood is what interests him. "And now I just follow your or the Physician's lead. Like a dog on a leash."

"People are looking. Put it away before it gets taken."

"Here," he says, holding it out to me, leaving only the blade to grasp. "Or you could use one of those plastic knives from the cafeteria, let Jaclyn cut into you with that."

I don't hesitate. If he's been born to cut, then I've been born to bleed.

Before I can grab it, he whips the blade away, neatly folding it back into the handle that hides it so well. He drops it into my lap, and then in one of those quicksilver changes that regularly flicker through him, he reclines on the bench, laying his head on my knee.

His blue eyes stare straight up into mine and are free of any hint of malice.

"Anna," he says, his voice soft and low like a little boy's. "Don't you love me at all?"

Tenderly, I run my fingers through his hair. He turns in to my touch like a kitten, nearly purring.

I once thought I loved him. But really I loved the thought of being loved. And he's the same. He needs to be loved. Desperately needs to be loved. It's what we have in common. It is what binds us. And it is what makes us hate each other. We are two people who only want to receive love and have no idea how to give it.

"No, Franky," I say at last, "not even a little bit."

He jerks away from my touch, sitting up, so that I am no longer looking down at him. And then he kisses me. A hard and passionate and completely loveless kiss.

I kiss him back. He is my boyfriend after all, and all the other kids having lunch outside on this almost-spring day are watching. Tomorrow they need to believe that we've run away together, just two crazy teenagers in love. It's a fairy tale, but easier to believe than our bodies crumbling to dust and disappearing completely.

And tomorrow I will be Jaclyn. Her ultraconservative mother doesn't believe in letting her daughters date. It'll take him a while to get around that one. And while he does, maybe I'll finally figure out a way to stop being anyone at all.

ROAD

RIDE

*"You can tell me anything,
you know that."*

*Mom says this.
And it's true.*

*But what does it help
to tell her
the awful thing
I am wishing for,
when I already know
what she'll say?*

*"Remember when you
wished for a pony?
Your sixth birthday
you wanted nothing else.
Please, please, Mommy.
You begged and pleaded
until we found a pony
for your party.*

And when the pony came,
you cried.
He was ugly and smelly
and not at all
what you thought
he should be.

Nothing we said
could convince you to ride."

She's told this story before
and always with the same
lesson at the end:

"Be careful what you wish for,
make sure it's what you truly want."

But I am not six years old anymore
and I know exactly
what I wish
and exactly
what I want.

I'm ready to change that
story's ending.
I'm ready for a new
lesson.

This time
I'm ready to ride.

—ARG

The dad came home sometime after midnight, and in the morning he woke me for school. I had to remind him it was Saturday. He ended up taking me out for breakfast instead. He didn't seem to notice that I mostly pushed the food around my plate. I couldn't eat, even though I was starving. A young couple cuddled together in a booth near the back had caught my eye when we first walked in, and suddenly the hunger stirred once more. I tried to ignore it. Tried to pretend everything was normal. It was nearly impossible. The hunger no longer growled—it was starting to roar.

"There's this great little bakery down the street from my work," the dad said, interrupting my thoughts. "I can order a cake Monday morning, and pick it up on my way home. Anything you want. They'll make it."

It was the first hint he'd given me about the mom's condition. She was an old-fashioned make-it-from-scratch type of person. No way would she choose to order a cake instead of making one. Which meant that she didn't have a choice. She was so sick, she couldn't bake.

I asked the dad for half chocolate, half white. I didn't know what would happen to me on Annaliese's birthday. But if I was there or not, I wanted the mom to have her chocolate.

By the time we finished breakfast, the hunger had finally subsided, and I could tell the dad was itching to get back to the hospital. He kept checking his phone. I told him to go, that I would do homework or whatever. He left, promising to be back later. Much later, I figured.

Still, I didn't waste time. I hurried over to Dex's. But my knocks on his crooked door went unanswered. Feeling lonely and rejected, no matter how irrational it was, I crept back home and crawled into bed. Amazingly, I slept vision-free. Most of the day was gone by the time I woke, and I fought the urge to run back over to Dex's to see if he was home yet.

Instead, I found my way back to the computer. This time I typed *Annaliese Rose Gordon* into the search box. I hesitated for a moment, then also typed *Jaclyn*. The two were connected, I was certain of it.

And I was right. Another girl had disappeared on the same night as Annaliese. TWO GIRLS GONE MISSING. The headline was hauntingly familiar. This girl wasn't friends with Annaliese, though. Didn't even live nearby. She was from a small town in the middle of Ohio. Turned out there was no connection between them. Or that was what the police concluded when the mother, still covered in her daughter's blood, confessed.

The girl's name was Jaclyn. Her mother confessed to cutting the heart right out of her daughter's chest. That was what she said. Except she didn't have the body or the heart. Both were still missing.

For a long time I stared at the picture of Jaclyn. And at the spelling of her name, exactly the same as the one I remembered scratching into the wooden handle of the razor blade.

I'd been Jaclyn. The memory at the locker with the twin sister had been real. And the name on the razor. Jaclyn was different, though. The other girls ran off with a boy and were never heard of again. But Jaclyn's mother found her. The flash of silver, slicing toward my forehead.

My fingertips found the spot where the metal point had crushed through bone to find brain matter. That had been Jaclyn's mother behind that pickax. Somewhere in the transfer from being Jaclyn to becoming Annaliese, something had gone wrong.

I needed to know how the mother had found them. How I'd found Jaclyn, and then Annaliese after her. Mostly, though, I wanted to see if Jaclyn's body had been found. If she hadn't turned to dust, then that was a first I wanted to repeat.

My eyes felt sticky after staring at the computer screen for so long, but there was something else I needed to do. I pulled up a few maps, and when the dad called at ten o'clock that night to check on me, I was ready.

The mom had to stay another night, he said, but he would be home shortly. They didn't want me spending the night alone again. The lie I'd prepared came easily: I'd talked to Gwen earlier and she'd asked if I wanted to stay at her place tonight. She could pick me up and drop me off tomorrow. No problem. The dad should stay with the mom.

The dad sounded so relieved, like a prisoner on death row who'd been granted a reprieve. He asked me once if that was what I really wanted to do, and when I replied in the affirmative, he said something about Gwen being a "good kid," and then assured me one more time that the mom was "fine and can't wait to see you tomorrow." A few minutes later we exchanged good-nights, and then I was free.

I headed straight into Dex's arms.

"You like late-night drives, right?" I said after we finished our hello kiss.

Dex shook his head. "Negative. Not anymore, anyway. I think the other night cured me of leaving home anytime after midnight."

"Oh, right." I could feel my master plan crumbling away without the cornerstone of Dex driving us to support it.

"Hey." He bent forward so he could see my face straight on. "What's up?"

"This is gonna sound crazy, but I need to go to Ohio. Like, right now. The mom will be out of the hospital tomorrow afternoon, and I need to get there and be back before she comes home." Dex was already nodding, and I knew he would take me without any further information, but it only felt fair to tell him a little more. "It's about the things I see, about who or what I am."

"Who you *used* to be," Dex corrected me quietly. Then quickly switching gears, he checked his watch. "Also, Ohio is a big state. Which one of its many exotic locales are we heading toward?"

I grinned, relieved he was willing to go along so easily. "A small town about an hour north of Columbus."

Dex nodded. "Okay, so we need to get to mid Ohio and back before noon. It's gonna be tight."

"Tight, but doable," I said, ready to pull out the maps I'd printed as proof.

"Then let's do it," Dex said.

Ten minutes later we were on I-90 heading west. And suddenly doubt crept in. No, it didn't creep. It busted in, kicking the door down SWAT-team style. The plan on paper had been one thing, but now in action it felt bigger. Less in my control. Time was ticking away, and instead of going off on this wild goose chase, I could be with Dex in his beanbag chair, getting the most of life out of every inch of Annaliese's body.

"Maybe this isn't such a good idea."

Dex grabbed my hand. "Hey, no freaking out. Whatever it is we're going to Ohio to do, I have a feeling it's the right thing."

The combination of his hand and his words steadied me. They gave me courage too. "My birthday—or Annaliese's—is Monday. It's some kind of deadline, I think. See, the thing is, Annaliese isn't the first girl I've taken. The one before Annaliese was a girl named Jaclyn. She went missing on the same night as

Annaliese. It said in the newspaper article that her birthday was only two weeks away. I think that I have to take another girl by Monday or else . . . Or else I don't know what."

Again, I was prepared for Dex to pull away. Even though he'd demonstrated his steadfastness over and over again, I still couldn't completely trust it. Now he proved himself once more.

At the next exit he turned off the thruway and parked at the far corner of a truck stop.

"Backseat conference," he said. Then he opened his door, stepped out, and entered the car once more—into the seat directly behind his. I followed his lead, and a moment later we were snuggled tight.

"Look," he said, as he pulled my razor out from his coat pocket. "I was sort of examining this for clues earlier today, and I noticed something, so I thought I'd bring it and show you." Dex turned the razor in his hand, so that the list of names stared straight at me. Lightly, his finger traced down the list. "All these names you can tell were scratched into here—"

"Burned," I corrected. "Or branded, or something like that. It was a hot bobby pin."

Dex nodded, as if this made sense. "Okay. Well, all these names look like they were done by the same person. The letters are formed the same kind of way. But this last one—"

I snatched the razor from his hand. "Don't."

A tense silence wedged its way between us.

I didn't know why I'd grabbed the razor from him. Maybe it was that I'd imagined it wrapped up and tucked away somewhere safe. It had never occurred to me that Dex might be studying it and seeing things in it that I wasn't ready for him to see. He wouldn't understand that though. Dex gave up his secrets so easily. They weighed on him but didn't eat into him, constantly taking tiny bites, the way mine did. His secrets were told; mine were extracted.

Or maybe that was all rationalization. We all lived with our secrets in different ways.

"I'm sorry," I said, holding the razor out to Dex.

He pushed it back to me. "No, I'm sorry. My mom always says—well, she texts actually—to stop wanting to fix everything. She says that sometimes she complains to blow off steam. It's not an SOS or a cry for help. She just needs someone to listen, not a white knight coming to the rescue."

Just like that, the little threads of anger that had been pulling at me fell away. "I love that you come to the rescue. That you want to fix things. I just . . ." I leaned into Dex, needing him solid and warm and close as I let a little more of the truth out. "That razor, it . . . I use it to . . . I—*it*—cuts my heart out. The next girl I'll become slices it from my chest, and then . . ." Coward that I am, the truly stomach-turning part of my confession gets stuck in my throat. Lamely, I finish, "That can't be undone. I'm not fixable."

"Well, let's try." Dex tilted backward, taking me with him. I wrapped my arms around his neck, wanting every possible bit of myself to connect with every possible bit of him. Dex must have been thinking the same thing, because he shifted, angling us into even more of a reclined position. I moved to let his long legs find space on either side of me, and then I fell back onto him, pressing my chest against his and sealing our lips together with a kiss.

Dex yelped.

I jerked away.

"Ow, shit." He reached toward his chest. My razor was there. And a growing circle of blood was spreading across his T-shirt. With a surprisingly steady hand, I pulled the blade from Dex's flesh. It was only half open; it hadn't cut him deeply. Even in the dark car I could see that clearly. But it could easily have parted his flesh and slid straight into his heart. The thought of that was enough to pierce mine.

The razor fell from my hand and thudded against the floor mats.

"Hey, Anna." Dex struggled to sit up and put his arm around me. I scooted away. "Anna, I'm okay. See? Just a flesh wound."

He held up his shirt, baring his thin chest. The razor had left a crescent-shaped cut. Blood continued to run steadily from it.

"This is not your fault, okay? It was an accident. And I was the one who brought the blade, so if it's anyone's fault—which it isn't—then it's mine. And look, I'm not even bleeding anymore." Dex pulled his shirt away. The blood flowed. "Okay, well I am still a little bit. But again, my fault. My family is known for our watery blood."

I said nothing. I knew it was time to confess everything. To tell Dex the full bloody history of that blade. The full bloody history of me. I couldn't. I looked away from him.

"Anna, come on." Dex's fingers grazed my chin, nudging it up until our gazes met. "Here's the plan. I am gonna find a bathroom and stop bleeding. I think that will make you feel better. Then I am going to buy several bags of junk food. That will make me feel better. Then we are going to get back on the road and drive to the middle of Ohio. And this whole"—Dex waved his hand around—"incident will never be spoken of again. Unless you want to speak of it, then we will. Or if you want to write ballads of it. Or put together a *Jeopardy!*-style quiz about it where we'll both have to answer in the form of a question. Any of those things. Okay?"

I still couldn't get any words out, but I nodded. It was enough for Dex. He kissed my cheek and then jumped out of the car.

Alone, I could feel sobs threatening. But I didn't want to be a snotty mess when Dex returned so I shoved some breath strips into my mouth and focused on inhaling the stale car air and replacing it bit by bit with my minty-cool exhalations.

Slightly calmer, I was ready to deal with the razor. I suppressed the urge to open the car door and chuck it out into the darkness. Instead, I carefully wiped the blood from the blade and pushed it back into the handle. Turning it in my hand, I could now see what Dex had been trying to show me. Someone else had carved the name *Annaliese*. It was so obvious now that I was looking at it. The curve and curls and hope were gone. *Annaliese* was written straight and hard and angry.

I knew that writing. I had just seen it on a tiny slip of paper. The Physician. He had put Annaliese's name there. There had been girls every year. So many girls. I had only added six of them to the razor, though, along with Anna. The Physician had added Annaliese's name for me, and I had no idea what that meant. Maybe it meant nothing at all.

I pushed the razor into my coat pocket, past all the other odd bits, not wanting to risk it cutting into someone else. I dug everything else out. A cough drop, a button, and a crumpled napkin with caramel-colored streaks that suggested it had been used to mop up coffee. Trash, tucked into a pocket and forgotten. Except even as I thought this, I pulled the wrinkled folds of the napkin open, looking for the writing I somehow knew would be there. It was another one of Annaliese's spitball poems, but this one hadn't been hidden so much as left behind.

Road trip with my best friend, Gwen

That was all I had time to read. A roar went off inside my head. I clenched the napkin tightly, not wanting to lose it. And then I was carried away.

IN PERSON

The automatic doors swoosh open, mechanically welcoming, oblivious to my hesitation. A few stuttering steps later, I am in the dank lobby of the Colonial Inn. There is no guesswork involved in finding the two girls who are waiting for me. Gwen and Annaliese stand side by side, the only other people there.

After another brief pause, I move in their direction, and with that their own uncertainty ends and they head toward me as well.

The shorter girl bounces, masking her nerves with a wide smile and outstretched arms. Short of pushing her back, there is no way to avoid her hug. So, this must be Gwen. It's awkward, as hugs between strangers always are, but even more so because this is supposed to be the first in a series of increasing physically intimate moments between us. The friendly hug leads to the lingering touch, and that gives way to the first kiss. Except it won't. This hug is it for Gwen and me.

Gwen pulls away, and behind her Annaliese has her arms crossed over her chest. No hugs from her then. Good. It would feel a bit too much like walking into a house before the previous owners had moved and measuring for curtains. We exchange friendly nods.

"Jaclyn, it's so great to finally meet you in person! At last!" Gwen's enthusiasm levels are cranked way too high, as if the idea of playing it cool never occurred to her. "So, I'm Gwen, as you've probably already guessed, and this is my friend Annaliese, who I told you about. Wow. It really is so great to see you. So great."

"Yeah, it is," I agree, but my mellow response seems almost sarcastic in contrast to Gwen's exuberance.

An awkward silence falls, and I wish I'd never answered Gwen's letter. It came the day after the two names fell from my locker. Annaliese or Lacey were the choices the Physician had given me this time. I would cross paths with both girls at some point in the month before my eighteenth birthday, giving me plenty of time to pick one and make the switch. Once—a long time ago—I'd written lists, debating which girl to take. Then I started flipping coins. Lately I go with the first one I meet. If I do the crossover quickly enough, I can usually miss out on ever meeting the second girl at all. It's become a bit of a game with me, being fast enough to not discover what's behind door number two.

"So, you and Gwen met on some kind of kids-of-shrinks message board?" Annaliese asks, still hugging her arms to herself, probably wishing she'd never let her friend drag her along on this trip. And yet she is trying to break the ice and salvage our weekend together. It's nice of her. She's a nice girl. She also has no idea why Gwen is really here.

"Yep, that's right." Gwen responds too quickly, too loudly. She sends me a look, part apology, part plea. In the email, Gwen had promised she would tell Annaliese.

My mom says she won't drop me off in some strange town to meet a total stranger all by myself, even if she is only FORTY-FIVE minutes away in Columbus having her conference. So, we compromised. I'm bringing my friend Annaliese. She doesn't KNOW about me, and I've never mentioned you before. But I know the whole point of us meeting is to be with someone that we don't have to pretend with—so, DON'T WORRY, I'm going to tell Annaliese. She has been my best friend forever, but as you know from our many talks in the past, that almost makes it harder to get the words out. Let me know what you think.

"Yeah, on a message board," I now agree. If they were staying the night at my place—with the falling-down farmhouse and Jaclyn's Jesus-freak mother—there is no way Annaliese would believe anyone there knows anything about mental health. That isn't the plan, though.

And what else can I say?

It wasn't hard once I got the letter from Gwen to trace back through Jaclyn's online history. Two years ago Gwen and Jaclyn met on a teen LGBT board. Lesbian, gay, bisexual, transgender. They must have clicked pretty quickly, because only a week after the email confirming Jaclyn's registration on the board, the long list of emails and saved chats began. At first they mainly talked about how and when they knew, and the difficulties of coming out to friends and family. But then it got a little flirtatious. There were references to phone calls and heavy breathing. Then Gwen wrote, "I think I love you."

Suddenly the emails stopped. I think I know why. About a week after that last email, Jaclyn made a deal with me to make a boy fall in lust with her. Then several months later Gwen's letter arrived. It must have taken her that long to work up the nerve to send it. She said that she loved Jaclyn and knew that Jaclyn loved her, too. She begged—"Whatever went wrong, please give me a chance to fix it."

Gwen claps her hands together. "Well, we should get going. Were you able to get a ride to show us around town? All we've seen so far is this and the Holiday Inn next door. My mom gave us money to stay there, but Annaliese and I agreed it would be better to use the money to stay here instead so we can each have our own room."

"Oh, okay," I reply, pretending obliviousness to Gwen's

hidden invitation to spend the night with her. And then because I believe in ripping off the Band-Aid quickly, I spin and march back out the front door. "I'm parked over here," I call to Gwen and Annaliese, who are following closely behind me.

He is leaning against the side of the car, impatiently waiting. I hate the very sight of his face, no matter how many times he changes it. The feeling is so strong I shouldn't be able to hide it, but I do because I have lots of practice. I run toward him and into his embrace. He captures my lips for an endless and punishing kiss. When it is over, he slings a possessive arm across my shoulders, his right hand dangling down so that his fingertips just graze my breast. I force my body not to stiffen.

"Gwen, Annaliese, this is my boyfriend, Steven."

I can't look at Gwen, so I simply gaze up at him with what I hope is an adoring expression. My betrayal of Gwen is finished, and now my betrayal of Annaliese can begin.

KNOCK-KNOCK

As promised, Dex returned with massive amounts of junk food, and then we got back on the road. I tried to smile, but the razor in one pocket and napkin poem in the other left me feeling leaden. My smiles never achieved liftoff.

Finally, after two hours of driving in near silence that had me sinking deeper and deeper into my grim thoughts, Dex reached over and tapped my knee.

"Knock-knock."

It took me a minute to understand, and say my line. "Who's there?"

"A little old lady."

"A little old lady who?"

"I didn't know you could yodel."

I groaned.

"Bad?" Dex asked. I nodded. "Okay, how about, Why did the midget get kicked out of the nudist colony?"

"I dunno."

"He kept sticking his nose in everybody's business."

I groaned again, but this time a snort of laughter also escaped. And Dex kept going, one terrible joke after another, until I laughed so hard I cried. Then I just cried, while Dex held my hand. And when there were no tears left, I began to tell Dex everything, laying out all the jagged pieces of memory.

Finally, I confessed all of my sins. And it was easy, because I knew they had already been forgiven.

TWIN

SPILLED

Road trip with my best friend, Gwen.
Gwen who never shuts up,
who says every thought that enters her head,
has been quiet ever since we left Wooster.

Actually she was silent most of yesterday
only I didn't notice, until we were in the car
and her mom asked how it was
and did we get along with Gwen's internet friend.

I said, "Great, great. It was great. She was great."

Gwen said nothing. Not one word.
Not yeah. Or eh. Or no.
Nothing.

Then there was only NPR news
and classical music
and Gwen's silence, which was somehow
even louder and more annoying
than her usual endless chatter.

"I wish you hadn't even come."
Those were the first words Gwen spoke
as she stabbed at the button on the
gas station cappuccino machine,
not even looking at me,
not seeing my mouth fall open.

She'd begged me to come. Begged.
But I didn't say that. I didn't say anything.

"She was great. Great. Great."
Gwen did that thing where she imitated me
in a whiny singsong voice.
"You don't even know her.
You just thought she was great
because she let you talk about Logan,
the love of your life,
and she didn't laugh.
And you were so impressed by her
pretty little boyfriend.
Well guess what?
That was all a lie.
She doesn't even like boys.
She's a freaking lesbian.
That's how I met her."

Caramel mocha flowed over the side
of Gwen's cup and over her fingers.
"Shit."
She flung it aside,
it hit the counter

then splattered out
at me,
hitting my shirt my jeans my shoes.
It stung against my skin.

"I'm sorry,"
Gwen said. She patted at me with
great wads of napkins.
I grabbed them away, and went
into the bathroom
daring her to follow me.

"Oh, Gwen, what happened?"
I heard her mother behind me.
"I just spilled—"
The bathroom door closed,
cutting her off.

Road trip with my best friend, Gwen,
who I think might've just told me
she's a lesbian.

It's gonna be a long ride home.

—ARG

The large farmhouse waited at the end of a bumpy and pitted drive. Behind it only the outline of an old barn remained. Weeds and wild grass swayed around us, brushing across my hands hanging limp and heavy at my side. A piece of plywood had been nailed across the front door, but it sagged on one end as if someone had pulled it away to sneak in. One of the upstairs windows had been broken, and gray curtains billowed out, waving in surrender.

"Seems like nobody's home," Dex said quietly. "Should we look around?"

It was six a.m. We'd spent the last hour in a Denny's at the side of the highway, waiting for the sun to beat back enough of the night's darkness so that we could knock on the door of a complete stranger. Except now we were here and there was clearly no one to answer our knock. And I didn't want to explore. I wanted to go home. But this sad and hollow place had once been my home. Kind of.

"Let's check the backyard first," I said, stalling, because I didn't want to step inside that house and smell the musty air and see what had been left behind.

Dex took the lead. I drifted in his wake, following the trail of beaten-down grass. We came around the side of the house, and the wind picked up, as if trying to blow us back. Low, thick clouds covered the still-rising sun, casting us in shadow. Shivering, I shoved my fists into my coat pockets and kept walking. Another, even stronger, gust of wind whipped by, and that was when I heard it. A tinkling, jangling sound. High little clinks interspersed with lower cowbell moans.

I looked up at Dex, and from the way his head was tilted, his right ear angled up toward the sky, I knew that he'd heard it too.

"Over here," I said, and this time I took the lead, away from the house. The land dipped slightly, a gentle downward roll that carried my legs faster. At the bottom there was a crease with a trickle of water running through it, and on the other side the ground swept upward again, disappearing into a tangle of trees. Now the sound was louder, and as the sun poked out, bits of silver glinted through the bare winter branches. Hopping over the stream, I headed into the trees, following a worn foot trail that wound its way through the weeds until it ended at a clearing.

I skidded to a stop. Stunned.

Wind chimes hung from branches all around the clearing. Little clay birds painted bright shiny red, seashells strung on thick white cord, and long silver cylinders that shook like fringe on a flapper's dress. All those and more created overlapping waves of music. And at the center of it sat a girl wrapped in a sleeping bag, a sketch pad across her lap. I recognized her immediately. How could I not? I had been her. It was Jaclyn.

My legs trembled beneath me, and then Dex was slipping an

293

arm around my waist, supporting me.

Jaclyn didn't seem as surprised to see me. She merely looked up from her sketching and gave one last flick of her pencil, before setting it aside and standing. All of her movements were languid, almost sleepy. Slowly she drifted in our direction, as easily swayed by each gust of wind as the chimes in the trees above her.

She came to a stop in front of me, and her hand floated up between us until it was at eye level. Index finger extended, the cold tip of her finger pressed gently into the fracture point on my forehead as if testing the depths of the damage. Everything went still. The wind stopped, and the chimes hung limp and heavy while she studied. A moment later another gust whipped through, and her hand fell back to her side, like a leaf being blown away.

Perhaps it was the shock of contact, but I realized then what I should have known immediately. This wasn't Jaclyn. It was Jess. The twin sister.

"My mother did that," she said, her voice surprisingly strong. "She did that to the girl she found Jaclyn with. Except that girl wasn't you, not yet, because you were still Jaclyn."

I nodded, admitting it. Not that I could have denied it. She knew. Somehow she already knew everything.

She looked back over her shoulder, and then gave one nod, as if she'd decided something between her and someone else.

"Come sit. All of you. You're here to find something, so let's see if we have it."

The way she spoke. "All of you." "We." It made me feel strange, like there were more people here than just her, Dex, and me. Craning my neck, I looked around but only saw the trees and the shimmering chimes that filled them.

Unzipping her sleeping bag, she spread it flat on the ground so we could all sit on it. Jess settled herself cross-legged at one end, and then waited while Dex and I followed suit.

"I've never had anyone here before," Jess said conversationally. "It's my place to be alone with my sister, but she thinks I am too much alone lately, which isn't true at all. This is the only place—" Jess stopped, as if someone had interrupted her.

She turned to the empty space beside her. Her head tilted, listening. Nodding, she held her right hand out in a stop motion, and then looked back to us. "Jaclyn doesn't like when I misrepresent her opinions. She says what she meant by alone was flesh-and-blood living people, like you two. She also thinks it's good for me to see that there are other freaks out there in the world, so that I'll know I'm not the only one. It's hard to feel alone, she says, and she should know because of the whole lesbian thing." Jess rolled her eyes. "You know, for all that she didn't want to talk about it when she was alive, it's the only thing I hear about now. And also, as I've told her, chatting with the dead is a little stranger than liking girls. There is no LGBT community for me. No real role models. She had Ellen. I have *The Ghost Whisperer.*"

"You know, that's an excellent point," Dex broke in, since it looked like this one-sided conversation between the sisters could go on forever. I could see why Jaclyn wanted her sister to mix with the living. The way Jess covered both sides of the conversation as if it was natural was strange, but even worse was how obviously thin her argument was. She didn't really care about finding a support group. She was at ease living with the dead, so much so that she didn't seem firmly attached to the earth herself.

"Thank you," Jess said, throwing a raised-eyebrows I-told-you-so look to her right.

"So," I said hesitantly, wanting to make sure I understood everything correctly. "Jaclyn is sitting next to you?"

"Not sitting. Floating would be more accurate. Just like the other girls."

"The other girls?" Again I felt the urge to look around, searching.

"Oh, you don't feel them there?" Jess asked. "I thought . . . They came with you. Of course, lots of people have stringers and never have a clue they're there." Jess jumped as if nudged. "Oh right, sorry. Stringers are what I call the ghosts who kinda attach to and travel around with one person. Like at a street fair where they're giving balloons away and every kid has one attached to their wrist kinda bobbing along behind them. The ghosts are like that, sort of. Except instead of being bright and round and bouncing, they're tattered and heavy. Even floating, they always seem so heavy." Jess's gaze locked on to the treetops, as if she were floating and lost among them. Dex and I said nothing, simply waiting for her to return. In another moment she did, her focus sliding back down to me. "But I thought, with you not being really alive yourself, that you would be more in touch with these types of things."

I didn't know what to say. I had stringers. Tattered and floating and heavy. I might be one myself. The obvious question was to ask who they were . . . except I already had a pretty good idea. Tucking my hand into my pocket, I grabbed hold of the razor handle with the names of eight girls. Maybe it should've been comforting, made me feel less alone. Instead, I felt haunted.

"Well, this is awkward," Jess said, not looking as if she felt any discomfort at all. "It's like I just told you that you have spinach in your teeth. Except it's invisible spinach that you'll never be able to pick out."

"It's fine," I lied quietly.

Dex, seeing my obvious distress, stepped in. "Can you tell us about Jaclyn? Anna has remembered bits and pieces, but it would help to have the full timeline."

"Of course," Jess answered immediately. "The full timeline." She took a deep breath. "Well, I'd ask if you want the short version, but you already know it. Jaclyn died, but her body didn't and then it did. So, the long version."

Jess fell back into the grass, and began to tell her story to the sky.

"My mom ran away from home when she was fifteen. For no reason as far as I can tell. Everybody round here says my grandparents were the nicest people, and it just about broke their hearts when Mom left. And Mom's never said nothing bad about them neither. Just that they held her too tight when she wanted to be free. She became an honest-to-God groupie. Followed bands and tried to fuck the rock stars, but usually ended up settling for some roadie. At nineteen, one of those roadies gave her twins and a pair of Mick Jagger's snakeskin boots. I guess the idea was to sell them for enough money to get rid of us. But she kept the pair of boots and she kept the pair of us, and came back home here. Grandma had died, and Grandpa was ready to sell the house and move to Florida, but Mom convinced him to give it to her instead. So she raised us alone, and I guess she gets some points for that, but not too many, because she never missed an opportunity to remind us of all that she had given up. Her glamorous life and her fabulous friends.

"I was seven years old when I told her to go back to them, and when I said it I was half certain she would, but even then I was damned if she was gonna hold that over my head for the rest of my life. Jaclyn started crying. 'Mommy, don't go, please don't go.' Mom slapped her for crying, and then me for making her cry. Or maybe she slapped us 'cause she liked to see the shape of her hand across our cheeks."

Jess paused and glanced to her right. "No," she said, shaking her head. "I'm telling my story the way I see it, and I don't wanna be fair to her right now." Putting her hands beneath her head, she gazed upward once more.

"Anyway, she didn't leave. Told us that type of life was for the young and beautiful, and she wasn't either of those anymore, not after we'd stolen her youth, and wrecked her body too. Not only were we responsible for her stretch marks, but we'd also pushed her up four clothing sizes. You'd think KFC might've shared some of the blame, but no, Mom didn't see it that way. Her being so unhappy and making us so unhappy, it just felt like the way life had always been and would always be. But Mom must've decided she needed a change. Some women might've found Weight Watchers and aerobics, but ours found Jesus and she gave herself to him and his great church of judgment and shame. But that wasn't enough. She had to give Jesus her greatest treasure, and burn her sins. When she told us that, I was pretty sure Jaclyn and I were going on a spit, and Jesus was gonna be wearing Mick Jagger's snakeskin boots. Turns out the boots went on the big bonfire in the backyard, and we were headed to Bible camp to begin our journey on the road to redemption. Except I wasn't going down that road, and nobody could make me. Jaclyn, though, she ran straight toward it, as if Jesus was the nice daddy we'd always hoped Mom might someday bring home."

Jess sighed softly.

"That was the first time I lost my sister, and I didn't even know it until it was too late. We were never those mind-reading, practically-share-a-brain type of twins, but we had something better. We saw each other clearly. Knew the other better than we knew ourselves. Our first week at Bible camp, Jaclyn asked to be baptized. They had a pool they used, so she went all the way in, and it seemed like they held her under for such a long time, like they literally wanted her to be reborn. I remember trying to see her face beneath the water and thinking that if she looked scared, I was gonna jump in and pull her out. But I couldn't see her, and even years and years later when I looked at her, it was like she was still underwater. Of course, some of that might've been from me, because my new motto was smoke 'em if you got 'em. And I almost always had 'em."

Pinching her forefinger and thumb together, Jess brought them to her lips and inhaled deeply as if taking a drag from an imaginary joint.

"The second time I lost my sister was the night she went on a date with Steven Benedict. His dad is a big deal at the church. He has lots of money, and used a bunch of it for this seventy-foot cross they built near the highway. I was there when Steven picked

Jaclyn up at the house, and Mom smiled at him even though we weren't technically supposed to be going out on dates. But this was Steven Benedict, and they were going to the teen prayer meet at the church—so it was okay.

"His eyes were too close together, and I didn't like him. I looked at Jaclyn. And for the first time in years I saw her clearly again, and I knew that she didn't like him either, and that the only reason she was letting him hold her hand in his sweaty little paw was because she was completely desperate and didn't know what else to do. And then I blinked, and she was smiling at him, and I thought I'd made it all up in my head. I told her to say a prayer for me. Those were the last words I said to my sister, because the next time I saw her, she was you."

"Wait," I said, not because the story was going too fast, but because the black was coming and I could no longer feel Dex's hand in mine. I was leaving this now for another, and that was all the warning I could give before I disappeared.

DOING IT

Jaclyn stands, a hand to her head. "I feel sick. Migraine, I think."

Immediately, the room goes silent. They stare at her, and I stare at them—gauging their reaction. She is green and trembling. You can almost see the headache pounding behind her eyes. No one can fake that. All the suspicions that flared up when she entered the room with Steven are extinguished.

Or not.

Steven's face contorts, trying to find the right way to arrange his rodent-like features so they express surprise and concern. He shouldn't even bother. In an instant he gives them both away. Jumping to his feet, he grabs hold of her with his grasping hands, as if she'd just called his Powerball numbers and was his winning lottery ticket too.

Everyone in the youth prayer group can see it as clearly as the outline of a condom in the back pocket of his crisp khaki pants.

The door clicks closed behind them, and the speculation begins.

They're doing it.

They've done it, she's pregnant, and now with nothing to lose, they're doing it again.

No surprise, everyone knows what her sister's like. Twins look alike. Act alike.

Everyone is talking, except me. Folding my hands in my lap, I pretend to pray, as if that's my true reason for coming here. Really I'm waiting. In a few minutes I'll walk out that door too, and they can whisper about me as well.

Right now they're wondering why I'm here, when the plaster Virgin Mary on my aunt's front lawn makes it clear that I belong at the Catholic church at the other end of town. They know how

I came to their school this year, transferring all the way from California. A world away and yet, thanks to Facebook, close enough for all the rumors to follow. Math whiz and cheerleader. Smart, pretty, popular, and—as if that wasn't enough—the nicest girl in school too. That's who I had been. Except that wasn't me. That had been Rose. The real Rose.

Her old classmates had been all too ready to spread the tale of how on Memorial Day weekend, right before the end of her sophomore year, she changed completely. She was at a friend's beach house up in Santa Barbara, and this freak boy from school showed up. A stalker thing, everyone agreed. He'd been her lab partner in chemistry. That's probably what made him think he had a chance with her. Couldn't be anything else, he was so out of her league. Half his face was all messed up from when his house, which doubled as a meth lab, exploded. His mom had died and his dad went to jail. Everyone figured he'd quickly follow in one of his parents' footsteps. The weird thing was, Rose left with him and didn't return until the next morning. No one knew that they'd fallen in love. Or that he was the one who refused to be with her, that he told her it would never work out. But Rose had never been denied anything she'd wanted, and she wanted him more than anything. So she got him . . . and lost everything else.

After that, she wasn't the same. They called it trauma. That was why she could no longer remember the cheers she'd done a hundred times. Why the advanced equations she'd easily solved the week before completely befuddled her. But that was nothing compared to the guy she chose to date at the new school her parents sent her to after that disastrous Memorial Day. Not that she chose. I didn't choose him either. He couldn't have been more different from the boy Rose had given her soul for. Her new boyfriend, Paul, was a jerk, best known for getting a Land Rover on his sixteenth birthday and for roaming the halls calling out "Hey, fag" to anyone he didn't like. He was different, too, though. He'd changed just a week after Rose arrived in Ohio. But nobody really noticed. Going from jerk to full-fledged asshole isn't such a huge jump.

My cell beeped. Speak of the devil. A text from my boyfriend the full-fledged asshole.

Is it done yet?

I don't respond to him. Instead I send a text to Rose's mother in California. A few weeks ago we'd made awkward small talk over the Thanksgiving turkey. I could feel her eyes on me constantly, searching for the daughter she'd once known.

I am in love with Paul. We are running away together. Don't look for me. You'll never see me again.

It is all a lie. Except for the last part. Her mother never will see Rose again. No one will.

I put the phone back in my purse. Everyone keeps talking, pretending not to notice me. I walk out the door and down the empty hallway. Slinging my purse over my shoulder, I feel the weight of the razor as it thumps against my back.

It will hurt me worse than that before this night is over.

The hallway is gray and has the same musty smell as the rest of the building. I go the way Jaclyn told me. Right out the door and then straight on. I want the last door on the left. Someone attempted to paint the words *Child Care* on the wood in a cheery bright red, but they were too heavy-handed, and wiggling lines drip from several of the letters. Above the words is a small square of glass. I peer inside.

Voyeuristic. As part of Allison Swan's SAT prep, her parents had her write out a page of the dictionary every day. My vocabulary grew expeditiously that year. I'd previously thought *voyeuristic* meant someone who liked to travel, but really it's a fancy word for a Peeping Tom. For me. It's funny to think I hate this part, when everything that comes after it is really much worse. But yeah, I hate this part and am relieved that the room is completely dark. I can't see a thing.

"Your boyfriend slept with my sister last night." Jaclyn had stood next to my table in the corner of the library I liked to sometimes hide in, needing a break from the whole high school experience. I knew who she was. Had made a point of finding her face in the crowd after her name had shown up as the first of two choices on a piece of paper. She was a grade lower than me, and this was my first time seeing her up close. Her frumpy clothes and the big wooden cross hanging around her neck instantly marked her as being part of the Fundies crowd.

"Um, okay," I'd said, uncertain if this was part of her religious beliefs—confessing other people's sins.

She went bright red, and her face scrunched up as if I'd just cursed her out or something. Then she turned and walked away.

"Wait," I called, and she did. I hesitated, pretending to think about what to say next, pretending the decision hadn't been made the moment I saw her crack. I could never resist picking the broken ones, not merely damaged but broken so badly they already had tiny little pieces missing.

Jaclyn waited, saying nothing, betraying no impatience with twitchy fingers or jangling knees. I felt it though. She'd come to me, wanting to shake things up. Wanting to change her life. Of course, she'd intended to piss her sister off, or get my boyfriend in trouble. I had something bigger in mind, and it told me to skip the soft sell. She was ready to buy.

"There's something you want. Isn't there? But you think you can't have it." I paused, letting her repeat my words in her head and make them her own. "But what if you could? What if it was yours for the asking?"

She stared at me, quiet and still. Her chest rose as she took a deep breath. "Then I'd ask."

Looking back, it was almost too easy. When she'd pointed Steven out to me, I'd known something wasn't right. It didn't add up. I could've backed out; there was still time to choose the second girl. But I hadn't, and now I am here.

"Sorry, Jaclyn," I whisper, and press the door latch.

"No, stop!"

I freeze, but the words aren't meant for me.

"I said stop. Steven, I don't want this."

"Yes, you do. You said you did. You're just scared. It'll be okay."

"No-oh—"

The single word is cut off. Muffled.

My initial surprise is already gone, or maybe I wasn't really all that surprised. Whatever her reason for choosing Steven, it wasn't love. I'd known that. But still, she'd made the deal. No returns or refunds.

On the other side of the door I hear the scuffling sounds of a struggle. Jaclyn is a small girl; five minutes and it will be over. If it bothers me to hear them, I just need to cover my ears. Then he'll leave, and I'll finish the deal. Yes, it's terrible. A new low after decades spent in quicksand.

There is a high-pitched squeak. Either his excitement or her fear. The twenty-pound weight that constantly sits on my chest, making it hard to breathe, shifts. It burns, beautifully. My breaths come faster, and they are filled with fire.

I push the door open. Fluorescent light from the hallway spills into the dark room. They are outside the brightest wedge of direct light, in a far corner, and haven't even noticed my entrance.

He straddles Jaclyn, who is facedown on a colorful rug. One of his hands keeps her arms pinned together, twisted behind her back. Her ankle-length jean skirt has been pulled up to her thighs, leaving her legs white and exposed. His other hand jerks at his brown braided leather belt, struggling to get it undone. Her eyes are squeezed close, and her mouth is free. She could scream, yell, and people would come running. But those people are just as likely to stone her as help. Instead she softly pleads. "Don't do this, Steven. Please don't do this."

He doesn't even hear her.

The door snicks closed behind me, and this is what makes Steven stop.

"What was that?"

I am already moving across the room. My eyes adjusting to the darkness, hunting Steven. The athletic body that I live in finally remembers how to high kick. Fluid and graceful. A shift of weight, and my foot flicks out, finding the sweet soft spot directly behind his chin. His jaw snaps closed with a clack, and his head leads the rest of his body in a backward arc, until he connects with the floor.

He groans; I advance. Grabbing two handfuls of his blue

button-down shirt, I haul him up and slam him back down. *Thunk.* His head hits the floor. He blinks blearily. I do it again. And again. And again. Until his eyes stay closed and his mewling mouth goes slack. Only then do I release him, even though it's not enough. I want to find my razor and slice him to bits.

One step back from him and then another and another. Finally my blood stops pounding so loudly that it fills my ears, and I hear the sound of hoarse and ragged breathing. Like someone desperately trying not to cry, and failing. I look toward Jaclyn, but she is wide-eyed and silent. My fingers find my cheeks and feel the wetness there. The last time I cried . . . it was quite a while ago. Funny, I remember it being a cleansing experience. A release. But this is just messy. And ill timed.

Tired of fighting my shaky legs, I sink to the ground beside Jaclyn. "It's time to pay," I inform her, but there is none of the usual steel in my voice. It's more of a warning. *Run now.* She only nods.

"Sure," she says. And then she snickers. "I'm an idiot. Why did I make him want me? That makes no sense at all. I should've asked you to make me want him."

Her laughter is sharp and cutting. I close my eyes against it. "I need you to say the words. 'Yes, I will pay.'"

She quiets, and I think that now she will resist. I am wrong again. "Of course. I always pay. Always. So, yes. Yes, I will pay."

After this, her fate is sealed. And so is mine.

Dex held me while I was away. And I had been somewhere else. Every time I found another piece of the past, I wasn't remembering it so much as reliving it. As I blinked back to the present, he stayed silent, giving me a few minutes to reorient myself.

"Where's Jess?" I finally asked.

"Right here," she said, and I looked up to see her stepping out of the trees at the far end of the clearing, a large glass jar in her hand. "I brought Jaclyn's heart, thought you might want to see it."

It was exactly what I'd come for. To witness with my own two eyes that some solid piece of Jaclyn still existed. But as Jess placed the jar directly in front of me, I didn't want to see. Not anymore. And yet I found it impossible to look away.

The heart bobbed in some sort of liquid. Who knew that hearts floated, yet there it was, doing just that. It was almost calming to look at. A muted pink, instead of dark red; throw some fake snow and glitter in there, and you'd have a macabre snow globe. As if showing off, the heart spun in a circle, and I could see the missing section from where Annaliese had repeatedly bitten in.

The nausea came quickly. I had only enough time to slap my hand over my mouth and rush toward the tree line before my bottomless cup of coffee came up and out. Even then I couldn't shake the taste of that heart. I closed my eyes and willed them to picture something else.

Bunnies. Butterflies. Bites of a bright-red bloody heart. There was no escaping it.

The worst part was, the heart hadn't made me sick. I'd puked because I'd been fighting against the hunger. Slowly I uncurled my hands. I'd had them clenched so tightly my fingers were stiff. Not giving in to the hunger was like trying to hold my breath until everything went black. It went against the body's instinct. We need air to live. And the part of me that was the hunger needed that heart. Needed to take another bite. Needed to finish it off.

Footsteps crunched behind me. "It's all right," Dex said softly. "She put it away."

"Okay," I said, but it wasn't. Jess had done it on purpose, had wanted to see me suffer. I couldn't blame her. Over the years I'd taken pounds and pounds of flesh; all she took was my breakfast.

After a few rounds of breath strips I was able—with Dex's help—to get on my feet again.

"We should go," he said to Jess, and I knew he said it not because of our time constraints but because he didn't want her to hurt me again.

"No," I said, surprising myself. "She has to finish her story. When Jaclyn left . . . for good."

Jess studied me for a minute. Then, looking toward the tree-tops, she smiled. "I can walk and talk. Wouldn't want you to be late getting home."

She didn't wait for us to agree but simply strode out of the trees, in the same direction we'd come from. Dex and I fell into step behind her.

"After Jaclyn became you, she started dating Steven—"

"No," I interrupted. "It wasn't Steven. Not anymore." The boy who I'd beaten senseless as Rose was the same boy whose arms I'd flown into as Jaclyn trying to send a message to Gwen. Eric must've taken him soon after I became Jaclyn.

Jess faltered for the space of half a step, but then with a nod began moving steadily once more. "Good. Good riddance. He deserved it."

I couldn't argue with that. I was glad that Eric had chosen him . . . even if it didn't make sense. From what I'd remembered, he didn't usually take the victims of the lust spell. If he had, then right now he would be Logan instead of the round little red-headed boy. Given a choice, I'm sure that would have been his preference.

"At first Mom was thrilled about Steven and Jaclyn," Jess continued. "They were both devoted to the church, and she believed they were only holding hands and praying together. Then she caught them making out. At the time I thought Jaclyn was so stupid, getting caught like that. Only later, when Jaclyn told me how you'd had it all staged, did I get it.

"Mom locked her away, told her she would never see daylight, much less Steven, again. Jaclyn ran away. I guess she would've disappeared and we would have always wondered what happened to her, except Mom wasn't going to let her get away that easily. She tore apart the house looking for some sort of clue. And she found it. Oh boy, did she find it. A letter from a girl saying she was in love with Jaclyn and knew Jaclyn felt the same way, and she wished things hadn't gone so badly between them. It was from some girl in Buffalo, and, funnily enough, when Steven's parents found out he was missing too, they used his cell to track him to the same place."

Jess laughed, and it had the same bitter edge as the one I'd heard from Jaclyn. "If she'd thought Jaclyn running away with a boy was bad, then the thought of her running away to a girl . . . well, that was just the end of the world.

"Mom left with Steven's dad on a Friday night and came back early Sunday morning in a rental car. I woke up and it was still dark out. Mom was standing over me. 'Get up,' she said. 'I need your help.' I followed her out to the car, and it was only when she unlocked the trunk that I saw her hands were red, and that the rest of her was too. The trunk opened and by then I knew that Jaclyn was dead and I expected to see her body, but there was only a wad of bloody rags."

Jess's voice was cold and emotionless. As if she was merely

reporting a story she'd been told, instead of one she'd lived. I understood that. The need to distance yourself. As much as I wanted to reach forward with a touch, I didn't. That kind of comfort—especially from me—could break her.

"'You killed her,' I screamed, and Mom slapped me. Then she told me that she hadn't killed Jaclyn, that she had saved her. Not her body, but her soul. She tried to bring Jaclyn's body home to bless it and bury it, but it had crumbled to dust in her hands. Only her heart survived. That was all we had left of Jaclyn and we had to keep it safe."

We'd reached the house, and Jess walked up to the sagging porch and sat on the top step, facing us. "She unwrapped that bunch of rags, and put Jaclyn's heart in my hands. I didn't know what to do, so I started walking toward the trees, and as I did I remembered an old hollow where we used to hide things when we were kids. I put it there, and by the time I was walking back to the house, I could hear the sirens of the police cars coming to take Mom away. Later I found out she'd called to hand herself in."

Jess stood and turned toward the front door. "I don't get to be here much anymore. They sent me to live with a foster family. On the weekends, I get a friend to drive me out here. It's home, you know? Anyway, I gotta go in and clean up after the stupid ghost hunters that like to get drunk and come down here. Drive careful, and tell the girls Jaclyn says hey." Reaching around the loose board, Jess pushed the door open. Instead of a horror-movie squeal, it slid open silently. Jess squatted down to duck beneath the board, but then turned back to me.

"Hey, Jaclyn wants to know. You get the name of the next girl yet?"

I nodded, feeling sick as I guessed what question was coming next.

"You gonna do it? Cut yourself outta this one and be eaten into another?"

The way she put it, I should have been on my knees puking again, but instead my stomach twisted with something else. Something worse. Hunger. Still I wanted to tell her no, act horrified and offended at the very suggestion.

And not just for her and Jaclyn. Beside me I could feel Dex tense, waiting for my answer. Make the right choice. I could sense him silently urging me on. My very own Jiminy Cricket.

The hunger screamed inside me, a growing baby demanding to be fed. Every day it became harder to make it hush. To pretend it wasn't there. But Jess's story was also inside me. Screaming in another way. Dividing me. Could I take another girl after hearing all that? After looking into Jess's eyes and seeing Jaclyn there too?

It was too late to save Jaclyn. It was beginning to look like it was too late to save myself too. Funny, because that was what I'd come here for—a way to save my own skin . . . or Annaliese's. It had never even crossed my mind to worry about the next girl up on the chopping block. But now I made myself remember her, not as a name on a paper but as a real girl.

Lacey. The paper said Lacey Lee Beals, but I'd known her as just plain Lacey. She was a real girl who had rolled her eyes at her mom even as she followed orders. A real girl who confessed she'd started smoking as a weight-loss strategy, but after six months of it still hadn't lost a pound. A real girl who complained that babysitting her brother was a chore, but who also would kiss his little head every time he toddled by.

That was her life, not mine. I shouldn't be able to put it on as easily as the sweater she'd given me to wear on my way to the hospital. The sweater that I'd thoughtlessly left behind, tangled in the sheets of the hospital bed.

I clenched my teeth against the hunger's wail, uncertain how long I could keep it locked inside.

Dex and Jess stared, still waiting for my answer.

"I hope not," I finally said.

Jess nodded. That wasn't exactly the answer she'd wanted to hear, or maybe she didn't believe me. I had no chance to convince her further. Without another word, she slipped into the crumbling house and the door thumped closed behind her.

"You hope not?" Dex said, and I could feel him pushing for something more concrete.

I didn't have any certainties to give him. "Sorry, should I have said, 'Definitely not'?"

Dex looked back at the house, and I knew he'd read into Jess's tight nod too. "Sometimes a tiny lie can be a big thing."

He was right, and that was why I didn't tell him how close I'd been leaning toward a yes, instead of my mostly no. I forced a grin. "Lie? To a ghost, a girl who talks to a ghost, and a boy who sees the future? I honestly didn't think that was an option."

Dex smiled at this. Of course he did; with all the burdens he carried, somehow his smiles were still so easy to coax out.

As one we turned away, retracing our earlier path through the overgrown yard. Glancing over my shoulder, I gave the house one last look. There was no sign of Jess. Or Jaclyn.

"Will she be okay?" I asked, wondering if he knew how things ended for Jess.

Dex shook his head, but I couldn't tell whether that meant he'd seen something terrible, or that he simply didn't know.

I decided to believe the latter. It gave her the benefit of the doubt, the same one I'd given myself. At least that option gave both of us a chance.

HOW

TOMORROW

Tomorrow is a lie
I have already told.

Tomorrow is a party
I am not invited to.

Tomorrow is a boy
I wished for and received.

Tomorrow is the virginity
I will be losing.

Tomorrow is three words
I must confess.

Tomorrow is hoping
I don't give more than I gain.

—ARG

"Home sweet home," Dex yawned as he drove the car into the garage. For the last two hours I'd watched him struggle against the weight of his eyelids, while he pushed harder against the gas pedal, determined to get me home on time. And he'd succeeded. The clock on the dashboard read 11:13.

"I should get inside, they'll be back soon." But I didn't move. I couldn't . . . until Dex leaned in to kiss me, and then I threw myself at him, clinging tight. It wasn't like our other kisses. My birthday was no longer Monday, a day somewhere in the distance. It was tomorrow. And that made this kiss feel like good-bye.

I didn't even realize a few tears had leaked out until Dex's fingers gently brushed them from my cheeks.

"Ugh." I scrubbed the wetness away. "Stupid blubbering. I'm sorry. It's just—there's not enough time."

"I know," Dex answered. "Why do you think I broke the speed barrier getting us back? I wanted to be able to spend some time with you without being squeezed into a car or in the presence of a girl who talks to ghosts." He tapped the clock, which had ticked away to 11:20. "Noon was your cutoff time, if I remember correctly. That gives us forty minutes. Want to join me in making the most of it?"

"Yes." My answer was immediate. As was Dex's response. He

threw his door open and slid from the car.

"Race you to the door."

I ran after him. Halfway around the house, he let me catch him. Or he caught me. Grabbing hold of my hands, he swung me out in a circle. Clinging tight, I leaned back and watched the world spin by. Then our lips met, and the world spun in a different way.

Without coming up for air we somehow found our way into the basement. Once the door closed, we pressed closer, wanting—needing—more. "Anna, we don't—"

"Yes, we do."

"But you . . ."

My fingers on his button fly stalled. "Don't you want to?"

Dex laughed. "Oh no, I do. I really do. But do you? Really?"

I kissed him again, pulling away long enough to murmur against his skin. "Yes."

And it was true. Maybe it could've-should've-would've waited, except the ticking time bomb of an eighteenth birthday made me think that I had a limited number of laters. Seize the moment. Seize the boy. I was frantic to be closer—to complete the bond between us. We'd shared secrets, horrible visions, and now . . . and now something else.

That seemed to be enough reassurance for Dex. Awkward and giggling, we pulled and tugged at our clothes until at last they fell away. Dex snagged a packet of condoms from his bottom desk drawer and presented them to me with a sheepish shrug.

"To be safe," he said. "And just so you know, I didn't have these here prepared, expecting this or anything. They've been here since the last time, my first time, kind of. . . ."

"Who was it?" I don't know why I asked. It was the last thing I wanted to think about right then. I was supposed to be seizing, not quizzing.

"No one!" Dex shook his head hard, emphasizing the point.

"No one?"

I didn't mean it as a criticism, but Dex took it as one. "Not like that. It was a someone. A girl someone. A friend. Well, a friend of a friend. Okay, to be completely accurate, the friend of a former friend. It was after I became notorious for supposedly leaking that video. The friend of the former friend wanted an introduction. I don't think I was exactly what she expected. She had the idea I was some dark rebel raging against the machine. But I guess she figured she was here so she should just make the best of it. . . . It didn't go well. I had a vision in the middle of us, er, you know."

"Oh no," I said. "A vision? Like, you saw her die?"

"Uh, no. I saw that when we first met. This was . . ." Dex went bright red. "She, uh, wanted to watch a movie on the computer while we did, you know, and it was someone in the movie that triggered it."

"Oh no," I said again. And then, curious, "Who was the

actor? Would I know the movie?"

Dex turned even darker. "Not that kind of movie," he muttered.

It took me a moment. Then, "Oooh. Oh-ooh."

He nodded. I giggled. Then he did too. In the next instant we were both clutching our stomachs, standing in only our underwear, and laughing so hard it hurt. His laugh was so funny, a deep chuckle with an occasional snort. I couldn't help imitating him, and that set off the tickle fight. Dex's long fingers found every sensitive spot on my body, until I flopped onto the gigantic beanbag chair in surrender. Dex fell beside me. Our bodies pressed together warmly. The desperate need of before had dissolved, leaving behind only the low and constant buzz of tension that had been between us almost from the beginning. Still, it felt like the moment I'd meant to seize had passed. I didn't know whether to feel disappointed or relieved.

Dex's head dipped toward mine, so our temples pressed together. "I'm glad it didn't work out with her," he said softly. "I know I'm a guy and supposedly need to sow oats or collect notches or whatever, and I do sometimes want that stuff, but . . ." I felt his shoulder shrug against mine. "I didn't even like that girl. She was weird." He laughed. "Like I should talk, right?"

I found Dex's hand, resting on his stomach, and gave it a squeeze. "You're a good weird."

Another shrug. "I think the former friend meant well. Two

weirds make a right, or something. Anyway, it wasn't good, and I knew it, but I had this horrible thought like this might be my only chance, like I'd never meet anyone who could deal with me, and that I'd have to settle for a girl who was willing to settle for me too."

My heart squeezed, not with sympathy, but with something larger. It hurt, and it made me want to say something stupid. Something like, "I love you." I bit back the impulse.

Dex sat up a bit, leaning on his elbow so he loomed over me. "If I'd known you were coming, I would've waited. I think I—"

Grabbing hold of Dex, I pulled him down on top of me. Our lips met and his unspoken words were swept away. Maybe he was going to say he loved me. It would be too much. Too soon. Or maybe it was only that he liked me. That would've been way too little.

The kiss, though, was perfect. It said it all. And yet it wasn't enough. We pressed closer, needing something more. And when we found it together, it was . . . Not perfect. No, it was simpler than that and infinitely more complicated. It was just right. As if it and we were meant to be.

Afterward, I curled up against Dex as he pulled a fuzzy fleece blanket over us.

"You okay?" He whispered the words, and this, too, felt right, like he wasn't quite ready to break the spell.

"Yeah, it was definitely better than my first time too."

Even as I said it, I realized that the first time I'd been thinking of wasn't mine. It was Annaliese's.

You were right. Love and lust are different.

That was what she'd said to me. And once more I could see her under Logan from where I watched, silent in the trees. But now I could also feel the tree stump digging into her left hip. And I saw the spider dangling from a tree branch, precariously close. Logan grunted, and I thought, Finally, but he continued pumping away.

It was Dex's heartbeat, still thudding heavily, that kept me anchored in the present. I pulled away from Annaliese. Still, it was almost as if I could feel her, hovering near, just like Jess had described the stringers.

Dex kissed me. The pull of the stringers faded as I kissed him back.

It was true what I'd told Annaliese. Love and lust were different. But I'd also been wrong. Because sometimes they could also be one and the same.

When it was time to leave, I had to force my feet to move. Turning away from Dex, I focused on the mechanics of lifting each leg, setting one foot down and then doing it again and again until the house came closer. Digging my hand into my pocket, I grasped hold of the key like it was a lifeline. The whole time I could feel Dex, waiting, watching me.

I turned back to him, refusing to let this be the end.

"I'll see you again," I promised, and as I said the words it occurred to me that if I became Lacey, I could still see him. And for a few more years—and a few more girls—after that too. As Dex got older we'd have to stop, but by then we'd have had time together—maybe not enough time, but more than the few hours that added all together barely made up two whole days.

I was horrified at the thought. But hopeful too. And then horrified again.

Quickly, I spun away, not wanting Dex to see, knowing he would hate the idea. And hate me for thinking it. For wanting it.

Dex was right. I had a choice; I'd always had a choice. And every time I'd chosen myself.

This time it would be different. This time I would make the right choice.

I didn't believe it though. Not really.

And a part of me still hoped for some way out of making any choice at all.

FOREVER

"Your mom is three sheets to the wind," Franky announces, walking into my bedroom without even knocking.

"She's not," I answer. A reflex. Deny everything. Even though

I've been lying on my bed, staring up at the ceiling, wondering when exactly she made the transfer to two o'clock.

For the longest time, since I was ten at least, she'd held steady at three p.m. If you caught her before then, she'd be hungover, but she got things done. Lunches were made, and laundry was loaded. Slightly after three, she was happy and tipsy. This was a good time to ask for something. A few dollars for a new shirt or permission to do something hungover Mom might've deemed too dangerous. As night began to fall, it was best to avoid her altogether—her moods were too difficult to gauge and shifted too quickly.

Franky throws himself onto the narrow bed beside me, pressing his body against mine. "I told her your brother left something up here for me." Sliding his hand up beneath my shirt, he whispers into my ear, "I don't think she guessed that it was you."

I slap his hand away. "Not now."

"Well, then I'll go." But he doesn't move. He wants me too much. It is one of the things I most like about him.

Several moments pass. Downstairs the TV blares, carrying the sound of canned laughter up to us. "I thought you were leaving."

He sighs, as if his heart is breaking. "I love you, you know."

I do know. The words make me feel warm inside the same way a few sips of my mother's drinks will. It fades, though, and leaves a terrible taste in my mouth afterward.

Franky pushes himself up on one elbow. "Anna, say you love me too." His eyes boring into mine are intense and demanding. It would almost be frightening if I hadn't known Franky since he was a little boy. We grew up in the same neighborhood, and he is my older brother's best friend. Often my own best friend, Katie, and I made a foursome with them, tearing through one another's yards in a never-ending game of follow the leader. Tommy was always the leader. I followed because he was my older brother and only sibling. Katie followed because she'd been born with a crush on him. But Franky followed because he was shy, clumsy, and not much good at anything besides following someone bigger and stronger and brighter.

Except then he'd gone away to college, once again following Tommy—to the state university this time. A year later, it was like he was a different person. He'd finally ditched the Coke-bottle glasses and let his hair grow out like the rest of the boys. But that wasn't it. He walked differently, talked differently, and looked at you differently. Like he knew something you didn't, and thought it was a great joke.

And he no longer followed Tommy. Apparently, they'd had some sort of falling-out. Something to do with Tommy losing his football scholarship, although I don't know how that could possibly be Franky's fault. Typical Tommy. Not taking responsibility and blaming it on poor Franky. Truth is,

Tommy has never been a very good friend to Franky, and I suspect that half the reason Franky is in love with me is to get back at him.

"You don't love me," I tell Franky now. Testing him. Wanting to hear him say the words again.

At this his mouth curves into a smile that makes him seem totally unlike the Franky I knew growing up. He looks almost evil. It's scary, but also exciting. His fingers pluck at my shirt.

"You're wearing Tommy's old high school jersey."

I shrug. "He left it behind on one of his washdays, and I stole it. It's comfy."

"You look like one of his girlfriends. Wearing it and thinking about how you'd like him to screw you."

I laugh because I know it will annoy him. This is one of the games we play. He tries to shock me with his new bad self, and I refuse to be impressed. "I think you're jealous."

"I am. Makes me miss my sister. When I was a sickly little kid, she was the only one who would touch me. She'd give me sponge baths with this rough old cloth and horrible lye soap, but she didn't scrub hard like some people would have. Sometimes I would purposely make messes, just to have her clean me again."

I push him away, suppressing a shiver. "You're sick."

He smiles at me. "You remind me of her, you know."

"You don't have a sister, idiot." Still I feel chilled. Suddenly not wanting to be so close to him, I stand and take a few steps away.

He follows, putting his hands on my waist and pulling me close. "Maybe I did. In another time, another life. Maybe I've lived a hundred years, and a hundred different lives."

We've made out several times, and in baseball terms have been closing in on third base, but now I feel another shiver of revulsion. I don't want him to know, though, don't want him to think he's won.

"Nicotine craving," I say, slipping away. I cross quickly to my desk and flip open the lid on my faded childhood jewelry box. The tiny ballerina begins her pirouettes while the *Nutcracker Suite* tinkles. Digging into the space below her, filled with ticket stubs and earrings with no matching pair, I finally find the pack of cigarettes I've hidden away.

"Eureka, my Winstons!" I say, overly enthusiastic as the box tips to its side, spilling everything out onto the floor. "They taste good like a cigarette should."

I toss the pack to Franky, where he is leaning against the window frame. "Light me one."

Quickly, I shove the odd bits back into the box in large fistfuls. One paper eludes me—a movie ticket stub from years ago, probably one of the last ones I saved before I decided that kind of junk wasn't worth keeping. Or maybe I saved this one, despite thinking that, because I wanted to remember.

Tommy and I went together. Just the two of us off to an early Saturday-morning matinee. We'd wanted to get away from Mom, and ended up seeing Disney's *Pinocchio*, even though we were too old for cartoons. We both remembered seeing it at a drive-in, when we were still little enough to watch the movie without worrying about how much Mom was drinking and whether she would get loud or sick or angry. A long time ago.

"Good movie?" Franky plucks the stub from my fingers and holds out a cigarette to put in its place.

"You forgot to open the window," I say, once again crossing the room away from him. With a grunt I yank it open and lean out, taking a long drag of my cigarette. "It was okay," I finally answer his question, as he joins me. "Everybody makes it like the whole movie is about his nose growing. Like it's a story about not lying. But that's a small part of it."

"And what's the bigger part?" Franky peers at me intently, like the question is a test.

I shrug, make a joke. "I don't know. What to do if you get trapped inside a whale."

Franky laughs, and smoke billows from his mouth.

"Kinda dark and scary for kids," I say as I flick the ticket stub out the window. The wind catches it, carrying it away.

"Nothing's scary for kids. They don't know enough to be scared."

"Hmmm," I say, not agreeing or disagreeing.

Franky smokes fast, sucking hard on his cigarette, quickly reducing it to ashes. I like to savor mine. As he tosses his butt out the window into the weedy garden below, he turns to me. "I'm not going back to school next month."

I almost drop my cigarette in surprise. "What? Why?"

"Isn't it obvious? I want to be with you. Forever. Starting now."

He has that intense look again. I focus on the red tip of my cigarette instead. "I don't believe in forever."

His fingers close over my cigarette's hot tip, extinguishing it. "Okay, then how long will you give me?"

My stomach clenches. I want to move away, but his hand locks around my wrist, holding me there. Letting my finished cigarette fall, I force a little shrug. "My plan is to leave this town the minute I turn eighteen, and not a second later. So that gives you exactly one year, three months, and nine days with me."

"Eighteen." Franky nods, dead serious. "I'll take it. Our love is endless until then."

"Hey, wait." I make myself laugh. "I didn't say love. I'll share my stolen cigarettes with you, and maybe a little bit more."

His fingers tighten, and I wince, but he doesn't seem to notice. "So you don't believe in forever, but you believe in stealing. I bet you don't believe in love either, but you do believe in lust."

"I'm a modern woman." The words come out wobbly, not confident like I want. I feel like a child, small and frightened.

Franky releases me, and then his hand is soft and concerned against my cheek. "You're all white, Anna. What's wrong? You afraid of something?"

You. I'm afraid of you. But I don't say it, because he looks so sincere, and I wonder if I imagined it. Katie once accused me of being afraid to love. Maybe she was right. I look at Franky and think that I could love him. That maybe I already do. He's exciting and dangerous but familiar and comforting all at the same time. And he loves me, and I keep pushing him away. Taking a deep breath, I let him in. Just a little.

"I'm afraid of being stuck here, like my mom."

He gathers me close, but it isn't pushy this time. His arms hold me loosely. I could easily get free, but now I don't want to. "I won't let that happen to you, Anna. You'll never be stuck anywhere if you stick with me."

"Okay," I whisper into his shirt.

Then we kiss, and I think that maybe this really is love.

Franky leans away slightly, and reaching into his pants pocket produces an old-fashioned razor. The kind a barber would use.

"Hey, that's my dad's," I protest, recognizing it.

Dad keeps it on top of his dresser along with his collection of silver dollars. Both have to do with his father, who worked as a barber his whole life, just like his father and grandfather before him. My grandfather wasn't working to make another barber. His son would go to college and become successful. The blade was a gift from him on the day of my father's high school graduation, to remind Dad where he came from. The silver dollars were to show him where he was going—to the rich world of banking.

"Hush," Franky says, snapping it open, and for some reason I do. My father never lets Tommy or me near the razor. He keeps it sharp and oiled the way his father would've. When we were little he told us it would take our fingers right off.

Now Franky holds out his wrist and with a flick of the blade slices right across one bright blue vein. For an instant nothing happens, as if his blood has been as taken by surprise as me. Then it gushes out, spilling down into his cupped hand.

"This is me making a promise," Franky says, and then he holds the razor out. "Will you promise too?"

I don't take the razor. Instead I reach for the bedsheet or paper or something to stanch the flow of blood. "Are you crazy? You're bleeding everywhere." My hand closes on one of my old T-shirts and I push it toward Franky, but he jerks his hand away.

"You promise, too, and then I'll stop the blood."

It is half threat, half dare, and totally crazy. I want to scream at him to get out, but without him I will have to get through the rest of the summer in my bedroom alone listening to my mom getting wasted downstairs. It's just a little blood, I tell myself, nothing much worse than the blood sisters' oath Katie and I took as children. And look at how well that stuck.

"Fine, I promise." The razor is heavier than I expected, and as it slices through my skin it hurts no more than a paper cut. Then the blood begins to flow and it burns. Franky brings our wrists together and wraps my old T-shirt around, binding us.

"Now we share the same blood again. And forever after," Franky says, his eyes intense.

Nothing is forever, I think, but the ridiculousness of this whole situation hits me, and instead I start to laugh.

"Sure," I say. "Forever and ever and ever and ever."

MONOPOLY MONEY

The mom's eyelashes were gone, set free by her constantly plucking fingers. Propped up against pillows, she sat in the center of her and the dad's huge bed, looking tiny and tired. But when she held her arms out in a silent demand for a hug, I dived straight into them without hesitation. If she had lost any strength, I couldn't detect it. Her hug was a bubble that held me suspended in space, safe.

In that one moment I was found, and more lost than ever.

"Oh, sweetie, I missed you so much," the mom said, slowly loosening her hold, even while I still gripped her tightly.

"I was worried," I said. It was true, more than I had even realized. A part of me had worried that I would never see her again.

"Oh, sweetie," the mom said, and her eyes looked past my shoulder to where the dad stood. "Your father wanted to bring you, but I—I didn't want it to be too scary for you. Especially after you'd just been in a hospital yourself. And they kept telling me I'd go home soon, but I think we had different definitions of soon, because I thought it meant a few hours and they seemed to believe it meant a few days."

"It's okay," I said, but my voice was small and hurt.

The mom swept her fingers across my forehead, and I couldn't help but lean into her once more. I wanted to tell her how I just woke from a terrible dream. Curling up beneath the sheets, I had thought that I would dream of Franky and Anna. The memory of them had grabbed me after I'd walked into the house. Instead, I'd had a normal nightmare. Well, maybe not normal.

I was Pinocchio, a girl version of him. I still had my puppet strings, though, and I was tangled in them. The more I struggled to get free, the more twisted and trapped I became. Finally, I simply lay there, crying, "I'm a real girl. I'm a real girl." Every time I said it, my nose grew longer, until it went from being a twig to an entire tree with separate branches that all grew up from my nose. A different girl sat on every branch, and each one held an apple plucked from the tree.

Bright red apples that dripped blood. I recognized each girl, could've called them all by name. Except I couldn't say anything, because I was underground, twisted into the roots of that horrible tree.

When the dad had gently shaken me awake, I'd jerked away, thinking he was part of the tree. "Annaliese, it's me. Sorry to wake you, but I wanted to let you know we're home. Took us a little longer than we expected to get checked out of the hospital. You have fun with Gwen last night?"

It had taken me a moment to pull out of the dream—the nightmare—and make sense of the dad's words. Even then all I could manage was a trembling "Uh-huh."

He studied me for a long minute as I packed my mouth full of breath strips from my bedside supply, but in the end he only said, "Your mom's in bed and she's gonna have to take it easy for a while. Okay?" I nodded. "She really wants to see you, so when you wake up, you can go on in."

I sat up. "I'm awake." Really I didn't feel fully awake until the mom's arms were wrapped around me. They should have reminded me of the strings, tying me up. But the opposite was true. I didn't have to tell her I was a real girl—she already believed it.

"I hope you didn't think we forgot about your birthday tomorrow," the mom said now.

I didn't want to talk about that. Couldn't talk about that.

"Why were you in the hospital?" I demanded instead. "Why won't you tell me?"

The mom and the dad exchanged another look. They both looked guilty. Caught.

"It's nothing bad," the dad said, sitting on the other side of the bed, next to the mom.

"Good news actually," the mom agreed.

I said nothing, waiting.

The mom nodded to the dad, as if giving him permission to speak. He shook his head. It was almost funny, the way they both didn't want to say it. Finally I took pity on them.

"You're pregnant, right?"

The looks of surprise on their faces. As if there were all that many medical problems that could be classified as good news. Also, her hand was pressed against her stomach, cupped gently, as if holding on to something precious and hidden.

The mom recovered first. "We found out a few weeks before we got the call about you. It was like two miracles at once, but we weren't sure how you . . ." The mom turned to the dad, uncertain. He tried to help her out.

"You'd always told us that you wanted a little brother or sister."

"That's true," the mom said, nodding. "But we didn't want to spring it on you. Everyone said you needed to slowly ease back into your old life. So we were waiting for the right time, but then

I thought I was miscarrying and I didn't want to tell you and upset you, if the baby was lost."

The mom choked up and the dad grabbed hold of her hand.

"The baby's fine," he said. Then he grinned, looking happier than I'd ever seen the dad before. "Babies actually. We're having twins." Through her tears the mom smiled too.

"Oh, wow, that's great." I said the words. I pushed my lips into a smile. I even clapped my hands, like a seal performing a trick for a piece of fish.

And it was great. Tomorrow was my deadline. Eighteen. The cut-off Anna had chosen. Then Annaliese would disappear from their lives once more. But this time they would have a replacement. Two of them, instead of one impostor.

A part of me hated those little unborn babies. She'd lost her eyelashes worrying about them. One for each eye.

"Your mom has to stay on bed rest until they're born," the dad said.

"Yes," the mom groaned. "And it's already driving me crazy."

"Well, Annaliese and I will keep you entertained, won't we?" The dad looked to me as if we were coconspirators.

I agreed, and to show the mom we meant it, the dad produced a pile of dusty board games from the closet. We played Scrabble and then Monopoly, laughing as the pieces slid off the board anytime one of us shifted on the bed. If the silences sometimes felt strained and the laughter forced, none of us mentioned it.

We were all determined to play at being the perfect happy family together.

Maybe they did it for the same reason as me—they just so badly wanted it to be true.

FAMILY

HAPPY BIRTHDAY

They sang happy birthday
and as I blew out
sixteen candles
I made my wish
that this year
will be different,
that this year
everything will change,
and that next year
when I blow out
seventeen candles
I'll be such a
crazy sexy cool
new kind of girl
that no one will
even know that it's . . .

only me.

—ARG

CAUGHT

"If the poor doctor hadn't taken pity on me and finally used the forceps to pull you out, your birthday would've been tomorrow instead of today. As it is, you were born at eleven fifty-three p.m. You just made the cutoff."

This was what the mom told me Monday morning when I went in to see her before leaving for school. I found myself wishing the doctor had been a bit less accommodating and given me one more day in the womb. Perhaps I was as unready to leave then, as now.

On the way to school, the dad gave me a different kind of birthday message.

"I received a very strange anonymous voice mail last night, saying that you've been spending some quality time with the boy next door. I also called Gwen's mom this morning to thank her for letting you stay over there the other night."

I was caught. Totally caught. And even though I knew it didn't really matter—it wasn't like it would make a difference if he grounded me after I was gone—I still tried to cover. "Oh yeah, I forgot to tell you. After you called I was so tired, I decided to stay home."

The dad said nothing, just put on his signal to turn in to the school. It was a damning silence. As we pulled up to the curb in front of the building, the dad sighed. "Okay, Annaliese.

Today is your birthday so you get a pass. But tomorrow I want the truth."

I could have just agreed and run away, but I couldn't resist pushing back. "And what about Mom? Does she want the truth too?" He hadn't told her, I'd bet anything. She would be too upset, and that wouldn't be good for her or the second-chance babies.

The dad's hand slammed down on the middle console. I'd never seen the dad mad before, but now he was pissed. At me. "Annaliese, I expect you to be a better person than this. I understand and I appreciate that you've been through a lot. But that is no reason to behave this way. Do you understand me?"

Face burning, I nodded.

"Good. Tomorrow all three of us will discuss this."

"Okay," I mumbled, fumbling for the door handle, feeling horrible and caught in my tangle of lies. As I slid out, the dad grabbed hold of my hand. I froze, afraid of what else he might say.

"Anni, I'm sorry for getting upset," he said, surprising me so much that I turned to meet his eyes. All the tension and anger were gone, and he looked almost chagrined, as if his anger had caught him unaware too. "I don't want to ruin your birthday. It's not every day you turn eighteen."

My smile wobbled along with my voice. "No, it's not." He squeezed my hand, and I squeezed his back. "Thanks."

Quickly, I climbed out and swung the door shut behind me, not wanting any more anger, any more understanding, and definitely no more *happy birthdays*.

Keeping my head down, I hurried toward the front doors. The only reason I was even bothering with school was to find Eric—quickly. I needed to know exactly what was supposed to happen today.

"Hey, Birthday Girl!" Gwen called, waving as she trotted across the parking lot.

I was ready to blow her off, not wanting to waste the time, but I remembered her trip to Ohio with Annaliese. And our moment of laughter in the hallway. She'd been Annaliese's friend, and now she was sort of mine too.

"Hey," I said, waiting for her to catch up.

"How was your looonngg weekend, you skipper, you?" Gwen asked as we walked into school together.

"Weird," I answered, scanning the hall for Eric.

"Well, mine was just boring. So entertain me with the weird."

"Well," I said, uncertain whether to say what I was about to say. "I think I might've remembered something."

"Oh my gosh, that's amazing!" Several people turned to look at Gwen's enthusiastic outburst. She didn't even notice; all of her attention was focused squarely on me. "So tell me. Tell me!"

I wavered a moment longer and then let the words come out

in a rush. "It's kind of random, but did we go on a road trip to Ohio together?"

Gwen's normally bouncy walk flattened out. She kept moving forward, but it was as if her feet were dragging against the floor now. "Yeah, we did," she answered cautiously, looking straight ahead.

I pretended not to notice her sudden change in behavior. "And did we have a fight too?"

Clutching my arm, Gwen propelled us into an empty classroom. Once there, she released me as if her hand was burning. Noticeably agitated, she walked several paces away before turning to meet my gaze. "What exactly did you remember, Annaliese?"

I gulped, feeling the hot coffee spilling over me, forgetting that the memory wasn't even mine. "I remembered that I was sorry. That I hadn't been a very good friend, and that I wished I'd been better." My shoulders lifted in a helpless little shrug. "That's all."

Gwen stared, her eyes wide, her lips trembling. For a second I could see tears threatening, and funny enough, I felt like a few of mine might escape too, but then she got a hold of herself. "Well, that's a great sign that you're having real memories and not those strange fantasies we talked about before. It's a breakthrough." She made a big show of looking at the clock on the wall, but she stared at it for too long, as if she'd forgotten how to tell time.

"We should get going," I said softly. "The bell's gonna ring soon."

"Yeah," Gwen agreed. She didn't move, though, and I waited with her. Then all at once she flung herself at me and wrapped me in a shaky hug. It was so quick, I had only a second to hug her back before she was heading out the door.

I followed her to the hallway, and we fell into the flow of students. A minute later the bell rang and we split off in different directions with a promise to see each other at lunch. But I didn't go to homeroom. Following an instinct that I was learning to listen to, I went to the bathroom near the cafeteria, the same one where Eric had once trapped me. As if my wish had made him appear, when I swung the door open he stood in front of the mirror, frowning at his reflection.

"I'll be glad to see the end of this face," he said, not even turning to look at me.

"And when will that be?" I hated having to ask him questions, being at his mercy.

He smiled. He knew it too.

"Soon." From his back pocket he produced a note folded into a neat little triangle and flicked it toward me. It bounced off my chest and onto the floor.

I nudged it with the toe of my shoe, as if it were radioactive. "What is it?"

"A note from Lacey. Telling you where to meet her tonight. And thanking you for all your help and boy advice. You two have really bonded over email."

"No." My shrill voice echoed off the bathroom walls, mocking me as I heard the uncertainty in that one word.

"Your mouth says no, but I think the hunger is gonna say yes." Eric laughed. "And once you accept that, you'll be a good girl and go to Lacey."

"No." I said it louder this time. He ignored me.

"She's just up the road at Buffalo State. Tomorrow she—well, by then you—will go home to Oklahoma. She's on a school trip, by the way, so you'll get to take a bus. I bet that will be fun for you. And while you're making new friends, I'll shed this fat kid and tie up a few other loose ends before meeting you down south. After that the only thing left is for us to fall in love all over again."

He held his arms out, as if I would run into them.

Instead, I picked the note up off the floor. Dropping it into the sink, I turned the water on and let it pour over the paper until it was limp and soggy. Then, using my fingernails, I shredded it to bits. This still wasn't enough. Carrying it into a stall, I scraped it off my hands into the toilet bowl. I flushed three times so that every last bit was washed away.

Eric lounged against the sink, watching me with a smirk. "You think that means something? You'll find her anyway. The hunger will take you to her. You already found her once. The only difference is that this time you'll know what to do."

I sagged against the stall door, defeated. He was right. The gentle tug that I'd once followed to Lacey's door was gone, replaced by something much stronger and more insistent. It was becoming painful not to give in and follow it.

"And what if I don't?"

"If you don't go to Lacey?" Eric shook his head. "Then I won't want to be near you when the hunger takes over, 'cause it won't be pretty. And anyone who is in the same room—they probably won't survive it either."

I shuddered, but it wasn't me. And it wasn't a shudder of repulsion. It was excitement. I could feel the hunger, like a snake curled up at my center, slowly unwinding and stretching out toward the picture Eric painted.

I tried to swallow the hunger back down, at the same time the green tiles of the bathroom walls went gray. "No," I gasped, grabbing hold of the sink, anything to hold on to the now. It was no use. The past had a hunger of its own that sucked me in and swallowed me whole.

FIRE

I am in the belly of the whale, building a fire to make him sneeze.

No, that's not right.

Where am I? Who am I? I used to tell myself I was Anna,

no matter what. Lately, it doesn't seem to matter as much. Or does it matter more?

I push my sticky lips apart, seeking moisture but tasting gas. With effort, I force my sticky eyelids open. A dark shape hovers above me. I bat at it, and it swings, hinges squeaking softly. Back and forth. My fingers grip the grass beneath me. I know where I am.

Home.

Or what was once my home. My family. Mom. Dad. Tommy. It's been three years and almost four girls, but still I thought I could go home again. Just climb into my old bed and tell them I was their daughter. Never mind I didn't look the same.

I told him I'd rather be dead than take another girl, and I was prepared for his fury. He surprised me, though. He tricked me. Smiled and told me it was okay. Took my hand and led me home, rang the doorbell for me when I was afraid. And he spoke, too, when I couldn't figure out what to say. "We have information about your daughter." Those were the magic words. We were in.

Oh God. What did he do?

Franky. It feels unfair to the memory of Franky to keep using his name, but that is where it started. Usually I try to call him nothing at all. Strip him of his name, the same way he took mine.

I scramble to my feet, but only make it to my hands and knees. My head bumps against the swing, and my clothes are wet and clinging and cold. Fire rages in the belly of the house, pushing out the windows, burning up everything inside.

And everyone.

He set the fire. That's what Franky did. But not to kill them. They were already dead.

I killed them.

They invited us to have dinner with them, and with every bite of food the hunger got stronger. It made me nauseous. Gagging, I ran toward the bathroom, while Mom asked, "Is she okay?"

I didn't make it to the bathroom. The hunger was tearing its way out of me, and I fell to the floor shaking with it. Franky must have known. He was already gone.

But Tommy. Mom. Dad. They gathered over me. Worried, wanting to help. As their hands reached down to gather me up, my teeth found them.

I tore them to pieces.

The hunger receded, and then Franky was there once more, drowning them in gasoline. I screamed that I wanted to burn too.

Sirens sound in the distance.

"Time to go."

He has been here the whole time. Watching me. Waiting.

"No," I say. I try again to stand. And fail again. So, I crawl. There's still time; I can end this. End myself. Along with that thought comes the realization that even now, beneath the gasoline taste, there is the flavor of blood . . . and the hunger wants more.

"You're soaked in gasoline, you know." There is laughter in his voice.

I remember then. He laid me on my bed, in my old room. It all looked exactly the same. They had left it that way. I thought he was giving me back to them. Returning me to where I belonged, and I felt so grateful to him. I cried and thanked him as he left. But then he came back and lifted the red container over my head, and gasoline poured from the spout.

A window bursts, and the heat inside reaches toward me. I shrink from it, whimpering, scrambling away. Suddenly having a taste of what it means to burn, and not wanting it. Not to die that way. Not to die any way.

"I'm not afraid to die." That's what I'd told him. "Death would be better than living this way."

I'd lied. When he lit the first match, I ran from the house, out into the cool night air.

He lifts me until I am upright and leaning on him. Arms wrapped around each other, we cross through the neighbors' yards, toward the waiting car. I pretend he is pulling me away, that I would rather be inside that house ending this, instead of walking toward the next girl whose time to pay has arrived.

I could save that girl. Save her from me.

But I am clinging to him, desperate not to let the flames catch me.

No one will be saved tonight.

My head pounded and the smell of gas still seemed to taint every inhalation.

"Have a nice trip?" Eric sniggered.

I stared at him blindly, blinking stupidly as the last big missing piece fell into place.

I finally understood. I could feed the hunger—feed it with Lacey—and it would hibernate inside me once more. Until the next year and the next girl. But if it didn't get that girl, then the snakelike hunger wouldn't be inside me anymore. It would be me. A more monstrous and hungrier version of me.

Eric watched me, waiting for me to admit defeat, to realize there was no escape. Except even then, even knowing how bad it would get, I couldn't let him win.

"I'm not taking Lacey."

Something flashed in Eric's eyes, and he rushed at me, knocking me into the stall. I tripped against the toilet and fell back into the corner, scraping my head against the toilet paper dispenser. Eric's fingers found a fistful of my hair and twisted until I cried out.

"Listen to me," he hissed, his sour breath hot on my face. "We've got a good thing going. You already fucked it up once; you're not going to do it again."

I should've been afraid, but Eric's desperation was palpable, and instead of feeding my own, it did a funny thing. It made me feel powerful. We were tied together—the two of us together forever. That's what Franky had said to Anna. He had made the decision to connect his fate to my choices. I could let the hunger consume him too. I could make him a monster. And he knew it.

"Why did you do it?" I asked softly. "Why did you take Franky and why did you choose me?"

In response Eric pressed his lips to mine, keeping them tightly closed this time, but even without his tongue it was just as invasive and unpleasant. Not caring if he left a bald spot, I twisted my head away. He released his hold on my hair, but only to free his hand so he could slap me across the face.

"I love you," he said, slapping me again. And again.

I scrambled to get my feet under me and, using the wall at my back, pushed myself up so that I stood above him.

Then I was on the attack. Grabbing hold of the little red curls, I shoved his head down and brought my knee up to meet his nose. There was a satisfying crunch and then his blood ran out. It wasn't enough. As he clutched for his face, I pushed his head down again, but this time toward the toilet.

"Don't," he said, struggling to stand, but I kicked the back of his knees, forcing him to lunge forward. His hands gripped the edge of the bowl, holding his face inches away from the dirty water.

"Why me? Why Franky?" I demanded again.

"I didn't want Franky, I wanted your brother. What was his name again?"

"You know his name." I kicked at the back of his knees again, bringing him lower. He squealed like a little pig when his nose touched the water. "Say it. Say his name. Say it now."

"Tommy! I wanted Tommy. It was gonna be easy."

"Bullshit." It felt so good to press my hand on the back of his head, pushing his face into the water, listening to him splutter when I finally let him come back up for air. "Tommy could have any girl he wanted." As I said this, I remembered his broad shoulders paired with a killer smile, and knew it was true. A terrible and deep pang of loss, of missing him, ran through me with such power I could've sat down and cried from it.

"No, no, no," Eric said, for once looking like the pathetic freshman who had once lived in his body. "Not a girl. I don't get them like that. I do revenge. Don't you remember?"

I let him stand and then spun him around, needing to see his face. Pushing him against the stall wall, I took a few steps back, out of range of any retaliatory violence. "No, I don't remember. So tell me."

Ignoring me, he swiped at the toilet water dripping down his face, mixing with the blood still seeping from his nose.

"Tell me," I said again.

Eric's fists slammed against the walls of the stall. But he

talked, a thick Irish brogue fading in and out with every other word.

"My sister, a good Irish Catholic girl, got herself knocked up. Gave it away to the barber who lived at the end of our street. Him a fucking Protestant too. He said he'd marry her to get in her pants, but when he found out about the brat, well guess what? He pretended not to know her. And who was gonna stop him? Father had drunk himself to death when we were still babes, and my mum was too humiliated and tired to do anything but look the other way. This was when people still had a sense of shame and long before anybody thought of planning parenthood, and so that left me, the crippled little brother, in a body too twisted to cross the room by himself, much less beat the shite out of anybody. That's when the Physician came, made me the offer. All I had to do was cut out my own heart and make that dirty Protestant bastard eat it bite by bite by bite."

"And you became him," I said softly.

"No. That's the part you never got. I became me. The me I had always been meant to be. Bigger. Stronger. And indestructible. I took care of my sister. Married her, made sure she had the babe, and then filled her with another before I had to move on."

"Move on," I whispered, too sickened to say any more.

"Yes, move on and on and on and on. It's what we do, and what I did for years before you. I crisscrossed the country, watching it grow faster. I saw man fly into the sky, and then beyond it all the way to the moon. And I'll still be here when they learn to take us farther than that too. And I want to see it with you. It's what I've always wanted." Eric moved out of the stall toward me, no longer angry, but wooing. He held his hands out, as if he honestly believed I would take them. As if I would willingly join him.

I inched toward the door, but before I could leave, I still needed to know. "Why me?"

"I told you, Anna. Long ago and right from the beginning. You made me think of my sister. Made me wish I'd found a way to bring her with me. But in you I found her again. Many a generation later, a little branch grown out of the same family tree."

His hands grabbed mine, clenching them too tight. I felt Franky in that grip, or the boy who I'd thought was Franky. What had he said then? "Share the same blood again"?

Family. The Protestant barber. My father's razor, handed down through several generations. I reminded him of his sister. It all made a terrible kind of sense. He'd held that razor in his hand with such familiarity. Was the razor how he figured out the connection? Was that why he'd used it to bind us together forever?

I didn't ask. Instead I jerked away, spinning blindly toward the door and then out of it. I ran through the empty hallways, with Eric's blood still wet on my shirt.

Although separated by who knew how many decades, Eric

had found a piece of his original family and had given up the greater portion of his freedom to have it back. To have me. And now our fates were intertwined. Whatever I chose for myself, I chose for him as well.

Which meant Eric would be coming after me to make sure that I took Lacey and that everything went back to the way it had always been between us.

Half blind and dizzy with dread, I skidded and tripped down the halls. Instead of going for one of the side exits, I headed toward the front doors on autopilot, forgetting the monitor who was always stationed there.

"Young lady, do you have a pass?" he called out. Sunlight poured in from the row of glass doors behind him, turning him into a scowling black shadow. I pushed right past, throwing my whole body at the closest door. As the cold air hit my face, I heard him behind me. "You can't run forever."

Ignoring the words and the chill they sent down my spine, I escaped from the school and kept going. Without breaking stride, I glanced back. There was no sign of the hall monitor. Or Eric.

But I was caught anyway. Feeling the telltale signs of a past I couldn't outrun, I quickly ducked behind a car, before another memory descended.

NOTHING

CROSS MY HEART

Cross my heart
and hope to die,
stick a needle in my eye.

If this vow I do break
then no more breaths
shall I take.

Lips sealed, I promise true
I won't break my word,
my word to you.

It is Franky's idea. Tommy came home this weekend, and ever since he got here, Katie has been walking past our house every two minutes hoping to accidentally bump into him. Little does she know he was out until five a.m. and isn't likely to resurface again until it's time to start getting ready for another night out.

Franky and I watch her from his front porch as we chain-smoke and tried to outdo each other in describing the odds of her ever hooking my brother. Then Franky calls her over.

"Hey, Katie, c'mere a second."

"What?" she says, walking toward us. Her arms are crossed against her chest, defensive, ready for us to pick on her.

"I thought you might be interested in knowing that Anna's been practicing a little black magic lately. And most recently she's learned a love spell that she's been dying to try out on somebody. Right, Anna?"

"Go to hell." Katie walks away, and I wait for Franky to crack up, but instead he is pushing me to run after her.

"What?" I hiss at him.

"Help the poor girl."

"You're an ass."

"All right." He smiles in that way I've come to think of as dangerous. "Then help yourself. You keep whining about wanting your dad's razor back. Well, you can have it . . . just convince little Katie to solemnly swear she will hand over her hot, beating heart in exchange for Tommy's love."

"I think you forgot that I don't believe in love."

Franky smiles. "But she does."

"Stupid," I mutter, not specifying whether I'm referring to him or her. Or maybe me. Because even as I say it, I'm hopping off the porch steps. "Hey, Katie, wait."

I catch her on the sidewalk beneath the wide branches of the same tree we'd used as home base during our childhood hide-and-seek games.

"I'm sorry about Franky. He's such a jerk sometimes. Right?" I glance back to where he is watching us.

Katie looks toward Franky too. "Why do you hang out with him then?"

I shrug. "Better than being alone, I guess." Her eyes widen with sympathy, and before she makes an offer to be my friend again, I cut her off. "He also kisses pretty good."

"Oh." Katie hides a titter behind her hand. "I didn't know you liked him like that. I mean, you were always kinda secretive, but I never even got a hint."

"Always did," I lie. "But I knew he didn't like me that way, so . . ."

I heave a big sigh and she answers with a matching one. "Yeah."

As our wistful sighs slowly melt away, I realize that mine was not a total lie. I understand longing. Not for a boy, but I understand wanting something you cannot have.

"Well," I say, shuffling my feet, getting ready to turn away, go back to Franky, and let him know what I think of his stupid dares.

But Katie's words stop me.

"You're lucky, Anna. You're really lucky." Her eyes are shining and sincere and so very stupid.

I smile, shrug, push away the urge to cry. "A little lucky, but maybe I used a little magic too. Well, not magic, not really. More like the power of thought. And channeling it toward what you want, until you get it."

I don't even know what I'm saying, but Katie has always been gullible, and now her arms have loosened and she's looking at me like she believes every word out of my mouth.

"You can make Tommy want you. I can help you. It's easy. Of course, by *want* I just mean sex. But love can come from that, and hey, it's better than having him see you as a little sister, right?"

"Sex." Katie says the word slowly, drawing it out. I am certain I've scared her away, but then, "What would I have to do?"

I look up, thinking. I could tell her to strip naked at midnight and run beneath the full moon. She'd probably think better of it by then. So instead I take my inspiration from the boughs above me.

"It's easy. Like when we were kids," I say, holding out my hands.

Another moment of hesitation, but she takes them. Of course she does. It wasn't long ago that we were best friends, and even though that friendship has crumbled away, I don't think she realizes how much I hate her. How I hate the way she idolizes my whole family. My banker father in his crisp suits, my made-up mother with her model good looks, and Tommy. Perfect all-American Tommy. A stand-up guy who went off to college without a second thought and left his poor sister behind. I hate them and I hate her for not understanding why I am so desperate to escape.

"Anna?" Katie asks, her soft voice bringing me back. Her warm hands clasp mine, and I realize that mine have gone cold. My stomach turns, but I don't back down. I have come this far, and I can feel Franky watching, egging me on.

"Cross your heart and hope to die. Remember?"

Katie nods. Of course she does. During sleepovers, on the school bus, and beneath this very tree, linking our pinkie fingers together, we would solemnly repeat the childhood rhyme.

"Say it with me. The whole thing."

And she does. We do. Together we recite the worn words. And if Katie feels a chill go through her, she doesn't say anything about it to me.

But I feel it. My teeth chatter with it for the rest of the day.

I looked up and saw Logan kneeling in front of me, a frown of concern on his face.

"Annaliese, are you okay?"

I ignored the hand he held out, standing on my own power. Peering around the side of the car, I saw no sign of Eric or anyone else. Gulping air, feeling like I would never get enough, I found my breath strips and emptied the pack, putting one after another into my mouth like a chain-smoker. Only when they were all gone could I focus on Logan.

"Did you follow me here?"

Even as his face reddened, Logan lifted his chin in defiance. "I saw you run outside. You seemed upset. I wanted to make sure you were okay." He looked me up and down. "Is that blood?"

I brushed at the marks on my shirt as if I was seeing them for the first time myself. "It's nothing." Spinning away from him, I started to walk. I had to get home. It was now chillingly clear. It was time to say good-bye.

I turned to face Logan. "Look, I'm sorry. It's been a bad couple of days and I just want to go home. Can I borrow your cell to make a call?"

Instead of producing a phone, he pulled car keys from his pocket. "I can drive you."

I wanted to hit him for being concerned and nice and

obnoxious. Except after today Annaliese would disappear once more, and he would have the rest of his life to replay our last conversation.

"Okay," I said. "I'd appreciate that."

Logan grinned, as if I'd granted him some amazing gift. And his smile stayed in place even as he turned out of the parking lot.

"Wow, your car is really clean." I had meant to say something meaningful that would make him feel better about what had happened between him and Annaliese. But nothing came to mind. Also, his car was insanely clean. Two layers of floor mats were beneath my feet and there wasn't the slightest smudge of dirt on either one.

"Yeah, I know." Logan shrugged. "It's my mom's car but she lets me use it as long as I drop her off and pick her up from work on time. And I have to keep it clean. And when my mom says clean, she means superclean."

He didn't say it in a complaining kind of way like some guys would have. It made me remember that Logan was a good guy. The way he was with his mom reminded me a lot of Dex. This was the guy Annaliese had fallen for.

"Logan, look, I want you to know, I'm okay."

Logan's gaze drifted to my blood-spattered shirt, but he said nothing. He didn't have to. I was a mess inside and out. I decided to try another tactic.

"Maybe I'm not okay, but that has nothing to do with you. I

know you want to fix things, but you can't. Some things aren't meant to be fixed. Some things deserve to be broken."

Logan opened his mouth to protest, but I held up my hand, stopping him.

"Bottom line, Logan, what did you do that was so terrible? Yes, you cheated on your girlfriend. Yes, you had bad sex with a girl who you knew had stronger feelings than you did for her. And yes, you left her alone in the woods after the bad sex, and something terrible happened to her. But that part wasn't your fault. And you need to let it go. And you need to let me go too."

I could see him mulling over my words as he pulled up in front of my house. He shifted the car into park but still remained silent. I didn't want to linger in case the mom looked out the window and wondered what I was doing here in the middle of a school day, but I needed to know that Logan was okay.

Gently, I placed my hand on his arm. "I gotta go now."

Finally, he turned to look at me. "Was the sex really bad? Is that something you remembered? Because at the time you seemed to, I don't know, enjoy it."

"Seriously? That's what you have to say?" I nearly choked, and was tempted to choke him too.

"I'm sorry, I'm sorry. I didn't mean . . . If it was bad, I mean, I guess you would know, if that's how you remember it. And I know it's not the most important thing, but I want to know for next time, so we can do it right." Logan quickly backtracked—in the wrong direction. "I think we can figure that out, though, along with everything else. It doesn't change anything, Annaliese. I still want to be with you. After everything that's happened, I think we belong together."

It was so horrible, it was funny. Almost.

There was no getting through to him. Leaning across the seat, I brushed a kiss against his cheek, and then quickly retreated before he could turn it into something more.

But not quick enough.

"Annaliese, please." He grabbed hold of my hand. "I just want to make you happy. I'd give everything for that."

"Don't." I opened the car door, stepped out, and then leaned back in. "Giving everything is what got us here in the first place."

Slamming the door, I walked away, hoping that Logan understood. Everything was too much to give anyone. And yet somehow still not enough to get what you really wanted.

SEE

"What do you see? For me. What do you see?"

I hadn't meant to say this to Dex, and certainly not for these to be the first words out of my mouth. But now that they were out, I didn't take them back. I needed to know if I had a future.

The smile of greeting that had been on Dex's face faded. "Don't."

I pushed my way past him, down the stairs. In the dim interior my eyes were immediately drawn to the glowing light of the computer screen. Instead of its usual scroll promoting free will or choice, a video played. Curious, I stepped closer.

"Anna, wait," Dex called. I ignored him, already transfixed.

A young girl stood on a street corner, a backpack at her feet. She didn't do much, just stared into the distance, waiting. Then a bus pulled up, hiding her from view, and the video ended.

I whirled to face Dex. "Are you nuts? That's the girl that creep is gonna kill, and when he does, people are gonna remember seeing you hanging around, videotaping her. Holy shit, Dex, are you trying to frame yourself? People are already suspicious of you because of the whole YouTube thing."

Stalking past me, Dex grabbed the mouse and minimized the screen. "This is what I do. I record it."

He moved toward one of the large metal cabinets and flung open the doors, revealing rows and rows of neatly labeled DV tapes. "I know it doesn't help them, and I know it makes me look like a crazy person with a fetish or some kind of predator. But I have to do something. And I tried to do more—going after that guy. You already know how that worked out. I thought maybe if I'm there when he grabs her, I could stop him or record some detail. It's stupid, I know, but I have to try."

He threw the doors closed, and took two steps toward me, looking into my eyes. It seemed like he could see to the darkest parts of my soul. I cringed, afraid of what he might find. "I thought you of all people would understand that."

His words cut right through me. He thought I would understand saving someone else, when the only person I'd ever saved was myself. Guess he couldn't see into my soul after all. After everything he knew, he still believed in me.

"What do you see for me?" I asked again, my words soft this time. I held out my hands. "Please, Dex. If you can't tell me, then show me." I took a step toward him, palms up and open. "It might help me figure out what to do. How to make the right choice." I had no such hopes, but I knew that these were the words Dex couldn't deny.

I played him. Played him right into my hands, his fingertips gently connecting with each of mine and then the heavier weight of his palms settling upon my own.

I had time to feel the warmth of his flesh against my ice-cold hands before everything sank away.

STATIC

REC. The red abbreviation appears at the bottom of the screen. The noise is that of an angry librarian. *Shush. Shush. Shush.*

I wait for a picture to appear, and then realize that I am seeing it: the static scene of gray ash being blown in endless waves across the screen.

NOTHING

"I'm nothing," I said, pulling my hands from his.

Blinking, Dex looked away. It was all the answer I needed. And now it was time to tell him what he'd already known. Time to tell myself too.

"I'm gonna take Lacey. I know you think I have another choice, but I don't. I remembered what happens when I don't take someone. I remembered what the hunger is, and I can't . . ." I couldn't finish.

I expected Dex to nod in understanding and maybe express his regret. I was wrong.

"That's it then?" His hands gripped my shoulders hard, hurting me. He was fierce and angry in a way I had never seen him before. "You're giving up?"

The always-understanding, supersupportive Dex had disappeared. I shook my head, wondering if this was another dream. "Dex, you don't understand."

"Because you aren't telling me anything. You're afraid of the hunger. I don't even know what that means."

"It's something inside me, and if I don't jump to the next girl then it takes over, and..." I glared at Dex, hating him a little bit for making me say it. "I killed my parents. My real parents. My brother, too. It was like I was an animal. I ripped them to shreds. That's why I'm giving up. I can't stay here and risk hurting the parents or you."

"I'll take my chances."

My own anger rose to meet his. "Oh well, great. That's just super for you, but maybe I don't want to live with the memory of having ripped your face off with my fingernails." Dex flinched, but it only made me madder. "Why can't you get it? There's nothing else."

Dex shook his head. "There's always something else."

"Like what? Huh? Tell me, since it's so damn easy for you."

"What do you mean, easy for me?" Dex stepped back, crossing his arms over his chest and tucking his hands into his armpits instead of reaching them out toward me. Another barrier between us.

I threw my own hands in the air. "You know what I mean. Doing the right thing. It comes naturally to you, like you were born with a Boy Scout badge of honor." I sounded snarky. I didn't even know why. Dex's goodness and honor were the best parts of him.

He turned away, as if he could no longer stand to see me.

"How can you think I always do the right thing? When I've

told you how many times . . . Anna, I've done the wrong thing again and again. All the people I've seen die, and I just let it happen. And even when I try to do something, it's not like I want to do it. Do you really think I want to go after child molesters? You think I get off on acting like some sort of superlame superhero? I don't. Maybe I did once, but a few punches aimed straight at my gut quickly cured me of that."

Dex kicked at his desk chair, sending it flying. It didn't seem to make him feel any better.

"And you know what the worst thing is? I'm not doing it because I want to save that little girl. I'm not doing it so that she'll die after a long, happy life. I'm doing it to get her out of my damn head. I'm doing it so I don't ever have to see those little pink sneakers again."

I wrapped my arms around myself. "Oh, Dex." Wishing I could hug him, I shook my head instead. "You've done your best and it's a lot better than what most people would do. But what I've done—"

Dex slammed a fist into the metal cabinet, making it clang loudly. "What you've done. What about what you will do?"

"I don't have a choice, Dex." I could hear the whine in my voice and hated it. Yet I couldn't shut up. "You know it's true. You see it."

"So what. You're a blank. No death scene. No nothing. That doesn't mean you have to take this girl. Maybe it means you've already died and can't die again. It doesn't mean the choice is made. My visions change. People change."

Dex paced the room, a whirlwind that I felt tiny and lost inside of. Still I tried to make him see, if not the vision—then me.

"You saw nothing because I'm nothing. Not dead. Not alive. Just a monster." There. Not whining. Not making excuses. I was almost proud of myself.

For a moment he stilled, and then he came straight at me. I thought he might hit me, try and fight me the same way he had that horrible man. Except I wouldn't fight back. I would let him do the right thing.

I was wrong again. Dex pulled me toward him, hugging me close with a tender brutality. And then he kissed me in the same way. I kissed him back, wishing it were enough to keep me from turning into something hungry and terrible. I felt tears, wet on my cheeks, salty on my lips. They weren't mine.

That's when I broke free. I shoved Dex away and dashed up the steps, across the lawn, and around the fence, knowing it would've been better for him—and maybe for me too—if I had never crossed that fence line at all.

DAUGHTER

BEING 16

I hate my life.
I hate everything.

That's what I screamed
before running to my room
and slamming the door.

You gave me ten minutes.
I could almost see you
counting with the clock.

Then you came
and Dad too
but mostly you.

Holding me
petting my hair
while I sobbed
that I
wanted to die.

It's not true.
I think you knew
'cause you didn't lecture.
You just let me cry
and think how
being sixteen
—and nearly seventeen . . .
but nowhere near eighteen—
is sometimes enough
to make you
want to die.

—ARG

Walking into the house, I knew what had to be done. I'd severed ties with Dex, and now needed to do the same with the mom.

I'd done it before. Staging a fight with a mom before disappearing, making it look like I was a runaway. My conversation with the dad this morning gave me the perfect opening too. They had sabotaged my relationship with Dex, and because of it, he had broken up with me. Now I was broken . . . and would leave them the same way.

Taking a deep breath and two breath strips for courage, I let the performance begin. "Hello?"

"Annaliese?" The mom's voice came floating down the stairwell. "Honey, is that you? Are you okay?" Her worry and concern, almost palpable, came directly behind.

"I'm fine," I called back. Not the best way to start an argument, but I didn't want the mom to get out of bed. Didn't want her to be more hurt than she had to be when this was all over. Too late. When I reached the bottom of the stairs, she was already standing at the top, waiting.

"How did you get home? You're supposed to be at school."

"You're supposed to be in bed," I countered. It wasn't the direction I meant to take this argument, but I was so afraid that she would tumble down the steps. I could've gone up there, forced her back. But I didn't trust myself to get closer. She might hug me, and I didn't have the strength to push her away like I had Dex.

"Annaliese Rose, I am not moving until you tell me what is going on." The tone in the mom's voice said she was ready to go to war in her big fuzzy robe and slipper-socks.

"I had a fight with the dad this morning. Over Dex."

Confusion clouded the mom's face, and I remembered that the dad hadn't told her about the whole Dex thing. I was ready to backtrack and explain, when the mom held up a shaking hand, silencing me.

"What do you mean"—I held my breath, waiting for it—"*the dad*? Since when do you call your father 'the dad'?"

She didn't care about Dex at all. The boy she had built a fence to keep away. Surprise spoiled my prepared script. "Since always. Or as long as I can remember." I laughed bitterly, and it was frighteningly real. My improv was veering away from acting, and straight toward the truth. "He's the dad. You're the mom. Not my mom or my dad, because I don't have a mom or a dad. And also, I am not your daughter."

I couldn't believe I said it. Watching the mom's face crumble, I wanted to take it all back. I pushed forward instead.

"It's all a lie. I'm not the daughter you lost, and you don't need me anymore anyway, because you have the two new kids growing inside you. It'll be better this way."

That was it. I couldn't say any more without a rush of hot tears giving me away. Spinning around, I made a run for it. Again.

Away from Eric, Dex, and now the mom, and diving toward a wave of darkness determined to drown me.

There was a loud thumping on the stairs behind me, and I hesitated, certain the mom was lying broken at the bottom of them. Except she rounded the corner like a linebacker with the ball, and before I could even think to run again, she slammed into me, dragging us both to the ground.

"Mom!" I screamed, certain she had killed the babies, and maybe herself too.

She dragged herself up, still keeping her weight on me, so that I couldn't move away. "*Mom.* Yes, that's right. I am your mom. And you are mine and you can never be replaced. Never. You are my daughter. And I don't care if you don't know me and I sometimes don't know you. You are mine. Do you hear me, Annaliese? You are mine."

I tried to shake my head, tried to tell her that Annaliese had been replaced, but I couldn't. It didn't matter what I said anyway, she would never let me go.

And I was her daughter now. After tonight she wouldn't just lose me, I would lose her as well.

Her fingers gripped my face, making me look her in the eye. "Annaliese, I want to know that you understand me. I am not moving until you do."

"Yes, Mom. Yes." I was crying, and then she was too. We sat on the floor together for a long time, not saying anything. She put her hand on her belly, and I did too. Those little babies inside that I would never meet were sort of my brothers or sisters. I tried to send them a message through my fingertips. Telling them to live and be strong. Letting them know that even though we never met, I missed them.

Then I helped Mom back up the stairs and into bed. I gave her one last hug and offered to make us some tea. The chai kind we both liked with extra milk and sugar. Her hand slipped into mine and gave it a squeeze. Time flickered in front of me. Mom's hand was holding mine the same way, but she was sitting at the kitchen table.

"Have fun with Gwen tonight. It's been a while since you girls had a sleepover."

"Yeah." I shrug. "We've been busy and stuff."

"And stuff." Mom nods wisely. "And here I thought you two had some sort of falling-out after that trip you took to Ohio."

"Nope, no fights. We just needed a little space after that." Another shrug, as if this small movement might be enough to remove the weight of my lies. So far it hasn't helped.

"All right, well, if you decide to come home early, just give me a call."

"I know, Mom." I am impatient to get away before she sees through all my flimsy fabrications; already I can feel my fibs

beginning to tear at the seams. "Can I go now? Dad's waiting in the car."

Mom's hand releases mine. "Go on. I'll see you tomorrow."

"I'll be here," I say.

Annaliese didn't even realize it was another lie. Her thoughts were already turning toward Logan and meeting him in the trees that night.

Releasing Mom's hand, I told another similarly small and devastating lie.

"I'll get the tea and come right back, okay?"

I didn't put the kettle on, though. Instead I slipped silently out the back door, leaving my mom alone in the house to wonder forever after what had become of me. Her daughter.

FIGHT

I hold the bucket as she retches into it. Again.

Withdrawal is what Dad calls it. We've been through it before, he says, meaning him and Mom.

I remember it, but not well. I was nine and he told me she had the flu. Then after she got better there were four whole months when she didn't drink. Not a drop. Later, Tommy told me she'd embarrassed Dad at some work party, and he'd said enough was enough. But then, of course, it started again.

Now, seven years later, enough is enough once more. This time, though, I am the one left holding the bag. Or the bucket.

She broke her leg, that's what got it all started. I was the one who found her at the bottom of the basement stairs.

She's dead. That's what I'd thought. She lay on the concrete floor, all twisted and broken and white. Our dirty laundry that she'd been carrying had cushioned the fall. Her head rested on a pair of my father's dirty boxer shorts. They had probably saved her.

At the time it hadn't been funny, but now remembering it, I smile.

"What's so funny?" she snarls. She's been in a nasty mood all day. It's a good sign, I guess. Before she was in too much pain to do anything but vomit and moan, then vomit again.

I tuck the smile away, knowing she hates to be laughed at, to be the butt of a joke. "Nothing," I mutter.

She pushes the bucket away. "Get that thing out of my face. It stinks."

Yeah, from you. Clenching my teeth, I keep the words from coming out. As I carry the bucket to the bathroom for the hundredth time today, I remind myself how I'd begged God not to let my mother die in those first frightening moments after I found her.

"Anna!" She calls my name like a military drill sergeant, expecting me to come running.

And I do. The bucket is only half clean, but I slop the rest of the dirty water into the tub and rush to her side with it, already knowing that as distasteful as cleaning the bucket may be, it is much worse to deal with dirty blankets, sheets, rugs, and clothes.

She isn't retching, though. Instead, she reclines back onto her pile of pillows like a queen.

"What? Are you okay?" I gasp.

"Where's Tommy? Why do I never see my son?"

"He went back to school last week, remember?" I try to keep my voice patient, but can hear the resentment bleeding through. He's only an hour away, close enough to come home to do his laundry every two weeks, but apparently not so close that he can check on his mom after she breaks her leg in three different places. Instead he calls. He must have a timer somewhere because the conversation always ends a bit past the fifteen-minute mark. It's enough to make her happy. He called, he cares, and if only he wasn't so darn busy he would love to talk with her all day.

"Of course, I remember, and please do not use that tone with me." She gives me the imperious stare, the one that has caused stomachaches my whole life.

"Sorry," I say, but cannot resist adding, "He'll be home this weekend, but don't expect to see him much. He'll be inside Katie's pocket the whole time I'm sure."

She clucks her tongue at me. "Oh, Anna, don't be so small. You act like he stole your best friend."

Actually it was more like my former best friend stole my brother. After a lifetime of benignly ignoring Katie, suddenly it was like he'd been hit on the head with something. He was all googly-eyed and glazed over when he looked at her, the same way she'd always been toward him. And she looked so satisfied with herself.

I hate them both.

Even worse, I can't shake the terrible feeling that maybe I am the one who pushed them together at last. My fault. And Franky's too, with his stupid games involving blood oaths and promises that chill the blood.

But I don't tell Mom any of this.

"Whatever, I don't care," I only say. "In a year, I'm outta here anyway."

"Outta here?" She hates lazy language, and repeats my words with disdain. "And what exactly does that mean?"

Too late, I realize my mistake. Disappointed by my poor grades, my parents have decided that a college education will not be a good investment for me. Mom wants me to go to secretarial school like she did. Then she'd gotten a job, and then she'd met my dad. And look how happy her life turned out. Still, I pretend to go along with it, even as I become more set on a one-way bus ticket out of town.

"Nothing," I stutter now. "Just, you know, I'll be eighteen. Not in high school and stuff."

Her eyes narrow. "But you'll still be living under this roof."

"Yeah?" Somehow the word comes out as a question.

She eyes me in a way that makes me squirm, and I bite down on my tongue, resisting the urge to say something, to try and fix it. If I stay quiet, there is a 50 percent chance that she'll go the other way. It happens all the time: the death stare is fixed on me and I am writing my eulogy, when suddenly she is so sorry, she loves me more than anything, she doesn't know what got into her, and can I please please forgive her. And I always do. This is the good mom, the one who makes me think that maybe I should stay and become a secretary.

Then there is the other 50 percent.

"Why don't you pack your bags now, Anna? Nothing is stopping you from walking out that door right this instant if you hate it here so much."

"No." I shake my head, afraid of how serious she looks.

"No? Does that mean, no you don't hate it here? No, you don't hate me?" Sitting up, she flings a pillow at me. "Is that why you were smiling before? Were you thinking about how you were going to leave us all behind? Was that it, you selfish, horrible girl? Is getting away all you think about?"

She throws another pillow and I dodge it, but I am not ready for the glass on her bedside table. It thunks against the side of my head. And that's when I break.

"I hate you!" I scream the words, emphasizing and feeling each one. God, I hate her. I hate her, I hate her. I can't imagine hating anyone this way, as if my hate is enough to push them down the stairs to a concrete floor below. The bucket is still in my hand, and I fling it at her, watching the leftover dirty puke water splash across her and the bed.

She hobbles out of the bed, grabbing for the crutches that she's refused to even consider before now. One of the crutches she uses to stabilize herself, but the other she brandishes like a cattle prod as she thumps toward me. "Get out," she says. Using the crutch, she pushes me toward the door. "Get out!"

"Fine," I yell back, but I retreat slowly, and wouldn't move at all if she didn't jab at me, steering me through the hallway, until the stairs are at my back.

"What are you waiting for? You need me to show you where the door is? Go!" The crutch comes up over her head, as if she is about to bring it down on me.

Turning, I flee. I can feel myself wanting to cry, but in a distant way. Mostly, I wonder if this is really happening. I open the door and feel the fresh autumn air on my face. The leaves are just starting to change. Stepping out, I close the door behind me. This is happening. The tears start to fall.

"Anna!" I think I hear her calling for me as I stumble down the driveway. She doesn't sound like the drill sergeant. This time she sounds like the good mom, trying to say "I'm sorry."

I keep walking. I can't trust that version of her.

I turn left toward Franky's house. I'll stay there until I'm sure that Daddy has returned home from work. Then I'll slip back home and into bed, pretending nothing ever happened. She'll do the same. And on the surface everything will be okay.

TIME

PRAYER TO SAINT JUDE

Saint Jude, glorious apostle, faithful servant and friend of Jesus, the church invokes you universally as the patron of hopeless cases, of things almost despaired of.

Pray for me, for I am so helpless and alone. Please help to bring me visible and speedy assistance. Come to my assistance in this great need that I may receive the consolation and help of heaven in all my necessities, tribulations, and sufferings, particularly (state your request) and that I may praise God with you always.

Amen.

Like a tornado, the past had grabbed me again, and when it spit me back out, I was left dizzy. In the span of thirty minutes I lost my mother twice. But there was no time to fall apart. I was still in the shadow of the house, and any moment now Mom would be out looking for me.

I stood on shaky legs, and then rubbed my eyes, trying to bring them back into focus. That was when I caught sight of a man running across the front yard. I leaned back into the shadows, not wanting to be seen. But he didn't look left or right, just ran straight toward his car parked at the side of the road.

Straining to see against the glare of the sun, I took a step forward.

It was Logan's car, still in the same place as where I'd last seen it when he dropped me off. And it was Logan now jumping into the driver's seat and peeling away from the curb. As the car flashed past, I saw someone in the passenger side. A boy with red hair. Eric.

Drawing an imaginary line, I traced back across the diagonal Logan had been moving along. It led straight back to Dex's house. My stomach clenched with fear as I sped across the grass.

Both storm doors were flung wide open.

"Dex?" I called, taking the stairs in two leaps.

A clanging from inside one of the metal cabinets answered me. I yanked the doors open. Dex and a river of videotapes came spilling out at my feet. White masking tape bound his wrists and ankles and was wound over his face and hair, creating a sticky hood covering his whole head, except for a small gap at the base of his nose for him to breathe through. It was like some kind of terrible locker-room prank calculated to ensure the maximum amount of discomfort and embarrassment without causing too much real physical harm.

"I'm sorry, I'm so so sorry." I kept up the steady mantra as my fingers picked away at the tape. Finally, a long layer peeled free, and there was his mouth.

His perfect crooked smiling mouth that I could've kissed, except he croaked out, "Hands. Scissors. Desk."

"Right, right." I retrieved the scissors and carefully cut through the tape that was keeping his arms twisted behind his back, then I moved down to his ankles, while he flexed his long arms with a low groan. After freeing his legs, I set the scissors down and moved back toward his face, where Dex's long fingers scratched blindly at the tape, trying to find the seams.

I wrapped my hands around his. "It's okay, Dex. I got this. Just let me do it, all right?"

"No." He shook free, and if I'd thought I was beyond absorbing hurt, I quickly realized how wrong I was. Because his rejection hurt. Badly.

"Sorry," I said, shrinking back.

His hands flew out, reaching for me, and I moved toward him, letting him find me. Needing to be found. He pulled me close into a hug and rested his mummified head against my chest. "Anna, no. I didn't mean . . . I just, I need you to get the car. It's Logan, he's—"

I interrupted Dex with a kiss. The kiss I'd been wanting, no matter how terribly timed it might be. "I don't care about Logan. He did this, he can deal with the consequences. I just want to get you free right now."

Dex faced me straight on, as if he could see me even through all those layers of tape. "I saw him cut Eric's heart out."

I shook my head in denial even as I felt the truth of it spread through my body.

"I saw Eric turn to dust, and I saw Logan die and then get up and walk away."

"No! No no no." The words finally tumbled loose and I sobbed them into Dex's shirt, as he reached for me and drew me close once more. It was only a flash flood, and ended as rapidly as it had begun. The drumbeat of danger pounded inside me, dragging me back to the present.

"Can we stop it?" I asked.

Dex nodded. "We can try."

STUN

The last time we'd been in the car together had been after we'd seen Jess. Our hands had been entwined for most of the ride home. Now we sat on our separate sides, hands to ourselves as if an invisible line divided us. Funny, because we needed the comfort now more than ever. Maybe it was this thought that made me reach out toward Dex, placing my hand on his jiggling knee.

"You okay?"

He went still, and I retracted my hand, hoping he would grab it back. He didn't.

"I should've been better prepared," Dex said in a low voice. "I knew he was coming, and all I did was make sure I'd have lots of soft places to land."

"You mean Logan? You knew he was coming?"

Dex stared straight ahead. "A while back, I saw it. In a vision. Logan attacking me in the basement. We struggled, and then I hit my head on the corner of the desk."

"Saw," I repeated, as I put it together and realized what this meant. "You saw it because he killed you. You died when you hit your desk?" I gripped my hands tight to keep from reaching for him again, this time to feel that he was alive, that his vision hadn't come true.

Dex shrugged. "Freak thing, I guess."

"When did you see this?"

"I don't know, a while ago." He stared straight ahead, concentrating extra hard on watching the road. I had a suspicion as to why he wouldn't meet my eyes.

"That day I first came down to the basement, when you disappeared? That's when you saw it, wasn't it? We decided to be friends, and then you saw yourself die."

"It wasn't like that," Dex protested.

I didn't believe him. "Why didn't you stay away from me, and tell me to stay away from you?"

Dex shook his head. "I didn't want to, okay? It seemed like an acceptable risk to take."

"Dying? That seemed like an acceptable risk?"

"I took precautions. You saw them. I thought it was enough. I knew Logan didn't want to kill me, it would've been an accident. The only problem was that I didn't know what he did want. Turns out it was my tapes. He took four of them. It was like he knew which ones would be the most damning. The one you saw today with the girl. Another I had of a car accident. A couple of others too, all of them bad."

"He did know. The Physician gave the information to Eric, and then Eric told Logan. He's like me, except instead of the perfect love, he sells the perfect revenge," I said.

"Shit," Dex said, slumping in his seat.

Gathering my courage, I reached across the divide once more, took hold of his hand, and squeezed it tight. He could try to pull back, but I wasn't letting go. It was the only way I had to communicate how everything inside me could feel so happy and so sad at the same time, because he had stayed with me . . . and because I couldn't stay with him.

Dex didn't fight me, though, and our hands remained clasped together until we pulled up in front of a well-kept house in an otherwise run-down neighborhood.

Dex reached for his door. "Wait," I said. He turned to me, raising what was left of his eyebrows. "I think I should go in alone. If I tell Eric that I'm planning to go along with things the way they always were, he might leave Logan alone."

"I'm not letting you face him by yourself. Either of them. Look, I understand that twice now you've rescued me after I've been beaten up pretty badly, and that might lead you to think that I'm pretty fucking useless protectionwise. Maybe I am, but I don't care. I'm going with you, and that's it."

I took in Dex's face, proud and desperate and sticky with tape residue. Even if I lived the lives of a million girls, I was certain that I would never meet another guy like him.

But all I said was "Okay then, let's go. I lead."

He nodded tightly, and we climbed out of the car and started up the neat little brick-lined walkway. At the front door, I rang the bell, feeling faintly ridiculous.

Dex and I exchanged glances as we heard footsteps on the

other side of the door.

"I'm scared," I whispered to Dex, staring straight ahead.

"Me too."

There was the grinding sound of a lock being turned. "I'm glad you're here."

He took a step closer, so that our bodies were just barely touching. "Me too."

The door swung open soundlessly.

"Hello again, my girl," Logan said. The slightest hint of an Irish brogue lingered below each word.

I flew at him, fists pounding his chest. "You bastard. Why? Why? Why?" He retreated a few steps, drawing us farther into the house, and then when I could no longer feel the sunlight at my back, he grabbed my wrists and threw me against a wall.

"I think you forgot that I'm bigger than you now." He smiled and leaned in close.

"Why?" I asked once more. "If I become Lacey, you'll just have to move again. Why take him?"

"Why not? You did such a good job setting him up for me. He wanted so badly to make things right, and you wouldn't let him. I can't remember the last time one of them was this ripe for the picking. He wanted you and couldn't have you. The next best thing was to take Dex out, and all I did was tell him to steal a few incriminating tapes. It was almost too easy. And so what if it's only for a month, or a week, or just a day—it feels good to be in this skin that fits so well."

I spit into his face, aiming for the spot right between his stolen eyes.

His hands tightened on my wrists. "That reminds me. I owe you a trip to the bathroom, so we can even things out between us." He smiled. "Or I could forgive everything for a kiss."

We were so close, I could smell the blood on his breath. The thought of having his lips on mine, much less his tongue pressing inside my mouth, was more than I could take. I turned my face away.

He laughed. "Fine by me. We'll find out how long you can hold your breath."

His punishing grip transferred to the soft part of my upper arm. I cried out, and at the same time heard an electrical buzzing sound. Logan's body shuddered and then locked tight.

Dex stood behind him, pressing what looked like an electric razor into the base of Logan's skull. Pulling my arm out of his no-longer-solid grip, I watched as Logan went into rigor mortis mode once more. The whole time his eyes were on me. It was easy enough to read the message in them—I would pay for this too.

I think he sometimes underestimated me. As Dex buzzed him a third time, muttering something about, "Supposed to knock him out," I kicked his feet out from under him. Stiff and straight, he tipped backward as if in the midst of a trust fall. But nothing was there to catch him . . . except the tiled floor. His head cracked loudly against it, and his body finally went limp.

I stared at Logan's unconscious body, the only thing that was left of him. The slack face was once again his own. I knelt down, and gently laid my hand against the cheek that had once belonged to Rice Sixteen. His skin was warm and the pulse in his throat was steady, proof that his heart was still beating. Proof that he was alive. Except he wasn't. But only I knew that. With Franky walking around in Logan's body, no one would remember the real Logan; instead they would know a strange and lesser version.

If I had any courage, I might've taken the razor from my pocket and slit his throat right there, letting the last bit of his life bleed away before it could be tainted. Instead, I patted him down. Three of Dex's DV tapes were tucked into one pants pocket, the other held one more tape, car keys, and his prayer card. The prayer Logan had been saying for Annaliese. The one he should've been saying for himself.

"He could wake up any second. We need to go." The sound of Dex's voice snapped me back to the present.

"Okay," I said, but I didn't move. Instead I bowed my head and prayed the words on the card, trying to believe that Logan's gran was right—that there could be hope even for the hopeless. And then I picked up Logan's limp hand and placed the card into his palm. Gently, I laid his hand back down and pressed each finger, curling them inward until they enclosed the prayer.

Swallowing past the lump in my throat, I shoved the tapes and car keys into my own pockets and then, for one last time, looked at Logan, trying to fix this image of him in my mind. The day folded in on itself like origami, as I bent forward and kissed his cheek in the exact spot I had earlier. Once again it was the only way I had to say that I was sorry. And then I stood and marched out the front door with Dex right behind me.

"What now?" I knew he was asking if I'd changed my mind and my plan.

Having no good answer to give him, I simply said, "Thanks, Dex. If you weren't here . . ." I shrugged, not having to say the rest.

Dex shook his head in this sad way. I think he was wondering if he should've saved me at all.

"Stun gun" was all he said, looking down at the object in his hand as if he was surprised to see it still there. "I bought it after that night with the failed letter delivery. I didn't have time to grab it when Logan came in, but I thought maybe I should bring it along here. Thought it might come in handy." He opened the passenger-side door for me.

"Can I see it?" I asked. With a shrug, he handed it over.

It was only as my fingers brushed against Dex's and the stun gun slipped from his hand to mine that the thought of what I needed to do next entered my mind. If I'd second-guessed or hesitated, I wouldn't have done it, but staring down at the boy who had once been Logan, something inside me had slid as easily as that stun gun did from one hand into another, changing ownership.

As I pressed the stun gun to Dex's chest, the smooth plastic handle was still warm from his hand. I purposely avoided his eyes, not wanting to see the betrayal there, knowing he wouldn't appreciate that I was doing this for his own good, especially when he knew it was for my own good too.

I had to pull Dex's limp body into the car, and the whole time I couldn't meet his eyes.

I drove us to the closest McDonald's and parked in the back near the drive-through speakers.

"Anna," he croaked as I put the car into park. I zapped him once more, holding the stun gun to his skin until his eyes rolled up into his head. I was protecting him. I couldn't take the chance that he might follow me. It was cold comfort.

As I stepped onto the pavement, hunger gripped me so hard that I actually groaned aloud. It wasn't a Big Mac and french fries that I was craving either.

I breathed through it as I walked to the back of the car and opened the trunk. For once luck was on my side. A camera bag sat in the middle of the otherwise empty and perfectly clean trunk. Rifling through it, I found a sweatshirt similar to the one Logan had given me, except this one was smaller and more worn. And it was Dex's. That made all the difference. I pulled it on, keeping the hood pulled up to cover my head.

After throwing the keys into the Dumpster, I took a moment to consult my own inner compass—the one that led straight to hell.

And then I started walking.

PAY

WHAT WOULD YOU GIVE?

What would you give?

Anything. Everything.

For a boy?

Yes.

Then I'll make him want you.

How?

It worked for me, it can work for you.

How?

It doesn't matter how, as long as it works.

How will I know it's working?

You'll know. He'll know.

What'll it cost?

You'll owe me.

Owe you what?

Nothing more than what you took.

And then he'll love me?

He'll want you. But love can follow.
If you're lucky.

Is that how it happened for you?
Were you lucky?

She smiles, almost sadly.
Luckier than a cat with nine lives.

—ARG

START HERE

Katie is crying. I am crying. I had wanted to make her pay, it's true. But not this way. Never this way.

"Do it," Franky says, pressing my father's razor into my right hand. "Start here." He points to the tiny scar on my left wrist, where I'd cut myself with this same blade weeks ago. It had all seemed like a game then. A terrible game. A sick game. But not something that could be of harm to anyone.

I look at Katie again, wishing she would scream or run away, but she is frozen except for the steady stream of tears flowing down her face.

I'd been so angry, I'd been almost feverish with it. First the fight with my mom and then Franky told me that he'd just seen Tommy walking out of Katie's house. Apparently, her parents had left this morning for a weeklong trip—a second honeymoon in the Poconos—and she was home alone. Except not alone, because Tommy had come to visit. While I was getting screamed at and kicked out of my own house, right across the street Tommy and Katie were fooling around and having a good old time. That's when I finally said the words to Franky—"I love you." I loved him for being there for me and for telling me the truth. I loved him for being as angry at the world as I was.

He'd said he loved me too. And then with him at my heels, I'd come marching over to Katie's, determined to make her sorry.

"It's time to pay," I said to Katie, pushing my way inside.

That's when it all changed. Katie hadn't told us to leave, but just stepped aside as if she'd known we were coming.

"Yes, I will pay," she'd said. Then Franky brought the razor out, and I knew something was definitely wrong. I tried to run, but my feet became tangled up beneath me, and I fell to the floor instead.

"It's okay, Anna. I'm right here," Franky whispers into my ear now. He squeezes my hand and I squeeze back. "I'm with you. Are you with me?"

"Yes," I answer. "Yes." I say yes because Franky loves me. And I love him. And being with him is better than being alone.

I say yes, and he presses the razor into my hand.

I am standing in a pool of blood. My blood. It spills down my arms, where I have cut a line into each of them. That amount of blood loss should have me on the floor, but instead I feel so light. If Franky wasn't holding me, I think I would float up and away, through the ceiling and into the sky.

He takes the razor from my sticky hand and places it in Katie's. The part of me that can still think expects her to cut herself too. Her blood will spill out like mine, and then it will be Franky's turn, and the three of us will float away together.

"It's okay," I want to tell her. "It hardly hurts at all."

Except she doesn't cut into herself. Instead, with the razor blade extended, she comes toward me, and the blade slides through my clothing and skin, making a perfect X over my heart. Then it slips between my ribs, cutting and twisting away, until she extracts my heart. There is a tugging feeling, like something has grabbed me by the belly button. I watch my body start to sway, but can't feel it. I am outside of myself, floating. So this is what it feels like when you die. I stare down at the hole in my chest.

I am the Tin Man. Maybe I should find a clock to stuff in there.

It's not too bad, but then another tug, and I feel again.

Thudding heart, and shaky breaths, while I chew something terrible. In my hands, there is something warm and sticky. My heart. Except Katie has my heart. And then I feel Katie's horror and fear. Experience them inside myself, as a part of me. Along with her, I gag on the chunk of heart in my mouth. Together we feel Franky's fingers in our mouth, shoving in a chunk of chocolate. It melts, sweet and waxy, mixing with the heart.

"Just a spoonful of sugar," he coaxes.

Somehow we swallow, and as we do, there is less of Katie. More of me.

"Almost there now, Anna my love."

Bite by bite, she disappears, and I can feel how grateful she is to go, to escape, leaving me behind to live with this. Across the room my body crumbles, and the blood evaporates, until there is no trace of me at all.

Somehow, though, I am still here. And Franky too.

He smiles at me. "Hello, my girl."

MEANT TO END

I walked from congested roads clogged with rush hour traffic to quiet suburban streets, and then the houses spread out even more, interspersed with wide fields. It wasn't that long ago that I'd endured a similar journey, when I'd been a girl with no name. Now I was a girl with too many.

Footsteps suddenly sounded behind me. I spun, expecting Eric, forgetting the redheaded boy was gone. But it wasn't him. Or Logan either.

Just a middle-aged man in sweats, jogging along the side of the road.

"Nice night," he said as he came up beside me, slowing his pace.

I nodded tightly, not wanting to encourage conversation.

He held his hand out, like he wanted to introduce himself. But instead there was a slip of paper between his fingers.

"Think you dropped this," he said.

I stuck my hands into my pockets. Not wanting to touch him. "I don't think it's mine."

"I definitely saw it fall from your pocket, young lady." His eyes twinkled at the "young lady" bit as if assuring me that he was only playing at being stern. "Come on now, I'm not gonna give it to you again after this."

I took the paper to appease him.

He smiled, a grin so big it was almost a grimace. "See, now isn't it lucky we ran into each other? I usually run inside on a treadmill, like a rat going around in circles." He laughed. Not in a self-deprecating way, but like he was thinking of those rats and feeling superior. "Today, though, I decided to do something different. Not that I didn't like doing things the way I always have, but I got these three sisters. They keep yapping at me to give change a chance. Sometimes you go a different way, and it can change your whole life, is what they say. So I gave in. Just this once, and then it's back to the treadmill."

I kicked at a stone in front of me, not reacting to his too-much-information chatter, not wanting to encourage him.

After the silence stretched on for several long moments, he seemed to get the message. "All right, well, you have a nice night now." He sped up once more and pulled away from me.

"See ya," I called after him, hoping that I wouldn't.

He lifted a hand and looked back over his shoulder. Head-lights flared behind me, spotlighting his face, and somehow twisting it. Making him look like someone else. Someone I knew and remembered too well. A man who had once called me a monster. Dr. Grimace and Gloom. The light spread and then he was Mr. Hardy, warning against calling the parents. And one last bend of light cast his face in shadows exactly like the scowling hall monitor at school.

The car behind me revved loudly, but when I glanced around, nothing was there. As I turned forward again, the road stretched wide and empty in front of me. The man was gone.

With shaking hands I unfolded the paper he'd handed me and held it out to see it clearly in the fading light.

It was the same paper that had fallen out of my algebra book. The one with Lacey's name. And the watermark on the back. The kind of note the Physician always made sure fell into my hands. The ground seemed to shift beneath my feet as I stared at the empty place where the jogging man had been. Dr. Grimace and Gloom had called himself a physician. Had he known I was a monster because he'd made me one? How many times had the Physician spoken with me while hiding behind another man's face?

Shaken, I grabbed hold of a weathered mailbox at the end of a gravel driveway, the only thing in the whole world that wasn't spinning. My hand clenched tight around the paper, even as I tried to make myself throw it away.

Didn't the Physician or Dr. Grimace and Gloom or Mr. Hardy, or whoever he was, get it? I wasn't taking orders from his little slips of paper anymore. I'd been walking in the opposite direction of the hunger, even as inside of me it chewed away in protest. But I wouldn't let it out. Not this time. I'd throw myself in front of a speeding car first. Or fill my pockets with rocks and walk into the nearest lake. And if all else failed, I'd find a gas station and buy a lighter. Then I would do what I had once been too afraid to. I would walk through fire.

It didn't seem as difficult as it once had. I had been ready to let the hunger lead me to Lacey's door. Even when Dex begged me not to, I couldn't see a way out. Now, though, after seeing what was left of Logan, dying seemed like the easiest option. Anything to not have to live with that memory.

No, I wasn't afraid of dying. Not anymore. But what I did fear was a niggling suspicion that the Physician might not let me die. That no car would be fast enough, no lake deep enough, and no fire hot enough to break his hold over me and kill the hunger for good.

Except. The treadmill. "Sometimes you go a different way." That's what he'd said. Was there a way other than Lacey? Other than the hunger taking over? Other than trying to find a dozen different ways to die?

I unfolded the paper once more, using my fingertips to carefully iron out the wrinkles. There was Lacey's name again, and on the opposite side of the paper—the watermark. I squinted to read the barely there words. Albion, NY. I'd remembered that part. The street and house number though . . . A car came by and, holding the paper out toward the light, I was able to read: 1306 Rural Route 16. I knew that address.

That terrible instinct, connected to the hunger that I'd

spent the last several hours walking away from—but different too—gave me a little poke. I leaned away from the mailbox far enough to see the numbered stickers on the side. 1306. Teeth bit into the letters. They weren't shark teeth, like I'd thought the first time I'd seen this mailbox. Now up close, I could see those teeth came from the mouth of a monstrous whale, its tail curling around the back of the mailbox and its blowhole spouting a cascade of black pinpoints that resembled shrapnel more than water. I shivered, and as if my movement had woken it, the mailbox door fell open. Taped inside was a square bit of paper with the full address typed out—free of artistic additions. 1306 Rural Route 16, Albion, NY.

I was always given two choices. Two different girls to choose from. But this wasn't the name of a girl. This was an address and a place that suddenly seemed to suck all the hunger away. I took a step back from the mailbox, and the hunger flared up again. Tugging me, wanting me to go to Lacey and far from here. Ignoring it, I stepped toward the mailbox once more.

The last bits of dying sun barely came through the trees that crowded either side of the driveway. I walked slowly and carefully, not wanting to twist my ankle in one of the deep tire ruts. By the time the drive opened up into a small yard, the darkness was complete. The lot was large and mostly empty. Front and center sat a squat brick house that had seen better days. The screen door didn't close all the way, and a light breeze kept swatting it open to crash against the outer wall.

Behind the house I could just make out a weak light. I inched toward it, this time my slow steps due to the heaviness and growing dread inside me. The shed door was fully open, and kept that way with a brick. The same monster that had attacked Dex stood haloed by the bare lightbulb hanging over his head. He hummed softly to himself while he sawed at a long piece of plywood.

There was a roaring in my ears, except this time it didn't take me back to the past—it carried me forward, closer to the monster.

Inside me all the pieces came together. I was always given the choice between two different people. Lacey's name was on one side, and on the other—my second option. Not a name but an address. Not a girl but a man.

Lacey or him. That was my different choice. That was my way off the endless treadmill.

I dropped the paper. It skittered across the scrub grass in a series of endless somersaults until a gust of wind picked it up and carried it away into the shadows.

Without even knowing it, I had already chosen. My childhood was long behind me, and my girlhood had stretched on for much too long. It was time to grow up. It was time to become what I was truly meant to be. Or what I'd always been. I would become the monster, and in doing so make sure that he never hurt anyone else again.

Entering the tiny shed, my senses were overwhelmed by the man's sour smell. He glanced up and, after a moment of surprise at seeing someone there, smiled. His eyes ran up and down my body.

"You lost, little girl?" Finally his eyes got around to meeting mine. He smiled wide, showing off a mouth full of gray fillings. "Hey, I remember you. Where's your friend? He here for another ass kicking? Or you come alone, ready for a real man?"

That was when I wanted to flee. Cut and run from this terrible place. From this terrible man. After this I would not be anything like Anna or Annaliese or any of the other girls. There would be no Mom or Dad or Dex or best friend. It would be a whole new kind of loneliness.

"It's just me. And it's time to pay," I said, forcing the words from my mouth, sealing his fate. And mine.

And he did pay, exactly the same way so many others had. Except that he enjoyed it. The warm blood gushing out. Sawing through flesh that moved beneath his hands pulsating with pain. And the power of holding a human heart still thrumming with life in his hand. He was enthralled.

He bit in with an enormous grin, and even as his jaw worked at the tough tissue, it didn't budge once. The heart was half gone, the transfer half done, by the time he felt someone else in his body. At first he thought it was heartburn and giggled a bit at the idea. I heard that thought, too, and shuddered. It shivered through his body. He struggled then, trying to hold on. But it was too late. He'd already given himself away. I forced the last few bites into his no-longer-smiling mouth and pushed them down the back of his throat with his own stiff fingers. In the dirt beside me, Annaliese withered, fading from the inside out until she was only a husk. Bit by bit, I watched the wind carry her away.

He was gone. She was gone. And once again, I was still there. Always the last one standing.

And then not standing, as my new legs buckled beneath me. Fully spreading out into his body, I became aware of the pain. The bones ached, the skin itched, and the heart was like a gasping fish flopping around my chest, searching for water and a way to breathe. This body was poison. His soul had left the walls stained inside. I could feel that residue burning through my new legs and up out of my fingertips. Every exhaled breath stank with the rot. I would have to fight the rest of his life to keep it from getting out.

No, not his life. Mine.

This was my new life, and it was agony. I could've let myself be burned to bits and it would've been quicker. I could've been selfish one more time.

The poison seemed to bubble up. I breathed through it, and would continue to breathe. My new fingers twitched, and

I forced them to be still. This horrible place was where I was meant to be. This was what the *brujas* had meant. I had chosen to fall into the dark and dangerous waters. Now I just had to try not to drown.

I had made my choice, and as horrible as it was, I would do it again. A hundred times if I had to.

With this thought, some small glimmer of peace sparked inside me. I focused on it, as one would a dim light at the end of a long tunnel. It was enough to let my foreign eyes drift closed. Enough to sink down into a dark and troubled sleep. And maybe even enough to get through this night, and after that somehow face what remained of this miserable new life.

ANEW

The *brujas* gather around me, crooning softly a song with no words. Or perhaps they simply don't translate.

They briskly rub their hands along my body, chafing the bad skin away until I am raw and oozing. Then they dig down deeper to the aching bones. *These bones are bad*, I hear one say. Every last one is snapped like a twig from a rotting branch.

Together as one they lean over me, their heads forming another constellation in the night sky. "Look at us," they say. "Look at us and the stars beyond. Don't look down as we dig into your chest and pluck out this crushed and battered heart, bit by broken bit."

Then they pull out long needles. Silver and sharp, they are threaded with strands of hair. The same hair they'd cut from Annaliese's head and thrown to the wind. Every last strand that was lost has been hunted and gathered. Plucked from birds' nests, from swamps, from storm drains, and the last one they found wrapped round a lightning rod at the top of a skyscraper.

In and out. The thread weaves through skin, back and forth, on and on, rebuilding the body they'd broken down.

Snipping their last threads, they lean in close. Lips softly pursed, they blow. It is more than their cool breath that makes my skin tingle. With each puff, a cyclone of dust erupts from their mouths. As it settles over me and into me, I recognize it as the remnants not just of Annaliese, but of the girls I've watched get blown away. The girls whose names were on my razor.

Finished, the *brujas* are pleased.

"This is right. This is good," they say, as they observe their work.

"You made the choice.

"The Physician, he waited, ready to take you out of the man and into the new girl.

"He only gives second chances to those certain to fail.

"But you didn't fail, and now you are ours, and we've made you anew."

They smile, soft and sweet but with steel beneath.
"This is right. This is good," they say once more.
Then six fingertips press my eyelids closed.
"Rest now," they say.
"Be at peace.
"Now you begin anew."

BIRTHDAY

POETS OF TOMORROW—FIRST-PLACE POEM
HIGH SCHOOL DIVISION

I am . . .

I am not the sum
of my imperfections.
Scars, pimples, and excess fat
do not define me.
I am not your opinion
of who I am.
Smart or smart-ass,
loquacious or shy—
only I know
all that I hold inside.
My failures of today are not
the measurement for the
success of my tomorrows.
Now I appear weak
but I am not always
what I seem to be.

*This is not even close
to all there is
of me.*

*I dare you to
underestimate me.*

—Annaliese Rose Gordon
East Lancaster High School
15 years old

FUTURE

She woke a few minutes before midnight. There was no clock to tell her this, but she liked to believe it was true.

Anyone who saw her walking along the side of the road in the middle of the night might've recognized her as Annaliese Rose Gordon. The girl who had been lost and found, and now was lost once more. On the news they said that this time she was a runaway. Or perhaps she'd been involved with that other boy. Logan Rice, the high school football star who'd nearly died this same dark night. His heart, they said. Some said the lost-and-found girl had broken it. A strange boy and a foolish missing girl. How many times could one girl expect to be searched for and discovered?

She wasn't missing, though. And she wasn't Annaliese either. She hadn't been for some time. Nor was she Anna. Someone new lived inside her, a third person, made up of the girls she had chosen and whose names she had etched onto the razor handle. They had been holding her together all this time, filling in all the missing little pieces. But now they were one. And whole.

Although the night was dark, she did not worry about losing her way. Her pace was steady and she moved with purpose. She marched toward the future, almost experiencing tiny pieces of it with a crystalline kind of clarity, the same way she'd once relived bits of her past.

She saw the boy who had brought her into his awful game, the boy she would always think of as Franky. She saw that she would no longer have to fear him. She saw that he could no longer follow where she had gone. At the moment she'd made her choice, the strong athlete's body he'd stolen had broken down around him. Palsied then paralyzed. He once again became the same sick boy he'd sought to escape.

When the *brujas* visited his hospital bed and offered to free him, he accepted without hesitation. They sucked him out through a tiny hole in the once strong but now sick and weakened heart. Without a body to hold him, what was left of Franky was small enough to fit in the bottom of a thimble. Having no use for a thimble that could now hurt them more than the needle it was meant to protect from, the *brujas* sent it along to their brother overnight express. The Physician would find some use for it, they were certain.

And all the while the machines attached to the stolen body of Logan Rice Sixteen screamed, and the doctors and nurses crowded in, trying to save him even though they were all secretly certain it was wholly hopeless. But the unseen *brujas* didn't despair. Gentle yet relentless, they coaxed Logan back, using the words on the prayer card he still held curled into the palm of his hand. The doctors were ready to turn off the machines. They checked the time and cleared their throats, ready to declare his hour of death . . . when the flat line spiked and his heart beat once more.

Logan lived, although, like Annaliese, he would not be the same person he had once been. Perhaps, like Annaliese, he would come to prefer it this way.

And Annaliese, now with eyes wide open, began to see beyond. Beyond to the rain that had not yet started to fall and beyond to the sun that was only beginning to rise. Shortly, she would walk and then begin to run through both, seeing her mother, armed with a black umbrella but soaked anyway. Searching. For her daughter. For her.

They would meet in the middle of the deserted street, and sob and hug and think to themselves how they would never let the other go, not ever again.

Her father would be there too, dragging them out of the street to safety, holding them up when they might've collapsed. He'd insist on carrying her mother home, and her mother would only agree after she was solemnly promised that her daughter would keep hold of her hand the entire way.

As they got closer to the house, the neighbors who had been out searching, seeing them, would begin to call out, "She's been found. They found her. She's okay."

Dex would be among them, and he wouldn't—couldn't— believe. Hours ago he had watched the monster from his vision die . . . and then somehow live again, the images flashing before his eyes. A movie with no stop button. He'd watched the monster consume Annaliese. He'd watched the monster die, and he'd thought that he might too.

So when he saw her flesh-and-blood in front of him, he couldn't believe. Not until she kissed him. And he touched the place on her forehead where a starburst scar had once covered a missing chip of her skull. The skin was smooth and clear now. The bone beneath it solid.

Then he believed. Then he saw. He didn't notice the change, the new her. The real girl. This was the same girl he'd always known. This was the girl he loved.

They joined hands, palm to palm, fingers intertwined. All the futures he held inside flowed through him and into her.

She didn't see death, though.

She saw all the life to come before the end.

And it was full of possibility.

ACKNOWLEDGMENTS

I am terrible at asking for help. And I am even worse at sharing my sometimes insane aspirations for fear I will be laughed at. For everyone who helped, and for everyone who didn't laugh but instead said, "You're writing a book? That's cool. Can I read it?" Thank you. This includes: my sisters and their husbands; my amazing in-laws; and my friends Melissa, Jenny, and Matt. Thank you all.

I also want to thank:

My big boy, Jamie, thank you for taking two long naps a day starting at five months of age. Those nap times gave me the opportunity to not only start a novel, but to keep working on it until, ninety thousand words later, I typed *the end.*

Zoe, my beautiful daughter, thank you for being a monster and insisting you're an angel. You make me laugh every day.

My husband, Andy, for being a modern man who takes the kids to the park to get them out of my hair, does the laundry, and helps in the kitchen. Thank you for being my brilliant, creative collaborator and partner. What would I do without you?

My parents, for always being supportive and understanding, even when you really wished I would just go to law school. And for driving me back and forth to the library so that I could constantly replenish my source of new reading material. And for letting me read whatever I wanted without interference. Especially that last one. That was huge.

My grandma Karyus for letting me raid your stacks of paperback novels. You introduced me to everything from Mary Higgins Clark and Sydney Sheldon to *The Thornbirds*. My reading life would not have been the same without you.

My crit partner Alyson Greene. Thank you so much for taking the time to read and for all of your thoughtful comments. Hopefully someday we'll meet and I can thank you in person.

My amazing editor, Erica Sussman, and everyone at Harper-Collins. Thank you so much for making me an author.

And finally, to my brilliant agent, Alexandra Machinist. I feel so incredibly lucky to have you in my corner. Thank you.